The Dazzle of Day

The Dazzle of Day

Molly Gloss

TOR®

A Tom Doherty Associates Book
New York

For Ed

kamarado

THE DAZZLE OF DAY

Copyright © 1997 by Molly Gloss

Edited by David G. Hartwell

A Tor Book
Published by Tom Doherty Associates, Inc.
175 Fifth Avenue
New York, NY 10010

Tor Books on the World Wide Web:
http://www.tor.com

Tor® is a registered trademark of Tom Doherty Associates, Inc.

Design by Lynn Newmark

Library of Congress Cataloging-in-Publication Data

Gloss, Molly.
    The dazzle of day / Molly Gloss.—1st ed.
       p.   cm.
    ISBN 0-312-86336-5
    I. Title.
    PS3557.L65D39   1997
    813'.54—dc21   96-53693
                                                    CIP

First Edition: June 1997

Printed in the United States of America

0 9 8 7 6 5 4 3 2 1

Acknowledgments

For the descriptions of leaf-cutter ants, and for details of tropical birds and tropical farming, I am indebted to the published writings of Alexander F. Skutch, a naturalist of profound compassion and thought.

In the mid-1970's, argument over the feasibility and desirability of funding the O'Neill space colonies was an ongoing matter for discussion in *The CoEvolution Quarterly,* and eventually that material, including the invited responses of several notable people, was gathered together and published under the title *Space Colonies* (Penguin Books: New York, 1977). Some of the arguments and insights spoken by characters in this novel (addressing a rather different question) have been abstracted from the discussion in that book.

All epigraphs in this book are from the writings of the sometime-Quaker Walt Whitman, his lifework, *Leaves of Grass.*

Author's Note

Esperanto is an artificial, international language favored by many Peace churches for its facility at clearing the way.

There are no silent letters; every word is pronounced as it is spelled.

Vowels are sounded ah, eh, ee, oh, oo—as in "Are there three or two?"

The semi-vowel ŭ is like the English w, and combines with a preceding vowel to form a diphthong:

aŭ = ow *(landau)*
eŭ = ew *(euphemism)*

Consonants are sounded as in English except for these:

c = ts *(prince)*
ĉ = ch *(cello)*
g always "hard" *(goat)*
ĝ always "soft" *(gypsy)*
j = y *(hallelujah)*
ĵ = zh *(Taj Mahal)*
r always trilled
s always sibilant *(sensible)*
ŝ = sh *(sugar)*

-j is the plural ending.

Among some Esperanto speakers, female children take the family name of the mother, and male children the family name of the father.

Questions asking whether a thing is true or not (yes/no questions) are formed by the use of the particle *ĉu*. Here, that usage is suggested by the colloquial English interrogative, "eh?"

VERANO

Darest thou now O soul,
Walk out with me toward the unknown region,
Where neither ground is for the feet
nor any path to follow?

My family once considered themselves Tico, but the old Hispanic tradition of community has so long ago disappeared from
this continent, subsumed in the monoculture of the West, that
I consider my only culture to be Quaker. Still, the Friends who
are joining us in this migration have Japanese names, English,
Norwegian—these *Friends* are strangers to me. Moreover I
don't speak Esperanto very well, and maybe I'm too old to learn
it better, or maybe too tired. Esperanto is a language without
much grace: In the rainy season, who would want to give up
saying *invierno,* which lies sweetly on the tongue, in trade for
the crabbed little sound of *vintro?*

I am sixty years old, and afraid the arthritis in my knees,
which is a new thing, may before long make me no use to anyone—or worse, an encumbrance, which would surely be a
vaster problem in that young ship than here on this old land.

It might be, the matrix that's been used is too diminished
after all for species survival. With the first of these toroids it was
something like that, the one named *Crommelin,* built for the

rich man, Jon Crommelin, a scrupulously beautiful, flauntingly private refuge put to circling the earth just above this poisoned sky, every grain of dirt disinfected, every person and object sterilized, unpleasant insects and reptiles shut out. In a year, less than a year, there was a collapse of the organic life, and the dead construct was abandoned. It was sects of the counterculture— Carsonites and bird-watchers and Rodale farmers, Quakers and Mennonites—who understood the microbial needs of a closed system, guessed the conceit that must have killed the life there, and joined in bargaining for the *Crommelin* and attempting its renascence, as a kind of public proof of the connectedness of all life.

A decade of seeding and reseeding, trials of species-packing and of minimalism, emending and remodeling the nexus, and now there is a modest proliferation of these small forged moons, these hollow wheels with their interior, tubular landscapes. I, for one, had thought every isolationist party from Aryan Nation to Doomwatchers would soon flock up to the sky, but what has been proven by these toroids is only the absolute unmindful benightedness of the greater part of the human race. The very difficulties and economics of a closed circle of recycle and reuse have kept the stations, against all expectation, in the hands of the patient and whole-minded; our *Miller* is the only one yet to make preparations for casting off moorings—setting sail for the farthest shore. What if, in ten years or twenty, when we are too far away to get back, all the trees and the birds begin to die?

The toroid takes its plain Quaker name, *Dusty Miller,* from the reflective sail's whitish aspect in the sun's transparent light, and I have lain awake and imagined it; the small circle of raft— the houseboat, as people are saying—at the center of its great circle of flimsy sailcloth, moving soundlessly across the blackness of space like a moth, a leaf, a little puff of pollen adrift on a solar wind, which is an image that sits well with me. But I shall not see it thus except in my mind's eye; I shall live within its ceiled and narrow view, in a circumscribed world lying under fields of lamps. Never to see the sky! The stars!

The closed circle of the hollow torus can be walked round

in fifteen or twenty minutes, a bare two thousand meters from starting point round again to starting point. Big as some islands, people say, and they tell me of balance and proportion, scale and siting, the compact order of a Japanese garden. But other people have said there is a melancholy that gets into the soul of an island people—and, indeed, into the souls of migrants, for among the pilgrims of the *Mayflower,* and at Plymouth, there was black discouragement and suicide. There still are mornings in the Fourth Month rains when I get a yearning to tramp out to the horizon, a wanderlust so palpable it makes my breast ache. Where, on the *Dusty Miller,* would I tramp to?

Quaker people have endured on this old estancia on the Pacific slope of middle America for 240 years, steadfastly practicing love and faith in the midst of chaos and wars. My parents are buried in this soil, my sister, my sister's daughter, I always had thought I would one day be buried beside them. Who would have thought it would come to this—sitting among the boxes of my possessions waiting to be taken up from this house, the house in which I have lived the whole of my life until now? Who would have thought I would one day be sitting on the floor of my house in the oppressive heat and drought of the *verano,* indulging myself in qualms and skittishness, thinking and now writing about the forepart of my life and the after, on this day that separates them?

I always have considered myself strong-minded, someone who would act on her feelings without faltering, and it has been a surprise to realize: I have been thinking of changing my mind, and hiding the thought from myself in this flurry of last-minute, agitated misgivings. Tonight, the last night for sleeping under this roof, I have been thinking of changing my mind, and looking for peace or clarity or certainty by trudging round in circles, sleepless, through the dusty night.

Tonight I walked along the cart road across the Rio Pardo and through the east-side fields and houses up onto the rocky ridge of the Ojo de la Luna, and home again by way of the goat-paths—a long looping tramp. The cart road is a rutted track; we have deliberately kept it poor and unpaved to discourage non-

Quakers from coming onto the *estancia*, a tactic that has been only a little successful. There have been killings, crazy wildings, here as everywhere, but we have gone on using the road after dark on Quaker principles, bearing witness to peace, trusting in the unknowable justice of God. *What happens, happens,* people frequently say, meaning not only murder and rape on the roads but death by plague or by cancer, which seem in these days to be distilled from the very air and water. I went along the road through a breathless darkness, slapping my sandals down briskly in the dust.

My old house stands alone, but a little way up the road the houses of my neighbors stand in the manner of Friends, gathered up in a hamlet, and there I was kept company by the voices of people who know me, calling my name from their porches. Children were playing in the road in the still night, and some of them made me a little escort as far as the edge of the river where the road drops down in the rocky channel and begins to follow the low water. The air was darker there, cooler, more silent, a comfort of another kind: In the daylight the Rio Pardo is a grief, scummed yellow along its margins, but in the darkness tonight the sound it made was soft and easeful, and there was only the grayish bulk of the boulders against the colorless blackness of the water.

The heavy forest has been shorn from the steep slopes higher on the watershed, and in the flood season the river is every year more ravaging. Where a bridge had once spanned it, I waded across following the cart tracks between the old concrete footings, pushing my bare ankles through the dead and tepid water. Afterward, on my skin, the slime itched and stank, and finally I had to stoop and rub my sticky legs with handfuls of dust.

Where the track climbs from the gully of the river and turns east toward the rocky *arista,* the houses are scattered among their fields in the old Hispanic manner. People have been moving up to the *Miller* for months, and many houses are vacant, abandoned. Tonight even the occupied homes stood dark and mute, seeming to ghost the landscape. I imagined people lying inside their houses in the hot, torpid darkness, asleep or awake, measuring their breaths on the still night.

We are at the height of the dry season; no rain has fallen for weeks. The ground is fissured, the grasses brown, shrubbery stooped and withered. At this time of year, the *verano*, it is easy to imagine the death of the Earth, easy to believe in its imminence. Walking along the road, my sandals raised a fine pale powder that hung in the night, and I remembered suddenly, it had been in the *verano* the year before, when I had said I would go onto the *Dusty Miller*. It had been in the *verano* that I had become afraid I would live long enough to see the end of the world.

Species are extinguished by the hundred a day in the name of hungry people; wholesale obliteration of human cultures has been the history of the world for dozens of generations, in the name of human rights. By the time governments and corporations, those grindingly complex and malignant machines of human culture, have finally broken down under their own weight and can no longer deal destruction on the Earth, what of value will be left? It was in the *verano* that I began to dream the *Dusty Miller*'s dream of a world in which people respectfully take part in their landscape, and go on doing it generation after generation.

But tonight, walking up the road through the fields of empty houses, I thought: If I see the end of the Earth, I see it. And I wondered why I had been afraid. "Now I am clear. I am fully clear," the prophet George Fox was supposed to have said when he died. It might be, there is only so much that can be learned from life; perhaps then one has to wait for what will be exhibited by death.

I never have married, have no children to persuade me. Quite a few people I know are staying behind—some of them consider themselves too old for this change, and some are frightened. Some people see a moral imperative in standing against government oppression of the Peace churches. Or they say this emigration extends a frontier mythos whose legacy is destruction and exploitation. I haven't any compunction that way. Quaker principles have been proffered to the world for many hundreds of years, and indifferently spurned or actively expunged everywhere. I am weary of trying to live a moral and religious life against the persistent oppression of an immoral, irreligious world. It has become a terrible, exhausting struggle. How much longer can we few go on sustaining a society based on joy and authenticity—defining success as an internal process in a world that defines it by power and wealth? What is the mythos that propels the *Dusty Miller,* if not Wholeness?

No, my qualms are secular, personal, banal. This weather they have made to be inside the metal skin of the houseboat: Will there be the Fourth Month rains? What if I want to go on calling the dry season *verano* and not have to call it *somero*?

While I was turning over these worries in my mind, a shape reared up in the darkness alongside the road-cut, and my heart sprang against the cage of my ribs. I stood up straighter and made a swift plan for escaping through the taro field, back to the last lighted house. The person looked toward me and lifted both hands in a peaceful or inquiring gesture—there was something familiar in the way he stood. In a moment, I came on along the ruts.

"Arturo?"

"Dolores!"

"You gave me a start. Were you just sitting there by the road?"

"I been walking but my feet got hot. I need a drink, you got one?"

Arturo Remlinger is a slow-witted man whose mother died in the rainy season this past year. He frequently goes walking up and down the roads looking for her. He understands as much as a five-year-old, maybe, and what do five-year-olds understand of death? Oh my dear, what does anyone?

"No, I haven't got water, Arturo. But come on with me, we'll walk up the road and get you some." Arturo's brother has taken on his care. The brother's house wasn't far off; probably Arturo had padded out the door after everyone there had gone to bed.

I took his soft hand and led him. He has a big, doughy body, a round face without angles. He is prone to unpredictable storms of temper—he wheels his big arms and stomps his feet, rolls his head on his thick neck. The sounds that come out of him then are rageful and wordless, terrifying, heartbreaking. Neighbors come when they hear him, and help his brother as they used to help his mother, gently press him out-of-doors where he isn't as likely to hurt himself. The house his mother had lived in was bare of ornament; she had learned to give up breakable things. The brother has a wife who is a clay artist, and two young children. I wondered: What hangs on their walls, what sits on their tables now?

We walked along the road together. "What do you think? Is the dry season about finished?" I asked him. One of his interests is the weather. He likes to repeat and repeat the accounts he hears on the satellite radio stations, of weather in Lithuania and Botswana, Kampuchea, Greenland, Chile.

He swung his head back and forth heavily. "No. Not finished. But we'll get some rain someday, ha ha." He grinned softly and used the hand I was holding to gesture for both of us, vaguely overhead. "Rains every night, just about, on the houseboat. I like raining. Hey, Dolores, I'm going to live up there, how about you?"

I had been present when someone at a New World Planning Committee Meeting had wondered aloud: Should impaired and disabled people be kept from joining the emigration to the *Dusty Miller?* The way of Friends is to think quietly and to listen. We ask the question, we consider how the answer is made by different people, we ask again, answer again, change our minds; we reach an understanding. The Meeting evolves this way, not by shouting each other down, not by the weight of the majority, but by the capacity of individual human beings to comprehend one another. So there was a pondering silence and then someone stood and said, "What is impairment, I wonder. Is it arthritis? If one eye is blind but not the other, is that disabling?" People considered this. After a while someone else, a surgeon, said, "There won't be the resources to treat serious health problems. No microtechnology for prosthetics, for the metered administering of insulin, for synthetic laryngeal voicing."

People went on in this way for quite a while—not back and forth but circling around. There was a Japanese woman sitting

at that Meeting, a young woman who had come over from
Honshu to talk to our Farms Committee about the growing of
kenaf and cilantro. This woman stood up after a long, listening
silence and said what everyone there already knew—one of the
four cardinal principles of the Religious Society of Friends:
"Something of the inner light of God lives in every human
being." I remember the precise pitch and cadence of her voice,
her precisely correct Spanish, and the way the air felt at that moment, charged and vivid. And afterward there was no further
questioning about the disabled.

"Yes, I'm going too," I said to Arturo Remlinger, before remembering I had been walking along the road doubting it.

"Hey!" Arturo said. "You know they got a hurricane in the
Philippines, and floods killed 82,056?" He went on telling
me about the weather—hailstorms in Azerbaijan, drought
throughout Africa, tornadoes in the delta of the Mississippi
River. He remembered or invented numbers of dead, rainfall
statistics, the projected paths of storms. I walked beside him
silently, holding his clammy, pulpy hand. I was thinking of
what I had said to him, and considering whether I had told the
truth. *I'm going too.* Well, if I didn't go, no one would be angry.
No one would ask me for an explanation. The heavy lift
launches always were deliberately overbooked, allowing for
the five or six who could be counted on to draw back at the last
minute. Some few people have even gone up and then come
down again. There isn't any shame in it. No one would want
people living on the *Dusty Miller* who weren't sure they wanted
to be there.

"Here, you're home," I said softly to Arturo when I led him
up on the porch of his brother's house. The door stood open;
Arturo had left it ajar, going out, or the family had left it open
to release the built-up heat from under their roof. I wouldn't
have gone inside, I didn't want to frighten anyone who might
wake and see me standing there, but Arturo kept stubborn hold
of my hand and brought me with him into the dark front room,
where there were shapes of things—cupboards and tables and
low cushions—but no shapes of people, who must have been
sleeping in the second room.

"I sure need a drink," Arturo repeated patiently.

"I haven't forgotten." I peered in the darkness for their cask of distilled water while Arturo went on holding my hand. I was groping with my other hand in the shadows along the shelves of a cupboard, hunting for something to pour the water into, when a barefoot woman came out from the sleeping room.

"Arturo, who is it with you?" the woman said with a loud, false boldness, and I immediately understood that her husband wasn't in the house.

"It's Dolores Negrete," I said. "Arturo was out on the road."

The woman's body released its stiffness. She said, "Arturo," and then tiredly, "He goes out after we're asleep."

Arturo released his grip from my fingers and, standing with his heavy legs planted, he swung from the waist toward his sister-in-law, and swung back, lifting his arms slightly. "Dolores'll get me a drink," he said.

I made a hand motion. "I can't find a cup."

The sister-in-law came across the dark room. She wore a thin cotton slip, white or ginger-colored, that seemed to move alone, luminous, through the darkness. The woman took a cup from a shelf and held it beneath the tap of the water cask. "Here, Arturo, here's your drink, but you know where the water is, and the cups. You could just help yourself."

Arturo drank the water swiftly down, holding the cup to his mouth with both big hands. His drinking was silent, neat. Afterward, lowering the cup, he said, "Thirsty," as an explanation.

"Go and pee and then go to bed," the woman said to him.

"I already peed. I did it on a tree." I could see the edge of his white teeth, the sly smiling.

"All right, then. Just go to bed."

"Hey, Barbara, Dolores wants to live in the houseboat and so do we." He swung toward me. "My mother isn't going," he told me.

"Go to bed now," Barbara said. She took the big man by the shoulders and turned him toward the door of the sleeping room. He came around with her slowly, his shoulders ahead of his hips and his feet.

"See you, Dolores," he said, twisting his head back.

"Good night, Arturo."

"They got a big storm in the Philippines today."

"Good night, Arturo."

"Okay, Dolores, see you."

He went out of the front room slowly. We could hear him in a moment, whispering loudly to someone in the bedroom, his words obscure. "Philippines," he whispered.

"Thank you for bringing him home," Barbara said. She stood with her thin arms folded across the front of her slip. She had a small face, short hair, there was no seeing her features in the darkness. I didn't know her except by her work—delicate clay pots painted with rigid, grimacing faces in dark colors of blood and jade and cobalt, and ornamented by bits of bone and feather. Burial pots, I think they are, and I have enjoyed the irony of their popularity at the souvenir shops, in the gambling casinos and whore houses along the coast.

"Your whole family is going up there? Up to the *Miller*?" I had to ask her. Other people's decisions in this matter seemed suddenly important to me—they might have considered things that had escaped my attention.

"We are, but Juan is on the Legal Committee and he wants to stay until the expropriation appeals are all turned down."

As people leave the *estancia* for the *Dusty Miller,* and as the numbers of people here dwindle, there will be a government expropriation of "underutilized" land—this was something that was generally known. The tactic of the Legal Committee always was to exhaust every appeal.

There won't be a need for attorneys on the *Dusty Miller,* surely, nor perhaps artists, as some people say there won't be the resources. I wanted to ask her, *What will your husband do in that place? Will you give up your art?* Then Barbara said, as if I had spoken, "He'll be glad to be out of law, he never was happy in it. He wants to take up teaching, now that we'll be free of government constraints on our schools. He can keep Arturo with him. It's to be all home schooling and tutoring and apprenticing there, you know."

I nodded as if I did know, though I hadn't paid much attention to reports of things to do with children, or families.

"What will you do?" I asked Barbara, now that I'd been made to feel the subject was open.

Barbara's thin shoulders lifted slightly. "I'm a potter."

"Yes. I have seen your pots."

The woman made a soft sound, a laugh. "Oh, not those. Not there. Art is craft, anyway, at its pure heart. I'll make plates and bowls and ceramic parts for machinery. And tiles." She sounded satisfied, and there wasn't any way to see, in the darkness, if her face spoke another truth.

I said, shrugging, "I've always only farmed, myself. I guess the farming will be the same, there or here. That's what people say."

"Only the weather will be better." Barbara smiled slowly, gesturing with one hand. "Arturo has been telling us everything about the weather up there."

"And in the Philippines."

She laughed again. "Yes. In the Philippines."

"Well, there won't be any hurricanes in that thing, I guess. And if they've thought it out right, the made-rain won't burn the trees."

There was a brief silence. Then Barbara asked me, "When is it you're going up?"

"I'm packed. A car will come for me in the morning, deliver me to the launch site." I thought of adding, *But I don't know if I'm going,* and discovered I had no wish, after all, to let anyone else look at my decision.

Barbara nodded. She shifted her weight silently, and it became clear she was waiting to go back to her bed.

I went to the open door. "Well, good night, then," I said in embarrassment. I would have kept on with our talk. I seemed to have this compulsion now, to discuss the environment of the *Dusty Miller.*

"Good night," Barbara said, without moving from where she stood, arms folded, in the middle of the front room. "Thank you for bringing Arturo home. We'll see each other up there."

"Maybe we will."

I went out again to the cart road and stood at the edge of the ruts and thought of breaking off for home; I thought of giving up this restless, useless night-wandering and taking my poor wayworn body home to bed. But then my feet went on up the track toward the rocky ridge of the Ojo de la Luna.

The air became thicker, freighted with smoke, and I fell to a plodding pace. I wished I had gotten a drink from Arturo's cup. Wished I had brought him to the door and said goodnight and gone quickly away from the tired woman's house.

The cart road, when it had gained the ridge called the Eye of the Moon, turned south along the face of the limestone bluff, but I left the road and followed dimly worn trails northward along the backbone. From the high outlook, in the smoky night, the neat checkerwork of fields in the valley seemed fashioned of bronze, copper, umber, terracotta. The darkness was starless and feverish, the moon a smudged, brownish ellipse behind the dirty sky.

Where will the smoke go on the *Dusty Miller*? I wondered suddenly. People say the bodies of the dead will be burnt and the ashes turned in with the soil, but where will the smoke go in a closed world?

When I was young, still a girl, in certain months of the year the sun would come above the Ojo de la Luna in cool mornings and flood the sky with transparent light, and the atmosphere on such mornings was clear at least as far as the nearest summits of the *cordillera*. But even in those years, the farming populations all up and down the narrow highland spine of Middle America were burning their fields, the hillsides too stony or steep for plowing, and in the sowing months the burden of smoke in the air would shroud the peaks, the sun would rise red, a glare. Now the vast forests of the Amazon burn throughout the year, making way for fields of cattle, and there never are clear days now, not in the rainy season, not even in January, which has traditionally held the year's most pleasant weather. In the afternoons in every month the air is hot, murky, oppressive.

We grow a maize, a small old kind with a dark purple husk that fits the ear tightly and trails beyond it in a long stiff beard, tough husks that for the most part keep out the weevils that de-

stroy so much stored grain in a climate prevailingly wet and
warm, and we go on planting our maize as the Indians must
have done on this same land before Columbus came, cutting the
old stalks with machetes, dropping the seeds into holes made
with pointed sticks, while elsewhere in this world people follow the pandemic, destructive impulse of technology: They
plant larger and yet larger hybrids that outgrow their clothes,
corn that keeps badly and has to be treated with pesticides,
fungicides, formaldehyde. In the rest of the world, huge machines with glassed cabs roll across vast fields of played-out soil,
and a bushel of corn is paid for in two bushels of topsoil, lifted
to the sky in voluminous brown scrims of dust. In March, when
the corporate farms are making ready to plant their fields,
columns of smoke rise high above the tops of the ridges all
around the *estancia,* and ash settles on the porches, the fields,
the jacaranda trees.

If they want to put my ashes in the soil, there is a clarity to
that, a circularity I like, but I don't want the smoke of my body
to foul the air. *What if there are no Fourth Month rains, and the
smoke from people's burned bodies is let out to darken the air?*

The goatpaths took me gradually down from the Ojo, northwest across a gravel wash and then westerly along the edges of
terraced fields where a branch of the river had once flowed—a
dusty channel now overgrown with shrubs and small trees. It
was this same long-abandoned side channel that divided my
own taro field from the maize, and finally, having decided nothing, I followed the troublous avenue of bare rocks in a long slow
circling toward home.

My house is older than the Quaker settling of the land—built
before The War, before the last several wars perhaps, a thick-
walled *bahareque* with white-washed beams and an idiosyn-
cratic placement: Its windowless back stands to the road, and
the unglazed "front" windows look behind to a field dotted
with orange trees, and a high-peaked shed roof that one time
housed a sugar mill. When I came through the orange trees in
the hot night, a Gray's thrush flew out from the *dulce* shed, and,
looking, I saw she had built her nest high up in a dark corner
of the metal roof.

I remember in the days of my childhood, my mother standing with her forearms resting on the wide frame of the window, watching birds crack apart the leavings of corn in their horned beaks, and she would name for me the doves and shy woodrails, the toucans and quails attracted to the spillage. In those days there had been cinnamon-bellied squirrels as well, and a pair of blue tanagers who year after year made a small soft cup on the ridgepole in the very center of the high-peaked *dulce* shed. But no squirrels have been seen on this land in the last decade, and the tanagers have gone too, after yearly failing to hatch or raise a single nestling. The native birds are steadily more rare as their sheltering forests dwindle and coarser, more commonplace species take possession of the land. In the recent days since my corn was laded up to the sky, only grosbeaks have flocked into the yard to glean the spilled grain, and this Gray's thrush is the first I have seen in a year.

While I stood pondering the thrush's neat little nest, the poor bird waited in one of the orange trees, her eggs undefended. She will hatch them, if any of the eggs are viable, after I have moved to the *Miller.* And standing there in the hot dimness at the edge of my fields, I realized that this bird brooding in my shed might be the last Gray's thrush I would see in my lifetime.

The fields of the *Miller* are in the ancient Pennsylvania Quaker manner, every seventh acre set aside for forest, but the plantings are deliberately various, a subtropical pastiche. Among the few trees familiar to me—kapok and paperbark, breadfruit, candlenut—are to be *banyan, bamboo, litchi, camphor:* trees that seem to me as astonishingly exotic as cactus or the stunted pines of a tundra. And the greater part of the fauna have come from a little parcel of mountainous land that was willed to the Japanese Society of Friends by the Nature Conservancy. No carnivores have survived on that steep little woodland nor any of the big, wide-ranging herbivores; those are gone, all of them, gone for decades. But the Japanese Friends have succeeded in protecting a native biology, a few dozen species of formerly hundreds of tortoises, snakes, lizards, toads, frogs, newts, birds, insects; and these have formed the core of the *Miller*'s living and creeping things. Whether a Gray's thrush will make its life in that polyglot forest among that little multitude of Japanese birds, Japanese animals, is not known to me. What birds will nest in the farm sheds of the *Dusty Miller*?

At last I went into my house and waited in the darkness until the wary bird came back to the eggs. When I put on the light, there were—almost a kind of surprise—the waiting boxes, and the loose drifts of uncrated belongings, things to be handed over to my homebound neighbors. I ought to have gone to bed. The long, absurd walking had brought me no clarity, I thought—had been only wearing and dusty and maundering. I was tired and someone would be at my door early to take away my packing. But I sat down among the crates and then got up again suddenly, restless, and went among my things until I'd found the books.

In early Meetings, worries were raised, and laid to rest, about the technology in the *Miller:* People wanted to go on living plainly, in the manner of Friends, and after all there would not be the resources for repairing or replacing complicated machinery, problematic instruments and appliances. But the balance that has been struck is sometimes odd, incongruous. Books, which are the plainest of human tools, must be housed in a manner to keep them carefully from the wet and warmth, and the limited space in that sealed and air-conditioned place, set against the necessary compass of knowledge, means a vast library of microfiche and videos, and just a tiny library of bound volumes. There are, in the two rooms of this house, many hundreds of books that will remain behind, and a single crate of twenty-six books that will travel with me to the *Miller.* The size of the box, the bulk and weight that are permitted to me, have forced me to providence: I have kept Zardoya's translations of Whitman, but nothing of Calderon. Have put aside *Le Grand Meaulnes,* kept *Les Miserables.* Now I was inexplicably, suddenly, stricken with apprehension: had I put *Song of the Lark* in the stacks to be given away, or the box to be taken up? *Adios, Mr. Moxley? Sigrid Lavransdatter?* I sorted through

the books, reading and rereading the indexing in a fever of sus-
picion. By what measure had I included *The Magic Mountain,*
but not *Pajaros del Nuevo Mundo?*

The air remained thick, hot. I knelt painfully before the box,
overcome with nostalgia and an indecipherable sorrow. How
had I imagined I could live the balance of my life without holding the pages of Cesar Vallejos in my hands? What if the people who had promised to include *Beloved, Ficciones, Historie
de ma Vie,* changed their minds or forgot their promises?

In my crate, one book is old, rare, has a value beyond words.
Elizabeth Martin and her husband had been among the First
Seventy who settled the old *estancia,* and her handwritten diary
is a family treasure. The First Seventy had been members of
Ohio or Iowa Yearly Meetings, had emigrated after one of the
first World Wars—escaping militarism, as they thought—thus
Elizabeth's diary is in English. I am even now making my slow
way through it for the third time or the fourth, my English still
as poor as my Esperanto. There is a rayon ribbon I use to mark
my place in it, and the ribbon now lies among painful pages:
She is waiting for the slow doctor, the slow lab, to say if she has
a cancer. She kept the secret, the little hard bead in her breast,
even from her husband, confided her dread only to the pages
of her diary. It is an old anxiety, made edgeless by familiarity,
and tonight when my hands brought that book up from the
bottom of the box I suppose my sudden brief weeping had as
much to do with birds and starless nights and the burned and
buried bodies of the dead, as with the worn old sorrows of Elizabeth Martin's life.

I have wondered: When Elizabeth wrote her secrets, who
were they meant to be read by? She always would identify people. "Mary (my mother)," she would say. Or, "Arthur, my
aunt's second son." Did she know, then, that her private words
would be read by strangers? Why else identify these people she
well knew? Who did she imagine would take the trouble to
work out her English words, her crabbed vertical hand? Who
would need the benefit of such naming?

Many people are keeping diaries again. They want to record
the momentous events of these times, and their feelings—

explanations, apologies, defense—addressed to children and grandchildren and the seven or eight generations afterward who must live out their lives within the hull of that houseboat until it fetches up on the distant rocks of Epsilon Eridani. I have no children, no one to whom I must apologize. I have wondered: What person would struggle to work out my spidery handwriting, my idiomatic Spanish, to read of arthritic joints, of the making of pottery and the growing of maize? For whom should I write?

But here, as you see, are the first pages of my diary.

Perhaps Elizabeth Martin imagined herself writing for a woman then unborn—for Dolores Negrete, who is only an old and childless woman descended from the Martins' family line, a Spanish-speaking woman who trudges through the night in order to circle round to the truth, a woman who sits on the floor of her house reading old painful confidences as she makes ready to begin her life again after sixty years. As I now imagine you, an Esperanto-speaking person unrelated to me, a person now unborn, who in 150 years, or two hundred, will be circling round again to the truth, beginning your life again. I imagine you sitting on the floor of your house reading my anxious musings about the smoke of burnt bodies and the leaving-behind of birds' nests, and as I am writing this, you are thinking of the forepart of your life and the after, in the days that separate them.

1

Inscriptions

One

JUKO

And you O my soul where you stand,
Surrounded, detached, in measureless
      oceans of space,
Ceaselessly musing, venturing, throwing,
      seeking the spheres to connect them,
Till the bridge you will need be form'd,
      till the ductile anchor hold,
Till the gossamer thread you fling
      catch somewhere, O my soul.

On that day, the go-down day, Juko Ohaŝi stood at the head of the weathermast—stood with her feet on the spindly seven-yard and her arms spread wide in the windless glare—looking sunward for her husband.

People who had never gone aloft imagined they might climb to a masthead and see the compass of the windship spread below them, but there was no seeing the whole of it from anywhere on the rigging; this was something every sailmender knew. You had to go out in a small boat, get five or ten kilometers away from it, before it began to be possible to see the whole configuration, the sails entire: Seven carbon-fiber yards thin as thread ringing the torus in concentric circles a kilometer apart, as though the torus had been a pebble dropped in still water; twelve wire-fine spokes radiating from the center in a complex reticulum of torsional support, intersecting the ring-yards and branching, branching again, until the twelve masts were fifty; two hundred panes of reflective vilar—a crowd of sail—each infinitely more tenuous than a soapbubble, each

broader than a corn field, bridging the delicate webwork of
yards and masts; myriad servos as fine as watchwork trimming
the sails in a restless canting with respect to the horizontal axis;
and all this immense diaphane supporting the small cumbrous
payload of the inhabited torus, a thick-bodied, eight-spoked
wheel lying at the center of the sails in a hammock of stays and
shrouds along the elliptical plane, like a moon at the eye of its
corona.

Among sailmenders, yes, there was a custom, a usual habit,
of standing at the outermost tip of a spoke, but not, as other
people thought, for a glimpse of the whole architecture turning in an elegant roundelay against the stars. From a boat, at ten
kilometers' distance, or twelve, the *Dusty Miller* was a vast
round mosaic of mirror, a great segmented disk rippling with
light and movement; but from the seven-yard, standing up from
the head of a mast, what you saw was a billowing field of sailcloth stretching wide and away beyond eye's reach, as the sea
must have stretched away from the eye of the blue-water sailor,
and the torus a small purplish atoll at the far horizon. Standing
at the head of a mast, people looked, not for the whole, but for
what must be the true aspect of a World: something larger than
the eye could take in.

Juko Ohaŝi, standing at the head of the weathermast, only
looked for her husband.

She had meant to keep from it. In the sixty-nine days since
Bjoro had sailed ahead of them in the *Ruby,* other people had
daily looked sunward from the fields of sail seeking a glimpse
of the far off boat, but Juko had not. She and her mother-in-
law both were inclined to eat sporadically and to sleep at un-
likely hours, and Bjoro inclined to push them toward more
orderly habits, so there was a certain narrow pleasure and freedom in his absence, and she always had taken to heart the old
axiom that you shouldn't expect your husband or your wife to
carry too much of the weight of your happiness. For sixty-nine
days she had felt very clear, very self-contained, unsentimental. She'd been comfortable not missing Bjoro at all, and had understood in a dim, restless way that looking for her husband,
or toward him, she might be stricken suddenly with loneliness.

She knew, in any case: From the rigging even the world they steered for was indistinguishable—three hundred days across the measureless distance: a minute light circling the small orange sun amid a turning field of stars, and the little *Ruby,* circling the world, an infinitesimally small mote of dust. Foolish to look for it—she had not meant to look for it. Had not meant to stand along the weathermast finding a balance in the compass of space, opening her arms as if she were offering something to God or calling up a spell against the night; had not meant to put her feet along the outermost rim of the fluttering array of sails and, spreading her arms to the black, windless firmament, to let in this fierce, this very precise longing for the smell of Bjoro's wet hair when he came from the bath, for the weight of his hands resting on her shoulders absently as he stood behind her in a crowd or in a queue.

It is the ŝimanas, she thought, and took a kind of mournful satisfaction in it. *All of us are gone a little mad these days.*

Her mother-in-law, Kristina Veberes, was apt to keep still about a worry until it was well past, and then she liked to complain to everyone how she'd lost sleep over it. She hadn't spoken a word of misgiving in the sixty-nine days, and wouldn't be wanting to complain yet with nothing known, no one safe; but Juko, standing at the head of the weathermast staring irresistibly, uselessly sunward, suddenly had in her mind that she and Kristina could get a little drunk tonight and comfort themselves with sarcasm, a habit they were both prone to. People believed the go-down day needed ceremony, and neighbors privately had given over to her two rare, small bottles of wine; she yearned suddenly to be sitting in the bath with her mother-in-law, drinking that wine, listing the son's, the husband's manifest faults.

They had an old, mother-daughter friendship, she and Kristina, years older than her marriage to Bjoro. Juko's own mother and Kristina had been childhood intimates, their families bound together in a tangle of distant kinship, of marriages several generations removed, and Juko had made a second mother of Kristina when her own mother was dead. She had been still married to Humberto in those days, but when their

younger son had died and she and Humberto had divorced, she
had moved her belongings into Kristina's house as a daughter
returning to her mother's family. Much of that unmarried year
was lost to her, a dull grayness, unremembered. She remembered the Plum Rains—the haloes around the xenon lamps in
the wet, humid nights. And Kristina's son, Bjoro, a man she had
known only as a would-be cousin—she remembered his gravity, his tolerant look, and the way that look had become un-
burdening, a safehold. Before the Plum Rains had come round
again, they were married. And their marriage had been knit to
that old friendship between Juko and Kristina—an inextricable web of family and familiarity.

On a little release of breath, someone said, "Ha! I'm up-top,"
and Juko, who was standing up-top herself, looked round for
the other. On the incom the voices always were burry, indistinguishable, and across the great distances of the diaphane the
sailmenders were gnats against the burnished vilar, but they had
named the two hundred fields of sail as farmers will name their
fields of corn, and she recollected some part of the sail chart for
this watch: There was Aric Engirt on the Weather-Beater, Al
Poreda on the Square-Away, Orval Wyho on the Rock-Bottom.
Someone was pulling swiftly out along the dark thread of the
spankermast, no telling who that was. The one who was up-top,
standing at the head of the skymast—Juko thought it was Marĉa
Negro.

In the earpiece there was a little sound, a sort of grunting dis-
gust, and the person crawling up the spankermast made a quick
slow-down, going clockwise onto the sail named the Far-Cry:
giving up a race.

"Who's racing? Is it Juko Ohaŝi? I seen Sonja go sprinting
by me with her eyes fixed on her hands, but you beat her good,
eh Juko?"

Sonja Landsrud was twenty-three or four, quick as a snake,
and it had been years since Juko had pulled out a mast on the
race, fast enough to beat Sonja Landsrud. She laughed. "No,
wasn't me," she said. "But I guess I'm not old, then, if somebody's thinking it could've been me."

"Could be you're still old, but fast," somebody said, and

people laughed. Then Marĉa said, "It was me—Marĉa. I'm the one beat her. I beat Sonja," and she let a little flourish be in it. *I beat her!*

"I was one-armed," Sonja said, a squawk. "Hey Marko, you saw me, eh? When I came out the hub? banged my wrist a hard one on that damned big fitting that sticks out beside the hatch."

"Get on, Sonja. Marĉa beat you, so don't whine." That was Marko, maybe, though hard telling on the vague incom.

Sonja said, surprised, "Whining's what I do," and that made people laugh again. It was an old aptness of Sonja's, become a joke she played to: She had always a particular reason for defeat.

Juko's ear became silent—they kept the incom mostly open for matters to do with the work, and for exigencies—and when the laughter had quieted, the weight of the silence carried her down past the moment of inertia and foolish yearning as she had stood at the vantage of the masthead. She fell softly onto the sail, the field called the Knock-Around, as softly as people, waking, fall back into the middle of their lives.

On the great sails there was silence, aloneness, as there never was in the crowded torus and maybe for this reason menders had a habit of coming together at the junctions where their fields joined—exercising their human connections. At the six-and-weather corner of her field she waited for Al Poreda, thinking he would come across the Square-Away in his usual steady plowman's pattern, lapping back and forth between the masts, monotonous, prosy. But maybe the *Lark* had brought his soul to poetry: He was covering the sail today with a loose, indecipherable chasing, a secret hieroglyphic. He kept at it, leaving out the corner, not seeing her there.

"Beauty," she said, her thumb on the incom, and that brought his head around slowly, looking for her. "Don't know what design you're making, but it has beauty," she told him.

There was distance between them, two or three hundred meters. He let himself come up from the undulating field, until his white exo was a small, drifting brilliance against the absolute blackness of the void. He opened his hands, a slow gesture, open-palmed, and brought his body around to her orientation.

"Looking for a pattern," he said. "Not finding it." Al Poreda had a grimacing, intent smile, like a man placing himself between fire and the body of his child. The skull of his exo was opaque, but she imagined his mouth letting the words out through that smile.

"No corner in your design, eh? I guess I'll quit waiting for you."

He was silent, his arms still open. Then he said in a tender whisper, "Don't wait," and let himself down on the sail, on the winding, unknowable pattern. *We are all gone a little crazy.*

A little retractable ribbon had a house in the waist of her exo, and when she pushed off with her hands against the weathermast the tether trailed her, sliding soundless on its endpin, following the curving track of the seven-yard. The *Miller* was braking, had been braking for forty years, and now they had come within the inner harbor of the new star their navigation had become an intricate, interminable equation of motion, a continuous contraposing of the outward stream of light, and of the solar wind, of the star's centripetal attraction, the perturbations of its four small planets, and the old momentum of the torus. The diaphane presented its face, like a blossom, always toward the sun, while the petals of shimmering sailcloth tilted their edges at shallow angles to the elliptical plane: finding their balance and then seeking a new one. Juko bobbled over the Knock-Around like a shorebird above a slow heaving sea.

Where there was a tangle in the halyard, she wrapped her legs over the yard's thin line and swayed there, picking the little knots in the fine carbon filament. Where an edge of sail was hung up in its rigging she pulled scrupulously at the jam until it was loose again, and with a flat-iron tool pressed out the creases in the cobwebby cloth. Where there was a hole in the sail she soldered the little breach—a dozen atoms expelled in a bead at the tip of the fine mending needle.

The mechanicals were ancient, deteriorating, the sailcloth and the rigging frayed and dilapidated. The *Dusty Miller* had borne sail for its first fifty years, gathering way in a stately, deliberate acceleration; but for eighty-five years, while the bare toroid coasted through the darkness between the old star and the new, the vast diaphane had been furled, its vanes contracted about the torus with some little hope the folds of mirrored cloth might shield them from the bombardment of cosmic rays. Then in Juko's childhood the great circle of sails was spread again for this long, difficult braking, and the Maintenance Committee blamed the poor condition of the old sails on the long closure, the reopening.

Juko had heard some people say they thought it was a decay of artistry as much as apparatus. She had learned the sail-mender's art, herself, from people who had, years before, gone up in the hub and hung a field of sail in that high-ceilinged space above the foundry and studied the servos for the spar devices, setting and resetting them, and watching the ways the little mechanical brain turned a halyard wrong or needed a hand to pull a yard down taut—setting and studying and resetting and watching again, figuring out the old art and then climbing out onto the black void, spreading the great sails for the long braking inward toward the new, the unnamed world. Most of those people were dead now, never had seen the new sun. Juko thought if you complained of lost artistry, probably you never had been out on the rigging; she thought people who had never been outside sometimes were inclined to criticize the people who had.

Where the jackmast joined the seven-yard, she went inward along it, girdling the big trapezoid of the Knock-Around, eleven hundred meters along the seven-yard, a thousand meters along the six. The Weather-Beater and the Knock-Around abutted one another along the six-yard and whenever the sail luffed under her, Juko saw Aric Engirt in the glimmering swale, working steadily toward her across the Weather-Beater. When he had made the corner where the jackmast crossed the six, he floated there with his legs wound round the thread of the yard, his face turned toward the little orange bud of the sun. Maybe he was keeping track of Juko from an edge of his eye: In the soundless sky, as she came down to him at the corners of their fields, he broke off his staring and let his body come around to her orientation.

"Phtt," he said, a wordless complaint, with his thumb shut-

ting out the others on the incom so the sound of it was closed-
up, a small-room sound. He made an exaggerated gesture with
his shoulders, a slumping, and she remembered he had been sick
lately, a cold or a cough, one of the nameless, catholic viruses.

She said, "You should have stayed home, kid, you look still
down with the bug."

He gave her a grimace, a ducking boyish look. "Should've.
Yeah." He lifted his gloved hands gently, numbering with his
fingers. "There's six babies in our damn house. People kept
wanting to put me to someone's breast. I've got this baby's
face, Rita keeps telling me."

Juko laughed. It was true, his face was smooth, dimpled; inside the fiberglass skull of the exo, his hair hung down in a thick,
childish forelock. "Six! You ought to tell Rita to let you alone."
Juko had not much recollection of this wife—a small woman,
dark hair? She remembered they had a new baby, maybe it was
a boy, born in the dry season.

Aric grinned, showing his teeth in a leer. "Too bad we didn't
make them all," he said. "Only one, and the rest are my
brother's doing, and the neighbors'."

"Six in the same house?"

"Six! Born in the same year, in the same damn domaro!
Maybe all the husbands laid down with their wives on the same
night, and in the morning all the wives got up pregnant. Anyway, now one of the chicks is ailing with something, maybe it's
what I've had—you know how a thing like that goes round a
neighborhood—so people are carrying that baby back and forth
and up and down, and a house with so many babies is prone to
be in a kind of rush regardless, eh? things never still. Rita likes
it. I guess I do, but this bug has made me surly." He grinned
again. "No crying kids out here, anywise."

Juko thought he wanted this to be a joke, but his pallid face,
grinning, drew up in a sort of pinch, suppressing a little dry
cough. She said, "So you thought you'd find some other people to be surly with, besides your neighbors? Come out here
and gripe at your friends?"

He laughed in a small way, looking at her shyly. "I guess I
just wanted to come out. Couldn't lay in bed, you know." He

moved his shoulders once more, eyeing her self-consciously from beneath the straight brow-cut of his hair. "The *Lark,* you know. I wanted to come out."

She didn't know why she skirted her eyes away from him. Maybe she had caught from him a kind of embarrassment. *Both of us are crazy then, I looked for it myself.*

Twice a day or three times, the radio people had been sending someone around to neighborhoods with copies of the *Ruby*'s voice logs, everybody wanting to know what was being said, even if the only talk going on was pointless and sentimental. *This from Arda,* the word had come down today. *We have a window thirteen o'clock for the go-down. Hans and me will stay on the* Ruby. *On the* Lark *there'll be Luza, Bjoro, Peder, Isuma. They'll mean to call again when land is made but they'll be busy so maybe not. Don't worry! Hans or me will call when we hear up from them. Now we'll have a real look-see!*

Not Bjoro's words—this was something Juko would have known without Arda naming herself. Bjoro was inclined to be methodical, mathematical; he'd have been more formal and more precise. Arda had a deep, loose alto, she always would say important things in an offhand, exclaiming way. *So at the window, will launch the* Lark!

For years, while the *Dusty Miller* had gone on making its slow and slower approach, they'd been slinging little scoutboats out ahead to learn what could be learned from brief robotic fly-bys of the sun and its small system, but now they had come inside the orbit of the star's outermost planet, and the slow old *Miller* was within a year of parking round the sun's second planet, its one livable world, and so they had sent six people in the fast motorboat *Ruby* sprinting ahead across the inner compass of the solar system for a first human glimpse. The *Ruby* had had a sixty-day traverse, and now for nine days had been orbiting the new world while they sent down the first two dozen tropospheric survey balloons; and today, finally, the *Ruby*'s tiny go-down boat, the heavy-lift launch the *Lark,* was cast off from the *Ruby;* and the four people in it—*Bjoro!*—must even now be making their quick, narrow crossing to close with the land.

"So you've had your look at the boat," she said to Aric Engirt with a tender grimace, "and maybe you should go in now.
There's no babies in my damn house, and I've got a small family, eh? and Bjoro gone. My mother-in-law will leave you alone
if you want to roll out my bed and sleep on it. When I come
off, I'll send you home to Rita."

He made a slight, sheepish hand sign, a sort of pushing away.
"No. Not that sick. Anyhow, I've just got started. I ought to
get the cross done so I don't lose track of what I've done."
Menders had each their own style of working a field, few of
them crawled the same sail in just the same way. It was Aric's
habit to run up a mast then down on the diagonal, go across the
yard and upward diagonal again, cutting the field into dia-
monds. "I'll quit when I've run the ex." And then, beginning
to smile, "It must be this damn baby's face, eh? You're aiming
to mother me, now your own has grown up and flown away
from you."

He meant Ĉejo, seventeen. He would not know—would
have been a child then himself—one of her babies had flown
away from her by dying. She hunched one shoulder up, de-
flecting the little irritation, if that was what it was. "Go on, then,
if you want," she said, and made a mouth, a smiling frown. She
lifted her hand in a quick, half-peevish good-bye, and pulled
out along the six-yard, taking herself off swiftly until Aric had
fallen out of sight across the luff of his field and she was alone
again.

She had an old, leathery callus that protected her in such moments, but he had got by it a little. She never had been inclined
to mother anything sick, that was the sore point. It had been
Humberto who had clasped their first son to his breast in the
first colicky weeks, muttering useless wordless sounds of comfort, walking round the room and round in his flat bare feet,
while Juko sat on the floor making wicker, or peeling oranges.
She had liked Ĉejo rather better at three and four, thin sweaty
arms wrapped round her neck, solemn kisses pressed on her
lips. But by then she and Humberto had made a second son,
and sometimes in those days she had gone on lying in her bed
with the heels of her hands against her ears while that son was

crying, crying, and other people had brought Vilef to her breast, brought him to lie over her unmoving heart, and it was only afterward, when he was dead, that she had felt the slow beating behind the bone.

People liked to say romantic love was a childish sentiment, something you ought to get over with in your green years. *To marry a lover is fatal,* people said. Everyone knew, the relationship of lovers was transient, electrical, while marriage above other things must be a durable partnering, a system of mutual reliance, a friendship. Family and neighbors were expected to indemnify a marriage by anchoring it in patience, affection, and support; and Juko's family had mostly followed that charge. She had been given, in Humberto, a husband who was melancholy, passive, prone to chronic physical complaints—but someone of tolerance and stillness, someone disposed to agree with her values and judgments, an undistinguished, predictably tender sexual partner, a conscientious father to their sons. The Senlima Clearness Committee had admired the tying of their wedding knot. And counseled its unraveling. People had blamed that divorce on Vilef's unhappy birth, but she and Humberto, both of them, always had understood: It was Vilef's death, not his birth, that was to blame. Humberto never had been able to forgive her for receiving her son's death as a gift, and she unable to forgive him for his unequivocal, stubborn devotion to grief.

Now her marriage with Bjoro, without children at its center, but tied to Kristina in a complicated gyre of mother-son, husband-wife, daughter-mother, was altogether unsentimental; everything between them was arguable, everything sufficient, abiding. She had, as she thought, reinvented marriage, and it had been years since she had thought of the Plum Rains at the end of her old divorce. But she was adrift, today, in the wake of a vague resonance. The narrow, explicit lonesomeness that had come up in her body when she had stood at the head of the weathermast had become a kind of homesickness, a bleary unfocused pining.

Her own pattern of mending was to circle a field at the yards and masts, repairing the halyards and smoothing the tangles, and then to drift inward slightly and inward again, spiraling toward midsail, looking for tears. While her body rose and fell on the slow breath of the sail, she made the wide smooth circle around the field and then around again, a chip of wood borne in on the eddy, circling. The silvery web of sails wheeled languidly, the star field turning with it. She kept from looking starward but she felt herself turning with the sails, felt the small orange sun holding steady in the vast blackness, and gradually she began to feel the muddy mood suspended about her like the depthless sky. She began to work well, to work habitually, not thinking of Bjoro finally nor the *Lark,* nor even of old marriages and dead children.

Someone said "Hans!" in a sudden yell drawn out long on a fading note. There was a small silence, a surprised dumbness among them all. Finally someone said, "Hey Sonja. What?" for Sonja and Hans were cousins—one of them had an aunt who had married the other's uncle—and everybody knew Hans was orbiting in the *Ruby*, waiting with Arda while the *Lark* carried the other four down to landfall.

Sonja laughed. There was not much timidness in that woman anywhere. "Oh hell. I can't hardly believe I did that. Oh hell. I guess I was just sending him a sort of kiss or a marker buoy or something. I'm up the head of the spanker and from here you can see forever or what passes for it, and I all at once had to send his name out on the wind, eh?" Juko, looking, made out the tiny thread-end trailing from the tip of the spankermast, Sonja Landsrud standing as Juko earlier had done, at the rim of the sail staring sunward. *We are all gone a little mad these days.*

There was only a brief silence and then it was Orval Wyho who said, flat and short, "The ŝimanas, I guess. It's put you over the edge." Orval always had a crabbed way of speaking; you knew his voice on the obscuring incom. Some of them laughed, making an indistinguishable noise.

"Hey Juko, you'd better leave a word for Bjoro too!" There followed a smacking sound, wet, a loud kiss.

"Who's to yell for Arda, then, and Peder? They'll be lost."

"Arda! Here's for you, dear!" "Luza!" "Hey, Isuma!"

"H-A-L-L-O-O-O the *Ruby!*" "Hey, *Lark!*"

Juko had no impulse to call to Bjoro, but she had liked Sonja hailing the boat that way, girlish, not grown too staid yet nor too reasonable. So on the little momentum of the other voices, she yelled once too, "Bjoro!," hearing it come out stiff and fierce-sounding.

There was a lot of laughter, a choppy noise. Then Romeo Thorkildsen, from the sailchart desk in the hub, sounded through it with his steady voice, unamused. "Can't hear a damn thing, you know, mid that racket," and made them subside. In the short silence afterward, it seemed to Juko that their little stopped-up breaths, their sighing restlessness, must be the sound of the *Dusty Miller,* sails and torus all, falling light as a milkweed seed inward toward the sun. Then Romeo said, a closed sound only for her ear, "You see Alberto there, Juko, from where you are?"

Her eyes followed the black edge of shadow slipping smoothly clockwise, the luff of her own field casting its umbra across the Square-Away. "No. What."

"He's clockwise of you. On the Square-Away."

"Sure, but he's hid in the dark." Looking for him, waiting for the ebb of the shadow, she said, "Al?" and then, "Hey, Al."

She had known Alberto Poreda a long time, been a child with him in the Senlima ŝiro, been a little in love with Al once, when she was eleven. In Senlima, in that neighborhood of their childhood, the Ring River cut two shallow channels, and the footings of the Fiddle-Spoke rose straight up from the gravelly island to pierce the high ceiling. When she had been eleven, she had sat on the island in the shadow of the spoke with a boy whose name she no longer remembered, and she'd let that boy touch her flat brown nipples. She had told this to Al afterward, without knowing why she had wanted him to know, but she remembered the reddened look his face had taken on, and that he had kept away from her for weeks—maybe it was from panic. Why was she remembering that now? All this looking backward.

"Juko," Romeo said, "he's gone offline is all, see if you can get him to answer up, wave his hand or something."

She made a reply, wordless, and left the center of her field for the weathermast, sculling across the open sail without hurrying, and then coming in along the mast beginning to pull swiftly hand over hand. There was no wind, only the steady small light of the little sun, and the star field skipping a dim shine off the facets of sail. In the absence of windrush, Juko heard the beating of her own blood in her ears.

She and Al had used to sail tetherless, all bravado and foolishness when they were young, twenty, sweeping across the face of a field in long, heart-stopping glissades, imagining other sailmenders watching them must be struck with envy and respect. People who were twenty still sometimes went onto the sails without a tie. *Young, stupid, reckless,* Juko thought now. She knew, though, why they were doing it—remembered her own body's voiceless yearning to belong to a larger, a less coherent pattern. She hadn't loosed herself from a sail tether in years, she and Al both having become more careful after their children were born.

And she remembered suddenly: Where Al's son should have had a hand there was a smooth rounded nub, very pink. She could not remember the child's face at all, but very clearly the look of that nubbin, and the use he made of it, deft, delicate. Or she was remembering her own son Vilef, the single finger of his ill-formed hand climbing her chin.

When the mechanism of the sail drew the edge of shadow back smoothly across the Square-Away, she could see Al's small dark shape on the shivering field of vilar, and another little beetle, it would be Aric Engirt over there on the Weather-Beater, pulling slowly out along the six-yard.

She said, "Al," and no one answered, but then Romeo said something, not to her, and she heard several voices but not the words, and then Romeo again, the others falling silent as he spoke. He was a balding little man with a big voice. "Juko," he said. "I guess you'd better go on in to him. Aric, you go too, eh? until you can see him? what he's up to? One of you get an answer out of him, so we don't worry."

"Going," she said—for Romeo, an answer—and then heard Al's soft word, the echo unexpectedly in her ear, "Going."

In the small silence afterward there rose in Juko an uneasy

remembrance of Al Poreda's dark narrow face, the line of his white teeth below the edge of his burning smile. And then in her ear the little hissing as in a closed room, as if he had put his body in the fire at last. She was struck by a preposterous fear, something to do with Al sailing tetherless across his field as they had used to in the old days, all bravado and foolishness. And now she was crossing over the long bright sail to him, dropping like a bird, a bead of rain, a stone into his open hands, when she saw the sudden stiff spreadeagle puff of his exo, and the shape he made bobbing on the tether like a New Year's kite, bright cloth on a wire frame standing out stiff in the windless cold.

"Oh!" Aric Engirt said, in a surprised, childish voice, and Juko saw that he had checked his momentum, had hooked his legs around the rigging of the Weather-Beater. She went on a moment longer, falling toward Al, the mast passing swiftly under her in a thin blurred thread, and then she tripped the dragline with her thumb and when her body had ceased moving she felt something still moving within her, a jittery excitement in her chest.

"What," Romeo said, steady and gentle.

"He's breached his exo," Aric Engirt said, still filled with astonishment.

The silence had its own quality of surprise. "He's dead, then?" Romeo said, dumbfounded, without truly asking anyone anything. In a moment he said to someone else, not to any of them out on the sail—perhaps turning to tell the others gathering behind him there in the hub—"Alberto Poreda has got himself killed." Juko thought she ought to say something to Aric or to Romeo on the incom, but what she felt, still felt, was that breathless flutter, and no words came.

She had bathed her mother's body when the soul went out of it, had watched or helped other people do the same for their own family members—she wasn't afraid of looking at someone who was dead. But the tumid body seemed not Al's, seemed only ambiguously human. She waited, looking, from a hundred meters, and then went on slowly out to the end of Al's tether, and in a little while Aric Engirt came on too.

Al was bobbing above an edge of field that had tangled hard in the lines. The exo had a glossy look, solid; there was a long straight rift in the left forearm of the exo, and a distended blip of Al's arm was extruded into it, an egg-shape, taut and shiny, bruise-colored. The knife was still in the fist of his right glove. Juko fixed her eyes on his closed hand, the narrow serrated knife, and kept from looking at the clear skull of the exo, the fierce grin in the blood-swollen face.

"He's cut through his exo," Aric said, whispering this as if it might be a secret other people weren't listening to.

Romeo Thorkildsen, his voice going on being surprised, said, "Oh! My dear God!" Then, becoming steady again, "Well, you'd better bring him in, eh? Aric? You and Juko bring him in."

Aric Engirt looked to her in alarm. The soft pouches below his eyes were dark, the way Ĉejo's had used to be when he was needing sleep or coming down feverish. Baby's face. Something moved again in Juko: It was her jumpy heart contracting, tightening. "Yes," she said. Then she put her hand out deliberately and took hold of Al's big wrist. There wasn't any feel of a limb inside an exo. The thing she had hold of had a smooth slick softness, rubbery. She opened Al's hand and took the knife from it and folded the knife and put it away in her own tool belt. Then she took a better hold of his wrist, and the old marks of her fingers remained impressed in the exo.

Aric watched her, or he watched Al, not coming up to take hold of the other wrist. His need not to touch the body made her feel obscurely admirable. She didn't speak to him—what would she say?—but then a few murmuring words spoke themselves, not for Aric's sake. "It's still Al. He's just got himself killed, is all."

She sculled gently, starting down along the mast, bringing Al's body by the one arm. It twisted slightly, trailing behind her as a stubborn child twists to have a hand let go. Aric opened his mouth to let a breath in, and the air going down in his body made a little sound in her ear, a sigh. Finally he came and took a gingerly hold on the other arm. They went slowly inward, both of them, with Al Poreda carried buoyant between them.

People were waiting at the ring-yards. Without speaking, they fell in behind, a few and then a few more, until it had become a sort of cortege.

"He has that father sick and set to die," someone said.

Someone else made a small answering sound, a sort of clucking of the tongue.

"What," said Orval in his flat, recognizable tone. "I don't know about that."

"A cancer," someone said. "He's not old yet. Maybe he's sixty, sixty-five."

Juko cast around for something to say. She had learned from that dying old man, Al's father, how to roll sweet brigadeiros in cinnamon and the zest of an orange; should she say that? She found that she had got used to the feel of the body. After a while she took a new, firmer grip, and looked down with mournful curiosity to see the old marks of her fingers where they remained imprinted on the exo.

"It was the sîmanas, eh?" someone asked them all tenderly.

It was a sort of madness, an exquisite pain of utter and unspeakable aloneness. Their own. It was not a small thing. In Juko's memory, perhaps a dozen people had killed themselves to end unbearable, unspeakable alienation; and when the clerk read the names of the dead at Yearly Meeting, these suicides seemed to lie at the center of all their lives, a heart of inexplicable grief. But they had all got to calling any least sadness or fear by its name. *It is the sîmanas,* they said, blaming that mind-sickness for quarrels and forlornness and names cast like bottles into the void. Maybe they meant to enfeeble it, giving its name to other, slighter insanities. It was plain, though, that this question was asked in the old way, true and narrow. *Has he gone crazy, then? killed himself?*

Juko's eyes sprang with tears, a short stinging that was not grief, she thought, but tiredness and an obscure fear, something to do with madness, with bad weather, or the Plum Rains. She didn't look at anyone.

"He maybe meant to cut the halyard," Aric said, low and sick, a boy's voice. "There was a big snarl. Maybe the field swung up and put him off his balance."

It was Orval Wyho who said, "I never have tried it, but I expect you'd have to saw quite a bit to cut through an exo." On the incom his voice had that crabbed sound, grumping.

Juko had known people to die on the sails—three, now four, in twenty years—but it was not those people she thought of. She was remembering poor Tual Mendoza, who had gone mad one day and cut his tether, had folded out his thin sailmender's knife and carefully, neatly, sawed through the cord and kicked himself adrift. Juko had been in the tugboat that had taken him in afterward. She remembered how he had stared at them all with great child's eyes, bewildered, terrorized, inarticulate.

At Meetings for Business, people every day were reporting the bleak particulars gathered up from the balloons, the first real details of weather and landforms, the discouraging measurements and jargon of glaciation, of vulcanism, of storms. What Juko had felt on hearing all this bad news, these bad reports, was just a failure of her imagination. Maybe she never had believed it would one day come to this—people standing on the new world. *A hundred and seventy-five years. And now people standing on the land.* She remembered how, in the tug, looking for Tual Mendoza in the black depths, all the grandness of the sails was shrunk to triviality: From a thousand kilometers, the *Miller* was a silver bead on a dark starred field.

Things began sliding around in her head, a random disconnectedness, none of it to do with death, now, none of it to do with Alberto Poreda. She was thinking of a long rattan table she had in mind to build; of asking Leo Furuso for the necessary bundles of reed; of getting some smaller works of hers finished before the big table could be started. Leo Furuso was one of those who'd made her a gift of wine, straw-colored, distilled from the skins of mandarin oranges, or mangoes—she wasn't able to remember which, and fretted over this in a useless way. I don't like waking alone in bed, she thought, as if in defense of herself, as if this fact was to blame for the earlier, bluesy pining for her husband. *People shouldn't expect their husband or their wife to hold up too much of the weight of their happiness.*

The torus gradually took on size and effect. It had a quick gravitational turning, and at its circumference it lapped the slower diaphane of sails with a tireless constancy. From the one-yard, the periphery of the torus rose from the horizon in a long, lustrous, reeling palisade, with the globe-shaped hub at the axis seeming to stand unmoving behind it like the inner keep of a castle. A small confusion of cupolas and knobby spires projected north and south from the hub, and these poles spun swift or slow or not at all, according to their uses. People climbed out to the sails or back from them along the cat's cradle of lines between the one-yard of the diaphane and the docking ports at the north pole. It was the usual thing to trip a dragline and leap over the thwarts of the torus in one long splendid planing: In that one moment, the gray fastness of the wheel became the nucleus about which and for which those two hundred fields of silver-gilt sail were spread. But now, having Al Poreda's swollen body in their hands, they climbed the hawser with deliberateness, with gravity; and the torus, revealing itself incrementally beneath them, seemed unrevealed, flat, jejune.

There were long apertures chasing the inner circumference of the wheel. The apertures had been baffled against the dizzying turn of the starfield—there was no seeing in or out of them. There had been mirrors once, corresponding to the apertures, for letting the light of the old sun into the world, but they had been disassembled early on and the mirrors sold off, and it had been a myriad of xenon fixtures that had brought them ersatz daylight in the long years between suns. There was a spangle of lights at the hub, in the few small windows and defining the docking ports, but the wheel and its spokes were dark, windowless, arcane. Juko, looking down on it through the architecture of Al Poreda's stiff, spreadeagled legs, felt bitterly its lack of a human reference.

She thought all at once, inexplicably, of the big, yellowing camphor tree standing on the high side of her house. The altejo aqueduct ran in a narrow channel up there, but where the roots of the old tree shouldered it to one side, the water spread out shallow and slow. It was a favored place for birds to come, drinking and bathing, though the water was brown and there were bits of twig and dead leaves in it. The camphor tree was inborn, but old for all that, a crown ten meters high, shedding leaves now in great dry drifts, the limbs displaying themselves against the ceiling. People in the ŝiro had had the young forester to look at the sick old tree, but it occurred to Juko now: The camphor might be dead before her husband had gotten home again. He'd be four days, five, surveying on the ground, then thirty days sailing back here in the *Ruby*—at least that. *Al Poreda is dead,* she thought, as if that ought to keep the death of the camphor tree from surprising her.

Two

ĈEJO

To think that the sun rose in the east—
*   that men and women were flexible, real,*
*   alive—that everything was alive,*
To think that you and I did not see, feel, think,
*   nor bear our part,*
To think that we are now here and bear our
*   part.*

In the lift, Ĉejo stood with a woman who was mournful and silent—he thought he remembered she was a relative of Al Poreda's. He didn't know if he should speak to the woman—he was in an agony of fear—but finally he said, "Are you Ina's sister?" She was fair-skinned, narrow-eyed like Al's wife, Ina; they had the same stoopy shoulders on a long torso.

The woman's face was red in a blotchy way, but if she'd been weeping she was done with it for now. She nodded gravely. "You're Humberto Indergard's son. You look his image. Your mother works the sail with Alberto. Is she Juko Ohaŝi?"

"Yes."

She nodded again. "Do you know about Al? He got killed just now. I'm sent to meet the body."

The bad news, which had been vague, became at once more specific. He felt a quick, excruciating relief: *Alberto Poreda.*

One of Ĉejo's cousins had spent his green years with Al and his wife. Ĉejo had used to spend a little time there too, with his cousin, when he had been nine, ten. He had gotten from Al and

Ina a short-lived, very fierce interest in Jesus Christ. But when the word had come round the neighborhood, *someone on the sail was killed*, his heart had turned over; he had thought it was his mother.

Ĉejo and Al Poreda's sister-in-law came gradually buoyant in the lift, turning round to new positions relative to the floor, the door. The exit opened in what had been the ceiling. At the egress of the lift there was a corridor yoked to other corridors looping out to the docks and into the warren of labs and manufactory. Ĉejo didn't know the way. He followed the sister-in-law, who went ahead of him slowly in a long, drifting stride. It was cold in the hub. He rolled down the sleeves of his shirt.

Against the bright-green field of the curving wall were mahogany-colored people, yellow lions, stilt-legged white birds, all dancing long-limbed with their teeth bared, their feet turned out; then he passed a row of peak-roofed brick houses standing with shoulders adjoining, women sitting in bunches on the steps before the cherry-red doors; and a person in yellow trousers walking along a dry road beside a tile-and-plaster wall, beside trees arrayed high-crowned against a vivid blue firmament. On the long, windowless passageways of the hub, without an orientation to ceiling, to floor, people had painted a kaleidoscope of murals. Ĉejo had painted here, himself, two or three times. There were thousands of meters of intersecting corridors, no lack of surfaces. People had been painting on these walls since the beginning of life in the *Miller* and the murals beside the lifts were very old—maybe they were the work of people who had been dead for a hundred years.

When he and the sister-in-law came out to the periphery of the north pole, windows were set at rare intervals, letting on the docking ports. The ports had been meant to receive the big heavy-lift vehicles that had used to come up from Earth launches. They were used now chiefly by individual sail-menders entering and leaving the hub, for which use they seemed cavernous, out of scale. There were strands of lights framing each of the portals, a frame for wheeling stars, but within them was blackness, hugeness. In one, finally, Ĉejo saw a lit torch and shapes drifting inward seeking the human-scale hatch in the deep darkness of the interior wall. Their shadows fell away long and utterly black in several directions at once, jumping up the walls, the ceiling, down to the floor, in the great cave of the docking port. He put his face to the glass, looking for his mother.

"Is that Al they're bringing in there?" the sister-in-law asked him, coming to look also. There was no telling yet. He saw tiny shapes, five or six, in the bright white of exos.

"I don't know," he said.

But it must have been. When they followed the curve of the corridor, they saw other people had got there ahead of them, crowding the space in front of the hatch. Ĉejo knew most of them, by face at least; they worked the sailchart room or the sail, were friends of his mother and of Al. Some he didn't know. One was dark like Al, an old man, his skin close to his bones. The sister-in-law didn't speak to the old man but took hold of his arm as she came alongside him.

Ĉejo thought he should wait out of the way, at the edge of the group. Someone he knew, a sailcharter named Anĝelo Jutaka, held a wall strap away from the others. When he was next to him, Ĉejo said, "Do you remember me? I'm Juko's son."

Anĝelo nodded without smiling. "You're grown up. I remember you, a little child. Did you hear about Al Poreda?"

"Yes."

"It's Juko who's bringing in his body."

Ĉejo looked toward the door. There was a small round window set in it, letting on the pressure chamber. From where he was, he could see nothing through the glass. He waited, imagining his mother and the others crowded into the little room with Al Poreda's body, their white exos bumping silently together in the whispering room.

"They've let the *Lark* down, did you hear?" Anĝelo Jutaka leaned closer to him, speaking the words softly next to his ear, a solemn whisper. "Nobody should be surprised if it was the ŝimanas killed Al—it's the anxiousness does it, that's my feeling, and these are anxious times, no denying."

Ĉejo didn't know what he should say to that. He had been wild with restlessness earlier in the day, feeling on the cusp of great change. Now his anxiousness had an immediacy he didn't think Anĝelo was meaning—he wanted his mother to come out of the hatch. He wanted to see her face, let her see his.

"Isn't that Ina's sister?" Anĝelo asked him, murmuring into his ear. "Isn't her name Ajlina?" He bent his head toward the sister-in-law.

Ĉejo had not remembered the woman's name until now. "Yes. She's come to meet the body."

"Well I don't know him, but I guess the other, the old man, must be from Al's family too. He looks like Al, eh? Dark and short like that."

The hatch door released a little breath and then swung slowly inward so the people next to it had to move out of the way, some of them pressing their backs against an old wall painting: the graying spines of books in untidy rows and stacks among oddments and keepsakes. It was Orval Wyho who had opened the hatch, but he didn't come all the way out of the chamber. He unfastened the skull of his exo and drifted to one side, bareheaded, solemn, waiting for the body to be taken ahead of him into the corridor. Ĉejo's mother and a man named Aric Engirt guided Al by the elbows as if he were a child or an old man with frail legs, but the shape in the exo was unliving, sufflated, the image behind the clear faceplate tumid and black.

The old man of Al's family slid his look gently over Al's poor face, shook his head, said "Ah, ah" in a sorrowful way. The woman, Ajlina, when she saw Al, expelled her breath in a sound loud and clipped as a bark. "Oh! God! Who can believe this?" She began a harsh moan, and the old man embraced her, his own lament become a condolence, "Ah, ah, ah." Ĉejo could see it was a pantomime of grief for his mother: She and Aric, while they went on holding Al's wrists, his puffy elbows, were shut inside their hardhats, not able to get out of them one-handed. People came together around the body, supporting the father, the sister-in-law, and in the narrow, crowded space Ĉejo lost his view of Juko. She had not seen him, hadn't looked toward him.

It was Ajlina, suddenly, who gave up her hold on the old man and took Al's hands deliberately in her own. Her face was stiff, tearless, she was abruptly finished with her outcry. "They have got a bier waiting at the foot of Esperplena, eh?" She said this to no one specifically, but looking around at them all hopefully. Then she gave over one of Al's hands to the old man, who touched it to his lips and said "Gift of God" in a trembling voice. The two of them led some of the other people in a little procession down the corridor. They were tenderly guiding Al's buoyant corpse between them, as if he were a blind man.

Then Ĉejo could see his mother. She had at last unfastened her headpiece and was holding it in the crook of one arm like a parcel. Her face was pale, mournful, her hair sticking up in a ridge along the crown of her head. When she saw him, she grimaced silently. She said something to Aric Engirt, a few low words, and spoke to others as she made a way through them slowly to where Ĉejo waited with Anĝelo Jutaka. "I guess it was the ŝimanas, eh?" people said to her anxiously, and she shrugged a shoulder.

"Juko," Anĝelo said.

She touched Ĉejo's arm lightly, but she looked at Anĝelo, said to him, "What did Romeo hear, do you know, Anĝelo?"

Anĝelo looked away. "I guess he said a word, 'going,' or something like that. That's all Romeo heard."

She shook her head. "Before that, eh? What made Romeo think there was trouble?"

Anĝelo shrugged. "Just a little sound is all. Maybe it was the air going out the hole, or the knife against the exo, sawing. He hears everything, Romeo does." He looked at her. "Al never said anything to him, if that's what you were meaning."

"I guess it was."

"No, he never said anything." He shook his head. "He never said a word. Not on the income, anyway. It was the ŝimanas, eh?"

Juko grimaced, lifting her shoulder again.

"Do you have to log out?" Ĉejo asked her.

She squeezed his hand. "Yes. You don't need to come. Will you wait for me?"

"Don't get started talking to people." He wanted Anĝelo Ju-taka, hearing him say it, to help her go in and out quickly from the sailchart room.

"I won't. A little while. Wait for me."

She and Anĝelo and other sailmenders went off without him and he found the long, complicated way around to the gallery of the spokes. He waited. When she finally came, she was free of the exo, wore an undyed flaxen shirt and the kenaf trousers she favored, the ones dyed red. He liked the trousers himself, but not the shirt: The yellow at her throat made her skin look sallow.

She made a face, screwing up her mouth again. "People wanted to talk."

"It's okay," he said. In the hub of the *Miller* the fluorescent lights were garish, equivocal. He had waited alone, in the cold lights, the cold air. What time was it? You had to go outward to find the day, the night.

They held on to the wall silently, waiting for the lift, their bodies insistently adrift. After a while she said, complaining, "I'm tired, I want to sit. There's no sitting up here."

He said, "No."

She looked toward him. Then she put her arm out, reaching for him, and let her head rest against his ear. Cêjo's eyes sprang unexpectedly with tears. "I thought it was you," he said, his voice breaking helplessly, and she made a sound of distress, wordless, without lifting her head.

They went down from the hub silently, heavily, in the lift of the eightspoke. People liked to name every mechanical thing, and they had named this spoke the Way-Around: At its foot on the east side, the Ring River completed its circling of the world and went under the ground, where a pump lifted the river to its beginning again on the spoke's west side, and released it in the short steep cataract of the Falls From Grace. When Cêjo and his mother came out from the lift into the high, upcurving vault of the torus—out into the damp heat and yellowish light of afternoon—the clamor of the falls was a sudden steady noise, obscurely comforting.

The earth in the *Miller* was impounded on the slopes—

terraces and steps that followed the long curving geometry of the torus. People in his mother's ŝiro, the Pacema, lived on the high banks, the altejo, their houses built along the curve of the walls, near the bones of the ceiling. In the rainy season, Pacema houses stood above the fog, looking out through the tops of trees to houses and fields on the other side of the short arc, sixty-five meters across, or down the long, narrow, embowed vista to the houses of Bonveno ŝiro, westward, or the footings of the sevenspoke, the Violin String, which stood at the top of the rise to the east.

People in the terraced fields were weeding the flax or tying up the seed pods of onions with little sacks to catch the seeds as they dried and dropped off, but as Ĉejo and Juko went by them on the little path between the river and the maltejo fields, they stood up from their work and spoke to Juko anxiously, wanting to know if it was true that someone on the sail had been killed, or wanting to know who was dead, or asking if it was the ŝimanas that had killed him. Ĉejo's mother nodded or shrugged, answering people impatiently without speaking, walking with her hands pushed down in the pockets of her red pants. Ĉejo wanted to say something to console her, but didn't know what it ought to be.

"I came up in the lift with Al's sister-in-law," he said uselessly.

His mother, with her eyes fixed on her sandals, said, "Do you know Armando? The old man who was there with Ajlina? I think you met him once at Yearly Meeting." She made a dismissive gesture with her hand. "Well, it was a long time ago." Then she told him, "Al is the old man's son."

"I can see it. They have the same look," Ĉejo said.

"I guess they do. People say that, anyway." She looked at Ĉejo. "People say you look like Humberto."

This was something he always had refused. From habit, he made a grimacing face. "I don't look like him. I don't know why people always say that."

In a moment, another old habit, she said to him, "You're prettier," and gave him a sliding look, a little smile. She brought one hand out of her pocket and reached for his. They walked up the footway between the fields, their clasp of hands connecting them.

People trained vines to go up the posts of arbors but often kiwi and ĉejote had a habit of ranging out, unruly; in Alaŭdo fields, where Ĉejo lived and farmed with his father, he had been tying up the blind vines, helping them find the poles. No one in Pacema was doing this, or they had fallen behind in the work. Where ĉejote had come snaking out in the path, Ĉejo stooped and pushed back the tender stems. He felt his mother watching him. She was still getting over her surprise at seeing him a farmer. Her look made him feel proprietary, adult.

"Are you solidly moved in?" she asked him.

He had only lately come back to live with Humberto. He had spent his green years in his mother's brother's household in Senlima, but when he had made up his mind to farm, he'd come back to his father's house.

"Yes. I'm in. We've got the loom moved, that was the worst thing. Four of us carried it."

"Who all is in that apartment now?"

"Leona and Petro"—these were his father's parents, Ĉejo's grandparents—"and Heza Barfor." When Juko looked toward him, he added, "She's a divorced woman without children. She was living in her sister-in-law's house but they didn't get along. Alfhilda, too, she's living with us now."

Juko looked at him again. "Alfhilda's twelve, then? She's a good girl. She and her mother were always my favorites in that family."

Children, when they were twelve, moved out of their parents' home to spend their green years with other people—uncles or grandparents or the parents of friends—and Alfhilda, who was a cousin of Ĉejo's, was as new to the house as he was. He had been fond of her, himself, when they'd both been children, but he had left the green years now, and imagined he ought to put a distance between himself and twelve-year-olds. "She leaves things where they land, never picks up," he said.

Juko maybe wasn't listening to his complaint about Alfhilda. "It's a small house," she told him, murmuring.

"It's all right. We get along, all of us."

She nodded. "Yes." There was something in her face, a look; maybe she was feeling shut out.

"You get along with your household, too," he said, without knowing how it could help her mood.

She nodded again. "Yes." He didn't know if she was thinking of Al Poreda.

The weight of their bodies fell off a little, going up the steep way onto the slope, but Juko went up the easeful climb slowly, looking into the darkness beneath the crowded houses. Houses were built to stand on poles, to let the air flow from below, let the heat and the damp out; the sutaĝo, the underneath, was used for a threshing floor, and chickens sometimes roosted there. Under one house some children were scratching something in the cool dirt, squatting with their sticks, whispering, and that made Ĉejo think of something he had forgotten.

He never had lived in the house his mother lived in now, but from his childhood Kristina Veberes had been an auntie to him, a third grandmother, and before his mother had moved her belongings into Kristina's house, before she had married Kristina's son, Ĉejo often had slept, played, visited in the two rooms of that apartment.

He remembered suddenly, there was a little low-roofed alcove in the front room that borrowed its space from under the stair of the sadaŭ, and he had played and slept in that odd little cranny with Kristina's grandchildren, who had been as cousins to him. Ĉejo had not paid much attention to Bjoro in those days—a man his mother's age, the father to one or two of Kristina's grandchildren. But Bjoro's wife had died, and Ĉejo's brother; and his mother and father had ended their marriage. Now the alcove Ĉejo had slept in, the little cave where he had scratched his name in the floorboards, was Kristina Veberes's sleeping place; and Ĉejo's mother slept with Kristina's son in a room that looked out on the incurvature of the world.

When Ĉejo led his mother up the ladder of her house, neighbors were standing there on the loĝio with Kristina. Four or five families divided up the long U of a house, and people liked to bring their handwork out of their apartments and make the common middle, the loĝio, a place for gossiping and arguing, for coming together to visit with their neighbors, and for children playing. Now they had made it a place for waiting to hear bad news.

Ĉejo's father was there, too, a surprise. He turned and looked at Ĉejo coming up the ladder, and Kristina's look followed his, white and stiff, and other people turned, and then they saw Juko coming behind him, and there was a loosening, a relief. One woman said, "There! Not Juko, eh?" Kristina pursed her mouth and then opened it silently.

The divorce of Ĉejo's parents was old, the edge worn from it, and Humberto had kept up a quiet friendship with his once-wife, and with Kristina, but Ĉejo was surprised to see his father's eyes fill with tears; he was surprised when Humberto put out his hand and touched the crown of Kristina's head, stroking the old woman's hair, and she put her hand up, too, and patted his fingers.

In a moment she said, "Who is dead then?" and Juko said quietly, "Al Poreda. It is Al Poreda."

The people who knew Al began to shake their heads, to make small sounds of regret. Some people cried. Ĉejo cried a little himself, a guilty sorrow: He was glad it was Al who had died, and not his mother. Kristina put her hand out and drew him in, wiped his eyes on her shirtsleeve. "Well, I'm sorry for his family," she said flatly. "But I didn't want it to be my daughter-in-law."

Someone said mournfully to Juko, "It was the ŝimanas, eh?" and she looked away in irritation, not answering. Then she went into the little apartment, leaving her neighbors and her family standing out in the loĝio. Ĉejo went in too, feeling still a helpless wish to comfort her. Humberto and Kristina went on standing out there a little longer, speaking together in a murmur Ĉejo couldn't hear, but finally they came in too, and Kristina slid the wall closed to keep out the neighbors.

Juko had filled a kettle for tea and plugged it in, had begun to measure the leaves. Kristina unfolded a repozo but she wouldn't sit against it herself; she brought out little cups for each of them and sat down with hers in the middle of the rug.

Then Juko left the tea kettle unfinished and sat down against the unused repozo, her legs folded under her. She let her head fall back against the wicker rest and shut her eyes. Ĉejo sat too. It was Humberto who went to stand in the corner of the room, the little galley, to wait for the kettle to get done with heating itself.

The daylight through the open casement was yellowish, warm, stirred by a small draft. Ĉejo closed his eyes as his mother had done. A brief dark dream was imprinted behind his eyelids: Al Poreda's broad brown face swelling suddenly and blackening, eyes widening to let fear swiftly out, and his mother's face contracting, taking the fear in through her open mouth, the holes of her eyes.

"I should go and see Ina," Juko said, in a tired, flat voice. Probably she was waiting for someone to forgive her for not going. Ĉejo looked at her.

"Her family and her neighbors will be there," Kristina said. "You don't have to go right now."

Juko made a small, indeterminate sound. In a moment, Humberto brought the pot of fragrant tea. When he was pouring for Ĉejo he lifted his brows in a vaguely questioning way, nothing to do with the tea. Maybe, like the others, he was asking, *Was it the ŝimanas then?* Ĉejo shrugged his shoulders. He only half remembered the last time there had been an accident on the sail: A woman named Ĵulia? Ĵunio? had suffered an emobolism, something to do with her air mix, a faulty exo. He remembered someone's words, "Choked for breath," but then he realized: He didn't know if these words had to do with Ĵulia, or if they had been spoken to explain the death of his brother, Vilef.

Juko and Kristina began to talk quietly about Al's wife and son, Juko telling and Kristina asking tedious particulars to do with that family, and both of them relating anecdotes about Al's distant relatives, people Ĉejo didn't know. They went on with it for a while and then fell silent. Ĉejo sipped his tea, looking down in the little cup. All at once he began to hear the slight, distant rush of the Falls From Grace, and then in other apartments two women talking, and the scraping of a table leg or a cane against the floor, and children calling to one another, and chickens fighting, and birds vocalizing in a multitude of languages.

He had recognized in himself, for a long time now, a deeply morbid curiosity to do with the rare violent deaths, and gradually it became too difficult not to ask his mother: "Will you say how Al was killed?"

She looked at the vertical poles of the wall, or through the casement to the dry crown of a tree framed there. Ĉejo looked too. Above the lineaments of the tree, he glimpsed a delicate cluster of xenon lights in the arching scaffold of the ceiling. "Maybe he was looking for the *Ruby*," she said, sighing. "We all were, I think, but maybe it was too far off for him, eh?"

In a moment Ĉejo said, "Yes," though she may not have meant to ask anyone anything. She had brought him out on the sails once, pulling along the hawser from the hub of the torus to the oneyard, and then out the gallantmast the long distance toward the masthead. They had seemed to float on the vast array of sheets, rocking, below an infinite field of wheeling stars. His mother had warned him: "Don't look at the stars," but how could he not? He had vomited inside the exo, sailsick, and they had had to turn back at the three-yard without reaching the head of the mast. All the way back, he had kept staring out at the dizzying turn of the starfield, and the undulating, unimaginably distant horizon of the sail. *It was too far off.* He thought he knew what that meant.

"There was a cut in his exo," she said after a moment. She said it in such a way, tiredly, that Ĉejo felt a quick waxing of his guilt. But at a certain age—eleven, twelve—he had liked to imagine the effect of vacuum on the human body. He had not thought, then, that the swelling corpse maybe would seal a hole in an exo. He used to imagine a body freely dilating to the point of dispersal of the atoms, keeping a human shape with infinitely widening interstices until, like the universe, its form became too vast to perceive.

"He cut it himself," Juko said, and Ĉejo found a brief, terrible appeal in imagining Al Poreda cutting at his exo, trying to let his shape out upon the stars. After a brief silence, low-voiced, she said, "But maybe it wasn't meant. He might have slipped, cutting the tangle out of a halyard."

Kristina Veberes made a small, chaffing sound, *shuh*. Ĉejo saw the look that went between his mother and her mother-in-law. Kristina and Juko's friendship was old, they got along with few words. This was something to do with Al's death, but he was excluded from its meaning.

"Do you remember Karlina Remlinger?" Humberto said. He had been silent until now. Ĉejo looked at him, but he had been asking Juko. She rolled her head slightly against the head of the repozo.

"You know her. She repairs electrical things. She carries around her tools in that high-sided red cart with the rope handles." He waited for Juko's face to tell him she remembered. Then he said, "She has a theory to do with persons whose ancestry is equatorial, being more prone to ŝimanas than other people. She thinks racial memory or something, a tolerance of artificial daylight, is on the side of the Norse line, the English." Ĉejo saw him glance sideward at Juko. "She's doing a compiling. Maybe she'll ask people about Al's family line, and whether he is from Costa Rican people. If it was the ŝimanas killed him."

Juko moved restlessly. She set her tea on the boards of the floor, pulled her feet up under her and sat on her toes, sideways. "Where does this theory come from, eh? She might be wrong about this, about a racial tolerance. People who lived in those winter-lands, they were known for unhappiness, I thought." But then she said unhappily, "He's Costa Rican, I think. His father, Armando, is dark, anyway, his name is Poreda. I don't remember Al's mother. Do you know her family?" She looked at Kristina.

Kristina's old face gathered. "Linda Florencio," she said. She made that abrading sound again, *shuh*, and looked at each of them. Her hair was white and long; she habitually pulled it back and tied it with a bright piece of yarn or a ribbon, but it was coarse, frizzy, the unruly ends stuck out in a halo. "There's been endless intermarrying, eh? There can't be many families who are mostly of one line, do you think? Anyway, hardly any records are kept. Do you know Armando's parents, or Linda's? How can Karlina know they weren't Norse, eh? or English?"

"She has found some old disks," Humberto said. "They kept better records early on, I heard. She asks the old people, makes family trees. I don't know how many families she has found that are mostly one ancestry." He had a habit of smiling crookedly while squeezing his brows up high above the bridge of his nose: a quizzical look, unconfident. He was prone to use it when he thought he'd be disputed. It had a childishness that vaguely irritated Ĉejo. For a couple of years, he had been watching himself for that look, in case it might be inherited. Now, when his father made that face, Ĉejo studied him. He had straight black hair, long eyes, slightly folded lids, though his family name was Norwegian. Juko was Juko Ohaŝi, though he thought there was less Japanese in her family than in Humberto Indergard's—her hair was brown and fine, her eyes were blue. Ĉejo usually didn't see his father's face in mirrors; he was more than half serious about that. Only sometimes, unexpectedly, he glimpsed Humberto's long eyes looking back on him from the glass. He had not thought of them as Japanese eyes until now.

"Why's she doing it?" he asked his father. "Nothing's to be done, only we'd worry about everybody we knew who was Costa Rican, and they'd worry about themselves."

Humberto said, "Well, we're worrying anyway, I guess. It might not hurt to know who we should worry about." He still kept his little smiling frown.

Ĉejo shook his head, unpersuaded. "I think it would just push them over the edge, anybody who was leaning that way." He felt a sudden indisputable certainty. "If I was prone to ŝimanas, I wouldn't want to know."

Humberto shrugged softly. "Some people would want to know. How can some know and some not?"

Ĉejo was impatient with this reasoning but not able quickly to rebut it. He was a slow thinker, he felt; he would realize his answer tonight or tomorrow, too late.

"Maybe Karlina is thinking about the long run," Juko said.

"She might be thinking to keep equatorial peoples from parenting with each other."

"People should marry whomever they choose," Ĉejo said fiercely. He made ready to argue this conviction if his mother took the usual view. Families and neighbors liked to arrange marriages, but he had lately fallen in love for what he felt sure would be the last time, and his feelings ran high on the subject. A small look passed between his parents but there was no telling what it meant, whether it was something to do with him, or with their own marriage, the finish of it, or the beginning.

"No one would stop anyone from marrying," Humberto said. "But people would know, if this theory of Karlina's is true, that a person who was Costa Rican should try to marry someone from another line, a northern line. If you were looking for a good husband or a wife for someone in your family, you wouldn't suggest that a Costa Rican marry another Costa Rican. It would just become a known thing."

Ĉejo said nothing. He didn't know why he felt boxed off, defeated. It hadn't been an argument. Helplessly, he began to worry whether this girl he loved, Katrin Amundsen, might be equatorial.

The others were silent as well. It had begun to be dusk, and in the lowered light they sat on the floor without touching, without looking at one another. Humberto still held the little cup of tea in the hollow of his hand, and he looked into it. Juko, with her head pressed against the repozo, watched the slow darkening of the ceiling, the rafters that were the floor of the sadaŭ.

"What can be grown in that cold," she said after a while. She said it flatly, not a question.

Humberto looked at her with his brows squeezed up, that quizzical look. "There is some native flora," he said. "Woody plants, mosses, lichens, small trees in the stream valleys."

"Can you grow kiwi fruit? Ĉejote?" she asked him irritably. "What will you eat? The woody plants? The mosses?"

In the next year they must settle on a way of going. They must swing around the sun to get up speed for leaving—for going on fifty years to the next likely world—or iris the sail and make an anchorage around this one—settle on this world now and forever. Cêjo felt a thrill of fear, that his mother might have made up her mind already, on a question that was so momentous.

Humberto drank down the little bit of cold tea and examined the inside of the cup. "Nils Truhijo and many others are drafting designs for plantodomo. There is a library of frozen agricultural cells; people are looking for species suited to a tundra. Or there may be more temperate zones—where the balloons failed, eh? in the southwestern islands, the eastern midlatitudes." He glanced toward Juko, perhaps gauging the quality of her discouragement. "For twenty years we've known there was not much hope of a mesothermal climate," he said, watching her.

Cêjo looked at Juko too. "You haven't made up your mind, have you? How can you find the sense of a Meeting if your mind is made up?"

Juko shook her head angrily. "No. My mind isn't made up. I only want to be gloomy today. Let me cry over my cêjote and kiwis, and tomorrow you can tell me about greenhouses and temperate zones." Suddenly she did cry a little, putting her fist to her cheek, and a few tears ran down the path between her curled fingers. Cêjo stared at her in surprise. He could not remember when he had seen his mother cry. Not even on the occasion of his brother's death.

Humberto looked at her too. "There are some hardy kiwis, I think," he said in astonishment. "But you can cry for the cêjote."

Kristina, without speaking of Juko's tears, stood suddenly and picked up people's cups from the floor. "I have some tortillas. I'll find something to put in them. Cêjo, maybe you would come and slice things."

She put on the little light in the galley and brought things out of the cold box: bits of pepper and mushroom and steamed rice left from another meal, cilantro, peanuts, sprouts of lemongrass. On the narrow pocket table, Cêjo cut the peanuts and the cilantro with a knife. The tortillas were dark, Kristina liked to

make them from breadnut; she built upon them slowly, array-
ing the food on the flat rounds, while Humberto and Juko
went on talking quietly, asking and answering things to do with
Juko's now-husband, Bjoro, and the go-down boat, the *Lark.*

"She was crying for Al Poreda," Ĉejo whispered to Kristina
when he had thought it through.

She didn't look up from what she was doing. "I don't know,"
she said. There was a distant quality in the sound of her voice,
and Ĉejo felt suddenly excluded from something. He was
afraid, while they all had been sitting together drinking orange-
scented tea and speaking of tundra plants and closed minds, the
others had experienced a different conversation.

They sat around the low table and Kristina, with a look, en-
couraged them all in a brief, religious silence: gratitude for the
meal. Then while they ate, they talked of the health of several
people they knew, and slightly sordid hearsay about a woman
who was an old enemy of Kristina's, and gossip about Humberto's cousin's daughter who was marrying a man none of
them knew. When the table was cleared they might, on another
night, have played Obsession, or got out the chess board—it
was rare for Ĉejo to have his mother and father in one place,
under one roof. But there was Al Poreda, and the cold tundra
planet, and his mother's mood was dark. He kissed Kristina's
dry cheek and Juko's, and received their kisses, while Humberto
stood watching, shifting his feet. Then he and his father walked
home from Pacema in the darkness.

The daylights had been extinguished. In the narrow lanes between the houses, light fell out of casements and made the air
visible, but in the farmed land the darkness was whole, un-
compromised. Humberto went ahead of Ĉejo, finding the way
carefully on the beaten tracks. He was silent. Only when they
had got at the edge of the Alaŭdo ŝiro he said suddenly, murmuring, "Is there soul in a plant, do you think? Why do you
suppose we honor the food by a silent grace?" with the end of
it dropping so it became less a question. He had a habit of
doing this, brooding on small mysteries, but when Ĉejo looked
at him he looked back squinting, as if he were surprised to have
asked it, and he said quickly, "I don't know," as if it might have

been his own answer, or the unfinished beginning of something. Then he put his hand to the back of his head and ruffled
his own hair fiercely. In a moment he began to lay out the next
day's work tying up the ĉejote vines, harvesting leaves and
flower buds from some of the doan gwa melons, repairing the
runoff piping under a bed of radishes and en-kai, and it wasn't
as if he had asked Ĉejo anything.

Ĉejo's grandmother and her friend Heza Barfor sat together
under the lamp in the front room of the apartment. Leona sat
against a repozo with both her feet extended in front of her. She
was a little lame from an old accident, a bone broken when a
pipe had fallen on her; she was a sewage engineer. Her lap was
full of milkweed and she was picking it clean with swift skill,
the seeds raining in her bowl with a tiny, steady patter. Heza
sat on her hips and heels on a cushion and knitted.

"She is only a couple of years older than us," Heza was saying, "but look at the difference. If she wasn't so cross-grained,
I ought to feel sorry for her."

Since Heza had come to live in Leona's house, she had complained ceaselessly about her sister-in-law, using always the indefinite "she," as if the woman's name was a sour fruit she
didn't want in her mouth. Ĉejo didn't know the sister-in-law,
and had got swiftly tired of Heza's complaining. If his grandmother was tired of it, she didn't say; she would listen and nod
while Heza let her bitterness stream out. Leona's tolerance was
storied.

She lifted her head to Ĉejo and Humberto and said over
Heza's complaint, "Do you know? a sail mender was killed
today, but I heard it wasn't Juko, eh?" Her eyes narrowed,
looking at them.

Ĉejo's father crouched down on the floor beside her and
busied his hands with the milkweed. "It was Alberto Poreda,
panja. It was Juko who brought in the body." He glanced at his
mother. "We went to her house and stayed a while. We ate our
supper with Juko and Kristina Veberes."

Leona looked away. "Well, Juko takes a death without much
trouble, eh?" She had a long-standing bitterness toward Juko,
and her bottom lip curled on it.

These were matters that weren't spoken of except left-handedly, but Ĉejo understood that the anger between his mother and his grandmother had to do with Vilef's death, which had also been the beginning of the end of his parents' marriage, and not an occasion for Leona's tolerance. Because no one had told him an unambiguous account, Ĉejo had no position, and tried to hold back every malign outbreak. "My mother has an old friendship with Al Poreda," he said in defense of his mother, and then, "She was crying, eh?" because his grandmother was prone to complain of Juko's insufficient tears. Leona looked sideward at her son but not at Ĉejo, and did not speak. In a moment, Ĉejo deliberately sat down at his loom and took up the half-finished stringing of the warp on his warping board.

His grandfather wandered into the apartment with a handful of figs in his hand. He said, with his mouth chewing, "I heard somebody killed himself on the sail. Was that it? The ŝimanas?"

Leona said without bitterness, "If he was a religious man, God knows where his faith was when he let this happen."

"It's not so easy as that," Humberto said to her, but he made no effort to untangle it.

"Nothing, not even God, is greater to a person than their own self is." Heza pronounced these words solemnly without lifting her eyes from her knitting needles. All of them looked at her. Heza had a well known habit of stating things without seeming to connect them to what other people were saying. Ĉejo wasn't sure if her declaration had anything at all to do with Al Poreda's death.

Leona answered as if it did. "I would have said he didn't value himself enough," she said sorrowfully, an abrogation.

Ĉejo's father and his grandparents and Heza got gradually round to their old argument about Alfhilda, who was spending a night in her parents' house. She was like Leona, a science-minded person, and she'd lately taken an apprenticeship to Anejlisa Revfiem, the plant geneticist. The whole family liked to argue mildly between them whether this was a field one could learn well without first having farmed. Ĉejo thought Leona's and Alfhilda's understanding of hybridizing and cloning was abstract, not rooted in the soil as his was, or Humberto's, and he had brought this up before. But he kept out of the argument now, absorbed in the unvoiced counting of the warp ends; and when he got up from the loom, he went out to use the toilet and brush his teeth. Then he unfolded his bed in the room he shared with his father and his grandfather. He was in a mood for thinking about dying.

Against the darkness, lying on his shoulder and hip on the mat, he saw Al Poreda's tumescent face, swollen black with blood. Once, lying waiting for sleep, he had experienced a kind of flashing intimation, had glimpsed the absolute and unending loss of himself that must be death. He had thought that he believed in the enduring of souls, but at that moment, and while the streaking white afterimage still burned behind his eyes, he had believed in nothingness. Now he lay deliberately remembering that moment of meteoric fear and astonishment, but not able to reproduce it. He turned death over and over in his mind, listening morosely to his own heartbeat and imagining carefully that men and women would be real and alive, continuing to take a great interest in food and sickness, stringing a loom, love, when he, Ĉejo, would be dead. He imagined Katrin Amundsen grieving for him, but then his mind led him away from there.

He followed Katrin to a hidden place she knew of up the ladder of her domaro into the rafters of the sadaŭ, behind baskets and a stored piece of a split bamboo wall. It was dim and dusty, a narrow triangle of space with the sloping bamboo making a sort of low roof. They sat down close together on the sadaŭ floor, facing one another. Ĉejo was anxious, filled with heat and longing, and he whispered to her, *I love you,* and put his mouth on her throat, his hands at her waist, at the neat fold of her hips. She arched her head back, lengthening her throat for him, rocking her hips toward him. Katrin was twenty, had a woman's rich lust and experience. She pulled her shirt loose from the waist of her trousers and he slid his hands along the skin of her ribs, kissed her throat and her hair, her ears, her eyelids. *I love you,* he whispered, and helped her take her shirt off, then his. She was thin, her breasts small neat cones, the nipples very dark and peaked. He cupped them tenderly in his hands. She took a shuddering breath, arching her back, pushing her breasts into his palms. They stroked each other, her fingertips tracing his ribs and nipples, twisting the few wiry hairs in the hollows under his arms; his thumbs scribed her breasts as his hands closed slowly, fondling her. She lay back with a low sound. He kissed her throat and shoulders, the soft inner flesh of her arms, held one of her nipples lightly in his mouth, the areole springing under his tongue. She cradled his head, and her hips stirred against him. They took down each other's trousers, and when she touched him, held him gently, a yearning fire ran under his skin. He said *Katrin,* whispering and urgent. She pulled his head down against the delicate skin of her belly, and he moved his mouth over her, into the heat and darkness of her opening legs. Her whole body moved to him, shuddering, a kind of wildness in the pent sound of her moaning, *ah, ah,* and later when she sat on him, clasping his hips between her thighs, when she put him inside her and rocked, he deliberately tried to make that same sound, *ah, ah, ah,* wildly whispering, moaning, as he pushed up to her in a sweetly aching undulation, but his body filled with the roar of his own blood and he sank into the red booming and wasn't able to remember afterward if he had made any sound at all.

A door slid quietly and his father said something, a few words, and his grandmother answered, or Heza, soft words, shapeless, who knew what they said? After quite a while he heard the rain beginning to fall on the roof and the trees, the earth, a sound as alive as the streaming of blood.

Three

BJORO

I see, just see skyward, great cloud-masses,
Mournfully slowly they roll, silently swelling
and mixing,
With at times a half-dimm'd, sadden'd far-off
star,
Appearing and disappearing.
(Some parturition rather, some solemn
immortal birth;
On the frontiers to eyes impenetrable,
Some soul is passing over.)

Bjoro realized he had made a sound, dreaming. When he opened his eyes, Peder's long eyes were open, watching him through the faceplate of the exo. He looked away from Peder's stare, sat up shaking, and the little dream washed out of him in a flood: the long black breathless dive, he was nauseous, astonished, afraid, he said, "What!" or "Wait!" and struck the bottom of the blind slide in a burst of noise and percussion. In the dream, as in life, he had known he would die. He had thought, *This is how people feel when they are dying, this surprise.* But none of them were dead. If they had struck the lava field or the mountain, maybe it would have killed them; anyway Luza said it might have, she was the medic among them, and she knew dynos and forces, she'd studied physics as well. But they'd come down in water, the big lake at the edge of the old lava flows, clear of the mountain, clear of the stony field, and had saved the blown hatch door and a broken cupboard of tools, and Peder, who was broken too, and so none of them were dead yet. And they had still the finder-seekers: Bjoro's made a pip every little while, he felt it moving his blood like an ersatz heart.

They had leaned the hatch cover against piled-up rocks to make a roof between them and the sky, and a wind blew, rattling gravel or pellets of ice against the metal. Bjoro sat under the eave of the hatch with the heels of his gloves against his eyes, and only slowly let his hands down and looked out across the lake. The prevailing color of this world was gray, the patchy snow and the gravel soaking up the colors of the sky, the lake fuliginous with silt. While he had briefly slept, there had come a thin streak of violet and cobalt blue across sixty or seventy degrees of the western horizon, obliquely defining the serrate peak of the mountain. It seemed a bruise on the sky, a sign of something dire.

Luza said, without looking toward him, "We'll have night, eh?" and then she did glance toward him, she may have looked to see if he feared the darkness.

This world had a long slow turning, thirty hours forty-seven minutes in a revolution; they were not yet at the spring equinox. At this season of the year, there'd be seventeen hours of night. Bjoro wasn't afraid of night, he knew what a vast blackness looked like. It was the sky that daunted him, its great tenebrous clouds sweeping toward them ceaselessly from behind the peak. The air was incredibly cold, bristly, it smelled of sulphur; he could feel its cold and its enormity in his chest, his mouth, when he took in a breath.

"Where is Isuma?" he asked Luza. He didn't mean *where* but something else. He could see Isuma walking away from them following the icy margins of the lake, keeping to the rocks that bound the shore. She looked small and distant; her white exo against the grayish landscape made him think of Juko on the sail and filled him with sudden, helpless grief.

Luza kept looking out at the long lurid edge of the overcast, the night falling. "Walking down the lakeshore. Seeing is there a flat place to lay an aerostat down."

Before they'd ever left the *Miller* they'd constructed a hundred elaborate emergencies and worked out a hundred elaborate responses: If the *Lark* was lost on landing, they would get a balloon to ride them up one at a time in its gondola. The *Ruby* hadn't any other heavy-lift craft but the *Lark*. There were three on the *Dusty Miller* but they might as well be useless; it would take forty days to get one here on board the *Ruby*'s twin, the *Dream*. They had conceived the balloon rescue seriously, the six of them lounging on the floor in Isuma's house, pushing beads around on an abacus and interrupting each other with gestures and details. If they dumped the survey equipment, there'd be room for sixty kilos; none of them weighed more than that in the .8 gravity. They'd wear exos. It would take a while is all, rising a meter a second. Would be best if they had a good landing space, flat and unimperiled, for the montgolfiere, the open balloon below the closed one, to settle its voluminous sheets out in vast array when the cold nights sank it down to them. There was a spinnaker the *Ruby* could deploy for steering the unmanned balloon to their finder-seekers, and when the mild day-heat lifted the thing off the ground Arda and Hans would steer by remote again, bring the *Ruby*'s low orbit to intersect with the apogee of the balloon.

It had been a crazy construct. They had been playing, pretending, none of them had believed it, and here was Isuma walking over the snow after a place to land the damned balloon. Bjoro laughed. But Luza's startled look brought his fear out, and instinctively he stood up to walk away from it. Then he found he was climbing the back of the lava field to look for a landing place himself.

The ridge of stones was vast, a couple of hundred meters high, bounding the northern lakeshore in both directions out of eye's reach, a great bulk of gravel and basalt boulders, obsidian sand. Likely the stones had spilled down molten from the shoulder of the mountain and dammed the lake; from where they were, there was no telling how wide the field was spread, no way to guess the direction of the old flow. He went up slowly on it, laboring.

His legs quickly ached; he had to stand every little while and pull the cold air in his chest. It was opposite to his whole experience: On the *Miller* there was diminished effort with altitude, the hub was "up," free of gravity, effortless. He felt a wave of homesickness, standing alone and broken-winded with the storm-driven clouds and the immense mountain at his back. He had spent much of his life making ready for this venture, for this crash, even; he hadn't expected to be rotten at it, to find his mind occupied childishly with a desperate ache for his wife and his home. He had thought, in the filmcards he had studied of unbounded landscapes, of storms and snows and seas, there remained no surprises. It hadn't occurred to him, the vast depth of the third dimension. He hadn't thought he would fear the sky.

Ronaldo Inomoto had made boots for them all from studying old clothes and old landscapes. Bjoro had to think about his walking, had to set these heavy boots with care among the rocks; they made him feel he was stumping on numb feet, clumsy, no sense of the ground through the thick soles. They had near drowned him. He'd splashed his arms and gotten to the floating tool cupboard with his weighted feet hanging below him, worse than useless, dragging down the buoyant exo, and Luza had got out of her boots, let them go down in the water, but she was sorry for it now, hobbling in the thin-soled feet of the exo. The ground on this world was stony and gnarled, even the snow sharp, crusted—Ronaldo had guessed some things right.

Bjoro stood, finally, hunched and wheezing at the top of the ridge of rocks, and found the view north was an immense sweep of world, beyond imagining, many hundreds or thousands of hectares of broken ground, lava fields blackish and denticulated, dirty snow in the clefts of the teeth. There was no dust in the air; the edges of things were sharp, utterly clear. He could see to the northeast a green thread raveling through the canyons of lava, maybe it was a river, and almost at the sky's edge a line demarking two shades of gray—he had a sudden remembrance of the topo map of this continent and knew that line for the edge of the sea. Staring toward it, he felt a sort of vertigo, a dream image: He was standing on the slope high up under the ceiling of the torus but the trough of land below him slipped downward forever without a turning up. The land was immense, alive as an animal, unutterably powerful. The big mammals had been gone, all of them, decades before the *Dusty Miller* was built, Bjoro had seen them only on filmcards; but he thought this must be what people had felt once, staring in the face of the bear, the cat, the wolf—this terrible humbling before the thing so beautiful, and breathing death. He stood stricken, his breath gusting in white clouds.

He was a long time going over the rocks down to the lakeshore, stumbling slowly in the failing light. There'd been a handlamp in the tool cupboard; he saw Luza under the roof-hatch holding the lamp so the cone of light fell over Peder. On the cold wind he heard her voice, wispy, without words, and then Peder. "Enough," he said, or "Rough." When Bjoro crouched on the groundsheet beside them, Luza was holding Peder's hand, saying the end of something, ". . . ought to sleep; are you keeping warm?" and Bjoro was struck with a brief, pathetic wish to be the injured one, to lie dependently under the sheltering roof and be tenderly comforted and guarded.

There were flocks of little dark birds or bats working the surface of the lake now, grazing the water and wheeling upward and then dropping to it again in close throngs. Isuma, who had come back ahead of him, was crouched under the metal roof on her haunches, looking out at the big flat sheet of the lake, and the flyers. "What is behind us?" she said in a loud voice, a voice ringing unnecessarily across the water. None of them had spoken of anything but concrete matters—what they had saved of tools, what time it was, was it Peder's rib that had put a hole in his lung. But this bluffness in Isuma's voice was something new; maybe she'd become angry at their situation, or blamed one of them for it, or anyway Bjoro imagined that was it and not shakiness she was hiding. She was fearless, Isuma was, and solid. He thought if he heard her voice break, it would break him.

He meant to keep his own words flat, steady, but they jumped out too quick for him, mimicking Isuma a little, edgy and loud. "This field of lava goes on north to the horizon," he said. "Northeast a little river cutting it, and then maybe the ocean. There's no place that way."

"Well, no place round this lake is flat enough, big enough,

and anyway all sharp stones," Isuma said. She looked at Bjoro. "How far would you say, to the ocean?"

Bjoro shook his head. "Far. I don't . . . My eye . . ." He shook his head again. "What's between is bad land, old lava," he said angrily. He realized he was grateful for Peder's flattened lung. They would need to carry him, and that would keep them from crossing the vast black canyons to the river delta and the sea.

"South is the mountain," Luza said in a moment, the only one of them with a mild voice. She looked at them both. "So we're left only the east and the west, between the peak and the lava bed, either end of the lake." She gestured vaguely.

Isuma said, growling, "We ought to find a place quick, and get our selves and our finder-seekers onto it, before they bring the damn balloon down in the middle of the lake."

"They'll wait, I bet," Luza said. "They'll wait to see if the seekers move: If the seekers don't move, they'll be thinking we're killed." She grinned slowly, baring her teeth. The plan had been to mark a diamond of landing field by the four finder-seekers. No one had said what the plan would be if the seekers never were made to mark a diamond.

Isuma grinned too, and finally Bjoro did, something to do with not being dead.

They agreed they would do turns with Peder, two would sleep while one sat up, getting a pulse and a breath count every little while and clicking on the handlamp to feed him pain-killers. There was a med box that had been kept in the tool cupboard but no respirator in it, no possibilities for reinflating the lung. Luza wasn't a surgeon anyway, and the lung had a hole in it. She said he wasn't bleeding much into his belly, only the rib gave him pain and the empty lung made him wheeze. She said they ought to keep a lookout for ashy color, bubbles in his breath, blood from his mouth or his nose.

They fell silent, and in a while, without speaking again, Luza put out the handlamp and they faced the cold darkness. Their own weather was a Costa Rican analogue, humid subtropical, its two seasons warm-wet and warm-dry. The hub was the only cold place on the *Miller,* it was ten degrees there, or even less;

but Bjoro's imagination hadn't made him ready for a true cold-
ness of the air. It was zero in the daylight here, would drop to
minus ten or fifteen overnight. The exos were proof against the
cold, but a bared scalp, the back of the neck, one's eyes, let the
heat out of the torso as if the exo had been breached. There had
been skullcaps made by the Fiber Arts Committee, tuques knitted tight from kapok yarns, but lost in the crash. Escaping the
Lark, they'd thrown off the hardhats and afterward only recovered two, the things cumbrous in the gravity anyway. They
put one on Peder because of its respiratory assist, but none of
them used the other, they crouched together, shaking, with the
black wind blowing to their bones. There were no stars. The
wind shook the air noisily. It was, after all, not the blackness of
space.

Luza and Isuma lay down together on the groundsheet behind the windbreak of the tool cupboard and Bjoro hunched
himself into the close space between Peder and the women, with
his arms clasping his knees to his chest, and his head sunk down
between his arms. Gradually he found he couldn't keep from
tears, and it was only the touch of the others, an arm, a leg pressing against him, that saved him from crying out loud. His mind
felt crowded with an ill-defined horror, wordless, inchoate. He
worked his mouth silently. After a while the repetitive action
comforted him. He began to think about his wife, an aching,
aimless jumble of details and remembrances.

He had a habit, when Juko wasn't with him, of recasting a
gossip he'd heard, an argument, an occurrence, for later telling
to her. He liked to imagine elaborately where they would be
when they were next together, at supper or lying in bed, and
his words, and Juko's face listening to him, her voice making a
response. The actual telling never was much like his imagining.
He knew he went over these resumés and over them, to extend
his enjoyment of some events, and to get a sort of control over
others. In his mind he had told and retold Juko every consequential thing that had happened to him since the *Ruby* had
gone ahead of the *Miller.* But he had done little of it in these
hours since the *Lark* crashed. What he had seen from the ridge
looking out toward the sea was unspeakable—*I don't . . . My*

eyes . . .—and Juko wasn't where he could find her in his mind anyway. He'd lost track of real time, didn't know if it was night there now, or day, if she was on the sail, or eating, or sitting in the bath, or saying his name in her sleep.

He realized suddenly: By now she might think I am dead. He imagined her, imagining him killed, lying on her back in their bed, looking up blindly into the ceiling. She was not prone to tears, but he imagined her weeping for him, and for a childish moment he felt contrite, as if he must apologize for living on. But then it wasn't childish, and he was apologizing for something else, something to do with the vast gray landscape and the frigid wind blowing out of the sky.

He never slept. When he had done his third of the night sitting up, he lay on his hip behind the windbreak, his body clasped together with Luza and later with Isuma, his eyes shut and his teeth locked against the cold, waiting for daylight, which was only a thinning of blackness to gray.

The wind had subsided in the last hours of the night and now the air felt depthless, bated; Bjoro felt its slight tremble when any of them made a motion through it, or spoke a word. He had a sense that their movements would rouse the wind again, that they ought to lie still and silent, becalmed. But in the scant early light, Luza and Isuma took turns walking away along the stony shore to empty their bladders and then he had to do it too, stumbling stiffly in the big, hard boots and standing to relieve himself on the piled-up rocks. He kept his back to the flat, lead-colored field of the lake, the great bleak sky, the mountain. From where he stood watching the steam of his urine, he could hear Luza and Isuma speaking to one another, breaking loose the stillness.

They ate tubes of lemon paste and, while Bjoro fed one to Peder, Isuma and Luza went over their little bit of saved rig. Isuma piled up tools: a big, light hammer and a theodolite; a narrow rock pick; a seismograph; a sack for rock collection. She cut a corner out of the ground sheet and found in the tool cupboard a pen that would write on the plastic. She was a geologist, and knew a little about surveying, so it became clear: She meant to do some of what they'd planned, meant to get sam-

ples and take measurements and make maps, while she looked
out for a place to bring down the aerostat.

Luza was gathering together Bjoro's tools for measuring climate. His field was mechanics and after that meteorology; the
machine they had was dead, drowned, but he had spent years
studying weather and Luza was methodically piling up his
pressure tester, anemometer, hydrometer, the old-world devices unneeded for 175 years—accoutrements of another people, another place, and utterly alien to him, he realized now.
Bjoro wanted to laugh at these women's scrupulous diligence,
had to set himself against a rush of anger and despair. What were
they thinking? That this was a world they might, in fact, want
to live on?

"There's only the one binoculars," Luza said. Her brow was
drawn up, worrying over this. She was a fussy person, she liked
to arrange things systematically. Bjoro didn't want to take the
little instrument onto his stack, hadn't any wish to see this
world writ larger. But Isuma was quick; she pushed the old
Japanese binoculars at him. "I see farsighted," she said. She
squinted her eyes, then widened them childishly.

Luza kept looking at the organization of their choices,
adding to one pile and then the other some of Peder's things—
specimen kits for soil and water, packets of biological sample
sheafs—and her own things—a rad counter, a flat little thermocouple. When she was satisfied, she pulled her mouth out
slowly. "Don't get lost," she said, and let her teeth show.

It was Isuma who laughed, expelling whitish clouds of her
breath. It sounded like, "Ha! Ha!" and the loud, hard words
reporting across the lake startled birds into the sky, not the flyers of the night before but three big water-birds, long-necked,
beating their wings in hard, slow effort. Bjoro started too. He
hunched his back, anticipating the wind, but the birds wheeled
and gradually settled again, the air closing like a skin of water,
shivering, and then seamless.

Without a word, Isuma went away along the edge of the lake
toward the west, carrying her tools in the rock-collecting sack.
She appeared resolute, walking short-strided, not swinging the
sack. Bjoro, pushing his own tools in a duffle, looked after her

with sudden desperate loneliness. Luza stood to watch her go. Then she looked at Bjoro. A tear had run down beside her nose, though her mouth was still set in a kind of smile, earnest, intent. He couldn't smile, himself. He stood up and walked away quickly east, shaking.

He looked back every little while. The ridge and the lake lay in an oxbow, the curve hiding Isuma from him, but he could see Luza standing before the tipped-up hatch cover watching after both of them, one and then the other. The daylight had come into the sky by then and the air was shadowless, pellucid, under a flat overcast. The light in the *Miller* was yellowy, rich; he didn't know why the shallow gray light here, the colorlessness, seemed blindingly bright. He was able to see Luza's face clearly, the faint line of frown, her pursed mouth, even from a distance. Once, he raised his arm to Luza and in a moment she lifted hers in a broad sweep. He might have been a kilometer from her at that point, but the clarity of the air allowed him to see her bare open palm, the spread of her fingers. The sight of her standing small and distinct and familiar against the unfamiliar, outspread, scabrous landscape, evoked in him something like awe and tenderness.

When he had finally got beyond seeing Luza, when he was alone with the variously gray, utterly empty fields of dirty snow and of rock extending boundlessly before and behind him, the sense of his solitude flooded him with anguish. For a moment he was paralyzed, his breath letting in and out in quick, choking huffs, the clouds of his respiration remaining sharp and white and motionless in the air. At last he heard the finder-seeker, its steady slow pip inside his exo, against his skin, and he put his hand to it, spreading his fingers, pressing until he could feel its beat against his palm, irrationally reassuring.

The lake was incalculably long, stretched out along the depression at the foot of the mountain. It was slow and effortful getting across the old snow and the rocks, but the quality of the cold was changed without the wind—it had a purity that he suffered more easily than the blowing—and he found that walking between the skirts of the lava ridge and the long impoundment of the lake gave him some little sense of narrowness, of margin. He felt himself steadying, settling into a work. He became used to the sound of his own breathing in the stillness. A couple of times he climbed the rocks partway and looked out unwillingly upon the long sweep of the lake, the high, serrated chine of the mountain, and ahead along the edge of the lava field—everywhere rocks—but he didn't use the Japanese binoculars, and he kept his eyes mostly away from the horizons.

The lake was shallow at its eastern end, a margin of water weeds and gravel, and he took a weed as a specimen. Where the shore curved away to the south he thought he would go on following it stubbornly, feeling if he kept to the lake's edge there wasn't any way to lose his own trail. But there was an outlet—an incredibly white chute of water falling away steeply downhill from the lake into the canyons of the lava field—and he was stopped by it, had to stand at the fall line of the swift little river and consider where to go now. After a while, a chill slid down along his spine and he started to shake, so he turned and went on doggedly, following the bank of the stream now, east into the lava.

It was difficult to keep the river in sight. Anxiously he pulled out his compass every little while and took a line on a pile of stones, a hummock of ice, the shoulder of the peak, sighting out to the horizon and noting his place in the pages of a little notebook meant to record the weather.

Finally, from a high vantage, he looked out to the east and saw the land flattening gradually and the field of lava tailing off. Where the river slowed and widened, turning north to find the sea, there were plumes of white, a cluster of them. He sat down, shaking, and got out the binoculars. The focus was wrong: He fiddled with it until the horizon jumped up in front of his eyes and drove his breath out in a burst. There were six or seven sheer white columns against the gray, rising straight until they blurred and tore along the line of their joining to the overcast. He watched through the glasses, stricken for a moment with a wordless fear. For years they'd been making the unmanned fly-arounds. It was known there were no thinking beings living on this world: It was a young place, nascent, populated with birds and invertebrates and small mammals, small reptiles. What he saw was steam, or smoke, climbing up from a volcanic cleft, a solfatara. But for that one speechless moment he imagined the straight shafts of white were spokes holding high the ceiling of the sky.

The plumes stood together and far off for quite a while without his getting any nearer. Only when he came up on the first one, he could see the rest were spread out over dozens of hectares, the last of the six maybe another two or three kilometers north and east of the first, on the slope that fell off beyond the northern end of the lava field. What they marked was a company of stinking mud pots, the ground between them thawed and sloppy, yellow, spotted with tufts of brownish grass. The air was sulphurous, spoiled; he skirted around the field with his chin sunk down in the neck of his exo.

Where the lava field finally flattened out and was finished, the river sloped off northeastward across broken shelves of rock; he went on following it to the edge of the mud field. The view dropped off to the north suddenly, and there was the river spreading out, edged with low basalt cliffs, scattered with little islands, the water shallow, gray-green, the islands brownish gray, flat, pocked with hardened snow, or ice. Away from the canyons of rocks, the volcanic sweepings, there was a small wind blowing off the water, wet and smelling of salt. He stared out at the sudden vista, appalled, his eyes filling with tears. The edge of the sky was unbearably distant. He had to turn away from it until he had his heart back.

They had not spoken of how far to go, when to come back. He had come near turning back when he had first got clear of Luza—he had stood minutes there with his hand on the finder-seeker, intending it. Maybe, after all, the aerostat would lay out gently on the rocks, wouldn't be torn—he had thought of arguing for that. Now he thought of it again. He was afraid of the wind, and of walking away from the comfort of the lava field. It was a kind of relief that the widening ground south of the river mouth kept on stony to the horizon.

By an effort of will, he got the binoculars up and made a slow search north and east, the land sprawled vast before him now without the ridge of rocks, the lake to bound it. Through the eyes of the binoculars, he saw birds were nesting in the hummocks on the little islands. Water fell down in several narrow white lines across the face of the basalt cliffs—what did this mean? He had thought he had come to the delta of the little white river, but now he realized it might be the incision of a fjord.

As a sort of balm against guilt, he put a few blades of grass in bio sheafs, took little specimens of mud from the boiling pots, made perfunctory measures of pressure, altitude, humidity. And then he started back west along the skirts of the river toward Luza, and the shelter. He knew the few landmarks, going back, and ticked them off in his mind as he went past them—it was a reassuring exercise, it shortened the way. But the wind came on a little, blowing out of the east and down through the combes of the lava, and he feared worse weather. He pushed himself to go quicker, the long muscles in his thighs and his calves burning and shaky. He hadn't any sense of time of day, had to keep looking at his timepiece to orient himself to the long solar period, comfort himself that he had hours yet before the sky would blacken.

When he came in sight of the lakeshore, he kept watching for Luza until the watching became an anxious yearning. He got out the Japanese binoculars and searched up the long rockbound margin for her, and the empty sweep of shoreline raised in him an unreasonable, sudden fear he'd been left alone, the others gone off without him. After that he carried the binoculars in his hand, stumbling swiftly among the stones and over the patchy ice and stopping every little while, frozen with terror, to look where he remembered Luza had been, standing with her open palm raised to him. It was a while before he understood, he had all along been seeing the sheltering roof there among the big stones, the long white smooth hatchcover defined by the black gasket. He stared at it through the lenses, and when Luza came out from under it and walked down to the edge of the water, swinging a plastic bottle, he began to cry.

He put away the binoculars and wiped his eyes and walked deliberately down along the lake toward the camp. When Luza saw him, she came out to meet him, grinning madly in the unreal daylight. "Thought I'd been left forever!" she called to him. He shook his head, smiling dimly.

They sat under the hatch-roof with Peder and stared out at the lake. There weren't any birds. The wind made the water rough, its shine colorless. "It's rocky land, all of it. There wasn't any point going farther," he said to Luza when she asked him. "I thought Isuma would be back." For the most part they were silent, waiting for Isuma, listening to Peder's tired wheeze. Every little while Luza walked out to the edge of the rocks and looked off to the west and then walked back slowly without speaking. Bjoro watched his timepiece, and the edge of the mountain where the sky had shown color the evening before.

The daylight was thickening when Luza, standing out by the lake, shouted and lifted her arm in a broad gesture and Bjoro stood and saw Isuma coming at a fast walk, with the loops of the samples sack hung from her shoulders.

"Hey!" Isuma called to them from a long way off, and lifted both her hands above her head.

They sat under the hatch and ate tubes of corn paste and papaya and drank water Luza had distilled from melted ice and hand-pumped through the little medical filter. Isuma talked while she ate, describing the route to the western end of the lake—rocks, and rocks—and then the climb up over the saddle of a ridge and below the short scree the land unclenching finally in a lovely big plain, hummocky under a nap of grass. "It's a good field, but it'll take some getting to. Wouldn't choose it if you got a better place, eh?" She peered at Bjoro.

He let out a short, stinging laugh. "Nothing," he said bitterly. "I've found nothing." He kept his head down, telling what he'd seen going east—rocks, and rocks. He told about the mud pots and the river and the basalt cliffs, the water falling over them. It wasn't necessary to say he'd seen no place as good as Isuma's plain.

Isuma had made a map and she spread it out on her knees and showed them, tracing the tip of her finger along the way they would need to go, here the hard part, the saddle, it was rocky and a steep climb; getting Peder up it and down the other side was a worry, she said. She looked at Luza, and at Bjoro, and finally at Peder. Peder's face inside the clear bubble was a frown; he may have been sleeping, or his eyes were squeezed shut against pain.

They fell silent, in the manner of a Meeting when there was a difficult thing needing deciding. Bjoro sat with his gloved hands clasped in his lap and his eyes fixed blindly on his boots. He waited for the silence to enter his mind, so that he could focus upon this question of moving Peder the long distance to Isuma's field. But his thoughts were helplessly chaotic; since the crash of the *Lark* he had felt himself drowned in futile detritus and vague horror.

The wind rose suddenly in a little gust that blew sand against their backs and clattering against the metal of the hatch. "If it's a good flat field?" Bjoro said, low-voiced, hunching his shoulders stiffly. "There's no good place nearer, eh?" He was embarrassed to hear in his words a kind of impatient quality. He looked at the women and then out to the lake shore with sudden nameless anger.

No one spoke. Bjoro imagined himself on Isuma's flat field, watching the balloon's slow descent. He couldn't keep from thinking of himself rescued, embracing Arda and Hans in the close familiarity of the *Ruby*, weeping, speaking over the radio to Juko, waiting the crackly moments for her voice to reach him in return.

"It's a good field," Isuma said. "Just a long damn way." She looked from one of them to the other, grimacing painfully.

Luza was holding Peder's hand, rubbing her gloved thumb measuredly across his gloved palm. She sat hunched with her eyes on her other hand where it was clasped inside the bend of her knee. "We would need to make a kind of litter for carrying Peder," she said finally, murmuring. "Maybe Bjoro can get the hatch door to come apart, we could use a panel from it?"

An exquisite relief sprang from Bjoro's chest and out to the ends of his fingers and his feet in a quick, cleansing wash. He stood and got his tools out of the cupboard.

The sky had filled with grays, blacks; the mountain's peak and the edge of the horizon were lost behind the lowering overcast. Isuma held the handlamp for him while he backed out screws and turned nuts from bolts and cut metal with a little torch. He was comforted by the work. When he had the sheet of metal free of the hatch, he kept on in the utter blackness, with Luza or Isuma turnabout holding the light while he bent up a rim, strengthened the underneath, rolled a smooth edge on the handholds. He quit finally when the others asked for sleep, but afterward, lying with Isuma in the cold blackness, he imagined new improvements, and invented ways to get them done with the tools he had at hand. *I thought of lessening the weight by cutting out holes in the metal,* he would tell Juko when he was with her again.

The weather worsened overnight and in the morning a needly snow fell on the wind. There was no seeing the mountain now, but no comfort in the closing in of horizons, as the great black clouds came down to the southern margin of the lake. They got Peder into the litter and carried him west without waiting for Bjoro's remodeling of the metal. The wind was frigid, blown at them across the sweep of the lake so they were driven to walk with their shoulders twisted sideward, heads bent, crablike. Two carried the forepart, one the rear, changing about their places every little while. Bjoro thought the weight seemed light in the first minutes but then swiftly it was heavier. Isuma had guessed the distance to the landing field at eleven or twelve kilometers, and he had imagined himself walking the circle around the torus ten times. *All right. Not so far.* But it wasn't the torus they were circling, and Peder's weight was leaden, cumbrous. They had to stop often and let him down and stand over him, all three of them, gasping, with their backs hunched to the wind and the stinging, bitter snow.

Gradually Bjoro's hands began to bleed through the gloves where the edges of the handholds sawed against his palms. His back, his shoulders, his legs ached. He became grateful for Luza's blistered feet slipping in Peder's big boots, a reason for more and more frequent standstills. It occurred to him, none of them had ever carried a heavy thing more than a short way. Heavy work was in the hub, where tools and metal pieces and equipment weighed little or not at all.

He took to sorting back through his life methodically, seeking the times he had carried weight, but it was all trivial, occasional: He had used to carry his son, Eneo, his daughter, Abigajlo, years ago, home from someone else's house when they'd fallen asleep there; he'd pushed wheelbarrows piled up with dirt or oranges when the farming people were at their busy times; he had carried a box of tools or a piece of equipment from one ŝiro round to another. He was unprepared, inapt, they all were, for this terrible labor. A sudden new despair gripped him: Had anyone thought, before now, how they would get their hard work done on this world, without a freefall place for doing it?

Whenever they stood hunkered around the litter, Peder's eyes watched them through the clear faceplate, a childish look, confused, afraid. Once, his mouth moved, he was telling them something. Luza got the skull off and put her ear close to hear his whispery voice: "Where are we going?" His mouth made a strange twist, a sort of smile.

Luza's face was stricken with guilt. She couldn't find an answer. She looked at Bjoro, and at Isuma. A sudden heat rose in Bjoro's neck and his ears. He crouched stiffly. "Isuma's found us a landing place for the balloon," he said. He twisted his own mouth in a burning grimace. "You'll get the first ride up, eh?" Peder breathed a sound, shut his eyes slowly. Someone else made a sound too: Bjoro heard the low whining clamped behind teeth. It was Isuma, or Luza, or the sound was in his own throat.

When they went on slowly across the stony ground with the wind driving the hard snow against them, Bjoro found the distance between his body and his thoughts began swiftly to widen. He was aware of the voices of the others, and of stopping and going on, lifting and setting down, he knew he was chilled, that his hair was a wet mantle clinging cold along his scalp. He continued to turn things over in his mind—regrets and forebodings, imagined quarrels, reimagined events—but his body's discomfort separated itself from him, became dreamlike, transluscent. He imagined he was outside, floating directionless upon a gray space, in the silence and warmth and shelter of an intact exo.

He remembered that he had had a surgical repair when he

was seven or eight, a benign cyst, and coming up from the anesthetic afterward had felt as he did now: unable to focus on any visual image, detached from his pain. *If I spoke, I would be clear of it,* he thought, but could not get his mouth to move, words to come out. *This is how people feel when they are dead,* he thought. *This bodiless stillness.*

He heard a shout, it was Isuma, but there was a long slow suspension before he knew what she had said. "Here! The saddle!" And he shouted too, it was his own voice he heard, an incoherent yell of joy, as he broke the surface in a dazzle like sunlight.

They set Peter down on the ground below the ridge and Luza stayed there with him while Bjoro climbed with Isuma to the top. It was a hard steep going, they had to find handholds, footholds, on the icy stones, the frozen mud. Bjoro kept from thinking of how they would get Peder up this way. But from the swale of the saddle, the plain lay white and smooth under new snow, a great startlingly open reach, a landing field.

They had brought all of the finder-seekers, Peder's and Luza's and their own. They climbed and slid down the gravelly scree onto the plain and paced out a big diamond, stuck the little robot devices down in the snow at the four corners. Bjoro stood a hundred meters across from Isuma at the last corner, the snow falling between them, and lifted his arm, then both his arms, grinning madly. He was filled with a keen hope now. Isuma's shout came to him on the wind, a flutter like paper, he didn't hear it all: ". . . saved!" she said.

The scree was fine gravel, they had slid down it abruptly on their haunches; now the climb up was a ceaseless, inefficient struggle against the little sliding stones. The east side, the big icebound boulders, seemed to Bjoro to become abruptly less formidable, and getting Peder up that way began to seem possible. He went over in his mind a plan for rigging the litter— hanging it from a sort of harness at the shoulders so their hands could be free; two of them to carry Peder, one to steady the others, give a hand up, scout the best way. The balloon would be a while yet getting to them, there was time, they would go slowly.

Luza stood below, watching them climb down from the saddle. Her yell came up to them in pieces: "... okay?" they heard,
and "... set?" Isuma straightened and cupped her hands at her
mouth, shouted back, "We've done it!" Bjoro thought when he
saw Juko he would tell her the way Isuma's voice had sounded
then, fierce and joyous.

There were cords in the waists of the exos, tethers for the sail
work, and Bjoro made use of them for his rigging, though it was
little enough like his imagining. He made the straps short on a
first try, to bring the litter high enough to clear the rocks; but
it was too high to lift from the hips. When one of them let go
to seek a handhold in the rocks, or put a hand out for balance,
the sway was wild, Peder's face in the exoskull a white mask,
terror. So he had to fiddle with the length of the cord until the
weight hung lower, hip-height, and he rigged a waist yoke to
check the sway. Better. Isuma and Bjoro carried, Luza scouted
the path up, and came back to help them clear the rocks, lift the
weight over the worst places.

Bjoro's hands went on bleeding, and his knees now, his elbows, from crawling over the rocks, from stumbling to catch
the litter when Isuma fell, from falling himself. The cords of the
rigging dug into his shoulders, whipsawed his hips. He sweated
within the exo, and the suit gradually lost ground, could not
keep up with the diaphoresis. While he worked, he wasn't cold,
only wet, but when they sat to catch their wind, the sweat
chilled him swiftly and he would shake, was a long time building back the heat when they stood again to drag Peder on up
the ridge.

Luza led them an erratic way up, switchbacking across the
steep face following the flattest stones or the brief open ways
across little deltas of gravel drifted with the new snow. Sometimes she led them to an impasse; they had to go back and find
a new way, or muscle the litter up over the boulder that stood
in the path. They didn't speak, any of them, except as they had
to: There was little enough breath for climbing, and it broke
from them in loud, white explosions. They hoisted Peder's terrible weight above their shoulders, shoved it through old
crusted drifts, dragged it up through the great stones.

Bjoro began gradually to take a kind of offense at Peder's terrorized look and the rigid clench of his hands on the edge of the hatchcover. He found he couldn't keep from watching the sky for the descent of the balloon, irrationally fearful it might land and rise again without them if Peder's unwieldy burden kept them from getting over the ridge in good time.

Unexpectedly, Luza came back to them, shouting, her boots sliding little rocks down the hill. "We've got there! You're at the top, the catbird seat! Bjoro! Isuma!"

They went up the bitter end of it, shouting weakly, foolishly, and letting Peder's weight down at last on the other side of the saddle, along the south-sloping talus. The wind blowing fierce over the top drove the snow like sand, but they sprawled there in the lee of the ridge, spent and joyous, looking out on the plain, the landing field. They would lower the litter down the gravelly scree on a cord, it would be quick and easily done. They had got over the damned thing.

Luza said, "Oh," suddenly, in an odd voice, and Bjoro looked, blinking, wiping the snow-crusted sleeve of his exo against his eyes. There was a spray of blood on the faceplate of the exo; Peder was hidden behind it.

He watched stupidly while Luza pulled around the pack she had carried, dumped their tools and supplies, pawed through until she had the med kit. She slid the hardhat from Peder's head and, kneeling there on the gravel in the snow, cleaned her hands with the sterile packets of wipes and then swiftly rolled Peder's exo down, cut a hole in his neck and pushed in a little piece of plastic tubing. She cut a hole in the chest of the tough exo and in Peder's tender skin, and threaded in another plastic tube that filled immediately with pink, frothy blood that ran out in a stain on the snow. The sound of Peder's breath above the whistle of the wind stopped Bjoro's heart.

He remembered suddenly it had been Peder's wife who had been afraid. It had been Peder's wife, a woman Bjoro didn't know, a woman named Juanita or Juana, who had worn that smile between set teeth, on the day the families of the *Ruby* had sat down together on the matted cottongrass in the Mandala orchard and held a sort of celebration, a good-bye supper, though no one was calling it that. It had been Peder's wife whose eyes had followed her husband.

Bjoro had watched Juko privately to see if he might catch something like that in her eyes, but she was like his mother, autonomous, solid, not given to dreams of romance, or adventure; when he looked, she was intent on something told to her by Arda Mejina's husband, or she was laughing and pushing Hans Arnesen away from her for the bad joke he told. And obscurely, he had envied Peder Ojama his wife. Had not imagined, then, that any of them might really die. Had felt that Peder's wife's fear was a kind of pleasure, a prize. Now he was suddenly appalled by the childishness of his feelings, the incompleteness of his imagining.

He had not prayed, nor believed in the efficacy of prayer, since he was seventeen, but he began to repeat and repeat in his throat soundlessly, *God, please, please, please, God,* and finally, rocking on his heels in the stinging wind, he gave himself over to it, began helplessly to pray Hans and Arda hadn't gone away without them; that the balloon could be brought down accurately in the wind not once but four times; that the *Ruby* would find and retrieve the damned aerostat four times over when it rose again out of the sky. He prayed for life, and for home. What was prayer but the listing of hopes that were otherwise irrecoverable? *God, please, please, please, God.*

They went on sitting beside Peder, crouched shaking in the blowing snow in the scant shelter of the rocks along the top of the ridge, while Luza kept the tubes clear with a little pump she worked in the palm of her hand. She said she was afraid to move him further until he'd rallied. *Or died,* Bjoro thought desolately. He listened to his own breath and his heartbeat, and Peder's, and helplessly frowned out across the plain where the blown snow rose in immense gauzy curtains.

He was too cold and too worn out to keep on feeling things deeply, and fell into a tired numbness and then into a short, unquiet sleep. When he woke, the wind had died. The stillness of the air confused him; he looked out on the plain in bleary disorientation. The light had begun to fail. The sky and the snow were sooty gray, and in the vast midsky, the silvery sheets of the descending montgolfiere soaked up the dull ochre color of the horizon.

Isuma was asleep beside him, but Luza sat up with Peder's head on her thigh. The skin of her face was chapped, her lips swollen and fissured. She made a stiff, pursed grimace and shrugged her shoulders when she saw Bjoro looking. The skin of Peder's face was grayish, there was a line of old blood below his nose. Luza rested her hand across his brow lightly with the fingers spread as if she hid his eyes from the luminous shine of the balloon.

Four

Ebb, ocean of life (the flow will return),
Cease not your moaning you fierce old mother,
Endlessly cry for your castaways, but fear not,
> *deny not me,*
Rustle not up so hoarse and angry against my feet
> *as I touch you or gather from you.*

Because her shrunken old bladder couldn't be made to wait so
well anymore, Kristina sat herself in the doorway of the lavejo,
leaning against the jamb so she could get to the toilet if the
Meeting ran long. In the last year, Meetings for Business had
naturally been drawn out with all these matters to do with the
New World, but since the *Ruby* was gone ahead of them even
the weekly Meetings for Worship had been lengthening—
people were anxious or ebullient by turns, they wanted to speak
of the eventful times.

It was up to members of the Ministry and Counsel Committee to sense the end of a First Day Meeting and bring it to
a timely close, and increasingly they had trouble apprehending
the moment, erring always on the side of inaction. That was all
right—Kristina liked their inefficient spiritualness. This domaro had had counselors in the past who were without sufficient silence, people who would interrupt thoughtful quietism.
Luisa Jamaguĉi, who was clerk when the domaro held a Meeting For Business, and Iteja Peron, who was clerk of the Pacema

Monthly Meeting, were both of them better at bringing an overlong Meeting to an end, but neither would sit at a Meeting For Worship—Kristina considered it a weakness in those two, that they never had written a Minute having to do with the Holy Spirit.

There were six apartments in this domaro and twenty-four adults, but only twelve or fourteen who regularly came together on the First Day of the week: Meeting for Worship. What were they thinking, those other people, the ones who stayed away? Kristina wondered. Did they think there was an explanation for the soul, for its feelings of truth and beauty and goodness, for its moral imperatives and its intimations of wider scope—did they think there was an explanation for this that did not involve God?

She pulled her knees up to her chest and rested her forehead there, eyes closed, to allow the silence to take form. There seemed always a little while at the beginning of a Meeting when the silence was trivial—people would cough and squirm, it was clear in their faces that they were thinking about commonplace things. Only after the first restless quiet was there real silence— the silence of God, as distinct from the silence of people, Kristina thought.

She waited with her eyes closed, her forehead pressed against her knees. Her mind wandered, touching on large and small worries to do with her son, Bjoro, with the broken grouting between the floor tiles of the lavejo, and the piece of drafting work she had been doing for some people over in Kantado ŝiro, a plan for the rerouting of an irrigation aqueduct. Eventually—perhaps it was when the silence began to belong to God—she also thought of Linda Florencio, whose son Alberto had killed himself only the evening before. On Last Day, she realized suddenly.

She saw little of Linda now, but they had been friendly once, during the years their children were central to their lives. Linda had been on the Waters Committee, and Kristina had drafted projects that involved her; because their younger children were of like ages, eventually they had confided a few things, difficulties and satisfactions having to do with mothering. Kristina never had known Linda's older son, Alberto Poreda, so her allegiance was with Linda, and it was hard not to blame Alberto for causing grief to his mother. Death was inevitable, universal, and that rendered it meaningless, she felt; people had to look for meaning in the way they lived their lives. She never had given much credit to this thing people called the ŝimanas, was impatient with suicides generally, believing people just looked for too much happiness in their lives. Her own husband Aŭgustino had been that way, imagining that happiness ought to be a kind of reward for managing your life well. *God is love* comprised Kristina's whole system of ethics, and there was not much allowance in it for a husband who gave himself up to despair, or a son who killed himself while his mother still lived.

Perhaps other people were thinking of Alberto, as well. Kristina felt a damp, heavy mood among them, and an image gradually settled in her mind: the limbs of blooming locust trees slouching under the weight of rain.

"Today something has come in my mind of a very serious nature." It was old Arno Masano, who was often given to inward voices; he stood to speak rather more often than other people, and liked to cite ancient Quaker documents without attribution. He spoke with his eyes fixed on the hunched shoulders all around him on the floor. "I have had a revelation that I believe makes our obedience to God a very simple thing. It is this—that the voice of God comes through our judgment, and not through our impressions." He pronounced the words sincerely, solemnly, waiting for their understanding to come in on the following silence. Kristina waited for it too, in impatient confusion. "When people go by impressions, rather than judgment," Arno said, "they turn from the true voice of God, and follow the false voice of self. When they are led by God—that is, by careful judgment—they make very few mistakes." After a moment, with evident satisfaction, he sat down among the shoulders and knees of his neighbors.

Kristina rested her head back against the door jamb of the lavejo. She closed her eyes again. She had learned to give Arno's words as much regard as someone else's unborrowed leading— it had occurred to her, God might find it necessary to repeat some things more than once. But she thought Arno ought to have given them a little more help, this time, distinguishing between judgment and impression. If it was so easy, we always would make correct choices, she thought irritably. But in the lengthening silence after Arno had spoken, she began to think of Linda's son Alberto, following impression, and not judgment, when he killed his mother's son. *The false voice of self.*

After an interval, Silvia Troelsen stood slowly. She lived with her husband and his family over in Revenana, but until her marriage she had lived with her mother in the apartment next to Filisa Ilmen's. She had a new baby tied against her belly; one of her hands was cupped beneath the solid roundness of the manta, lightly balancing or guarding the child there. "I worry—" she said, with her eyes cast down, her voice thin, timid, "—is it impression only that makes me fear this New World we are coming to? How am I to know if it's my fear leading me from it, or God's voice warning me away from quakes and storms? If it's the weather scares me, is that good judgment, or only cold feet?" Smiles went around the loĝio, but Silvia's face was solemn, earnest, she may not have meant the little joke her words played.

For 175 years they had gone on talking and thinking and making ready for leaving this world. They had lived for 175 years in a kind of suspended state, a continual waiting for change, but it was a balanced and deep-grounded condition, an equilibrium. They knew their world, root and branch, knew its history and its economies. The human life of the *Miller* and the life of its soil and its plants and animals revolved together, in a society that was well-considered, a community that was sustaining. Some people thought they had lived for 175 years in a world that was a kind of Eden.

Now they had come to their sea change—it was an enormous revolution that was pending in all their lives—and it had become common for people to raise the issue of being afraid. Before the *Ruby* had gone ahead of them, before they'd known the dimensions of the unpromising weather, the stony landscape, when people spoke of fear, it was of direful dreams, vague apprehensions. Just lately, as a result of all this bad news,

these weather reports from the *Ruby,* people were more precise, speaking of the weather, vulcanism, rocky soil, instead of
dim dreads. Well, it's all right to be afraid, Kristina thought.
Only don't count it as judgment.

She found, though, that she held a certain sympathy toward
Silvia Troelsen, who had this new baby and a young child, and
had gone against good advice when she'd married a man without patience in anything, a man everybody knew was lazy and
short-tempered like his father. Her husband, over there in Revenana, wasn't likely to come to a First Day Meeting; Silvia may
have come to this Meeting in her mother's domaro to say this
one thing on her mind.

Kristina thought, *It isn't the weather you're afraid of, dear
girl,* but she wasn't moved to speak this thought, knowing it to
be opinion, which she was prone to put forward too often.
Only afterward, in the long silence after Silvia's witness, she felt
a gradual restlessness, an agitation she recognized: She would,
after all, eventually be driven to stand and share some leading,
though there was no telling what she would say; she never did
know that until the words were out.

After a while of increasing unease, Kristina stiffly got up in
the little space where she had sat. She looked at the broken
grouting between the tiles of the lavejo, just left of her left san-
dal. "I've been thinking of locust trees," she said finally. Her
voice was husky, its sound a surprise, though not the words—
now, it was as if she had known all along what words would
come out of her mouth. She kept from clearing her throat, she
let the speaking clear it. "They have blossoms like sweet peas,
they're violet-pink or white. They bear them in big loose
bunches, and when it rains, the weight of the water and the
blooms makes the limbs hang down, they're very yielding, even
the thick ones will droop as if they haven't any strength." She
sent a look around to her neighbors, considering whether she
had given them a sufficient image. "But the locust wood is very
hard—the young limbs, even, are strong wood—and proof
against rot. Some of you may know, the prunings are favored
for the carving of eave ornaments, and canes." She gestured to-

ward old Arno Masano, who lifted his cane and flourished it in the air.

She kept standing a moment, waiting as the others waited, to see if she might have any more to say. But the silence felt solid, comfortable, so she sat down.

The metaphor satisfied her. With her eyes closed, she turned it over in her mind, examining it, looking for ways it bore on Arno Masano's leading about judgment and impression. She had thought, hearing the words come out, she had spoken a straightforward symbolism of the strengths and weaknesses of their community. Now she saw, as well, a parallel between the locust tree and this unnamed world they had been steering toward for nine generations. It might be they should look for advantages in stormy weather, stony ground—maybe there was a hidden luck in them—canes to be made from broken wood. She wondered, also, if they lacked the information that would better their judgment—there were the two failed balloons. She thought, with something like stubborn insistence, Now the *Lark* is landing, eh? we'll see.

After a while, Hilda Fugate stood. She was a woman forty or forty-five; she and her husband had only lately come to live in the Pacema district, in the household of Virdela Rota, who was an aunt of Hilda's. Kristina knew Virdela Rota, but not this niece, yet. She had a broad nose, an intelligent face, not much like Virdela—maybe their relation was by marriage. "The image of the locust trees," Hilda said in a murmuring, diffident voice, "has made me think of the tree called mule's-kick. I don't know its botanical name."

Someone spoke out, "miconia," and another voice said, "styrax," which Kristina knew as snowbell, and not mule's-kick, though some trees had more than one common name. Hilda's eyes went briefly across all the heads, focusing upon no particular place. She nodded and said, "I know about this tree because my mother was a forester"—two or three old people nodded as if they remembered Hilda's mother's tenure—"and when I was eight or nine years old she had an apprentice who was killed, cutting one of those trees down after it had died on

its feet. Some of you probably remember that apprentice who
was killed, Rubeno, I think was his name." People nodded.
Kristina remembered it herself. The man's name had been
Rubeno Mendoza, he had been the young son of her husband's
cousin. "That mule's-kick wood is hard, but it splits, and if a
dead tree needs cutting down, then it likes to fall before it's cut
through, and as it goes over, the trunk splits lengthwise and
kicks out, or upward."

Hilda let a silence fall. She stood at the edge of the logio, and
Kristina was drawn to the outlook behind her. There was a draft
slightly stirring in the strands of a weeping willow tree that
stood beside the alteja aqueduct. When her children had been
young, they had liked to play in such places, under a willow's
trailing long tresses, in the secret dimness. She wasn't able to
remember what a mule's-kick tree looked like. In her mind's
eye, though, she saw the split trunk recoiling, and Rubeno
Mendoza's startled face.

After a long while of standing looking across all the heads,
Hilda said, shifting her weight self-consciously, "I don't know
what this means—my remembering that man's death, and the
mule's-kick tree—but his name I think means *ruby,* so perhaps
God knows." She said this in a voice of hesitation and tenderness and then sat down slowly beside Virdela Rota.

The silence vibrated slightly with Hilda's words. Kristina felt
it enter her own body and ring inside her skull. The mood of
the meeting was abruptly changed, but who knew in what direction? Afterward, Virdela, and old Arno, and then Leo Furuso spoke wildly various leadings, to do with cautious
decision-making, with precipitate death, with souls hiding a
malign bent, or a durable. Kristina nodded when Karlo Eŭbioso
stood and simply said, "The voice of the Holy Spirit, in these
times of anxiety and decision, must be listened for, both in
strength of spirit and the breaking of it."

In the very long silence after Karlo's witness, finally Arno
Masano and Kristina's neighbor Filisa Ilmen—both of them
were of the Ministry and Counsel Committee—clasped hands
and stood up, and the shaking of hands went around the room.
Coming onto the logio, people had been quiet, had come by

ones and twos, or by family groups, silently, establishing the hush of the Meeting, but now bunches of people at once stood and began to talk. No one tried to keep silence. The Meeting was finished.

Kristina used the toilet and then came out to stand and talk with Arno Masano. "It was a gathered meeting, eh?" Arno said happily.

It had been a while since a First Day Meeting had been Gathered Into the Light—not since the *Ruby* was gone ahead of them, Kristina realized suddenly. She and Arno believed with the old Quakers, when words were truly spoken In The Light, they didn't break the silence but continued it, the silence and the words all of one texture, one piece, so when the words ceased you had a sense of the silence continuing uninterrupted, seamless; and it was in such silences that God's voice could be heard. She nodded. "I guess it was." She had felt it herself, when Hilda Fugate had spoken, though afterward no one had seemed to know what her words meant.

Arno's look was serious, confiding. "It was after Hilda Fugate spoke her witness. She surprised me, when she stood up. I thought right away, it might be God's witness we'd be hearing out of her mouth because I don't think she used to speak at Meeting much, over there in Bonveno where she lived. That's what I heard."

He leaned his head nearer Kristina. "Somebody said she moved because her husband and his brother had a falling out. Her husband's brother is Ĉito Meĵia, you know Ĉito, eh? You drafted for him, I bet, because he was an engineer, or something like it. Now they've moved here from Bonveno because Hilda's husband and this brother lived in the same household and they have hard feelings or something, and he doesn't want to keep living with him in the same house. That's what somebody said." Arno knew everybody's business. There was an unfocused look of happiness that would come in his eyes when he was standing in position to overhear someone else's conversation.

Kristina wanted to ignore this talk of Hilda Fugate's family life—she was in a religious mood just now. She said, "You gave us the first words to think on, Arno," which was true.

"Well, it may be I spoke In The Light, myself," Arno said. He nodded and smiled modestly. "God does speak in me, from time to time."

She looked away. She never could make up her mind if his spirituality was honest—maybe it was just too forward for her liking. "In all of us, Arno," she said flatly, and moved away from him. She found other people to talk to, Filisa Ilmen and her husband, Leo, and then Karlo Eŭbioso made a beckoning gesture and she went to stand with him and young Silvia Troelsen.

"We were just speaking of locust trees," Karlo said, beginning to smile.

Kristina made a disrespectful sound with her lips; she thought Karlo might have been teasing her a little. "Don't chide God's words, Karlo, whoever speaks them."

Karlo laughed. "No, no chiding. We liked those words ourselves." His look became more tender, more serious. "Silvia liked them."

Silvia gave Kristina a timid look. She said, "A man I know, his father was killed yesterday, killed out on the sail—the ŝimanas, I guess, that's what people say. I thought of him—that man I know, and his father—when you told about the locust tree. Who knows why? But there was a little comfort in it. It was like poetry."

Kristina wouldn't have said anything so sentimental as that, even when she was Silvia's age. And she was suddenly angry with Alberto again. She hadn't thought of him leaving his own children. *What were you thinking of, damn your selfish eyes.* "Then it must be God who is the poet," she said irritably. "I never have had a facility that way."

Karlo nodded happily. "God's words, whoever speaks them," he said.

Kristina reached out to stroke the palm of her hand across the silky crown of the baby's head where it lay bundled against Silvia's breast. "Who is your husband—is it Ole?" she said to Silvia, and the woman said, "Ole Hiroŝi," nodding.

She'd had a slight notion to offer advice, or take Silvia to task for accepting a bad husband against the advice of her neighbors, her family, the Pacema Clearness Committee. *You can always divorce, take a new husband, but your children will have only the one father,* she thought of saying. But she kept still, and petted the child again. Sometimes a person would come right, when the job was rearing children. You could learn patience: It wasn't like left-handedness or poetry, something you were born with or not. Ole Hiroŝi might still master it.

When people began to leave the loĝio and go on with other things in their lives, she put on a clean shirt and collected her flat clay bowl and a little sack of ground breadnut, a lime, sapotes, a knife—there were always too many people at a mortafesto, and there was never enough food—and she hunted up her clarinet, because sometimes people would play music and dance at a funeral. She didn't know if Alberto Poreda's body would be laid out at his mother's house, or at his wife's, but she went over to Linda Florencio's house in the Esperplena ŝiro.

She kept a deliberate pace, swinging in one hand the battered old clarinet case and in the other the string sack with her groceries in it, and the shallow bowl. Her eye told an uphill way, the curve of the torus always rising ahead, and behind, following the architecture of the wheel, but it was flat to her feet, easy walking—it was only the distance that made her sweat a little, made her calves ache, now she was gotten old.

Esperplena was half around the circle from Pacema; it wouldn't have mattered if she'd gone east with the turn of the world or west against it. You could walk clear around the torus anyway in a few minutes, if you were young and in a hurry, though there were the fields and neighborhoods and the spokes to be got around, aqueducts and ditches to be crossed; and if you kept down along the maltejo, there was the bridging of the Ring River and the rebridging, as the watercourse was deliberately roundabout. There had once been woodland between Mandala and Alaŭdo, a belt of trees that stood across all the incurvature, and in that place the through path rose high up on the altejo. It had been, in old days, a narrow, shadowed, duffy track winding along the shoulders of the uncut forest at the edge of the ceiling. In Kristina's childhood, those trees still were living, but she remembered the quick plague that had killed them, and now the path along the altejo made a winding way among orchards of pear, sapote, persimmon, fig.

She saw people she knew, especially in Mandala where she had lived twenty-eight years, before marrying Aŭgustino Mendoza and moving to his mother's house in Pacema. But she kept walking steadily, just calling a word or lifting a hand to people who spoke to her, in a way that made it clear there was a place she needed to get to.

It had been years since she had been in Linda Florencio's house, she remembered poorly where it stood. At Esperplena she meant to ask the way, but there was a stiff yellow kite stuck on the roof of a house down in the maltejo, an old practice, and she knew it was Linda's house flying it, announcing a death.

People crowded the loĝio and all the apartments in that domaro, standing about in bunches or sitting on the floor, not many of them making themselves useful. Some young people were decorating a bier with flowers and the fronds of ferns, streamers of yarn and rag—they would put Al's body on the decorated bier and his family would carry it once around the circle of the torus before he was burnt. Among the children tying ribbons to the cart was Juko's son, Ĉejo Indergard, and a girl, a cousin by marriage of Kristina's granddaughter's husband. What was the girl's name? Kristina couldn't remember. She let both of them kiss her cheek, but she had come to visit the body, not to visit with her own relatives, she told them, and went off looking for the dead man. Alberto's body had been laid out on a rug in one of the rooms of his mother's apartment. The skin was blackish and taut—he had breached his exo, Kristina remembered. She looked at him critically, but the look he returned was pitiful, despairing, and she found after all she must forgive him. *Bad judgment.*

She went among the people until she found Linda Florencio. Their friendship was remote, disused, she didn't pretend otherwise. She looked in the woman's face—it was a surprise to find she had gotten old—and said simply, "I'm sorry for what's happened to your son," and embraced her until they had both quit crying, and then left her among her relatives, her neighbors. She pulled up a short table in a corner of the loĝio, sat on the floor and began to make tortillas. She could do it without thinking about Linda's son, or her own. The fast, rhythmic slip-slap, slip-slap, of the patties against the palms of her hands was a comfort, and it masked other sounds—she never had had much tolerance for the silly words that were spoken in sympathy at a mortafesto.

"I hadn't thought you were a friend with Alberto." Juko squatted beside her at the low table. Her face was sallow; she liked to wear that yellow shirt that had been resewn from her mother's old clothes after that woman was dead.

"I was a friend with Linda Florencio, eh? and Al killed her son," she said flatly. Then she said, "Did you go to Ina's house?"

Juko made a gesture with her head, not an answer. "People over there were coming over here."

"Did you see the body?"

"Yes."

"Somebody should have let the blood out of him. He looks bad that way, not himself."

Juko looked in the sack with sapote in it. She spilled the fruits out on the table and made a start at paring them, halving them, without speaking about Alberto's body. In a minute she got up and went to hunt for a plate. When she came back, Kristina said, "I had forgot you and Alberto Poreda were friends."

Juko shrugged, though her eyes became bright with tears that did not fall. Kristina kept patting the tortilla quietly, slip-slap, slip-slap. Juko laid the sapotes on the plate in a careful manner, spiraling the yellow fruit from the rim to the center.

"Did you know? my nephew spent his green years with Alberto and Ina?" Juko said this without looking up.

"Viĉente? Oh, I did know it. I'd forgot." She had forgotten Ina, the wife, too, when she'd been stoking her anger toward Alberto. *What were you thinking of? Selfish, selfish.* "Which is Ina? I never did know her."

Juko looked about. "I don't see her now." She set the plate of sapotes away from her and shook some of Kristina's ground breadnut into the shallow clay bowl, squeezed a lime into it, began to knead the dough and flatten it. "Alberto and Ina have a son born with only one hand," she said in a low voice.

Kristina looked at her. Juko seldom would speak about such children. *The fey ones,* people called those kids, and were chary of them—babies born without hands, or with toeless feet, twins joined at the ribs. It was blamed on insufficient shielding, cosmic radiation in the interstellar space. Juko's own fey child had lived four years? five? and Kristina had been harsh in her judgment of her own behavior, then. She had felt stiff and tactless and false-hearted, had believed that she was not a sufficient friend to Juko. This was something she and Juko never had spoken of—Juko was shrouded in her own guilt, in those days, brandishing a shield of anger. In the years since Vilef's death, looking back through a lengthening lens, Kristina gradually had become more forgiving of herself; but Juko deliberately refused to speak to her of those years. She spoke as if she had no other child but Ĉejo.

"I heard a man say, once, those children are touched by God's finger, and that way of seeing it has stuck with me afterward," Kristina said.

Juko's face became sour. "Is that a complaint against God? that God's touch always brings these calamities?"

Juko was someone who would not sit at a Meeting for Worship; if she once had followed a religious leading, she had turned away from it after the death of her son. She and Kristina often had argued about God, but they kept away from certain tender places, and this was one. Anyway Kristina could see in Juko's face that her daughter-in-law's irritability had nothing much to do with her. Both of them went on working the tortillas, slip-slap, slip-slap.

"Well, there is Ina," Juko said.

Kristina looked. The woman was forty or fifty, with fair hair, a tall body but her posture poor, her shoulders rounded over. Her face was anxious, tired, without grief. She hadn't yet felt this death, Kristina thought. Kristina's own husband had died young—she remembered standing among her friends and neighbors at that mortafesto, conscious of wearing sorrow like a garment, but feeling only confusion, and anger and fright. It was months before she had understood in her breast that Aŭgustino was dead.

It may have been one of Ina's children with her, a young man standing with his arm clasped about Ina's waist, inclining his head to listen to something Ina spoke. There was a likeness about their wide mouths, and the younger one was built like the older, muscular and long-waisted. The young man's face was blowsy from weeping, the tender skin around his eyes dark and swollen.

"Is that her son, then? That boy standing with her—is he the son without a hand?"

"Yes. Beto, his name is." And at that moment the boy flourished one arm, gesturing to his mother, and Kristina saw the smooth rosy knob at the end of his wrist. "There's a daughter, I don't see her," Juko said. "You wouldn't know either of them for Al's children, they're fair, like their mother, neither of them took Al's color." She looked at Kristina. "Do you want to speak to Ina?"

"No." She shook her head. "Yes," she said, and got up stiffly from the floor.

The widow Ina pulled her mouth out in a joyless smile when she saw Juko. "Romeo was here, did you see him? And Orval Wyho. They said you were with Al, eh, when he was killed?"

Juko made an uncharacteristic gesture, thrusting one of her hands back through the cap of her hair in a jerky movement as if she were fending off with an elbow the thing Ina was asking her. "Well, he was dead when I reached him, Ina." Ina stood with her son's arm around her waist again, the two of them leaning into one another, waiting, expectant. "He may have meant to cut a tangle in the halyard," Juko said after a silence. "None of us was there to see. Who can know?" Ina went on looking at her unhappily. Finally Juko said, "Maybe if the sheet had held flat, eh? then he might not have been killed."

Kristina was embarrassed for Juko's lie, but Ina leaned toward Juko with yearning and nostalgia, as if this lost opportunity were a gift she might still receive. The son looked at his mother sorrowfully. "Well," he said, and pushed the rounded heel of his wrist across his cheek, though there were no tears there.

Juko said to Ina, touching Kristina's sleeve, "Do you know my husband's mother, Kristina Veberes?"

Kristina had stood back, but she came up now, and stood alongside Juko. She had lately had to struggle with an old-woman's compulsion: She often wanted to share her painfully gained wisdom with people who weren't able to make use of it. *You'll get over being afraid, get used to being alone,* she wanted to say. *When my husband was forty-seven, he killed himself, so I know your feelings.* Stupid. She looked in Ina's stiff face. "I'm sorry for what's happened to Alberto," she said flatly. Ina's eyes strayed away from her, dry, skittish. That was all right. She hadn't cried much either, those first days.

After a moment, Juko came forward and put her arms briefly around Ina—the widow looked like a long bent pole Juko had got her arms around. Kristina didn't know this woman, but she knew what sort of loss she was living, so she also gave her an embrace. With her cheek against Ina's she found she was compelled to murmur, "When my husband was forty-seven, he went mad and killed himself."

The woman made a slow sound, a lament, let her head fall on Kristina's shoulder as a child will do, beginning to weep. Well hell, not so stupid then. She patted Ina's back and kissed her hair and murmured, "Yes. Yes. Yes," in a steady rhythm, the word empty, a mantra.

She and Juko made pots of tea and put them out for people to find, and they sat with tea themselves, on the boards in the open center of Linda's house, watching people, and talking with ones they knew, Sonja Landsrud and Virdela Rota, about the *Ruby,* and the little boat *Lark* that surely by now was set down on the world, and Kristina's son, Juko's husband, maybe by now walking under a sky, a sun's light, in unmade weather.

Later, Armando Poreda—who was dying, Juko said, and was Alberto's father—came and spoke with Juko nostalgically of childhood things to do with Al. This man Armando would have been Linda's husband during the years of their friendship, but his face was unfamiliar. She thought they had never met in those days, she had known him only through his wife's words. Now none of that was in her memory; he was an old man with smooth dark skin pulled close over a fine skull, and she could see in his eyes that he'd found some secret about death, and hadn't any need to grieve for the loss of his son.

He had been a handsome man, still was handsome if you took into account he'd gotten old, and was dying, and she liked his equanimity, a quality she still waited for in herself. She wished, not quite seriously, that his marriage to Linda and his dying were not in the way of her enjoying sex with him. She was ashamed of herself for the irreverence in this thought—it was First Day! they were meeting at the wake of this man's son!—but it had been a year since she'd copulated with anyone, and she wasn't ready to be finished with that aspect of her life, just yet. In fact, she had been surprised to find that, in her old age, she was relieved to be unmarried. She liked having the scope to enjoy sex with different partners. Anyway, marriages had to be remade, once your children were no longer children, and she had seen in other people that it was difficult work, something she was glad to do without.

The mortafesto went on being silly in the usual ways. People laughed and gossiped, children ran through, but every little while a self-conscious silence would fall in one of the rooms or a corner of the logio and then someone in the middle of it would be moved to stand and share some thought about Al, or about God, or death. Sometimes a person would fill one of these silences with foolish or pointless advice for Al's relatives— "God's will be done," people liked to say, but drawing it out to some dreadful length. Kristina, squirming irritably, would comfort herself with a conceit: She had kept her own words to them short and private, and had offered no advice.

She was impatient with melancholy music as with barren advice, and when a flute began to play a sad melody from the room where Al's body lay, and two women's voices joined it, a lyric about loss and truth, she took her clarinet from its case and spitefully toodled something amusing, a bit of a song. Let the sad people go and sit in that room with the body and the flute, she thought. Over here, we'll have a festo. Eventually Roaldo Forman brought his horn to play with her, and then someone with a guitar, a woman she didn't know; they settled into playing in earnest, variations on an old tune they all knew. A few people began to dance, and more instruments were brought out, and people who were sitting drummed the floor or their knees, or made timpani of the shoulders of the person sitting in front of them, and Kristina let go of her irritation.

After a while she had to give up playing and unbend her legs—she had an old woman's body, something she regarded as a betrayal. She stood up, flexing her knees ungracefully, putting her hands to kneading the small of her back, and when she was standing there she saw Linda Florencio and her dying husband dancing together, leaning into one another with the tenderness of children. When you move something, you discover new meanings in it, Kristina thought, watching them.

Juko found her again and said quietly, "I have some wine I got from Leo Furuso. I've been hiding it from you. People are getting ready to carry Al around the world; are you going? or maybe do you want to go home and help me drink up that little wine now?"

Kristina lifted her eyebrows. "You are damn selfish, eh? Didn't bring it for sharing at this funeral."

"No. Oh hell no," Juko said, and both of them looked sly, and smiling. They sat on the stoop of the domaro putting their sandals on, and then went up through the close-built houses. There was a wetland at the east edge of Revenana, the leaching field for that district's wastes, and the footway went high up on the wall to skirt it. Kristina's bones felt lighter up there close to the ceiling, and climbing up was a diminishing effort. It was the downhill that was hard, a thickening of weight on her old bones, her aged heart.

On the path between fields of jackfruit and bananas, walking swiftly uphill to them, was someone they knew, Leo Furuso's wife, Filisa Ilmen. Her face was pink—Kristina saw in it some bad news she was coming somewhere to give. She was a homely woman and not very bright but Kristina liked her; she was a good mother, and rightly had kept up a friendship with her husband's family even though Leo had some old grudge against them. She expected Filisa's bad news was for someone else, but then her round face, lifting, seeing them, darkened to red, and Kristina's heart began to drum in her ears.

"The *Lark*'s crashed," Filisa told them, and her eyes filled swiftly with tears.

Kristina hated the way her body felt when it was surprised by fear—light, breakable, shaken, like the rattles people made from gourds. She had not expected to find the attachment to one's child so strong after fifty years. *My son isn't dead,* she thought, but she couldn't make her body believe it. Her body waited for Filisa to say that Bjoro was dead.

Juko said, "Where does this come from? Who is saying it? Are people dead?" with her voice rising in a kind of anger. She didn't speak Bjoro's name, neither had Filisa.

She looked at Juko with her brows raised in appeal. "Someone from the Radio Committee came and said it. You know how they never tell clear things, eh? the radio always will break up." She shook her head, opened her hands out from fists. "They said there was a mechanical failure—something—and a short falling; there was water, they've come down in water, I guess."

Juko made a choking sound and Kristina was startled and frightened by that, more than by Filisa's chill words. She took Juko's arm, held it fiercely. "Now don't, don't," she commanded. Then she let go her hold and they all three stood without looking at one another, without speaking or touching. After a while Juko said, "I've got that wine," with her anger back again, and went on down through the fields toward the houses of Revenana, walking stiffly erect, swinging her arms. Kristina arranged her mouth. She said to Filisa, "The radio people believe they are killed, eh?"

Filisa lifted her brow again, childlike, sorrowing. "I don't know, Kristina." She put one of her arms across Kristina's shoulders. Kristina wanted not to be touched; she felt breakable, cracked, but didn't want to hurt the poor woman's feelings. She reached up and patted Filisa's hand on her shoulder. "Well," she said meaninglessly. "Well."

Five

HUMBERTO

A song of the rolling earth, and of words
*   according,*
Were you thinking that those were the words,
*   those upright lines? those curves, angles,*
*   dots?*
No, those are not the words, the substantial
*   words are in the ground and sea,*
They are in the air, they are in you.

Because it was May, farming was a work that wouldn't wait for grief or fear to be spent. In May there was rain every night, and long days of bright light, and the rain-washed air was charged with fertility. The rice was delicate, not as swift or as coarse as maize; if it wasn't to be overgrown it had to be kept weeded, and weeded again. It stood knee-high in straight rows of vivid green, and Humberto went between the rows, scraping the ground with a broad maĉeta curved like a scimitar.

Asian people had grown a rice that thrived in flooded fields, but it was the upland Costa Rican rice that had been brought onto the *Miller,* a kind of rice that sprang from well-drained ground, and yielded well on poor soil where heavy-feeding crops would sulk. For the latter virtue, Sven Fuĵino and Humberto had planted it to this field, the Shepherd's Crook, which was always impoverished by the old trees standing at the east edge of the ŝiro, the remnant of a woodland that once had separated them from Esperplena. Humberto had gone along, jabbing holes in the earth with a pointed stick, while Sven followed him with the rice seed in the hollow shell of a calabash gourd. Humberto's lines were straight as if he'd followed a cord strung across the field. It was something you had an eye for, or not; Sven always laid crooked rows.

Now Humberto went alone between the ranks of green, skinning the ground with the blade of the maĉeta in short, even strokes. His son had gone to work with Ĝeronimo Zea, digging up and chopping the spent stalks of okra now that that crop was finished, and Humberto had gone into the rice without asking anyone else's company in his work. He thought he wanted to be alone, and not to talk to anyone about the crashed boat. Weeding was not a job he liked overmuch, but he liked the small, repetitive sound, the scuffing the blade made against the earth, and when he straightened his back and glanced behind him, he liked the way the row looked, the soil clean and dark, and the cut weeds lying in little wilting windrows. It was work you could do without thinking about anything, your mind absorbed in the short, methodical swinging of the tool.

Houses stood nearby the field of rice, and the path between Alaŭdo and Esperplena went along the south edge of the Shepherd's Crook; people frequently walked by on the path or went up the ladder of a house or down from one. He kept at his work with his head down, meaning to give a message about his wish for solitude, but not many people respected it. Because he was related to actors in the event, they steadily brought him their well-meant sympathy and their speculations about the *Lark.*

Years before, Luza Kordoba had stopped his bleeding to death when he had stepped into the edge of Henriko Lij's canecutter. And though he and Luza had never had a sexual union—Luza was sapphic, her lovers all had been women—people knew that Humberto had loved her for a while, and tried to interest her in loving him, and that their friendship was charged with an old sexual energy. They wanted to bring him consoling words—he must be suffering grief for Juko's sake, eh? and for the loss of Luza Cordoba—but he was already tired of the weight of his sorrow. He wanted to find peace in his weeding and be allowed to let go of the people lost on the New World.

After a while Pia Putala walked out into the rice with another long blade and went to work beside him. She was silent for quite a while, as if she must have guessed his wish for privacy. But then she said, looking around, "There is a word just gone around from the Radio Committee, a rescue is being done. Did you hear?"

He hadn't heard that. He stood up straight. "No. They're not killed, then?"

"Well, maybe not, somebody among them has given a kind of signal. I guess it was a plan they all made in case this might happen. They've got a balloon going to bring them up one by one, people are saying."

Humberto stood looking across the several rows of rice at Pia. Since word had come of the crash of the *Lark,* he had secretly thought they were dead, all four of them, or would be shortly, as there wasn't any way to get them back up to the *Ruby,* was there? He hadn't imagined they could use the balloons. The idea startled him, made him feel stupid.

"When?" he asked her.

She straightened from her work and looked thoughtfully at the ground. "I don't think there was a time said. A balloon isn't something you can move precisely, I guess. But anyway they've started on it." She eyed him cautiously. "There's no sure telling this rescue will work, I don't suppose."

He was surprised again, feeling there must have been something in his face or his voice that made this woman, twenty years younger, think him so naive. "No," he said, in a tone of astonishment, and bent to his weeding again. He wondered if people had gone to tell this news to Juko and to Kristina Veberes, but was afraid of asking it, embarrassed.

He had thought there was only one possibility and now suddenly there were several. He kept on with the maĉeta, but his peace was now completely lost, he was preoccupied with imagining the manifold details and difficulties of this balloon rescuing. Deliberately, he kept from reimagining Luza and Bjoro alive. He was cautious of pouring much hope into a fragile vessel.

Once she had told her news, Pia became silent again, focused upon the repetitive weeding, and after a while Humberto surprised himself by restarting their conversation. He asked her, "Are people wanting to go on with Meeting for Business, have you heard?" He didn't want to go to the Farms Committee Meeting if people only meant to stand around and guess at how things would come out with the crashed boat.

"I don't know," Pia said. "I heard a clerk over in Bonveno saying, how could people come together on ordinary business matters until the *Lark* was a settled trouble? But he doesn't farm. I don't know what other people, farming people, are thinking. Maybe they wouldn't want to put it off. Nothing is ordinary these days, eh? There's a lot of studying and weighing of things that still needs to be done."

They had been studying and weighing for years, but now there was accurate information, useful detail. *The more known, the more is known to ask,* was an old maxim lately become timely. "The answer to every question is ten new questions," Humberto said unhappily, and Pia nodded without speaking.

He straightened, pushing a little stiffness out of his back, and looked across the field of rice into the woodland. For a while he had been hearing a ringing high whistle—a nunbird, he thought it was, objecting to their voices. He looked on the long slope at the edge of the woods, in the patchy, concealing shade under the trees, the ferns, for the bird's low nest. He had once been privileged to see the mouth of a white-fronted nunbird's nest, an inconspicuous hole a few centimeters wide with a long anteroom of twigs and dead leaves hiding it. It was Ridaro Rogelio who had shown it to him a lifetime ago, when he was still green and had thought he might want to take up Ridaro's work, be an ornithologist. For a while he had followed Ridaro at his slow, painstaking practice of netting and banding and counting and releasing certain birds, and then netting and killing others. When the cats had taken a plague and died, people had found they must act as keystone predators of some species, and this killing was part of Ridaro's work. Humberto never had been able to get a distance between himself and the killing and he'd lost his eagerness for ornithology. But he never had stopped watching birds.

"Are you doing a committee job?" Pia asked him.

He nodded without taking his gaze from the edge of the woodland. There had not yet been agreement on the question of whether new species, Earth species, ought to be introduced to the New World. People researching this question had brought up plagues of alien rabbits in Australia, of alien cheat-grass in North America; but evidently there had once been a landmass connecting America with Asia, and animals had crossed in both directions, some killing off others—how was this natural event different from human ones? While they waited for agreement, quite a few people were going ahead, looking at the *Miller*'s library of frozen cells for plants that would take cold weather, poor soils. Humberto's little committee studied the wild things—cold-tolerant natives that might, if cultivated, be edible, or pharmacological, or useful as a textile.

"I'm put to studying subarctic natives, the xerophyla," he said to Pia. "It isn't known yet, but if the water in the soil is frozen, a tundra, then when it thaws there will be too much water, the roots will stand in it."

She grimaced. "All these bad accounts."

Humberto lowered his eyes to the earth, his dirty feet, the toe strap of his worn sandals. "Some things will grow in those circumstances. I'm reading, looking." He began slowly to weed again. By the time he thought of saying something about esculant willows, the moment for it seemed to have slid by.

Pia let her maĉeta rest on the ground but she didn't straighten. She looked toward Humberto diffidently from her hunched-over pose above the handle of the long knife. "You have relatives on that boat, eh? Someone said you had a lover, or a brother, on the *Lark*."

Humberto shook his head, his face flushing. "I know Luza Kordoba, but not in that way. My son's mother is now Bjoro Andersen's wife." Pia's wrong information humbled him. He realized with embarrassment, maybe his links to the crashed boat had made him feel speciously self-important.

Pia said, circling backward a bit, "I guess I'd find it hard to keep a clear mind for a Business Meeting, myself, with the *Lark* still unsettled."

He seldom spoke in Meetings. He thought the clarity of his mind maybe wasn't the issue. "Whatever other people want to do," he said, straightening again so he could shrug.

Pia had two young children at home, one was a baby still sometimes nursing at her breast. Around the midday her nephew carried the crying baby out to the rice field to see if Pia's breast was what the baby wanted, and after that Pia quit the field. Humberto worked on alone until the weeding of Shepherd's Crook got done, then he went down to the tools house and washed and honed the maĉeta he had used, and rubbed a little oil onto the metal, and hung it up by the handle on a hook. He was tired, his back ached, his skin itched with sweat, but he had not altogether lost his wish for solitude, and this was a time of day when there would be several people in the baths. So he went up the ladder of the domaro to his own apartment.

There was only Alfhilda there, heating a soup. Humberto brought out the old books and the tapes he had from the borrowing library and sat on the wide sill of the casement with his back braced against the frame in the pasado wall and his knees pulled up to rest a librajo there. Humberto had lately begun a hunt for relatives of the tough, adaptive willows and birches whose stunted forms had once made a rug across the northern plains of the Earth. The possibilities he listed went to Kilian Bejrd, who studied each of them for their dietetic values, digestibility, or to Andreo Rodiba who was an herbalist, or to Edmo Smith, a spinster and weaver. And then to Anejlisa Revfiem who was tinkering with hybridizing different ones to see if they could be recast in a more useful or a more productive form. It was slow work—after a year of this studying and tinkering, they had two dozen possibilities that might furnish a marginal crop, might nourish or clothe or heal a person in need. But Humberto liked the difficult progress. He thought there was a certain satisfaction in untangling a small tight knot in a piece of thread—maybe more than in straightening out a big kinked rope.

He read the botanical works on the screen of the librajo with his eyes pinched to force the intricate old languages, the unwieldy namings, through a narrow strait. When his eyes or his mind tired, then he set the botanicals down and read old, general geographies about tundra soils, subarctic climes, their language of landscape by now comfortingly familiar. Much in those books was reiterative, but he wasn't tired of them. He had caught from some of the essays a kind of reverence for the strategies animals and plants had used, surviving in an arduous climate.

Alfhilda brought him soup and sat on the floor with her own bowl in her lap. She was his brother Pero's only child, a girl with a broad brown face, unreticent, impulsive, a songbird. She had a potter's wheel in the Alaŭdo work shed, and frequently went about with clayed hands, had to be reminded to wash. Her ceramics were plain and artless—her gift was for biology, and lately she had apprenticed herself to Anejlisa Revfiem. She liked to read from Humberto's botanical books, and talk seriously with him about the genetics of draba mustards and tundra grass and stunted mountain heather. He had had a quiet life for several years in a small household, himself and two old people. Now his brother's daughter and his own son had moved into this apartment, along with his mother's friend Heza Barfor. His privacy, his time for solitude, had become brief and erratic, but he wasn't sorry for it. He regarded, with astonishment and fondness, Alfhilda's swift mind, Ĉejo's earnest ideality.

"Do you know, there's this rescue to be tried?" Alfhilda said to him.

He nodded over the soup.

"They'll bring them up one by one in a survey balloon, dump the equipment and come up in the gondola," she said, without looking at him to know whether he had made an answer. "Avino went over to Luza Kordoba's house to tell them—in case they didn't know it yet."

Humberto's mother hardly knew Luza or her family. People would wonder why she was taking this upon herself, or they would guess: it was a slight, cunning gesture of malice toward Juko Ohaŝi. Maybe by choosing to bring the rescue news to Luza's family, she was deliberately, conspicuously choosing not to bring the news to Bjoro's wife. She and Juko had an old enmity, grounded in guilt and blame, dating from the death of Humberto's son, and he had long ago lost the energy for trying to heal it.

"What is it you're doing with Anejlisa just now?" he asked Alfhilda, by way of turning the talk away from the *Lark*.

"We're growing a hybrid from willow stock, a sort of mutation of the—" Humberto saw her tongue come forward, licking the soup, or the intractable word "—setsuka sachalinensis. Trying to get it to grow a root mass like the pussy willows, edible," she told him.

"On the setsuka? I never hoped much for that one." He lapped the soup thoughtfully. There was mushroom in it, and bright paprika; it was sharp, sweet. "I thought Anejlisa would go at it the other way, fiddle with the pussies."

"She's doing that too." Alfhilda lifted the bowl, maybe hiding her mouth, her beam of satisfaction, behind the rim. "But I helped with the setsuka. Fixed the plates, and the droppers, and scraped the cells." She looked at Humberto. "Are you reading the Kovalak book? I like that one."

"I'm reading it. What? Are you picking it up when I set it down?"

She grimaced. "Only sometimes. I read wherever your marker is, a page or two."

Kovalak's was one of the old books he had from the library, its pages rebound between stiff boards and the paper sprayed with something slick and inflexible, a fixative or a mold-inhibitor. People handled such books with care—they were talismans, holy objects, and Kovalak's work was lyrical, a kind of spiritual geography. Humberto read it not for instruction but for its gift of imagination, its passion and compassion for Earth's lost species, its informed evocations of storms and migrations, aurora borealis, icescapes. Kovalak had been dead for two hundred years, but in the photo image on the frontispage he was in his forties, hunkered down on his heels on a gravelly scree and peering off narrow-eyed toward something behind the camera. He was long-jawed, bearded, had a look of dignity and reproach. Humberto said, "When I'm finished with it you can read it yourself, not just pieces."

She made a childish face, rolling her bottom lip down. "Anej-lisa has given me a lot to read: eight books, one is French."

When they had finished the soup, the two of them took up reading companionably, though Humberto gave up trying to get at the complicated botanicals with Alfhilda asking him frequently the meanings of words, and reading things aloud when they struck her interest. Shortly Heza came in the house with a bundle of dyed yarn, and when she let her load down in the front room and started in about the balloon rescuing, Humberto had to finally give up trying to be alone. He put his reading away and got clean clothes and a towel in his arms and went along the pasado from his apartment to the men's bathhouse.

Two men were washing, and one man and a child were in the tub. He nodded to people, got his clothes off, crouched naked under the spigot of a shower beside Karlos Onoda and Edvard Penagos. Karlos and Edvard kept on with what they were saying to each other, something to do with thermostats and parabolic mirrors; both of them worked in the smeltering of metals. They were married, raising young children, their lives marked off different circles from his. The dribble of the waterspout was tepid and soothing; he sluiced it over the back of his head, his neck.

"Probably you heard about this rescue that'll be tried," Karlos said to him.

He pushed the water out of his eyes. Both men were looking at him. "Yes. A balloon," he said. Karlos's chest was extravagantly hairy. In the stream of the shower, the hair lay against his skin in a smooth pelt which Humberto admired from the edge of his eye.

"It seems a risky thing, eh?" Karlos said, raising his eyebrows. Probably Karlos wasn't asking a question, but Humberto felt he should nod, agreeing with a sort of wordless distress.

"Well anyway there isn't much mechanical can go wrong with a balloon," Edvard said. "I'd trust it more than another go-down boat, was it me." He said it in a grimacing way, as if he held mechanical things in high scorn. No one knew why the boat had tumbled, so people were placing blame on a vague failure of technology.

"How long will it be, before there's some word of them?" the man in the tub called out above the water of the showers. His name was Umeno Flagstad, he was short and thick-bodied, his skimpy hair stuck up in a wet cockscomb. Umeno ground lenses for eyeglasses and for laboratory microscopes. Humberto thought he had spoken generally, but the others seemed to wait for Humberto to answer the question, as if his relation to Bjoro or Luza gave him a kind of authority.

"I don't know," he said. Then he also said, "A balloon isn't something that can be moved precisely, I guess." He spoke up, so his words borrowed from Pia Putala would reach Umeno sitting in the tub.

"Those radio people are sending down stingy notices," Edvard said with bitterness. "There's only a few words of news comes out from the hub every little while, but people say there's a steady talking going on between the *Ruby* and the hub, should be ten people carrying the words down here if they were sharing it, but they're keeping the most of it to themselves. I don't know what they think they're doing, those people."

Humberto knew one of the people who worked at the radio, a man who had married a cousin of his. Before the *Ruby* had gone ahead, Noria's radio work had been a sometime talking with the miners who went out on the slow tugs to capture little asteroids. Noria was a furniture maker, the radio had been something he did seldom and unhurried. But when the *Ruby* was launched, all the people who worked radio had had to drop their other work, just to keep ahead of the listening, and transcribing—putting committees' belated questions to the *Ruby,* and running to get answers to questions that came back from the boat. What must it be like now the *Lark* was crashed?

"There's more work than they can keep up, maybe," he said, but Karlos was speaking at the same time, asking if there maybe had been a trouble with the radio. When Edvard complained again about mechanical failings, it became clear they had all heard Karlos's words over Humberto's. In discomfort, he waited for an opening to repeat himself, but they went on talking, and in a little while the talk got away from that matter, and there wasn't any reason for him to keep on waiting to say it.

He left the waterspout silently and sat in the deep water in the soaking tub, on the wooden bench beside Umeno Flagstad. The child was Edvard Penago's son, a boy about three or four whose name Humberto didn't remember. In a moment, Edvard and Karlos came into the tub. Edvard blew bubbles on his son's wet belly before he sat on the bench. When he was bent over the boy, his clean pink anus displayed itself for Humberto and Umeno.

After everyone was settled, Humberto closed his eyes. People were finally done talking, and for a few minutes he heard only the water lapping against the underneath of his chin. The bath was hot, it smelled of mint and the camphor wood of the tub. Shortly, behind his eyes, he began to construct wild, empty landscapes of rock and sky, his mind's work, dreamscapes that could not have been put into words. The person he placed in the world of the dream wasn't Bjoro or Luza but himself, poking holes in the pebbly dirt with the end of a pointed stick.

The little boy said loudly, as a sort of declaration all at once, "I have a penis." Men knew, three or four years old was an age for making these announcements, and they laughed or smiled. Humberto felt a brief pang of nostalgia. He was glad, usually, to be past his own child-rearing days; his friendship with his grown son felt easy as loose clothes. But sometimes, as now, he felt something like a loss. Where was that little boy, eh? vanished into the person Ĉejo had become.

"Bridge Troll has a penis that floats," Umeno Flagstad said to the boy quietly, and that got the adults to smile again.

The boy looked down at his own penis in the water. After a while he said to Umeno, "Mine floats."

Umeno studied himself in mild surprise. "I see mine does too." There was a silence, then he said, "Bridge Troll has a penis as long as his arm. It must be the size of his penis that got Bridge Troll into trouble, eh?" Some laughter went around among them.

The boy examined his penis again, and his long thin arms bobbing in the water. "What trouble?"

Humberto had told this same tale more than once to Cejo, and now he thought with sudden happiness, *I'll go on telling this to my grandchildren.* Umeno said, "Oh, it had to do with Koi, and the Plum Rains. Do you know that story? That time in the Plum Rains, it was hot and clammy and Bridge Troll lay down in the Ring River to cool himself. He was under the Tailed Frog Bridge where the water is very shallow, but he didn't remember: In the mornings of the rainy season people always open a gate on the Mandala dam. The little flood came along while Bridge Troll was lying there sleeping, and his big penis floated up and carried him along the water like a boat."

The boy's eyes were fixed wide on him through the wet scrim of his bangs.

"Old Bridge Troll," Umeno said, "thinking he might have to swim around the river forever, called out for somebody to rescue him. Koi swam up to see who was crying, and when he heard what Bridge Troll was worried about he laughed and said, well, he had lived all of his life swimming around the Ring River and it was a fine life. Bridge Troll, you know, has a short temper, and he had lived all of his life under bridges and wanted to go on doing it—he said he wasn't interested in living the foolish life of a fish. Well, this made Koi spiteful and sly and he said, if Bridge Troll wanted to stop floating around the Ring River he'd have to cut off his penis."

One of the other men, Karlos, made a scissoring gesture with his fingers in the steam rising from the water. "Ouch," he said, and there was laughing again. The boy fidgeted, looking at their faces, waiting for the end to be told.

"Bridge Troll by now had floated half around the Ring River," Umeno said. "And was just then under the Wake Robin Bridge. That bridge has a booming echo living under it, from the pump and the falls over there at the edge of Pacema."

"The Falls From Grace," Edvard said to his son, and the boy knew that place. He nodded solemnly.

"Fum-Grace, where Mario lives."

Edvard nodded too.

"Well, there's the pump brings water up to the head of the falls, and the water falling, the sound they make under the bridge is pretty big, eh? And when Bridge Troll heard it he got more afraid, and he told Koi to cut his penis off quick and save him from going up in the pump and down over the falls. So Koi cut off the Bridge Troll's penis with his teeth and carried it away for his children to eat—and Bridge Troll sank to the bottom of the Ring River."

Umeno waited for the boy's mouth to open in understanding surprise. Then he said, beginning to make a crawling motion through the water with his hand, "Bridge Troll had to crawl along the bottom like a crayfish going round and round the Ring River forever. Or anyway until drier weather, when the river got low enough for him to crawl out under the Tailed Frog Bridge." He began to grin slowly. "But later on old Bridge Troll stole one of Koi's children and stitched the little fish on to his body in place of his penis. So maybe Koi was sorry for that joke he played. Do you think?"

Edvard Penagos made a sound of fright and nipped his little son's penis under the water, between two fingers. The boy squealed and laughed, and began a game of holding his breath and crawling on the bottom of the wooden tub like a crayfish, pinching toes and penises.

When the boy and his father and Umeno Flagstad had gone home, Humberto went on sitting in the bath with Karlos. "Here's something new I've got to wonder about," Karlos said to him. He grinned. "Is there a bridge troll on that New World, eh, if there's no bridges?"

"Trolls are canny," Humberto said, smiling himself. "They might think of living under rocks."

"Oh hell, there's plenty of those, that much is true. What do you farm people think about it?"

"What? The rocks, you mean?"

"All of it. The ground, the weather. That world's got a short year, eh? How can a crop be raised in a month?"

People who weren't farming often didn't pay attention to the reports, or didn't remember them. Humberto looked away. "Fifty days. We can get crops to ripen in that time, if we have the long days. At the midlatitudes, summer daylight is either side of twenty-two hours."

Karlos raised his brows. "How would our bodies get used to that, eh? They say we've all got a clock in our bodies tells us when to sleep and wake and eat. I guess I wouldn't like to stay awake twenty-two hours, maybe plants wouldn't like it either."

Humberto began to feel tired and blunted. These were arguments he had heard many times. He said, "It would spur a plant to grow, I guess," but that was only what his instinct told him. There had been three or four mathematical studies without clear result, statistical remodelings to do with atmospheric pressure, surface gravity, irradiation, axial tilt; the research was built upon known agricultural responses. Not many people believed in the studies, anyway. Reports about what had been grown in the summers at Reykjavik, Iceland, or Yakutsk, Russia, seemed too remote from them to be any longer truthful.

Karlos touched his groin, smiling boyishly. "Maybe those long days would grow me a penis long as my arm, eh?"

Humberto answered without joy. "Well I guess we could get used to it, then."

When other men came into the bathhouse, Humberto dried himself and put on his clean clothes and went out, before the talk could get back around to the *Lark.* He carried his dirty clothes down to the laundry, and while he waited for the washing machine to finish its job he took a piece of needlework from his pocket, a square of linen he was hemming in a fine stitch. He sat on the flagstones at the edge of the path in front of the laundry, with his legs folded under him and the needlework on his knee. He had meant to give the finished piece to his cousin's daughter on the occasion of her marriage, but then had imagined it might be needed as a funeral gift for Juko on the death of her husband. Which, now?

The sewing was not an occupation for his thoughts, and because the path in front of the laundry house was not much on the way to somewhere else, he was frequently left alone to turn things over unsystematically in his mind. It was impossible to keep from thinking about the *Lark,* and gradually he began to worry along a new line. All the spacegoing boats were old, original equipment; the *Lark*'s failure maybe was age, or maintenance. He didn't know if it was possible for the people on the Mechanics Committee to warrant a reliable go-down boat.

Parts of houses were old as the torus, and many trees, wooden chests, tables, many of them were Earth-built. The clothes washers were old stock, a clever Japanese invention; they made an ultrasonic noise that shook the dirt off into very little water. In the kitchenhouse of the domaro Humberto lived in, the stove was Earth-built, it had a short phrase in Norwegian, raised in relief on the ceramic base. Cêjo, who was fascinated by it, had worked out the meaning. *Root and Leaf,* it said, and Cêjo, every little while, would offer some new sense he had made of that old, quizzical message. But original machinery had gradually become rare. The mechanisms that survived tended to be of two kinds: simple things with few moving parts, like the clothes washers; and things too problematic for their small manufactory to re-create—spacegoing boats, sewing-machine motors, the heavy equipment of manufacture itself. Humberto imagined an absurdity: After so long a course getting to this world, they might only lack the fundamental machinery to deliver themselves and their belongings down to it.

When he carried his clean laundry home his mother was there, delivering to Heza all the guesses and certainties and dreads she had gotten from the crowd of people at Luza Kordoba's house, all the people who were helping the family to wait, or bringing news about the rescue. Earlier, he had thought he might not want to go to the Farms Committee Meeting, in case the talk was all of the crashed boat. But now he went out to it—it would have been pointless to stay away, since even the people in his own house were keeping up their talk about the *Lark* and there was no escaping it.

The Alaŭdo Farms Committee for many years had made a habit of meeting in the field above the aeroponics shed, the one named The Whisper Behind the Tree. There were five carob trees standing in a rough circle in a field of cottongrass, and the committee fitted their own circle of people inside the circle of trees, people balancing tablets on their knees if they had to write something down, and bringing mats to kneel on at certain times of the year when the grass was stubbly or littered with St. John's fruit. There were twenty people who farmed in Alaŭdo, but not often twenty at a Farms Committee Meeting—today only nine. With the fate of the go-down boat at the front of people's minds, maybe quite a few were following the maxim that a person ought to stay away from a Meeting if not able to bring an earnest sense of listening and sharing.

Humberto seated himself between old Nores Panko and Ĝeronimo Zea in the circle, and let his eyes close for the beginning of silence.

"Ĉejo says, tell you he has gone to his mother's house," Ĝeronimo said, touching Humberto's sleeve, whispering hoarsely. "Waiting for word of the *Lark*, eh?"

Humberto nodded. "The balloon," he murmured, before Ĝeronimo could say it.

The committee clerk was a woman named Elisabeta Bojs, a good clerk with a facility for finding the open way. She liked to let the silence at the beginning and end of a Business Meeting go on a little longer than other clerks were inclined to, and in the long quiet Humberto felt a slow centering down, a sloughing off of his fretfulness about the crew of the *Lark*, until finally he was able to fill his mind with an expectant, living silence.

"Do people have concerns?" Elisabeta said at last.

After all, nobody brought up the boat. There were things to do with weeding, with getting the pejiba palm fruits down from the taller trees, and planting late mustard. People reported about the repair of the mezlando aqueduct, and raised pessimistic questions from the data sent by the *Ruby*. A query had been sent down from Quarterly Meeting about the possibility of burying heating cables underground to warm the soil for farming, and about the drilling of wells—whether people had considered the eventual problem of depleting the fossil water. Humberto reported on his own work with Killian Berd and Anejlisa Revfiem, and his second-hand information about the genetic tinkering Anejlisa was doing with the setsuka willows. Intermittently, Elisabeta stated her sense of the meeting, and if there was no disagreement with it, Gil Roko, who was the recording clerk, wrote it down as a Minute of the Meeting.

When there were nine recorded Minutes, and new issues weren't being raised anymore, she brought up the problem of the leaf-cutter ants, who had built two enormous labyrinths in the midst of a hedge of cinnamomum. This problem had been brought up before, without anything being decided. The ants were in a cycle of abundance this year—new colonies had been springing up suddenly in fields and in the woodland everywhere—and Aleda Laitowler thought, when the ants had exhausted the foliage of the hedge they would begin to attack the citrus trees. He thought people ought to act before this happened, to take the role that the extinct army ants once had taken, invading the leaf-cutter ants' subterranean galleries and chambers in the cinnamomum. Some people agreed with Aleda, but other people thought, in a few months or years the leaf-cutters would become suddenly rare again without farmers disturbing them. The population of insects was unpredictable, prone to puzzling fluctuations, this was something everybody knew.

Elisabeta had steered the arguments gently and let silence inform the spaces, but people had only put forward information to support one belief or the other, and no advance had been made. When they had last met, she had asked three particular people to study this issue, to gather information and reformulate it, set it forth in a clearer light. Out of the three, only old Nores Panko was there to make a report. He stood up slowly when Elisabeta at last raised the subject of the leaf-cutter ants. Nores never had been what people called a "weighty Friend"— someone whose voice was always worth listening to—but his old age had given him a kind of stature. He was seventy-nine years old, probably had seen other invasions of leaf-cutter ants, must have been living when the army ants inexplicably disappeared.

These leaf-cutter ants were a kind of farmer ant, he said, cutting pieces of leaves into tiny fragments like sawdust and heaping them up to make a compost in their underground chambers, which they fertilized with their own feces, and on which they sowed a fungus that produced nodules like tiny, fuzzy kohlrabi, that the ants then ate, just as human beings inoculated compost

with the spore of mushrooms, and ate the mushrooms. A female ant going off to establish a new colony carried in a pocket
of her cheek pieces of fungus for sowing in the new place, just
as human beings transported and preserved seeds, bulbs, cuttings, for propagating their own crops.

There was a silence while Nores kept on standing. He was
white-haired, but his bushy eyebrows still were dark; they
made a fierce line across his face. He had a wide tender mouth
that belied his brows, and a kind demeanor. He stood without
a cane, leaning a bit forward with his hands folded together behind his back. Humberto sitting below him could see the slight
tremor in his hands—maybe that was why he clasped them.
And looking at old Nores's hands, he began to imagine himself
a member of a guild to which the peaceful fungus-growing ants
also belonged—both of them vegetarian agriculturists. In the
midst of the quiet, he thought of saying this, but he kept silent,
waiting for someone else to bring it up. Too often he found he
wasn't able to give his values, his judgment, any coherent expression. He had formed a gingerly habit of not speaking when
there was serious disagreement.

Another clerk might have counseled a longer silence, for
people to consider the problem before probably tabling it again.
But Elisabeta Bojs said to Nores gently, "I feel maybe you have
something more you want to say, Nores," and he took a slightly
different grip of his hands and sighed.

"Well I guess I do," he said finally. "Here is something else
I will tell you. I was a boy when I saw this, and I'd forgot it
until I took up this reading about ants." And he told about once
seeing a colony of leaf-cutters invaded by raiding army ants. He
hadn't seen the battles, he said, only afterward the many hundreds of corpses of leaf-cutters' soldiers strewn dead around the
entrances to their galleries, and scattered for yards along the
paths to and from the city. Some of the dead and dying soldiers
had lost limbs or were cut in two, but there were scores without an evident injury—perhaps they'd been stung to death, he
said, or they might have simply fallen dead of exhaustion; who
knew how long they had kept up this defense against invaders?
The army was passing in a steady stream along the paths to and

from the leaf-cutters' chambers, in and out of its portals, carrying off to their bivouac the white bodies of larvae and pupae.

Though they had killed the leaf-cutter soldiers, Nores said, they only stripped the poor nursemaid ants of their charges and left them wandering about sorrowfully, uninjured. Who knew why? After a moment, Nores added, "I guess it wasn't anything like clemency made them do it. I suppose, in the natural way, they were leaving survivors so the ants' city would recover, and be there when they came round to pillage it again."

He loosed his long-boned old hands. "That's all I wanted to say," he said, making a shaky gesture. He sat down slowly beside Humberto, pulling his knees up slightly and resting his thin forearms across them.

There was a profound silence after old Nores sat down. Humberto thought he ought to refuse the shameless ascribing of human nature to these ants, but what he felt was a sudden deep ignorance of the quality of an ant's psychic life. He looked down at the ground in front of his crossed knees. There was a beetle with an iridescent carapace making a slow way through the cottongrass and the dry leaves.

Elisabeta let the silence go on quite a while. Perhaps she knew the direction of Nores's leading would make itself evident if they all waited long enough. Eventually someone stood and simply told about watching the ants on their narrow, beaten highways, endless columns of them homeward-bound, toting tiny pieces of green leaf that rose gigantically above their backs like great banners or rainhats. And someone else told of seeing a piece of leaf borne along by a big ant, with two or three small ants clinging aloft—the little ones had tried to help carry, maybe, but the big one had simply lifted the cargo, helpers and all, and marched away with it. And finally Gift Ŝu stood up and said, "I wonder. If we put leafy cuttings near their city, would they snub them, or be glad of the extra? When any of us have got fresh prunings, if we brought those over and laid them on their paths, maybe they would cut them up and carry them home and maybe that would lighten the pressure on the cinnamomum."

Elisabeta raised her brows in surprise. She looked at Nores.

"Will they take leaves cut fresh for them, Nores?"

The old man considered this before nodding solemnly. "They have a little preference for certain leaves, don't like every kind. But what they like, they'd take cut as much as not, I think. In that book it said they would take from downed branches."

And so a way was opened. Talk turned to the kinds of leaves the ants would accept, particular plants and shrubs, trees, herbs; and people made rough guesses about the kind and volume of pruning they'd be doing in the next weeks. Shortly, they got to speculating why some leaves weren't suited for the ants' use, and whether the ants' little species of fungus was related to mushroom, or to lichen. When the discussion seemed to get around to repeating itself, Elisabeta interrupted and stated her sense of this last part of the meeting: An effort would be made to minimize the defoliation of the cinnamomum by furnishing leafy cuttings to the colony of farmer ants who had taken up living there. No one disagreed, and Gil Roko wrote it down as the tenth Minute of the Meeting.

That was all the business anyone raised. In the silence at the close, gradually Humberto found he was adrift in the space behind his closed eyes, a sort of dream, himself in a cavernous black chamber on his hands and knees weeding a white field of woolly kohlrabi.

He meant to get away from the Meeting quickly afterward but people stopped him, wanting to talk now about the *Lark* and the rescue, and he was slow getting home again, the light by then already lowered for dusk. Heza was out of the house, she'd had a meeting herself, of the Fiber Arts Committee, and frequently was late from those meetings, was one of the people prone to sit around afterward and do handwork while catching up gossip. Humberto's father was playing cards with his cronies in the sadaŭ of a house over in Mandala. His mother and Alfhilda sat alone in the apartment, quietly playing Go. Alfhilda's soup was eaten up, so Humberto went round to the kitchen house and steamed some bulgur in orange and ginger, made a ragout of beets, leeks, squash, cold lentils. He left some of this in the refrigerator for other people to find and brought his bowl back into the apartment, but then his mother and Alfhilda complained and he had to go into the kitchen again and bring the rest of the bulgur and the ragout for them to eat while they played Go.

"Ĉejo is waiting at his mother's house," Leona said. She was focused on the game. "Until there's word of the *Lark.*"

He nodded. "The balloon." He ate slowly while he watched them play and then he took his turn at it, finding a kind of relief in the concentration on strategy. He won with Alfhilda and then lost to his mother, and while he was waiting out their next game he got up, carrying their empty bowls, and came back with a banana and a bowl of figs. He and Alfhilda ate figs and kept on playing after Leona had gone to bed, but when Alfhilda had lost twice in a row she gave up in frustration, and Humberto went to bed himself rather than sit alone with botanical reading. He was afraid Heza, when she came in, would want to talk with him about the *Lark.*

As soon as he lay down he was half-asleep, thinking suddenly, *I am too tired to worry tonight.* But he woke when the boards of the floor groaned quietly in the darkness beside him. Ĉejo was coming to bed. How late was it? His limbs felt rigid, expecting a blow.

"What has happened?" he asked in a low voice.

"Bjoro is rescued," Ĉejo said softly. "And Luza Kordoba. But Peder Ojama and Isuma Bun are killed."

Humberto rolled onto his back. He stared blindly up into darkness. He didn't know the two who were dead—he had been thoroughly spared grief. Immediately a kind of guilt settled on him, as if God had made this selection by considering Humberto Indergard's interests ahead of other people's.

"Isuma Bun is a second cousin to Katrin Amundsen," Ĉejo murmured after a silence.

Katrin Amundsen was a name Humberto knew without a face, the most recent of the girls Ĉejo had loved in the last year. She lived in her grandmother's household in Revenana, in the domaro where Ĉejo had spent his green years.

"I went to see if Katrin's family had heard about the death," Cêjo said. "Maybe Katrin is a close friend with this cousin, or her grandmother could be also Isuma's grandmother, and maybe they would want to know. But no lights were on in their rooms. I didn't know if I should wake anybody."

"It's all right if they don't learn about it until morning," Humberto said quietly. "What can be done anyway, but crying?"

In the darkness, Humberto heard his son's voice break. "I wanted to be there with her if she cried," he said, crying himself. Cêjo hadn't yet grown out of an overemotional romanticism.

He was fiercely monogamous and loyal but his couplings tended to be brief. Almost as soon as a girl returned his attention he would put her in a desperate, smothering clasp, and when the girl tired of the weight, she'd quickly wriggle free. Humberto himself had been a casual lover at Cêjo's age, had accepted copulation as a kind of gift from girls without imagining romantic love was being offered too. Now that he was forty-six years old and for the last six years unmarried, he found he was more analytical. He seldom had coitus with a woman without wondering if he loved her; and he wondered about the quality of the love, and if it might become relaxed enough to support a marriage.

He remembered suddenly that time he had walked into the swung blade of Henriko Lij's cane cutter, the long moment while Henriko gaped at him in astonishment and fear, and then the woman he didn't know, Luza Kordoba, pushing by old Henriko and past Humberto's own clutching hands to put her fingers deftly to his neck, pushing down in the hole through the spurt of his bright red blood, the swift, sure gesture that stopped him from bleeding out. While Henriko ran to get other people to help, people with surgical tools to close the hole, helplessly he had gripped Luza's wrist and fixed his eyes on her, and she had squatted over him with her hand at his throat, in his throat, talking to him quietly about farming and weather, and when she was short of those subjects, instructing him irrelevantly about things she knew in her own fields, kinematics and linear momentum, acupuncture pressure points and homeostasis, until the warmth and even pressure of her hand on his pulse had become as compelling and sexual as an erection. It was the single time he had loved someone as Ĉejo loved, brief and burning, urgently holding on.

2

Unnamed Lands

Six

HUMBERTO

After the dazzle of day is gone,
Only the dark, dark night shows to my eyes
    the stars;
After the clangor of organ majestic, or chorus,
    or perfect band,
Silent, athwart my soul, moves the symphony
    true.

Humberto had a habit of sitting together with Anejlisa Revfiem, Edmo Smith, and Andreo Rodiba at Meetings of the Alaŭdo ŝiro—this was something that had started when they formed a little committee to study arctic plants and they had thought they might be asked to give a report at Monthly Meetings for Business. Now their work seemed irrelevant and ignored at these big Meetings where the issues shaped themselves around larger matters than plant genetics, but they had gone on sitting together for the pleasure they all had in arguing together afterward.

There were something near two hundred adults, ten houses in Alaŭdo. By the natural order of things only fifteen or twenty or twenty-five people were likely to gather on the loĝio of one of the houses for Monthly Meeting if there was nothing needing deciding, nothing consequential. Not many things really affected everyone; most decisions were made in Meetings of a domaro, or in committees. But for more than a year the Meetings of Alaŭdo ŝiro had been preoccupied with the New World

and this was a matter that no one considered trivial. Habitually
now as many as sixty or seventy or eighty people, whole committees and households, would come to answer the Queries,
argue the Advices put to them by Yearly Meeting, or to raise
issues they thought should be sent on to the clerk of Quarterly
Meeting.

Isaba Aguto, who was clerk of the Alaŭdo meeting, had
taken to dragging a table out onto the loĝio and sitting up on
it so she could see faces and be heard in the crowd. Some people had complained about this, saying Isaba was putting herself above other people. But who knew the best way to guide
a Meeting of such size? Poor Isaba was doing the best she could,
some other people said.

Humberto wondered if all this arguing about Isaba's meth-
ods came from people being closed-minded, or afraid of the real
issues. He thought Isaba Aguto had a tendency to let an argument go on too long before putting the matter in the hands of
a committee, and she had some habits that annoyed him, nervous mannerisms, but he never had thought she was self-
important. When Isaba sat on a table, they all could see her and
hear what she had to say, even from the edge of the loĝio where
they were able to lean their backs against the outer wall of the
kitchen. Humberto thought if Isaba sat down on the boards of
the loĝio with other people, he and his friends might have to
move in closer to hear what was being said, and Edmo Smith
was stubborn, wouldn't bring a repozo for sitting against,
though he had a curved spine and couldn't sit for long without
support.

"Well, I don't hear a unity of judgment," Isaba said in frustration, and looked around at all their faces for someone who
might disagree—someone who might want to put forward a
leading that she hadn't recognized. She had a long torso, looked
tall while she was sitting, but when she stood she became short,
and her long waist thick and straight, hipless as a man's. She
never had borne children, but Humberto didn't know if this
was related to her narrow pelvis, or to her marrying a man who
already had been married once and had three living children.

People had been arguing about geothermal heat. There were

innumerable hot springs on the New World, thousands of surface vents emitting hot gases or vapors, and the Energy Committee of Yearly Meeting had delivered a report saying the steam from those hot springs could be used for running machinery, making heat and light, for warming agricultural greenhouses, and that this might be a simpler thing than the complicated and slow process of cold fusion they relied on in the *Miller.* The geothermal sites stood mostly on the flanks of volcanoes, were prone to quakes, and there was considerable disagreement about the jeopardy; they had sent a query to all the ŝiros asking whether people wanted to build houses on firmer, flatter ground, and then find a means to pipe the heat and the power to those houses, from springs, solfataras, fumaroles, which might be dozens of kilometers away.

Humberto felt himself caught in an anxious, muddled thinking, while he strained to hear something that would open a way, free him from doubt. But Isaba hadn't been able to keep people on the question. Inevitably the argument had deteriorated, sliding down to smaller and smaller issues. Who could say what was a reliably safe distance from a volcano? If houses were apart from the power plant, how would people who ran and repaired the machinery get from their houses to their work? Would they be expected to live, themselves, on the volcanoes, the fault lines? What if power-plant workers wanted to live at the power plant on the shaky slopes, but their families wanted to live in the houses on safe ground?

Isaba interrupted frequently, trying to broaden the question, to turn things upward, but people went on arguing logistics, making claims and counterclaims, and the important question was lost in ever-narrowing lanes and culs-de-sac. It was a compulsion they all had, a need to divide a question into its smallest components. Most people had given up the old wrangling over whether the New World would support human lives—they understood that it would, that the question was something else, something indecipherable, and that the scientific reports never would be able to explain the things that really mattered. But they went on suffering from a vague, irrational hope that if everything, every mystery of the New World, could be ex-

amined and known, then they would reach an understanding
of how they felt about it.

Isaba Aguto prodded her chin with her fingertips. "The committee that's been studying energy—are you on that committee, Lucina?" She gestured toward a woman and then returned
her hand to her chin. "Will you take this Query back to them,
ask them to restate it a little? Maybe if you bring it next month
in different words, or another shape, we can all find some way
to an agreement." She went on exploring her chin thoughtfully
a moment, pulling on it, looking out at people's faces, before
she tipped her head toward Samêjo Penaflor, who was the
recording clerk. "This geothermal matter is held over, then," she
said irritably, "until the question can be restated." A long sigh
went around while Samêjo wrote down this Minute—people
were frustrated by the inconclusive, discursive nature of the
Meetings lately—but no one objected to Isaba's conclusion, it
was obvious no agreement had been reached.

A silence settled on everyone after Isaba had stated her sense
of the Meeting. Humberto began to wonder if he ought to
speak, now that the main business was set aside. Since he had
been going on with his arctic studies he had lately had a dream:
his bookish imagining of something he took to be a glacial
tongue at the margin of a sea. In his dream, a bleak immense island broke from the edge of the glacier, fracturing slowly under
the weight and pressure of the ice. In a bluish tableau, people
stood on the ice floe and others at the edge of the broken shore
ice in separate, wretched confusion, while the distance between
them inexorably widened.

He hadn't yet told the dream to anyone, but he thought it
was rooted in his worry about the New World, or was something vaguely to do with their increasing disagreement and
paralysis. People sometimes brought up impressions and
inklings at the end of a Meeting, and he had been wondering,
in the last few minutes, if his dream might be that kind of vague
leading. But he seldom had spoken to a gathering larger than
the Alaŭdo Farms Committee, hadn't spoken at a meeting of
the whole ŝiro since the numbers of listeners had become so

many, the questions of such weight. He had little confidence in his judgment, felt himself easily swayed.

After a considered silence two or three people stood up abruptly and began to talk to one another, signalling that they considered the Meeting at an end. Humberto stood, and Edmo grunted and grimaced as he got himself up, pulling on the hand Humberto held down to him. Edmo wasn't old—his youngest child wasn't grown yet—but as he had aged his crooked spine had given him increasing pain. He had to stand up to spin thread, with his spinning jenny raised on a sort of platform. People made obscene jokes about Edmo and his wife, that they had intercourse standing up, and this was why his wife walked bowlegged. If Edmo had heard these jokes, he never had said. He reached around to knead the small of his back and straighten gingerly from hunching. "Well, hell," he said, complaining. "That was a useless Meeting, eh? When there's too many people, things get off the track. Here's what I think: Every house ought to send only its clerk and maybe one other person to Monthly Meeting. Twenty people. That's always a good size for coming to agreement."

"Everybody's entitled to a voice," Anejlisa Revfiem said irritably. "You can't tell people to keep home from a Monthly Meeting. They want to know what's being said, even when they don't speak out."

"Well, nothing will get decided, then," Edmo said grimly. "How can we get to any agreement, with so many people having a say in it?" He made a rude hand gesture that took in the bunches of people standing around them on the logio. "Must be eighty people, eh? ninety? a hundred people! A meeting will break down when we get these crowds, you know, that's something we can count on."

A rule by majority or by representation always had been anathema to the old Quakers, but it was mostly the size of the gathering that had kept Humberto from speaking, and he thought other people were daunted too—lately it was the same dozen or so who would stand and offer their voices, people not known for the weight of their judgment but for not being timid.

Still, he had been coming to the ŝiro Meetings himself because he didn't want to hear second-hand what was being decided or talked about now that the issues had always to do with the New World. He looked from one of them to the other but kept out of this argument between Edmo and Anejlisa, not knowing which side of it he stood on.

Andreo Rodiba had been looking down at his feet, considering. Humberto had a good opinion of Andreo. Often in the talking that went on after the Meeting it would be something Andreo said that would bring a thing into focus for him, make it comprehensible. Andreo wasn't known for his gifts as a speaker but for a penetrating wisdom, a seeing-through to the simple truths.

Now he said cautiously, "I don't know if it's crowds that break down a Meeting—or not *only* crowds. It's always been a spiritual method, eh? And it stops working when people give up being spiritual."

Humberto said, "Be quick to hear and slow to speak, and let grace season the words," which was an old Quaker maxim his grandmother had used to recite to him.

Andreo nodded. He had a long, fissured face, ears that sprang from his skull. When he gathered his mouth, the tips of his ears pulled nearer his head. "We've all been bringing quarrels to these Meetings and leaving grace at home," he said.

Andreo seemed to mean the four of them as much as anybody, though none of them had spoken for the last several Meetings. Maybe Andreo thought they had all given something intangible to the temper, the atmosphere of dissension—none of them had stood up and spoken of love, of fusing differences, of a desire for unity. Humberto was pierced by a belated wish to tell his dream.

Edmo was still fixed on what he'd been thinking about the size of Meetings. "Maybe a big ŝiro Meeting could be held in two or three parts; minutes could be read one to the other, so people would know what the other parts were saying."

Anejlisa grinned sourly. "Maybe you should tell that to Isaba, get her to put it on the agenda, next Meeting. But there's a double-bind, eh? We'll never have smaller Meetings because there's too many of us to come to any unity about how to have smaller Meetings."

They stood on the loĝio arguing and talking in this way without getting anywhere. Other people were standing around in little schools doing the same thing—assigning blame for the failure of the Meeting, and arguing about Isaba Aguto sitting herself above them. In the past, the time following a Meeting had been good for thinking and discussing and persuading—for people to move slowly toward agreement on a hard question. Increasingly, now, no one could agree on the question. Where was the foundation for agreeing upward?

Knuto Mursawa had been standing near them, seeming to listen to what they were saying. Knuto was an aeroponics engineer, a man somewhere in long middle age, with a flattened nose, moles on his face. He was as likely to say something scatterbrained as something that would open a way, but he hadn't spoken while people were arguing about geothermal power, or while Edmo and Anejlisa quarreled over the size of Meetings.

Now he cleared his throat and said, addressing himself to Andreo, "We always have lived in this world, in its body as in the body of God. It's a sufficient world and a blessed one, I would say, and I wonder why we ain't been thinking how we can go on living inside—build something like the *Miller* down there and live inside it." He may have wanted to say this momentous thing to the Monthly Meeting, and not been able to bring it out—it had a formal sound, rehearsed. Now he seemed relieved. He shifted, standing mostly on one foot, looking around vaguely without pinning his look on anyone.

None of them spoke. Then Andreo said, spreading his mouth down mournfully, "Well, Knuto, that's a pretty big question to bring up when we thought this Meeting was over, eh?" No one else spoke. Humberto looked in the other faces for a sign of what he felt, himself—a kind of stunned realization. He had thought he had learned to admire the elegant complexity of the subarctic ecosystem not less than the lush intricacy of the one he lived in, but now he felt his heart clench with a sudden, inexpressible yearning to go on living under a roof, without vagaries of weather, eating cerimoj and mangoes.

Andreo went off and brought back Isaba Aguto who listened to Knuto repeat his little speech, the same words brought forward in the same order, *as in the body of God.* A small bunch of people had gathered around Knuto by now, and argument began about whether the chronic mechanical failures and deterioration of machinery, the ŝimanas and plagues of illness, the steady irrecoverable loss of plant and animal species, would be prohibitive problems for a planet-bound biosphere.

Isaba said, interrupting, "We can't be talking this out today, do people agree? We had a long Meeting already, and some of us got to get on to other work. Maybe three or four people will meet with Knuto, and make a start at seeing if this idea is possible." A few voices called out. Isaba nodded, gripping her chin. "All right then." Knuto's lugubrious face was flushed.

After Isaba walked away, people finally began drifting off, going on with the other things in their lives. Then Humberto, who had been hanging back, talked to Anejlisa about the possibility of her brother-in-law's sister's second cousin maybe someday making a marriage match for Alfhilda. It was something that was still years away, but arranging a marriage was an important responsibility, and people who loved Alfhilda were already thinking about it and looking around unhurriedly for someone compatible. His brother Pero had asked him to talk to Anejlisa about her relative. Did she think this boy might be suited to Alfhilda? Would she keep an eye on this boy as he grew older, watch him to see if he might make a successful partner for Pero's daughter?

Humberto spoke his brother's request quickly and then struggled to get away from Anejlisa's interested, insistent scrutiny of the idea. He never had been comfortable with questions like these since his own marriage had come undone; he had a vague conviction that his divorce made him unfit to involve himself in other people's marriages. When his mother had talked to him about matching his son Ĉejo, he had felt a nameless fright, and had resisted having a hand in it. When she went on pressing him, bringing up names of girls, gossiping about this one or that one who might make Ĉejo a wife, he had finally, irritably, told her to bring her reports to Juko. Her face had flattened, as if he'd accused her of something—she hadn't spoken to Juko in years—maybe she thought he was blaming her for arranging his own failed marriage. But afterward he had gained a little peace: Now she and his aunt Lavka and Heza Barfor were looking at possible matches for Cejo without telling him about it.

He got away finally from Anejlisa and the ŝiro meeting, but he didn't go back to his own house. His mind was jumping helplessly from one thing to another, picking at odds and ends of worries; he wanted to go up into the altejo corn and be alone a while and turn things over systematically. He took the narrow path between the houses into the small terraced fields of pumpkins and beans, plantains, pepinos. A dead chicken lay on the dirt at the edge of the mezlando rice, and he squatted and turned the hen's stiff body over, examining it. There was a puncture wound in the breast, the feathers surrounding it black and clotted with blood. Chickens frequently disappeared—at daybreak they came for corn, in the evening they simply failed to go to roost; tayras carried them off, or opossums. It was rare to find more than feathers, but this one had made a brief escape, maybe, and then died alone. He sighed unhappily and carried the dead hen back down to his domaro, went into the kitchen-house and plucked it, eviscerated and washed the body carefully, wrapped it in a piece of linen and left it to cool in the refrigerator.

People came in the kitchen and went out again while he was working, and he was required to talk to each of them—to give a report of the ŝiro Meeting to people who hadn't been there; to listen to opinions about geothermal power plants from peo ple who had been shy of saying what they thought in front of sixty or a hundred people; to repeat what he had heard Knuto say about the body of God, to people who had already heard about it second- or third-hand. When he had finally, scrupulously, sorted the clean feathers from the bloody and left the clean ones in a basket in the sadaŭ for anyone who needed them and brought the offal out to the compost pile, then he went on with what he'd planned to do, going up into the altejo corn to be alone.

In the corn field he was hidden in the verdure, the maize rearing its powdery tassels an arm's reach above his head. Weeds had given up trying to grow in the shade under the spreading, strappy leaves, and he went through the field easily, pinching earwigs between his thumbnails, smearing aphids with his fingertips.

He had thought he would spend this time looking for a clear way—grappling with images of grace and unity, or turning over ideas to do with the body of God, or geothermal machinery, or Meetings that were too crowded for consensus; but the smell of the dry heated ground and the must of the corn at this time of year began to be linked in his mind with the scent of sexual intercourse, and helplessly he began to drift into the interstices of that connection.

People who wanted to keep their sexual relations private had to look for secret places or times, and when he was sixteen, seventeen, he had been embarrassed to bring a girl into his own bed with his family members and his neighbors listening on the other side of the wall. The corn field was a place of concealment, of seclusion—he used to lie down with girls on the stubbly dry earth among the stalks of the maize. That was so many years past, the memory of it so abraded, it might have happened to someone else. Now his mother teased Cêjo about his failure to bring a girl home, and there were places in the altejo field where the stubble of weeds was pressed down flat under the corn in a shapely nest, and twice Humberto had glimpsed a flutter of movement, not an armadillo, not a sloth, someone scuttling away from him through the brake. He had begun to keep out of the maize when he saw a girl of a certain age walking up the path toward his son in the altejo corn.

He remembered without nostalgia the heated urgency of those years in his life, and wasn't much interested in recapturing it. But he was sometimes surprised and obscurely worried when he realized he'd gone weeks without a real need for sexual contact. He missed the settledness of marriage, the casualness of its sexual relations. He knew people—his brother Pero and his wife—who had fallen into a methodical pattern of intercourse that didn't much allow for appetite. Pero once had said to him, looking sly, "When Natĉja takes my penis into her hands, that's when I'm hungry to have a little sex with her."

This made him think of a woman he had coupled with once, while he was still married to Juko. This woman, Naoma, had had a husband dying slowly from a cancer, and Humberto's younger son had only just died. Naoma had been a loud talker in those days, had a blotchy, coarse face, and she smelled of her husband's slow death; he hadn't thought of laying with her. But when she deliberately pushed her breast against his arm, put the tips of her fingers inside his trousers, he discovered after all a hunger for her, and they had copulated wordlessly on the floor of the tools shed. Afterward he had wondered if it was intercourse she had needed from him, and not something more generous. She had moved into her sister's household, after her husband's death, and become an ascetic—was this something he ought to be blamed for? he wondered. And his divorce from Juko must be blamed on other things, not on this adultery, but he had maybe stopped trying hard to find a clear way with his wife after he had had intercourse with Naoma Samuels.

When he cast around in his memory for the last time he had had sexual relations, he was only able to remember bringing the carpenter, Berta Ule, into his empty house while the members of his family danced at the christening of a neighbor's newborn son. That had been months ago, the baby creeping now, or walking, so he realized with a start that he had become celibate without planning it.

He didn't know why he had lain with Berta only the one time, and now that he was thinking of her he began to turn over the idea of seeing her again. He didn't know many people over in Revenana where she lived, didn't walk over there very often. Their meeting in the first place had been accidental; he'd gone to talk to someone who was on the Revenana Farms Committee, a man who was helping Berta Ule rebuild a shed. He thought suddenly of asking that farmer to ask Berta if she would welcome his company again; he didn't know if she might by this time have someone else in mind to become married to.

If you were out of the seed years, had been divorced or been widowed and still were wishing to marry again, you could make a reliable match for yourself, most people thought. By that time you ought to be free of the well-known tendency to choose a lover as a mate—perhaps even through being ruled by your sexual organs. But Humberto missed the assurance, the absoluteness, of having other people organize his partnering—it wasn't Leona's fault his marriage to Juko had failed. It might be a healing gesture, after all, if he asked his mother to find him a second wife—if he asked his mother, rather than that Reve-nana farmer, to talk to Berta Ule about renewing their friendship.

For a moment he stood in the close swelter under the corn, deliberately recollecting Berta's pendant breasts, the wide dark areoles, the nipples rising against the palms of his hands. He remembered her long freckled arms and a belly that rounded neatly above her pubic hair. Immediately his penis stiffened, suffusing with heat, reassuring him. The sound of a gamelan and of drums and people dancing at the christening had come rhythmically through the walls, and Berta had stood up playfully after copulating with him and had danced beside the bed, beating her feet against the floor, slapping her knees, her big teeth flashing.

Humberto swayed dizzily as if he were dancing himself, and the heat in his groin swept out to his limbs suddenly. His eyes watered, peering against a yellow blaze. He shut them, but the shimmer went on blinding and dizzying him. He felt himself absorbed in a kaleidoscope of fleeting movement, of impressions and shifting featureless patterns and colors, impermanence. For a moment, he wondered stupidly if he had become an infant again: He felt he hadn't yet mastered the intricate skill of seeing fixed three-dimensional objects in the great rushes of movement and light. Wonderingly, slowly, as a person born blind and suddenly sighted, he realized what hung before his eyes: the delicate arched bones of the distant ceiling, the array of the daylight xenon lamps.

His arms outflung, he was lying in a tangle of broken canes of corn. One of his eyes was shut, he realized, and when he opened it, the brilliance made his mind stop. The earth burned against the skin of his shoulder blades, his buttocks, his heels;

the bowl of his skull held a searing fire. In a flutter of confusion, he wondered if it was the whole torus that had flashed to apocalypse in a dazzling moment of heat and light. But then he understood what his ears were hearing: the hum of bumblebees, blackflies, mosquitoes, going on with their lives. He became aware of children laughing. A woman shouted something and she or someone else banged on a pot. The world was going on living, and he with it, lying on the ground. He thought he should be afraid but felt only a kind of surprise, and a flattened, distant interest in what had made him fall.

He sat, and in a moment realized that he had only imagined sitting up, that he was still lying there, looking through the blades of leaves and overarching tassels of corn to the ceiling. He put his whole attention scrupulously on the task of sitting, but his mind seemingly had separated itself from his body, and the body ignored the mind's decision, went on lying quietly on the ground, peering up at the glare of daylight. He shut his eyes; shut his one eye, because the other, disobeying him, went on looking into the sky. A mote swam into his field of vision, became a cowbird or a young starling flying against the distant girders. People once had examined the flights of birds for auguries of the future. He wondered what he should understand from this single cowbird flying across his single eye.

A wordless anxious shakiness moved into his chest. *Do you know what this means?* he thought desperately, but without knowing where this question came from or who it was meant for; it was nonsensical, unanswerable.

An involuntary tear scribed a slow arc down to the hinge of his jaw and into the nape of his hair. "Uh," he said, not a word but a vague protest, and the sound vibrated dryly on his tongue. He was surprised by the small hoarse moaning and tried to say something more definite, a coherent complaint or an appeal, but couldn't get anything more to come out of his mouth. And his mind, too, disobeyed him, becoming independent of his desires. He began helplessly, silently, to turn over and over the irrelevant repetitions of jumping-rope rhymes, of lullabies and work chants, ritual blessings for tools and crops, *bless this, bless this, bless this seed.* The center slowly gave way and he drifted into a jumble of unconnected words, a silent stream that flooded his brain with impression, with indecipherable meaning—*when show don't ever where next come call me come call heaven call to me don't don't*, and from that unknown place he slid seamlessly down to fragments, syllables, and finally into a silence that poured into him and washed his brain clear, and he lay mindlessly, not thinking at all, simply feeling in his bones, his blood, the swift wheeling of the earth, the weight of his body against the ground, the clammy June heat against his skin.

The dirt sifted dryly, and a snake came up on the rise of his ribs. A measureless time had passed. He was startled, muddled, as when he would sleep in the daytime and wake without knowing if it was early morning or twilight. The snake was black, very long. Humberto wasn't afraid of it—*musaranaj* ate other reptiles, even venomous snakes—but his skin shuddered involuntarily, a belated intent to move away, to let the snake get by him without touching. From the lower edge of his tearing eyes he watched the snake's head and forepart resting delicately on air, centimeters above the buttons of his shirt. It tasted his smell silently with a thin, scissored tongue.

In the snake's lidless eyes it was impossible to see its soul, and after a moment Humberto shifted his own eye away uneasily. What was this distance between human beings and snakes? He felt a closer kinship with ants and fish than with the utterly alien intelligence of snakes. There wasn't anything in a snake's life he was able to recognize: no family ties, sociability, playfulness, joy in living, no devotion to their young. It seemed to him, a snake was all predation, toothless jaws that took animals in whole. They were lengths of thick vine that had become unexpectedly muscular, fluent, blood-filled—who knew why?

If it ever had looked at him, the snake looked away now, the broad shovel-tip of the head turning indifferently as it gathered its thick limb to get over his obstruction. He was obscurely ashamed to be inanimate, to be taken for a warmed stone or a toppled tree lying between the rows of corn. The musarana insinuated itself languorously across his body but then settled into the triangular space between his outflung elbow and his ribs. The snake was heavy and sinewy, two meters long, but it coiled neatly into the small enclosure there, in the tented heat and darkness beneath a fold of his shirt.

He had touched wild birds, several of them, during the little time he'd been apprenticed to Ridaro Rogelio, the ornithologist. And a few times, in the sutaĝo beneath a house, gathering up drifts of leaves or taking a look at the kitchen plumbing, he had found sick opossums or porcupines recuperating or dying, had touched a few of them accidentally or because he had thought them dead. He had touched snakes and lizards in the rescue of chicks or chicken eggs. But he realized: This was the first time he had *been* touched by a living, unrestrained, undomesticated animal. He was inexplicably gratified by the snake's settling against his body, as if its trust in his innocence was something he could take credit for.

He was conscious of holding still, of holding in a breath, stilling a heartbeat; but gradually the unmoving weight of the snake began to seem an extension of himself, a massy benign tumor obtruded from his armpit, and his stillness became devotion, a kind of exaltation. When he shut his one movable eye he imagined himself imbued as the trees are, with silence and equanimity in the midst of irrational things. He began simply to wait, growing passive, receptive. Waiting for what? he wondered. For night? sleep? death? the stars?

His mind wandered, and he dreamed that he slept. When the weeds stirred softly and a draft opened against his shirt, he said, "Vilef," to keep his son from wriggling away from his side. Vilef was four, had been mobile for more than a year, could move himself small distances by an undulating flapping of his elbows and hips. Or he was dead, had been dead for more than eight years.

"There's beetles in the grass," the boy said, not wanting to be held.

There was a particular perfume he gave off when he'd been lying asleep and flushed with heat. Humberto breathed it in, the piercingly nostalgic smell of his son's skin. He opened his eyes. "Vilef," he said.

The boy's shortened arms were single-digited, atrophied, his body a kind of writhing divided limb without hips or buttocks, the thin legs flaccid and unjointed, but he rolled his skinny, pliant body on the canes of fallen corn, looking back at Humberto. His small head was slung sideward on the long thin stalk of his neck, his mouth open in that heartbreakingly familiar way, a sagging grin, the small rows of teeth straight and neat, perfectly formed.

"I want to look for beetles," the boy said, stubbornly pleading.

He was naked, his pale skin rosy where it clung to bone at elbows, heels, chin, the tips of his pointy single fingers; deep mauve where there was heat, darkness, dampness—his genitals, the cave of his mouth, the smooth hollows at the axilla of shoulder and arm. Humberto fixed his eyes on the small dark muscle of his son's tongue moving in the dark mouth. Vilef never had spoken in his five years of life. Whose voice was issuing from his mouth? "Come here," Humberto said. "Come and lay down here with me."

The boy wobbled as if boneless, as if he were a curved blade of grass trembling and swaying, weighted by a bead of rain. The leaves shook slightly with his nervous fidgeting. Humberto was helpless, must wait for his son to come or to wriggle away.

"You fell down," the boy said, explaining something.

"I'm just sleeping. Come here and sleep with me."

Vilef grinned foolishly, rocking up on his flexuous waist, and then he settled himself against Humberto's ribs again. He lay with his small head flung back, his face turned up to the daylight, his mouth open to catch the falling rays of the xenon lamps. His heated fragrance filled Humberto with an excruciatingly indefinable impulse.

Vilef breathed noisily. "Tell the names of birds," he demanded.

Humberto stared skyward where the spars of the ceiling were wound with thready clouds—a gathering of afternoon humidity, the incipience of the evening rain. A cowbird still flew there, beating back and forth within the frame of Humberto's view, the coarse fringe of leaves and tassels of corn.

"There is a brown cowbird," he said. He felt around for the nib of a memory, something he once had known. "They slip into other birds' nests, Vilef, and leave their eggs to be brooded and hatched by that other family."

The boy made a dry *cht,* birdlike, a sound of puzzlement. "Why?" he said.

"I don't know."

"Do those other birds care?"

He considered. "I don't know that either. They raise the young cowbirds with their own children. I don't know if they mind doing it."

He and his son watched the cowbird in silence. The bird drew a barely perceptible network of lines on the sky, its wing-beats snagging and trailing the mist.

"More," Vilef said solemnly.

"Gray's thrushes, and ruddy ground-doves," he said, "build their nests on the bananas, right on the ripening bunch, where the fingers of the fruit reach up and hold it cupped like this." He formed the intent to gesture delicately, stiff-fingered with one hand, but nothing came of it. His hands remained outspread, lying on the ground, inattentive. Vilef held one of his own formless hands up, the single finger pointing from his birdlike, truncated arm. "Like this," he said, and Humberto, smiling, feeling that he was smiling, answered, "Yes." Then he said, "Tanagers hide their nest in the center of the bunch, between the hands of the fruit. Sometimes, in the days between building the nest and feeding the babies, the fruit thickens, and the gap where they pass through becomes so narrow they finally can't slip in and out; then sometimes their children must starve."

"I would widen the doorway," Vilef said staunchly, and Humberto said, "Yes, I have done that."

"What else," Vilef said after a small silence.

He cast around in his memory. "Some woodpeckers live in families, aunts and uncles and parents and children all together sleeping in a single house. And the ani birds live in great shared domaroj, laying all their eggs together and rearing their children in a bunch without setting one apart from another."

"More."

"They perch in long rows, anis do, all facing the same way,

ten or fifteen or twenty of them crowded together; when a bird at an end of the long row wants to move to the opposite end, it walks over the backs of the others." Vilef made a wet loose sound in his throat, his habitual choking laugh, and Humberto's heart, from habit, clenched and released in a spasm of love. How easily the old responses reinhabited his body!

"I have looked for you," he declared tearfully, meaning something that was unfathomable even to himself. Vilef rocked his small round skull, and the heat of his breath blew intermittently against Humberto's ribs.

"Where did you look?" the boy asked dreamily.

Humberto felt himself caught in a mindless turbulence, a flood of echo, chord, vibration. Something latent and formless, long preparing, had arrived. "Where should I have looked?" he answered.

Vilef made a cunning sound, *huh huh huh,* the same dry, calculated chuckle he used to make in his sleep all those years ago, before the sheer weight of his own outsize heart had progressively strangled and killed him. Humberto strained to see his son's face; from the lower edge of an eye he watched the tip of a tongue searching the corner of a mouth, not able to distinguish whether it was his own tongue, his own mouth, or Vilef's. "You know where," Vilef said slyly.

He did know. Something turned inside him. He gave up straining to see his son's face; he looked up through the halo of light into the faraway framework of the ceiling, but then shut his eye, and through the transparent membrane saw the paths of blood in a carp's eye, in a dragonfly's wing, in the body of a tick.

"Paĉjo," his son said, and touched his outflung wrist. The heat in the touch startled him, jerked his eye open, and his grown son Ĉejo stood leaning down to him, his round face creased, worried—"Paĉjo, why are you lying here?"—and behind him, another face, an unknown girl with eyebrows thin as fingernail parings, her mouth an open bow. His other son, Vilef, had already slipped away from his side as swift and silent as if he'd been delivered whole into heaven.

On the old terms, he said, clutching his son's hand, or meaning to clutch it, meaning to say, *It must be on the old terms.*

A small hoarse croaking came out of his mouth, and the sound drained him of anguish—he felt suddenly empty and free, as if his soul could leave his body in the next moment. He hovered there, at that charged balance point of his existence, holding out to his son on the delicate upturned cup of his hand as if it were a construct of moss and twigs and brown maize, an unnamed land. Cêjo shook his head or shuddered, uncomprehending, and the moment went forward with a small stir of Humberto's heart. He fell back inside the days of his life as into a hollow vessel, full of familiar voices and people, of seasons repeating themselves, of sorrow and joy going out, returning, waiting, undreamed of.

Seven

BJORO

I sing the body electric,
The armies of those I love engirth me
*   and I engirth them.*
They will not let me off till I go with them,
*   respond to them,*
And discorrupt them, and charge them full
*   with the charge of the soul.*
Was it doubted that those who corrupt
*   their own bodies conceal themselves?*
And if those who defile the living
*   are as bad as they who defile the dead?*
And if the body does not do fully as much
*   as the soul?*
And if the body were not the soul,
*   what is the soul?*

When the airlock was opened, the quick rush of the draft was
like a wind, piercing cold, bitter against Bjoro's skin, and at once
he began to shake. He had had thirty-one days in the closeness
and warmth of the *Ruby* to get over his chill, but now his body
swiftly gave up its heat and he felt as he had when Luza had
strapped him in the gondola of the balloon, the bones of his
ribcage enclosing a central, numbing cold. Eighty or a hundred
people were gathered there in the south pole of the *Miller* in
the big open docking arena, a great daunting welcome, and it
struck him bitterly that this was a mortafesto as much as a celebration of homecoming.

When he looked for his wife in the faces suddenly crowding

him—a jumble of grins and moving mouths, unrecognizable—
he had a sudden, unexpected glimpse of Luza. On the *Ruby*
they had made an unspoken agreement not to say too much;
they had kept to things that were devoid of pain, had kept clear
of talk about the crash, Peder's dying, the pale, fluttery tangle
of Isuma's balloon pitching down the night sky. In the silences
between them there had been a kind of tender closeness. Now
all at once he wasn't able to bear Luza's look, bear looking at
her. When their eyes touched, he shifted his own away jerkily.
A clot of anguish and impenetrable rage swelled in his throat.
He knew if he let his mouth open, a thick dumb wordless shout
would fly from it.

Juko appeared suddenly among the faces. She was keeping a
fierce smile, her lips in a wide line which she pressed against his
ear. "Where've-you-been?" she said, whispering their old
homecoming usage. He wasn't able to answer: *out-of-the-way.*
He had imagined this reuniting, imagined that she might be
moved enough to weep, and he would taste her tears on his
tongue. But her face was familiar, unsentimental, and his body
was stiff and numb with cold, he wasn't able to bend it to his
will. He lowered his head effortfully and let his mouth down
against the crown of her head; on his tongue was the dry, acer-
bic taste of her hair.

Some of the faces around him became members of his family, his sister, niece, cousins, brother-in-law, an intricate web of
relations he felt helpless to negotiate. "Paĉjo," his daughter
murmured to him, and put herself under his armpit in her familiar way. He put his arm around her shakily. Juko had been
on his other side gripping his hand, but now she let him go, and
it was his son Eneo holding that hand suddenly and saying
something to him, and he was grateful for the cacophony of
people's voices relieving him of the necessity of hearing the
words, or of speaking. He felt distanced from his wife, his relatives, his children, as if years had passed and meanwhile they
had become other people.

Someone, maybe it was his sister Olinda's husband, said irritably, "Make them a way through. Let them go home, eh?"
and other people gradually took up this proprietary mustering.

The crowd opened a little, swimming slowly against the free-fall, and let the crew of the *Ruby* and their families go out of the docking arena and up the winding corridors to the gallery of lifts. When people spoke to him he tried to smile, but went on unable to speak, his brain filled with a jittery misery. The heat of his son's hand became his point of concentration. He felt mercurial, transient, was dimly grateful for Eneo's clasp anchoring him to a fixed base.

For years he had been piloting tugs, had made three or four space junkets as long as this one—longer. He always had dreaded the heaviness, coming down to the torus after those long periods of free-fall, had been days getting back his land legs. But now crowded in the lift with the nine or ten members of his family, he found an obscure comfort in the way his body felt taking on quick weight, substance, falling heavily down from the center. He thought, *All right. All right, now,* giving himself a kind of rebuke.

He looked for Juko. She stood holding the hand of his young granddaughter, but she was watching him with a look that was anxious and wary—a surprise. He reached for her suddenly, put his arms around her in a fierce clench. Her back shook briefly under his hands—she was letting go of a few tears—and when he understood this, he experienced a moment of exhilaration and loosening. "Ended," he said in a hoarse voice, and sobbed out loud. Other people in the lift began to weep too, their hands reaching to touch him, to stroke his cheek, pet his arm. "Yes. Yes," his family said, "the old *Ruby* has got home. Gift of God."

It was a vast surprise to come out into the *Miller*'s yellowish, humid daylight and find the jacaranda trees still in bloom, their lavender blossoms seeming impossibly glorious after long days and nights at the edge of the gray lake, weeks of incandescent lamps and tiny metal rooms in the *Ruby*. He was a technologist, not a botanist; a mechanic, not a farmer. It struck him that he had lived his life until now without ever looking on the landscape of his world. Now the brilliant green of the rice, the scarlet passionflowers against the rank verdure, the high-up ceiling, hazy with cloud and refracted light, filled him with helpless longing and love.

He hadn't thought of his mother being absent from the homecoming until he saw her standing in front of the house, squared on her feet, peering with her bad eyes down the path into the bunch of them coming up toward her. Maybe it was the hub she had stayed away from, she had a hatred of the free-fall now she was old. Neighbors, his mother's friends, his wife's relatives, were with her, standing about in the narrow path and the little garden before the house, waiting for him.

When he saw how many there were, a kind of exhausted panic made his legs suddenly unsteady: He wanted to be let alone, not be made the center of their celebrating. Kristina's eyes picked him out finally, gave him a long narrow look, and then he heard her dry voice suddenly over the others, she was turning to her friends, pulling at their arms. "My son is wayworn, used up," she was saying. "We'll let him sleep, eh?" It was a terrible moment, realizing his mother had seen this in his face as if he must still be a child. But when people started going off meekly, he was weak with gratitude.

He hadn't believed her advice to people was meant to be absolute, but when he came up the ladder onto the loĝio of the house she pushed him into the little apartment, the little room he and Juko slept in, and the two women rolled the bed out and put him onto it. His skin was rough with cold, and they covered him with a sheet, put a pot of tea on the floor beside the bed, closed the shutters over the window casement to shut out the daylight and people's voices. They behaved as if he were sick, and he let them behave that way. He submitted to everything helplessly, not having the strength for explaining, the will for protesting.

They left him alone in the room. As soon as the wall was closed, a burning anguish sprang up in his chest. He worked his brain, grappling to give a name to his feeling. He had yearned to be alone, but now, alone, he realized he wanted his wife to get into bed with him. He wanted her to lie with him on the bed without speaking, with the heat of her torso pressing against him in wordless, undemanding sympathy. He wanted her to hold him like a sick child until he slept, and he blamed her for not realizing this.

He drew his knees up and huddled on the mat, under the heavy weight of the air, shaking with cold and self-pity and irrational resentment. He could hear his relatives and neighbors talking softly on the other side of the thin wall, their voices an indistinguishable murmur. When he heard a word, it was meaningless, irrelevant. "Point," he heard someone say, and later, "Carry down." He realized he was straining to hear his own name, he wanted to overhear them talking about his health, his grief of heart, how much they had missed him, how much he had suffered.

He wasn't able to keep his eyes shut. His look jumped anxiously, distractedly around the room, not settling anywhere, not focusing on anything. The house had a quality not just of unfamiliarity but of transcendent strangeness, as if his whole experience had been a life in the branches of trees. He thrashed about, restless, until he was crouched on his knees with his forehead pressed against the mattress. He rocked on his head, his knees, the pressure behind his eyes making a wavery kaleidoscope of yellows and reds. Gradually the rocking soothed him. He slept a little in a milieu of feverish dreams and woke exhausted, sweating under the sheet. It was dusk, and the room's shadowiness, the dim light cast through the papery panes of the wall, disoriented and oppressed him. He saw that Juko, or someone, had gotten the room unaccustomedly clean, the individual motes of dust on the floor boards a testament to recent washing.

He sat on the mat, his body heavy and dull, and held his head in the cups of his hands until he was fully awake. Voices were still speaking softly somewhere in the house, a sound that made him feel excluded and vaguely sorrowful. He stood up and slid back the door. Juko sat in the dimming light beside the casement in the common room, braiding rattan. His mother sat near her, shelling beans in a battered clay bowl. When he opened the door, they both looked at him critically.

"When did you eat, eh? Are you hungry?" his mother said,

and made a movement as if she might be drawing her feet under her. Juko murmured something and stood up, put on the lamp in the galley, and Kristina settled again with her fists sprouting long fingers of beans. Bjoro stood in the doorway of their sleeping room, watching his wife heating soup, shredding cabbage, putting a thin knife to mushrooms and leeks. When she looked at him, he kept his eyes on the blade of the knife.

"People are worrying about you," Juko said. From the edge of his stare he could see his mother's face in a gathered-up frown, and between Juko's straight eyebrows a shirring of pleats. But the other members of his family had gone. What should he understand from that? That some people had become impatient, waiting for him to be over his suffering? He shook his head. Then he said, "It was all right," without knowing what he meant. The crowd of people at the dock? Peder's dying? Isuma's?

Juko, with the edge of one hand, swept the greens to his bowl, poured the soup over, brought the bowl steaming to the low table. "Bjoro," she said, reaching for him. "Come and eat." She had a gentle tone of voice, and her eyes touched him lightly as if he had become fragile. He sat on the floor with his knees under the table and ate Juko's soup. It was an unspeakable luxury after weeks of pastes and reconstituted freeze-dry. The two women watched him eat, their faces smoothing out, evidently taking pleasure in it. When he had emptied the bowl, Juko stood and filled it up again.

Bjoro said, trying to smile, "It was almost the worst thing, the bad edibles."

Kristina nodded firmly. "You can bear anything if you have good food," she said. This wasn't true but it had truth in it, and his mother doubtless believed it; she was someone who always would bring bread to a mortafesto, soup to the sick, though she never had liked to prepare daily meals. Her preference as cook was a breadnut tortilla rolled around scraps and leavings of food.

"And sleep, a good bed," Juko said, murmuring. The two women exchanged a closed look. They had a habit of leaving him out of certain things, never would tell him their meaning unless he asked, and maybe not the truth then. He always had resented such moments, and gradually had got away from asking for explanations. But he thought he understood this one. Juko, when she was divorcing Humberto Indergard, had moved in with Kristina and mostly stayed in her bed for weeks. His mother had had the Clearness Committee in to see her, but mostly let her sleep, and sleep, so long as she came out to eat healthy meals.

He said, his voice hoarse, "There was not much sleeping on the *Ruby.*"

Their faces looked at him in constrained surprise. "No. No, I guess not, Bjoro," they said to him, without either of them asking what it was that had kept him from sleeping. *It was dreams of the dead,* he had planned to say bitterly, and the unspoken words settled in his chest, constricting his breath.

They talked around him. Maybe they were resuming a conversation they'd been having while he slept. "Old Kelling is getting off the Advices and Queries Committee," Kristina was saying. "He's been telling everybody his health is broken."

"Oh, he always worries too much about his health, Kelling does." Juko's attention again was on the wickerwork. She worked the strands deftly, examining them under the lamp. "How old is he? Seventy? He'll get to be a hundred, but he'll complain every day until then, about his bad health."

Kristina nodded. "There's a man in my family who has a loose valve in his heart," she said. "He never has spent a minute of his life complaining about his health, eh?" She was back at her work too, shelling the beans. She took them out of a gunny bag two or three at a time. The pods were mottled, purplish, papery; she had made a little loose mountain of the empty ones beside one of her knees. The beans in the bowl were creamy beneath faint purple whorls.

"Is that Orid Finĉ?" Juko asked her, glancing up from the braiding.

His mother nodded. "Orid never complains about his heart. Only he has a pale look, and if you put your head on his chest you can hear a kind of whistling sound when the blood moves."

Bjoro knew Orid Finĉ. Orid was seventy, his hair white and silken framing a long face, without any resemblance to Peder Ojama except in the sound blood made, leaking behind a breast bone.

Juko teased Kristina solemnly. "You had your head on Orid's chest."

His mother showed her yellowing teeth. "That was a long time ago." Then she said, closing her mouth to a sly smile, "He is only a relation by marriage."

Juko laughed. In a moment she said, "When I was little there was a blind woman in our neighborhood. Did you know her? I don't remember her name. Maybe it was Pena? Or Lena?" Kristina shook her head. "Well anyway. This woman had a cane and walked about without any trouble, it seemed to me. I liked to play as if I was blind, eh? Shut my eyes and go out on the footway or the fields and find my way around. But I never could keep my eyes shut all the way tight." She smiled ironically.

They went on telling these stories of health and infirmity, first Kristina and then Juko, while Bjoro silently emptied the bowl of soup by spoonfuls. When he lifted the bowl to his mouth for the last of it Kristina said, eyeing him, "We sent everybody away. We swept them out of here with a broom, eh? They can come back tomorrow when you've got rested up. You know Leon Thorssen is clerk of the Yearly Meeting now that Guner Ĝohanesen has died? He maybe hasn't got old Guner's patience: He came with five people from that Planning Committee and wanted you to tell what you saw. What was he thinking! Some of them went over to Luza Kordoba's house, too, but I bet Luza's spouse—what's her name? Tereza?— pushed them out the same as we did. To come today, the very day you are home! the very hour! We told them to come back tomorrow. All that business can wait, eh? You won't forget how to tell what you saw. Anyway, they won't be publishing the Advices and Queries anytime soon. We said you needed a sleep. And to eat. Are you full now? Do you want to get into bed again?" She touched Juko's arm. "Put him to bed, Juko. He has something he wants to give you, I bet, something he's been saving." She flashed a narrow smile. She considered intercourse, along with food and sleep, essential to life.

Juko laughed and put her hand softly on his back. He didn't know what this touch meant—whether she was telling him she was anxious to copulate with him, or consoling him for being too tired, too filled with grief, to consummate his homecoming in that usual way.

He didn't feel interested in intercourse with Juko—moving his body was a ponderous effort in the unaccustomed gravity, and he had had only brief, edgy rest for weeks. But he had lost his craving to wrap his cold legs around his wife and lie in her arms like a sick child. Her hand on his back patronized and irritated him.

"I haven't needed fucking, only sleep," he said harshly.

This startled them, and they looked at him in a guarded way. It wasn't their usual practice, this tiptoeing around his feelings. The two of them always had shared a directness, a willingness to chide him, and their silence seemed a kind of humiliation. He felt a sudden impulse to say something else, to accuse them of something, but his brain wasn't able to bring it forward.

Juko stood with the empty soup bowl and washed it at the galley's little cold-water tap, put away the scraps of food, wiped down the chopping board. While she was doing this, Bjoro's mother watched him across the heap of shelled beans. Gradually his choking anger loosened, and he said tiredly, "I've not had much sleep for more than three weeks."

This was a condition they felt able to understand. They looked at him with affectionate tolerance. "I'll come to bed with you," Juko said, and reached her hand down to him. He stood slowly and let her lead him back into their room.

It was close and hot and dark, and smelled of his sweat. She went to the shutters to let the night air come in, but he said, low-voiced, "No. Will you leave them shut, Juko?" Her face searched him out blindly in the darkness.

"Are you not over being cold, then?" she said to him in a murmur. He wasn't able to answer, but she came away from the window again, left the room closed up.

He sat on the mat heavily. She knelt behind him and began to knead his shoulders. She was tender, thorough, she knew the places that held on to tiredness. He shut his eyes.

"Do you know?" Juko said softly. "Peder's wife dreamed her husband's death, before the *Ruby* was gone, but kept from saying so." Bjoro's eyes became hot with unshed tears. She waited, and when he didn't answer, she went on. "I'm sorry for what happened to Isuma and Peder." Her voice became almost a whisper. "I'm sorry."

He didn't know why her insistent sympathy, the urgency of her thin voice, angered him. He realized, he didn't feel grief for Peder's wife, but for himself.

"Dreaming of death is something we will do every day, on that world," he said bitterly.

She kept kneading his back and shoulders in silence. Her fingers were strong. Sometimes she flattened her palms and pushed the heels of her hands up and down the valley between his shoulder blades, either side of his spine. Gradually the rhythmic stroking aroused him a little. He was still wearing the caparajos they all had favored in the *Ruby,* and he thought his erection was hidden in the freedom of the loose trousers, but Juko whispered, "Do you want to lay with me now?"

"Yes," he said hoarsely.

He stood and pushed his trousers down from his hips. Juko laughed. "I guess you do," she said.

He lay heavily on the mattress, inert, and she knelt over him kissing his chest lightly and his soft belly and the urgent rigidity of his penis, stroking his cold skin with her hands and her mouth. She was patient, willing, and that built his inexplicable anger. He didn't know what he wanted from her, but when she took one of his hands and put it under her shirt, cupping a breast, prompting him, he convulsed suddenly with rageful passion. He seized her with both hands, rocking up wildly and then turning onto his knees to put her body under him. She braced her arms against his weight but she was pulling at her own shirt, working ahead of his pent-up rush. In an urgent fire, he grappled her trousers down, shoved her legs open with his knees. She was moving under him, murmuring, words he wasn't able to hear. He climbed on her, his elbows across the bones of her arms, and she twisted and her breath let out a high gasping sound of pain that made his skull hum. He pushed himself against her, groping, his penis beating against her pubic bone. Behind his teeth a whining sound arose, as he thrust against her uselessly, wild with defeat. He became aware that her mouth was open, that she was letting out a continuous whimpering complaint. She struggled under him, pushing against his weight.

In a frenzy he jerked her by the arm, the leg, onto her belly and hooked his arms under her thighs, lifting her buttocks to him. Another, higher sound came from her, or a word, *what* or *wait,* but eclipsed by the heavy booming inside his skull. It was another wife, it was Hlavka, with whom he used to have anal sex. But recklessly, uncontrollably, he forced himself into Juko's anus, and the sound she was making became a toneless, gasping crying, a thin wail that raised a singing under his scalp. He pumped against her with a terrible fury, his arms braced rigidly beneath her thighs, until his muscles loosened and shook with fatigue, until finally he was too heavy, too tired to keep on with it, and he rolled away whimpering, without release, and held his penis in both his hands, pulling on it in an exhausted rage until a short hot spurt of semen wet his thigh.

He released a few hot tears as well, and a clenched moan of misery. Then in the slowly cooling sweat of heat and fire, lying on the bed in the darkness with his hands still clasping his flaccid penis, he felt relieved of something, as if he had emptied himself of waste. When he realized he was searching for something in the blackness of the ceiling, he deliberately shut his eyes.

He became aware of his mother moving in the small alcove where she lay at night; and then he began to hear Juko's short huffing breath containing some louder sound of tears or fury. When she moved against his back, shifting away on the bed, he rolled his head toward her. She crouched on the mat of their bed, her hands pressed over her mouth, her knees flattening her breasts. Behind her hands was the sound of grievous breathing. Bjoro's limbs filled with a ponderous dull guilt and pain. Reflexively he began to go over and over what had happened,

conceiving other endings, other beginnings, words said or un-
said, until he was no longer certain what the truth was, though
he imagined the detail of gestures, silences, tears. *I forgot which
wife I was with,* he thought of saying. In his mind, in the peace-
making that had not yet begun, Juko was mournful and forgiving; she took some of the fault onto herself.

"Juko," he said sorrowfully. She made a sound, a catching of
air, and stood up, pushing away the tangled shirt and trousers
stiffly and going from the room naked. He lay in a heavy
lethargy in the darkness while water ran in the sink, and his
mother's voice asked something. Kristina knew the sounds people made, wrestling on a bed, she maybe had heard Juko's held-
in wailing and imagined—what? He wasn't able to hear what
she asked, but his wife's harsh answer, illuminating nothing:
"No, go to sleep, Kristina, go to sleep."

When the water was shut off, he thought he heard a door
sliding, and imagined Juko taking the old manta they kept hanging above the shoe bench, a cape against the rain for people who
walked anywhere after dark, and settling angrily on the narrow
boards of the pasado with the cape pulled up like a blanket over
her breasts. Then he imagined her putting on the cape and
walking around to Senlima or Alaŭdo, to her brother's house
or her son's, and a cold anxiety rose in his body. But she came
into the room again. Her shape moving against the darkness was
erect, stiff-limbed, her small breasts lay against her ribs. She
went around him lying on the mat, went to the casement and
pushed open the shutters. Then, in the night light falling into
the room, she got into a clean shirt and trousers, her arms
swinging in short, jerky arcs. He sat up on the bed and watched
her with a kind of thrilling dread.

"I haven't—" he whispered. "It wasn't—"

Without stopping what she was doing she said to him in a
furious whisper, "I won't have a husband who thinks I am a
hole to stick his penis into."

He put his head into his hands. "I have killed our marriage,"
he said piteously. Juko blew a wordless sound through her lips,
something made up equally of anger and amusement, as if she
considered this bathetic. He looked at her. She had taken her

dirty shirt and begun to push things unsystematically into the middle of it, unrelated objects from shelves and trunks: a hat, a hank of thread, old sandals, a scarf embroidered by Humberto Indergard. He stood shakily. "I was crazy," he said, opening his hands, murmuring. "There isn't any reason why you should forgive me. It was a bad thing to do. I was crazy."

She pulled the sleeves of the shirt into a bundle and held it against her chest. In the darkness her face was a shining mask of pain and bitterness. She said, thick and low, "I'll live in my brother's house until you are sane again."

He made a lost sound, and when she shifted her weight to move he put his arms around her desperately, the bulk of the bundle between them. She became rigid, standing with her face turned from him, waiting to be let go. Through the open casement of the window he heard voices speaking, the clack of a loom, someone's child crying, an enigmatic, quick patting of hands. He realized irrelevantly that the daylight was barely gone. In the incomplete darkness, not many people were sleeping yet. In Kristina's little grotto under the stairs of the sadaŭ, there was silence. She had a practice of intruding herself in their arguments, of taking Juko's part in any quarrel, and he felt her reticence now was a fearful sign. He stood holding his wife hard in his arms, unable to speak or act effectively. Her breath going in and out of her mouth made a bristly sound that he felt along his bones, like a scraping of metal.

In a while she said, "Let loose, Bjoro," her voice shaking under the weight of anger.

He said hoarsely, "Please, Juko, make peace with me. Please. I behaved in a bad way. I was crazy." He put his mouth against the crown of her head, whispering desolately, "I didn't know I was hurting you."

She reared against him, jerking her head, and his teeth rammed the inside of his mouth. He tightened his arms convulsively and went on holding her, rigid with fear. She twisted, turning her face toward him, her mouth misshapen. The bottom lids of her eyes brimmed with tears. *"Don't say you didn't know you were doing it!"* she said in a wild whisper.

He didn't have an answer. He looked away helplessly. "I was crazy," he said in a rising wail.

Juko sobbed suddenly, and this unexpected sound from her drove the air out of Bjoro's lungs in a hiccup of surprised terror. He hooked his chin over the pitch of her shoulder and turned his face into her neck. The heated, pungent, womanish odor of her skin overwhelmed him with grief. "I'm sorry, Juko. I'm sorry," he murmured repeatedly, and tears ran in his mouth and stung him where his teeth had cut the inside of his cheek. But when she had loosed three or four long roupy sobs, shuddering against him, he understood that her tears signaled a kind of yielding, an adjustment. His own crying became relief, and when she made a weak, insinuating effort to get out of his clasp, he loosened his arms. The bundled-up shirt slid down to the floor.

Juko brought the heels of her hands to her face and let them rest there, standing breathing hard over the little hillock of her goods. Bjoro stood, not touching her, with his arms still raised slightly, unfinished with letting her go. After a while she dropped her hands and made a slight, tired movement of indecision or despair and then lay down heavily on the mat, on her hip, crossing one arm over her eyes. Bjoro in a moment sat carefully below her feet. He waited, and when she didn't speak he put a hand on his wife's foot. It was bare, clammy.

The world moved under them in a ceaseless regulated sweeping. In the darkness, her smell was familiar, the sound of her breathing familiar to him. His fingers, closing on the small bones of her foot, warmed it slowly. Finally he came around the bed slowly and lay down beside her. He felt heavy and exhausted, tired of anxiety. Lying on his back looking into the ceiling, he realized he was waiting for the damp weight of the darkness and the silence to deaden their crisis. After a while she sighed, her little breath descending in him, rising out of him, sweeping up a windrow of weeds and old leaves.

He slept and woke, slept and woke. Juko lay unmoving, her eyes hidden behind her arm, her breath heavy and slow. It was impossible to tell if she was awake or asleep. The third or fourth time he woke and looked at her, her arm had slipped down and she lay with her mouth slack against the mattress, her eyes jumping behind the lids. He felt a brief spurt of shame, as if what he saw was intimate and revealing, but he wasn't able to stop watching her dreaming, the tips of her fingers spasming helplessly. A tenderness and love for his wife engulfed him suddenly, and when the dream slipped out of her, when her face became minutely tighter, less defenseless, he wasn't able to go on watching her, or loving her. In the darkness he put on his trousers and went softly out of the room, the house.

It was preparing to rain, the night air humid and heavy. The weak light cast out of houses threw black shadows along the walls. Chickens slept along the eaves of roofs, on the tops of walls, and among the yellow trumpets of the ajamanda vines that climbed over arbors at the edges of fields. Bjoro stood on the bottom step of his house, looking without holding anything in his mind, and then started downhill following the footway between the crowded houses, under the star-shaped shadows of the trees. The murmuring restlessness of people inside the houses was an inescapable field of sound. As he stood beside the clamor of the Falls From Grace waiting for the lift, a rain began, and his breath came hard in the clammy night. The ambient light was dimly yellow; the rain falling through it looked fine and white as snow. It was an unexpected summoning of another landscape, and brought with it a sudden, vast conviction: The division between himself and Juko was as impenetrable as death, this wife as lost to him as the first. He was choked with self-pity. At Hlavka's death he had felt a fear and knowledge that had overpowered his reason—it had been impossible not to blame her for dying, for succumbing inexplicably to an asthma she'd withstood for thirty years. Now he realized that he blamed Juko, too, in a vague but certain way, for not understanding what he had been unable to articulate.

He took the lift up to the center of the world. He had no expectations, no intentions, but he understood darkly: The metalline, strident, fluorescent chambers of the manufactory were a sacred space for him. Other people oversaw the machinery, kept up the ordinary maintenance and repair, but when there was a breakdown Bjoro was someone they asked to help them with it; he considered the glass kiln and the complicated apparatus of the paper mill and the foundry to be his province. This was a familiar landscape, manageable, ordered, and his yearning for it now seemed a kind of prayer.

In the hub, where certain machinery needed tending, there was work done around the hours: People fiddled at panels and boards, clambered over the machines, in rooms Bjoro looked into. He felt charged with loneliness, with separation, and kept away from the people he saw, kept to the Byzantine passageways in a kind of furtive agitation. No one stood by the keys in the glassworks. Without thinking of doing it, he scaled the batch hopper there, pulling up with his arms in the light air and retreating urgently into the narrow space between the ceiling and the furnace.

The air was hot, thick. When he had climbed the glass kiln, working, he always had protected himself, worn a stoker rig, but now he was barefoot, barechested, and the heat against the skin of his belly gave him an unexpected feeling of liberation, of abandon and risk. He put his hands down delicately, deliberately, against the feverish surface of the furnace and walked on his palms across the metal, his legs and feet following, drifting and buoyant. Beneath him the furnace made a continuous, hot susurration that entered his bones through the burning tips of his fingers.

At the center of the furnace where the batch was fed to the cauldron down a gullet and windpipe, he cooled his hands on the standpipe. There was a place among the conduits, an awkward cranny there, and he settled onto it, giving himself over to the effort of getting a breath into his lungs and out again in the dim heat. He felt pleasantly giddy, empty-headed. His body gave up a little of its lightness, and when his breastbone came down slowly against a gas pipe he reached through the webwork of flues and lines and siphons and scrupulously rested his palms, then his forearms, against the surface of the furnace.

He had once crouched in the narrow chamber of the kremaciejo, holding a wrench on a nut while Opal Nansen had slowly turned the bolt out from the other side. But the furnace had been shut down for days by then, and the crematory cell had been cool and dim. It was inlaid with heat-bearing tiles and there had been a minute dust of ash on the tiles. He had felt something integral and clarifying when he had run water in the sink afterward and carefully rinsed his hands, imagining the little trickle of gritty, grayish water in the catch basin delivered ultimately to the feet of cabbages, cassavas, mango trees. Inside the kremaciejo he had been able to slide down onto his back, stretch his legs out, without imagining his own death. It was now, in the heat and the narrow, dirty darkness among the pipes of the glassworks, that he had a sudden apprehension of his body consumed in fire.

He shut his eyes, with his arms laid trembling against the furnace, and looked inward, following the slight rush of air across the back of his throat, the intake and outtake of his breath. But he couldn't keep his attention there, his closed eyes following the breath out across his teeth and then flying loose in a gasp, and his arms betraying him involuntarily, recoiling. His eyelids started open, and he lay in the narrow interstice, huffing his breath. Clumsily he turned his palms up, examining them in the dimness; the fleshy pads of his fingers, the heels of his hands began to whiten and blister as he looked. He extended his arms, peering at them through a screen of tears. The tender skin on the inside of his forearms was striped ruby red. He squeezed his eyelids closed in an exaltation of agony. He had to push himself, clambering once, twice with his elbows, his heels, to get clear of the pipes, to free himself from the cleft space between the conduits before he had the room to pull his arms up, to clasp the pain like a pillow against his chest.

They had left Peder Ojama's body on the stony ridge, lying on one hip under a thin sheet of snow. Isuma had told them a body might lie more or less intact for months, or a year: The prevailing weather made a slow process of decay. Not many scavengers lived on this world. Bjoro had wondered if she was saying something else, something revealing—that there would be time enough for Peder's family to come back for his body, to collect it for burning. Was she saying, then, that this bitter place was to be their world? He had wanted to argue with

Isuma—he had wanted to set fire to the body there on the ridge, in the snow. But she had begun tenderly to arrange the limbs, drawing the knees to the chest, crossing the arms, fitting the hands under the armpits until Peder lay in the posture of a child protecting his center; and Bjoro's mouth had only filled with sourness and heat.

Afterward Luza and Bjoro had stood on the ridge in the blowing wind, watching the spectacular burning of Isuma's wrecked montgolfiere, the lifting flurries of sparks in the black night. And later, in the daylight, in the long waiting while the *Ruby* brought a second balloon round to try again, they had walked over the hummocky grass a kilometer or more to look for Isuma's body among the cooling ashes. The brief hot burning had left a blackish mass on a skeleton, and standing over it, Bjoro had felt something incomprehensible, something brutal and requited.

Eight

KRISTINA

I go from bedside to bedside, I sleep close
with the other sleepers each in turn,
I dream in my dream all the dreams of
the other dreamers,
And I become the other dreamers.

Because no one in her own household had taken sick, people were quick to ask of Kristina her time, her hands, in families where several people were down. She took on the fetching and the laundry for her neighbor Lavka Valen's household, and then the household of Jakobo Saldado—Jakobo was her dead sister's son—but when she was coming or going from those houses other people would catch her up, to ask if she would do a particular thing: carry the baby a minute; stir the pot; go and see if so-and-so needed a drink or had taken sick overnight. She found the urgent work of getting round to committees had to be done in the odd respite.

She had lately let herself be named to the New World Advisory—they were gathering a consensus on this matter of whether the New World would physically support them. It was this question that would shape the larger one, the question of staying or going, so it wasn't a light matter. Two or three more generations of people must finish their lives out and die on board the old, deteriorating *Miller,* if they gave up the idea of making a niche for themselves on this cold-weather planet and went on looking for another place more amenable.

It was her charge to listen to what people had to say in the committees of Pacema, Bonveno, Revenana. Farms and Waterworks and Science Committees she was seeing ahead of others, but in the end she must see all of them, even Fiber Arts Committees and potters, who would be thinking the point at issue was whether this New World had good seed hairs and stems for weaving, malleable clay for pots.

Eight people had been asked to be on the New World Advisory, their names settled on by agreement of the district clerks. Kristina, when she saw that five of the eight were old people, wondered if the clerks were thinking age was the same thing as wisdom. She didn't quite believe this herself, having known some foolish old people and some sensible children, but she thought people could turn a long life to good account if they worked at it a little. She wasn't unwilling to have this weighty work given to her. But there was a vanishing four-month window for making up their minds about it—it was a work that shouldn't be put off for plagues of illness, she felt.

In Pacema, there were forty people stricken; in Kristina's domaro, five. The sick people had a pungent, stinking urine; their kidneys ached; they took fever and lay weakly in bed, craving water and complaining of burning behind the eyes and on the tongue; and when they'd been sick for seven or eight or nine days, some few died and others began to be well again. No one in Kristina's domaro had yet died. Or only old Edita Salvera who probably would have died soon anyway, she had gotten to be more than ninety years old and in the last few months had slipped into a kind of dream, calling her children and grandchildren and great-grandchildren by the names of friends who had been dead for twenty years. Edita, when she took the fever into her body, simply fell into sleep and peacefully let go of life.

Grace of God, people said of Edita's death, which made Kristina twist her mouth in irritation. She wanted to be mindful and attentive when she went out of her body. She had an abiding curiosity about the moment of death and considered it a loss to die in one's sleep, ignorant, oblivious. But her irritation had more to do with platitudes than with God. She never had blamed or credited God for things that happened in the world, though it was hard not to hold Someone accountable for all this bad timing.

The accident of chronology had brought a persistent, wide-spread feeling that these particular microbes had come inside the *Miller* by way of Luza and Bjoro, though none of the six in the *Ruby* had come down sick, and the *Miller* always had been prone to epidemics. The population of micro-organisms always had been lively, capricious, unpredictable—in times past, this was blamed on the humid environment and irradiation and the two-thousand-some people living as close to one another as the pages in a book. But now, with a kind of plaintive urgency, people were blaming the New World. Ruby Fever, people were calling this new illness, and no one wanted Luza Kordoba treating the sick members of their family, though Luza always had been a well-respected kura.

It would have been hard enough work to make up their minds quickly without a plague delivered into the breach. *Better the brakes than the spurs,* was a well known axiom, and some problematic questions had gone undecided on the *Dusty Miller* for a hundred years, awaiting unity. Consensus was a method that was understood to be inefficient, cumbrous. It slowed down the introduction of new ideas, made sure that change was well-considered. No one had any experience with decisions that couldn't be put off.

In the press of God's bad timing, Kristina had become impatient with sleep. She had got in the habit of napping once in the daylight, once or twice in the night, and sitting under a lamp while other people were sleeping, holding a magnifying glass over pages of cryptic balloon data, Minutes of Planning Committees, replies to old Advices and Queries. Her own apartment at night was still, empty, no one objected to the light or railed about an old woman ill-using her body. Her son had made a frenzied mission of overhauling the steel mill robotics; he seldom slept in the house. Juko kept away too, was sleeping in her brother's house where someone—Naĵa, the sister-in-law?—

was sick and the old man, Juko's father, had a dementia and needed habitual looking after.

This had given Kristina's neighbors something to gossip about: Maybe Bjoro was working too hard out of a guilty conscience, something to do with his bringing home the plague in his body; and maybe Juko stayed away from her husband because she was afraid to catch a sickness from him. Or maybe she had a guilt of her own—her brother might have scolded her for always, in the past, leaving the old man, old Ŝilko, for him to watch. Of course, there was other gossip as well—neighbors had heard the whispered arguing and crying the night Bjoro came home in the *Ruby*—but Kristina kept herself from listening to it. She didn't know fully what was between her son and her daughter-in-law anyway, only that it had become thick, a shroud, and when both of them were in the apartment it had filled the rooms, silenced them all, kept them from looking in one another's faces. The plague had been a kind of bitter deliverance from that, perhaps one of God's small graces, the timing not off after all.

She turned the pages of the bound Minute book slowly, her watery eyes peering among the endless tedious arguments and petty deliberations of the Bonveno Planning Committee. A man Kristina knew, Gilberto Osborn, was the recording clerk, and he had a neat small hand but a compulsion to write everything down. There were long, irreducible harangues from people whose words would finally carry little weight, and people who would stand aside or be discounted when the sense of the Meeting was gathered up. She had to read pages to find the scarce words of clearness, of judgment, the communal leadings, the congruences. She always had had a short patience for drivel, and from too much reading of Minutes lately she had maybe become intolerant. It wasn't Gil Osborn's fault there were stupid people living in Bonveno district, she thought, but he shouldn't have written down their words. And the clerk over there in Bonveno, Toma something-or-other, shouldn't have let them go on talking after it was clear they weren't saying anything with depth or insight.

She pushed her knuckles against her eyes, a pleasant burning pain. *Oh hell.* She stood effortfully and went out of her apartment and down to the lavejo, as much for relief of tedium and stiff joints as relief of the little pressure on her bladder. The toilet box gave up a thin smell of rot and sweetness, a composting perfume she secretly savored, and once there she made herself comfortable on the seat and waited for a slow, small bowel movement. *What's the matter with them, over there in Bonveno?* she thought irritably. When at last she stood up from the toilet seat, a tiredness settled suddenly into her chest and her pelvis. When she came out from the lavejo and saw the small yellow circle of the lamp in her apartment illuminating the loose stacks of papers, her flattened cushion, her magnifying glass, she thought *Oh hell,* and put out the light and got into bed.

For a while against her closed eyelids there were dim traces on the darkness, the neat handwriting of Gil Osborn. But she wasn't able to apply her mind to those serious matters; she went helplessly over and over the trifling things in her day—the sorting of the Saldados' unfamiliar laundry, an unfinished piece of drafting, the words she had traded back and forth with her nephew about the sexing of chicken eggs. *Why are there so many stupid people over there in Bonveno?* she kept thinking uselessly. In the apartment occupied by Filisa Ilmen's family, some couple began to copulate—the little huffing of the man's breath broke the first delicate skin of Kristina's sleep. In the undefended moment she was struck with grief, and thought suddenly, heavily, *Who can know what he was thinking?*

She went round irresistibly in the early morning to see Luza Kordoba, where she lived over in Senlima. There was a heavy mist along the incurvature so the houses down in those neighborhoods were in fog. Because the gray mornings made her glum, she went above the warm drizzle, keeping to the narrow footway at the edge of the ceiling. Walking up there along the high curve, she was sometimes prone to see the world in a bad way—to catch sight of it suddenly as tubular, meager, ersatz. But she was too tired, today, for farsightedness: The view across the long roofs, the heads of the light poles standing above the fog, was utterly familiar, without the capacity for surprise.

She didn't know which house was Luza's and had to ask a person pruning a tree and then two people cooking on a brazier on the high narrow pasado of the domaro where people had sent her. Senlima houses were down along the maltejo in a tight cluster, with the terraces of their fields climbing up either side. The domaro that Luza Kordoba lived in was built at the edge of the maltejo aqueduct, and Luza and her brother's family and her spouse had a house with a view through the legs of trees that stood higher up on the slope.

Kristina climbed slowly up the stairs to them in their treetrunk house, standing on every second or third step to press a fist behind one hip where she was aching. Then she had to go from apartment to apartment looking for Luza until she'd found her, she and the woman who must have been her spouse, sitting puzzling over the parts of a little motor, maybe it was a refrigerator motor, that was neatly arrayed on the floor between them. Luza's foot rocked slightly, working the treadle of a cradle where a sick little child slept ruddy-faced, wheezing. The room was a storm of disorder. A strung hammock had become a landing stage for disheveled bedding and towels, unwashed clothing. The table was adrift with unrelated things— a dirty shirt, greasy cutlery, a tangled wad of yarn stuck through with needles.

From the threshold of the apartment Kristina said quietly, "I've brought a cold soup for that sick child."

People had told her there was a baby sick with the plague in Luza's household, and she had made this a reason to come, though she never had known Luza Kordoba more than offhandedly, didn't know her family at all. The sick child was a pretext. Among the Planning Committees and the business clerks of the Monthly Meetings, there was a mistrust of the balloon reports and a need to hear the weather and the landscape as human eyes had seen it. Her own son Bjoro had told a few things flatly once, and after that sent people away, but Luza had been patiently telling and retelling everything she'd seen. Twice, Kristina had listened to her long, thorough account and was ashamed that she had a compulsion to hear it again. She didn't know what she expected to get from the repetition except once more a glimpse of her own old bones standing in obdurate cold, her own watery eyes peering toward an unapproachable horizon.

The woman who might have been Luza's spouse murmured, "Dankon," smiling slightly, and Luza said to Kristina, looking up, "You are Bjoro's mother, eh? Kristina? Do you know my wife, Asa? Come in and talk to us, will you." She gestured over the scattered parts of the motor and grinned. "You can tell us how to get this put back together again, eh?"

Kristina considered her son's mechanical knack had come from her, but she made a polite mocking sound and said, "You're thinking I've got somebody else's know-how." She stepped out of her shoes on the doorsill and came into the house. The narrow galley table was pulled out, littered with rinds of oranges, slime and seeds of pomegranate. She had to pile up bowls in a dirty cooking pot to get a clean space at the edge of it, a place to set down the jar of soup. And then, because she was lately in the habit of making herself helpful in other people's households, she went on for a minute, gathering up the unwashed dishes. Luza's wife laughed quietly when she saw her doing this.

"Our mess hasn't got to do with any of us being sick, eh? Luza's the only one leans toward neatness in this household, and she was gone a hundred days—this is how we lived. Now she's got home and she's not rational, she thinks she's punishing us, not to pick it up." Asa wasn't sheepish. She looked at Luza in amusement.

Luza blew an obscene sound through her lips. "Come and sit down, Kristina. When they have mice making houses in their filthy towels, they'll pick things up maybe."

Kristina's own leaning was toward tidiness—it was all right with her if dust was on a shelf, but she wanted people to put things away in their places. She admired Luza's unflinching stubbornness. "Well hell, then," she said, and began deliberately to undo the work she'd done, to put the dirty dishes back where they'd been, and that got the two women both to laugh.

She came and sat down stiffly beside Asa, on the bare floor.

The tatami mat in the room was folded up so they could lay out their work on a sheet of plastic, and the floor was hard against her buttocks. She shifted her weight, easing her bony ankles cross-footed.

Luza was getting at the greasy dust in the motor's little intake, inefficiently poking a twisty rag down each narrow cell of the grid. There were two metal boxes sitting between them with the lids open: One was a tools box and one held a cache of nuts and washers, screws, wire. Asa rummaged in the tools box and got a wrong-sized wrench and tried it against the head of a bolt on a piece of motor that was in her lap. She held the nut on the other end with pliers while she tried another wrench and then the right one and methodically loosened the bolt. Kristina watched this impatiently, without comment. Luza's doorstep declaration might have meant, *Don't* tell us how to get this put back together.

The three of them talked politely about fractious refrigerators, and the view into the legs of the trees, and people's habits of neatness or of sloppiness. Every little while Asa's eyes went over to the sick child, and gradually this moved Kristina to forgive her jumbled house. She watched the baby herself. It had been more than half her life since she had sat watching a sick child of her own, but the sweetish smell of fever on the baby's skin and the whistle of air going in and out of the child's mouth brought a rush of vivid memory. Olinda had been prone to get infections in her ears, her sinuses, and Bjoro three times had grown cysts in his belly. She hadn't thought of those baby days in years.

"What is that child's name?" she asked them.

Luza looked at the baby. "Paŭlo," she said, and looked down again, watching her own hands working. "My brother's son," she said, and after a silence she added, "They have another one. My brother's wife has taken him—the other boy, Jeno—to live with her mother in Mandala until this plague is finished. She thinks maybe she can keep him from getting sick, eh?—no one's caught plague in her mother's house yet."

Asa lifted her eyebrows without raising her eyes to Kristina, and said, "She should have stayed in her own house, here, with her husband and her sister-in-law. People will be thinking all this shit-talk is reasonable, that the plague is rightly named. Ruby Fever—ha! *Luza's own family believes it,* people will be saying now."

Luza released a thin sound, a hissing, without looking up from her twisting of the rag. "People will say what they want. Some people will say, Luza and Bjoro were in the *Ruby* with Arda and Hans for twenty days and nobody got sick, eh?" She shook her head. "Shit-talk sinks to the bottom."

Kristina said glumly, "Sometimes it ought to have a weight tied on to it." She was ruled, these days, by the feeling of time urgently slipping away from them all.

When the sick baby whimpered suddenly and kicked his legs, Asa pushed the motor away from her lap and took the baby boy into it. His little fingers went straight into his mouth. Asa petted him, her spread hand lifting the fine damp strands of the child's hair. "So, so, so," she murmured, rocking on her hips. He lay listlessly with his eyes shut, his mouth loose around the fingers. He went on whimpering dully. Kristina stood up with a soft groan and crossed the room to the sink. Asa said, rocking the child, "Is it fruit, in that soup?"

"I put papaya in it. That's an easy thing to go down." She washed a spoon and brought the soup and spoon back to the woman sitting on the floor with the boy clasped to her chest. Asa coaxed the child to take a little, not on the spoon but on the tip of her finger, whispering in his ear.

Luza said, finishing a long thought, "If people want to blame this New World for the plague, they don't have to be saying it's a bacillus." She looked at Kristina. "It's all the worry and nervous strain puts souls out of balance, and then sickness is let in, eh?" It was an old belief—any kura knew it to be true—and in calmer times most people had faith in it. Kristina believed it herself, and it may have been Luza's words that made her see suddenly from the edge of her eye the aura of her world, a fluttering of colorless anxiety distilling until it became physical: red streamers. But when she startled and turned her head to look, there were the trees standing windless beyond the open casements, and rising above them a light-pole holding skyward its delicate cluster of globes, illuminating the vault of heaven. She had spent a lifetime striving to glimpse what was in the crack between her world and God's, but these small epiphanies always came at inattentive moments; they were shadows that vanished when she focused her eyes. She sat down again with painful stiffness and pressed a fist behind her hip.

"It wasn't sickness my son brought home with him," she said heavily. "I thought it was grief, eh? horror of those deaths, but people just die badly sometimes, I've seen one or two die badly, myself, it wasn't only that. I don't know what he brought home inside him—but something, I don't know, something." She shook her head helplessly.

Luza said in surprise, "I guess I know what it is, it was in both of us." Kristina was able to see the tender pale scalp between the individual hairs of the woman's head—a babyish look. She must have kept her hair cropped short as stubble while on the *Ruby,* and by now it had begun to grow out in a bristly dark corona. But her broad face was dour, intent, considering what she would say. "The weather was bad, and the . . . hugeness. We were afraid."

She looked at Asa first and then Kristina, frowning. "We killed Peder, carrying him, do you know? Ought to have sat where we were, brought the balloon down along the lakeshore. We didn't— We should have sat where we were." She went on looking earnestly from one of them to the other, as if she'd asked a question.

Her face had reddened a little. These were things she hadn't spoken of in other tellings. "I don't know what killed Peter, if it was the cold, or the carrying. We should have let the balloon come down there, right there in that damn field of rocks where we were, not carried Peder over the ice to Isuma's field, he'd maybe not be dead, eh? if we'd done that. But we thought . . ." She gestured blindly, lifting her hand and closing it in a fist, taking hold of something difficult in the air there in front of her— holding her fist out as if it represented the words she couldn't articulate. "I thought we would die, all of us, if the balloon tore." Then her voice broke a little and she said hoarsely, "I thought it would be better if Peder was the only one who died."

There was a silence. But after a while, smiling ruefully, Luza said, "Do you know? the sky on that world begins at your feet? People say you can see the face of God in the way one thing is connected to another, and I think I saw the face of God in that sky, the way it was connected to the ground, the way my body stood inside it!"

Kristina said furiously, the only matter she felt able to speak to, "God is in every place." The other matter, the culpability for Peder's death, frightened her in a vague way. She thought, *That's between Bjoro and Luza and their souls.*

"In the *Miller*, God's face is on the ceiling, eh?" Asa said with a narrow smile, glancing at the other two women across the restless limbs of the baby. Luza laughed, and Kristina after a moment made an appreciative sound with her mouth, *Huh*, feeling they were loosening something, all of them, coming out of a tangle. "Yes. On the ceiling."

Her eyes were burning painfully. She sighed and put the heels of her hands against them, rotating her wrists methodically, kneading. A universe of stars wavered briefly in the blackness. *Oh hell. Hell. Here it is now, and I don't have time for lying about sick in my bed.*

She stood up with difficulty, pushing on Luza's shoulder. "This is a hard floor, and I'm old," she said, and petted the woman's lustrous cropped hair. "My hair was black, black as that, you know." She touched her own wild white hair with her fingers, an uncharacteristically fussy gesture. "I never have learned to comb," she said, grimacing unhappily.

"Oh, I like your hair. It's thick, and I like the ribbons you tie in it, the colors against the white."

Kristina accepted this flattery without a reply—Luza was a kind woman. "My house is in Pacema," she said. "Come and visit me when this damn plague is finished with us all." She touched Asa's head too, and the sick baby's, conscious of a kind of blessing in this gesture, and then put her feet in her shoes and went down the steps of their house stiffly, clutching one of her aching kidneys with her free hand. She went slowly, beginning to shake already like an invalid, round to her own domaro and then to the door of Filisa Ilmen's apartment.

"Send somebody to tell my son, he ought to take care of his own mother before any damn machinery," she said tremulously, giving in to misery and self-pity.

Filisa, who had a sister-in-law sick in her own house, said, sighing, looking up from the little galley sink where she ran a bowl of water, "Well, hell now Kristina, I was thinking you'd got by without it."

It was Filisa's husband Leo who helped Kristina out of her shoes, her trousers and shirt, waited while she peed, helped her from the toilet, put her into bed. He was a man she always had liked, quiet and sweet-tempered, his cheeks round and florid in a lean face. She was ashamed to be seen by him in this weak state, her thin shanks trembling when she stood up from the toilet, and her embarrassment made itself over into bitter impatience, complaints, petty demands. *That's a good shirt, Leo, don't be letting it lay there on the damn floor. No, no don't fold it now, it's got too dirty, the way you let it lay.*

He was matter-of-fact, tolerant. When he stood her up from the toilet and pulled her shorts around her bony buttocks he said mildly, "Worst thing, eh? The way the pee stinks." She clutched him gratefully, though she was helpless to stop being petulant. "Oh hell, pinch your nose closed if you can't stand it, Leo, it's a damn little thing to complain about."

When he unfolded her bed and let her down onto it she groaned quietly and turned her back to him, clasping the thin bedsheet. She heard him clattering, dragging over the little table, arranging things within her reach. "Can you sleep?" he asked her, and when she muttered resentfully he pretended not to hear it, his hands fussing, letting her hair free of its red ribbon tie. His fingers raised a thrill across her back, something to do with fever or with anile foolishness. "I'll come back in a while. Or somebody will. They've sent off for Bjoro, eh?" He patted her shoulder and went away.

She struggled over onto her other hip, out of a childish need to see what he'd brought next to her bed. There was a bottle of water standing on the table, cloudy, drifting shreds of lemon, and a shallow bowl with a wet bit of sponge, maybe meant for cooling her face. At the edge of the bed he had put an empty pot for peeing into, and papers for wiping. She had a sudden longing for an orange, and resented Leo for not thinking of it. With difficulty, she lifted on an elbow and drank two swallows from the water bottle, her mouth burning, the tepid water a brief ease. She closed her eyes, let her body settle heavily on the mat. I don't have time for lying in bed, she thought fretfully, but fell at once into the vague dissociation at the borders of sleep.

"Panja," her son said. She wrenched up suddenly and clung to him, helpless even to control her tears. "Oh. Oh. This damn plague," she cried irritably. For only a moment, she had thought he was a little boy whimpering feverish and she his mother, sitting up drowsing beside his bed. But then she knew who was sick, who sitting by the bed, and his calling to her out of childhood with that old babyish name, *panja,* seemed a vaguely dreadful sign. What did he think—that she was dying? "Will you get me an orange?" she asked him impatiently, and she stopped her tears with her fingertips jabbed against her burning eyelids.

He went away and came back. "Here. Kristina," he said, crouching beside her bed. He began to peel the orange in his hand, piling up the little saucers of rind on the edge of the table. The piece he fed her was a mass of tasteless pulp; she pushed it around with her tongue and swallowed stubbornly. Her mouth was coated and sore, she'd lost interest in food. When he held out another finger of fruit she grimaced and looked away.

He put his hand against her cheek and then her forehead. She was parched, fever-ridden. Beneath her skin, behind her eyes, a dry fire was burning, and his cool hand sliding across her face was intensely comforting. "Do you want me to bathe you?" He was patient and kind but detached, a manner he took on when he tended to the sick—his first wife Hlavka's chronic asthma had inured him to invalidism.

"Let me have some water to drink," she told him.

He held the water bottle while she swallowed. Her own fingers curled shakily around her son's hands. When she let her head back onto the bed again, she said, complaining weakly,

"Oh hell. I don't have any time for being sick just now."

"No," Bjoro said indifferently. He began to bathe her limbs with the wet piece of sponge, drawing an arm and then a foot out from under the bedsheet. Her skin was tender, crawling with feeling, the cool wash delicately painful. She watched her son's face. He was forty-seven, had a long sloping bony brow, wide and thin mouth, not her husband Aŭgustino's look nor her's, but a family homeliness that had been in her own mother's face and an uncle's. There was no little boy in that look anywhere, and since he had come home in the *Ruby* there had been a defeat, an unknowability, a core of anger, a miserable unhappiness. Her eyes began to tear slowly, watching him, and in the blur she received a gift, saw him a lanky child again, with pale hair sticking up straight along the crown of his head.

"I want to see that world," she said, breathing out harshly. This had been at the edge of her consciousness for days, a numinous whispering that unexpectedly, suddenly, became coherent. A shudder went along her skin like a loosening of clothes: Her body's understanding of something still inarticulate, something that transcended language. *I want to lie down on that earth and embrace it.*

Her son went on sponging her skin. "I have seen it," he said contemptuously. Her own feeling was nonrational, beyond arguing, but she said, clasping his wrist, "God's face!"

He looked at her in incomprehension. He was angry, anguished. "There's no God in that world, Kristina, I have seen it! I felt when I was standing between the ground and the sky in that world, I was nothing, unremembered. There was so much space, air, emptiness, distance, and no meaning in it, eh? Where was God? When I was in that world, what I saw was—" He threw her an urgent look, flourishing his hands, grappling with something. "I don't know! What did the mountains mean? What were their names?" His eyes filled with sudden tears. "There was a wind!" he said wildly, as if that explained everything.

Kristina became inexplicably tearful herself. She was surprised and ashamed when the words that were in her mouth turned and came out banal. "We can't know all the meanings of things," her mouth said, and the sound of her voice shamed her too, seeming only flat and stubborn.

Her son blinked impatiently. His tears fled onto his lashes and vanished. He looked away, beginning again slowly to push the sponge across her fevered skin. "There isn't any meaning at all, Kristina. There's chaos." His voice was low, murmuring, as happens when you know an argument has gone past the point of usefulness. Kristina's shame deepened. She hadn't felt they'd been arguing.

"We must just try to make our lives coherent," she said sorrowfully. "To go on gathering ourselves into the Light."

"What does that mean?" he said harshly. "What are you looking for, in this Light? God's face? What does that mean? That it's implacable? Beyond knowing? Yes! God's face, then!"

At times in her life she had felt she had an understanding of God—for a few inexplicably clear moments she had recognized the essential value, the equal wonder, of everything in the universe. She had understood, there was utterly no distinction, no separation, between the parasitic beetle, the anibird, Wolfgang Mozart, the evacuation of a bowel. But it was easier to let this understanding go than to confront the terrible weight that lay inside it. And it was something like that that made her loosen her grasp now, made her let go her desperate embrace of the New World and withdraw into the frailty and effortlessness of her illness. "Help me onto the toilet," she said pitiably. "I don't want to use this damn pot Leo put by the bed."

She wasn't able to remember when she had last stood naked before her son, and she clutched the bedsheet ineffectually while Bjoro supported her by the elbows. "How cheaply we take good health," she said through her teeth. Bjoro brought his arm around her, murmuring impatiently, "I've seen naked old women, panja."

She tightened her hands tremulously on the sheet—a medicine bundle against her breastbone. "Do you think old women don't have any dignity to keep?" she said wretchedly.

But swiftly afterward she lost the strength for modesty, became indifferent to such things, undignified. She lay naked with the sheet bunched under her when the fever broke a sweat; she gave up the effort of getting into the lavejo and took to using the pee pot beside her bed. She no longer cared if it was her daughter-in-law Juko, or her grandson Eneo, who sponged her naked limbs; if it was her daughter Olinda who helped her to squat and pee, or Olinda's husband Axel.

She dreamed and woke, dreamed and woke, in a brief shallow circling. Objects in the room slid away from the walls and down into her dreams, allusory, intangible, transient. Or she entered the walls and became permeable, imbued with light. She was a person who always had tried to interpret her dreams, but was too sick to redefine these—or they meant nothing, they simply were. In a sudden feverish insight, she accepted them for what they seemed—another domain of life, having equal weight with her waking life. *The face of God.* She thought she might die, and it was a relief to let go her old dread of dying in her sleep—it had been an arbitrary habit, she realized, assigning more reality to the waking world than to dreams.

When she began slowly to be convalescent, it was Bjoro's daughter Abigajlo who kept her company in the daylight hours. They played Go, or chess, and in the long afternoons Abigajlo read to her, with the librajo propped on her knees: poems and moral philosophy, religious mysticism and the metaphors of physics. Abigajlo was twenty. All of her life, she had seemed to absorb from the air the shape of things unseen—intimations, flashes, whispers, bodings—and from that seed ground had sprung a lively interest in spiritual matters that her parents never would share in. Hlavka's beliefs had been narrow, she had been grounded in a concrete reality, was strictly humanist: A soul was the fundamental force for good in human beings, only that. Bjoro, if he ever had been open to hidden things, had shut those doors one by one until now he stood behind a stolid disinterest. He regarded his daughter's beliefs with remoteness. For years, Abigajlo had been bringing her spiritual interests to Kristina, as she never could do with her parents: She had a passion for the unknowable shadowy edges of things, and Kristina was a religious woman.

They argued mildly about the principle of *ahimsa,* which

wasn't a tenet of Quakerism but of Hinduism, and practiced by
certain Jains and Taoists. Abigajlo was fierce in her belief that
all living things sought their own happiness, and people ought
to do what they could to keep from interfering with that.

"What is your practice when the happiness of mosquitos or
little black flies involves your blood?" Kristina asked her in
amusement. "What will you eat if you give up cutting lettuces,
whose happiness is to flower and go to seed?"

Abigajlo had thought these problems through, and only
grinned back: If people went on struggling toward an ideal that
was unattainable, then in the striving itself they might find
something unexpected, an insight.

Abigajlo also flatly believed natural objects, rocks and ponds,
sky, had souls, and Kristina put forward a problem: On the
Miller, what was natural? The river and the lakes were en-
gineered. Was there soul in a cloud called to life by machinery? But then both of them began to trade apocryphal stories
about self-conscious vehicles and malevolent generating plants.
"There is anima in any damn machine, eh? If you ask a mechanic."

Kristina made an effort to tell her grand-daughter some of
her dreaming, but the brief, evanescent images became ordinary
or absurd when she impounded them in language. "There was
something I understood . . ." she said, muddling to a stop. She
waved a hand vaguely, irritably. "It's gone again. . . ."

Abigajlo sat beside her bed chewing on a loaf of bread and
swallowing it down with tea. "When you're in my dreams,
we're always arguing," the girl said, as if she thought this might
help Kristina to find what she'd lost. Kristina croaked a helpless laugh. She liked their amiable, discursive quarrelling.

In the evenings it was Juko or Bjoro, one or the other, who
came and slept in the house. Kristina was thin and weak but
driven by urgency: She coerced each of them in their turn to
read to her from the pile of Minutes, and Advices and Queries,
and sheets from the modem and the exploratory balloons, while
she lay in bed with her burning eyes shut. They were always
tired, themselves. They stumbled over words, lost lines, fell
into confusion. Bjoro, when he was fed up with boggling the

words, would say, "Enough," and shove the papers from his lap, go off to bed. But Juko sometimes would sit with a finger on the page, frowning wearily through long baffled silences, until Kristina finally would open her eyes and see her sitting there, and murmur, "Go on to sleep, leave that, it's all right."

Juko was private, withdrawn, and Kristina let her be so, afraid of something that remained vague, a shadow that was in some way an umbra of the new world. While they ate together, or while Juko combed Kristina's hair or shook out her bedsheet, they went on as they ever had, in conversation and argument about food and work, sewing, people they both knew. They went on telling confidences, Juko complaining about her brother, and telling the little oppressive details, the resentments and sorrows of seeing her old father, Ŝilko, circling back to childishness; it had now come round to peeing his pants and mashing foods with his fingers. But she and Kristina avoided speaking Bjoro's name, both of them did, and Kristina understood this slight scission was a gulf—they were isolated from one another suddenly, their friendship of twenty years brought down as easily as that, as if it had been a bridge made of paper and string, negligible, irrelevant.

"Do you remember Daĉjo Otersen?" Kristina asked her suddenly while they were standing at the sink in the women's bathhouse. Kristina gripped the edge of the splash board shakily, steadying herself while Juko stood in front of her soaping and washing her face, working the washrag deliberately into the hollows at the hinges of her jaw, into the crevices of her ears, the creases of her eyelids and cheeks.

"He was Helena Hajnzel's son, he was one of them on the *May Snow,*" Juko said after a moment. This man Daĉjo Otersen and two more had been lost on the tugship *May Snow* when it went out ranging for rocks and never sailed home. "I didn't know him, much. I knew Liliana Olavo, better," Juko said, naming one of the others who were lost. "Liliana's sister married a cousin of my father's, that was how I knew her." Scrupulously, she began to rinse Kristina's face of soap.

"He was in a dream of mine, I think," Kristina said. She didn't know why this dream had reappeared to her just at this moment. Or why she had dreamed of Daĉjo Otersen, a man she knew only slightly.

"Daĉjo?"

"He was . . ." Kristina felt for the thread of the dream. "There was a red sky and he was a bird, I saw his feathers, and the beak, his eye was ringed in black—I don't know how I knew it was Daĉjo." In the dream, he had sat on the lofty cap of a light pole with wings folded, one black eye fixed upon her, and then flown into the sun, which had become visible in the ceiling behind him, beating his wings in a hard, slow rhythm the way a heron flies, or a swan, though she had known he was neither, was only himself, Daĉjo Otersen, flying, feathered.

Juko said without interest, "What was he doing?"

She was suddenly irritable. "Oh I don't know, it was a dream." And then, irrationally, tears sprang in her eyes. She put a trembling hand to her mouth, and Juko let one of her own hands down and looked at her, alarmed. "What? The dream?" Kristina wasn't able to answer, wasn't able to understand what the dreaming or the crying meant. When finally her throat opened and spilled out words, they weren't any she'd expected. "I always have wondered, do you have poor Vilef in your dreams?" she said sorrowfully. She was surprised, both of them were, by her breach of an old, unspoken agreement not to speak of this dead child.

"I don't dream!" Juko said fiercely, and began to wring out the washrag. Kristina was startled by the scrim of fear in her daughter-in-law's eyes, and felt herself flooded suddenly with self-reproach. What was in her mind, to bring up that poor dead baby after all these years?

Juko folded the washrag neatly, hung it from the faucet. She took Kristina's arm and walked her wobbly back to their apartment. A burning silence charged the air between them, and this quickly was a pain Kristina couldn't bear. When she was settled in the bed and had her breath back, she said unhappily, "Are we finished being daughter and mother to one another, then?" and Juko looked at her in astonishment.

"No! Where does that come from? Because I won't speak to you about my dead son?" Her face became very bright. "Because Bjoro and I aren't sleeping in the same bed?"

An inarticulate dread rose in Kristina. "That isn't anything to do with me," she said crossly, and turned her face away. In that moment, she understood: It wasn't the keeping of these secrets but the baring of them that she feared.

Juko made a small frustrated noise and put out the light, went to her own bed. After a while, into the darkness and silence she said flatly, "Once, I dreamed the air was water and he swam in it, smooth as a fish."

A gift of fever and sickness, a lost memory, rose up slowly in Kristina. "Some of the world is visible to us," she said, sighing, "but some of it can only be seen in our dreams."

Nine

ĈEJO

And these things I see suddenly, what mean they?
As if some miracle, some hand divine
*   unseal'd my eyes.*
Shadowy vast shapes smile through the air and sky,
And on the distant waves sail countless ships,
And anthems in new tongues I hear saluting me.

Olava Morgan's hands were thick, blunt-fingered, the nails etched with indigo blue as if she might have been dying yarn before she came to lay her hands on Humberto. "This is holding me," she said, sighing. It wasn't clear if she was speaking to Humberto or to Ĉejo. Ĉejo was watching her, sitting cross-footed beside his father, who was lying on his mat on the floor with Olava's large hands spread across his eyes. "Right here, the eyes, my hands are stuck here, the pull of the energy is so strong, maybe it would pull some skin off if I moved my hands. It feels like that."

Ĉejo said earnestly, "One of his eyes won't close."

He knew that Olava knew this. She had been in their house daily since Humberto had suffered his stroke. He didn't know why he felt compelled to tell her, *One of his eyes won't close.*

Olava said, nodding, "I can feel that. This eye, the right one, eh? I can feel the heat." She shifted her hands, drawing the thumbs under, bowing the knuckles. There were twenty hand positions in the rijki healing art; Ĉejo knew this from his grandmother, who had learned a little rijki therapy from Olava in the hope that it would ease Humberto's sleep. He had been sleeping badly since this stroke had paralyzed him, and often, late into the night, he lay muttering and beating his motive left hand against the floor. All of them had had to learn to sleep with the commotion—Leona's inexpert practice of rijki therapy never had brought him peace.

"I can feel the heat," Olava murmured again, her hands making a shape like two long narrow mounds of earth hoed up for planting pumpkins. She narrowed her eyes and shifted her weight on her knees. She was a big woman with a cap of gray curly hair, pointy front teeth. She had a sloppy way of dressing, sometimes wore crumbs of food at the corners of her mouth—her untidiness put Ĉejo off, and he and his grandmother had argued over this in the past. But Olava had been kura to his father's family for more than thirty years, and in the first days after the stroke she had tenderly cupped Humberto's pulse in her palms for hours at a time while they all waited to see if his brain would swell enough to kill him. She had been daily explaining things, relieving anxieties, serving as a sort of clerk at their family Meetings. What was a doctor's chief work, anyway, after inoculations and setting broken bones? It was helping people through difficult times, even through dying. Ĉejo had lately given up thinking that sloppiness was an obstacle in those matters.

"Well Humberto," Olava said quietly, "I missed your face, eh? At my sister's grand-daughter's wedding." She sat behind his head, her fingertips resting on his cheekbones, his mouth spread out just below the tips of her fingers. Ĉejo had become accustomed to his father's crooked grimace, the one corner pinched and the other loose, but now with Olava's big hands over his father's eyes the mouth drifted alone, isolate and unfamiliar.

"That singer, Signe Pilsen, do you know her? She came and sang for my niece, a gift, a wedding song. Some people say she has a voice but it's a loud screech, that's what it sounds like to me. All the time she was singing at my niece's wedding, I was thinking, that would be a good song if somebody else was singing it."

Ĉejo had expected Olava to meditate while she was laying hands on his father. His grandmother always would shut her eyes and fall silent when she tried rijki on her son; Ĉejo thought if you were conducting the body's *ĉi* from one person to another, you wouldn't want to be talking about weddings and singing. He said cautiously, "Are your hands feeling anything now? Is any healing going on?"

Olava opened her eyes, beginning to smile slowly. "There's always healing going on, eh? Healing and dying both." She shifted her hands, flattening and spreading the fingers. "Here, put your hands on now, lay them on mine," she said, wriggling her thumbs slightly. Ĉejo placed his own hands scrupulously over hers. "There's heat," she said, "and a pulling. Do you feel it? Right here over the bridge of the nose."

The backs of her hands were cool against Ĉejo's palms. He closed his eyes and waited to feel something. Olava began a wedding tune behind her lips. Her hands carried Ĉejo's hands slowly outward; their four hands began to hold Humberto's long face, his skull, tenderly between their palms. Olava went on humming quietly, not seeming to need to be focused on the touching, though Ĉejo went on trying to meditate, his eyes shut. As his hands became slowly heated, filled with a kind of charged weight, then finally he had to look, had to say, "Do you feel this, paĉjo?"

Olava's hands, moving outward, had let his father's eyes come out from under. His left eye was following Olava, his right eye looking up to the rafters, the floor of the sadaŭ. He stirred restlessly and said something inarticulate, a quick glib collection of meaningless syllables. He looked at Ĉejo and Olava urgently, jumping his left eye from one of them to the other. Ĉejo shook his head, scowling, turning the sounds over in his mind. His father's tongue was thick, intractable, but some few words were clear, and sometimes a garbled word could be understood. *Pe! Jos duble!* he may have said. Ĉejo didn't know what these particular sounds meant.

Olava moved her hands and Ĉejo's with methodical care, lifting them from Humberto's face, setting them down on his right shoulder. She said quietly, "Well I don't know that language you're speaking, eh Humberto? You'll teach it to me, I bet, if I keep paying attention. Through the skin, though, I know what you're saying: *Sure Olava, I feel that healing touch there, that heat, and I'm sorry I missed that wedding, that Signe Pilsen singing those songs in her screechy soprano voice,* but I don't know if you might be saying that, something like that, with your mouth. Or something else, eh? I don't speak that fey language yet." She smiled sorrowfully.

Cêjo's father, watching Olava's face, stirred again and sighed. He was drooling from the loose edge of his bottom lip, seeming not to know when saliva had accumulated in his mouth. Cêjo had a habit of wiping it away with the pad of his thumb, but his hands were occupied resting on Olava's hands, on his father's useless right arm, conducting the heat and power of his own body into his father's, so he let the little dribble run down into the crease of Humberto's chin. "Right here," he said to Olava, "I feel this pulling right here."

Olava nodded solemnly. "Yes. It's pretty warm, I feel it drawing pretty strong." She gave him a look. "You got a good touch. Your grandmother, she couldn't feel it, couldn't get her hands sensible to the energy. Humberto, we can show your son how you like to be touched, eh? He can lay hands on you, himself, after this." She brought her hands down over his father's abdomen, lifting her elbows out slowly, linking her fingers in a thick mat. "The spleen," she said, murmuring. "You know the spleen? This is how to touch it, how to find a balance by touching. You make a path between your body and Humberto's and let the *ĉi* flow along it."

The warmth of the soul's energy moving from his own body into his father's was palpable, compelling. He watched Olava's hands and followed them. She went on showing him how to touch his father in a healing way, the pancreas, the stomach, the liver, and then his father's hips and legs, his feet. Eventually Humberto's right eye rolled up and he shut his left eye and breathed noisily, sleeping, but Olava seemed not to notice this—she still sometimes talked to him in a low, soothing drawl, telling inconsequential gossip and news, or asking him something and then delivering the answer she said she could hear through his skin. Cêjo listened intently without understanding anything through his palms, only the inaudible whisper of heat and life.

"Well, you got to listen awhile," Olava said when he told her this. She nodded. "You'll get to hearing it. But your hands are good. You got a healer's hands, I think. Anybody can learn it, get some of it right, but certain people are just born to it, they got a certain spirit, a certain touch that's right for rijki." She held her own hands up and examined them with unselfconscious pleasure.

Cêjo made a pot of tea when the laying on of hands was finished, and he and Olava drank it, sitting beside Humberto as he slept, the two of them talking quietly about the rijki therapy, what had been accomplished—harmony for disharmony, quietude for worry, ease for strain; and the harvest, what was being brought in—corn and breadfruits, pumpkins, pejibayes.

They traded certain gossip about Heza Barfor. Olava knew Heza from the Fiber Arts Committee, and Heza's sister-in-law—the one she always was quarreling with—had been in Olava's care for a while. It hadn't been possible for people to keep the sister-in-law from dying, Olava said, but that woman had used the energy from her illness to heal her relationships with her relatives. This was something Cêjo had wondered about. During the dry season, Heza had moved back into her brother's household—helping her sister-in-law with the hard work of dying, people said.

Afterward, Cêjo had expected the old woman to go on living with her widowed brother. It was a surprise when she came promptly back to their apartment again. "My brother's grandchildren are rude and loud," she had said, as if this explained it sufficiently. Cêjo, repeating these things to Olava, added thoughtfully, "Living in our house, maybe she had got out of the habit of being patient with children." He felt very distanced from his own childhood.

Olava said mildly, "I thought Heza came back to live with your family because of her friendship with Leona, eh? now that Leona's son has decided to have a stroke, and this family needs comforting."

Ĉejo hadn't thought of his grandmother in this way—a friend, having a claim to someone's loyalty. And he hadn't considered that Heza might be a comfort to them.

Their household had become chaotic, prone to storms. Humberto, who always had been a mild and tolerant person, was an impatient, irascible paralytic. He cried out unfathomable demands, and fell into a fury when no one understood his needs. His clear words were all obscenities: "Fuck!" he would shout in the spasms of his defeat, his left arm hurling out in a wild frenzy, his left leg beating the floor in rage. "Shit! Hell! Piss-you!" In these storms, Ĉejo's cousin Alfhilda was prone to burst into tears, and Ĉejo, who could not bear the crying and the rageful cursing, would pace helplessly up and down the pasado while his grandmother and grandfather lashed out at one another or shouted back at their son in frustration and misery. Now Ĉejo searched around in his memory: Was it Heza, after all—going on unperturbed, making reply as if Humberto's meaningless sounds were speech—who always would restore the peace?

His father went on sleeping in the middle of the floor after Olava Morgan had finished her tea and gone home. Ĉejo slid back the wall of the apartment to listen for him if he woke, and sat on the loĝio in front of his loom. He laid down the narrow lines of brown tapa, and wider ones, quince yellow, the border of a woven rug, while he followed people's arguing and haranguing with each other, their whispering of scandal, without taking part in it himself. He had lately made up his mind that he was a person with a brooding disposition: He liked to practice sitting out on the loĝio, not joining in people's idle talk. He liked to work silently, watching other people in an abstracted way as if he didn't know who they were. When no one was saying anything that interested him, he turned over solemn thoughts in his mind—not the old, weighted questions to do with death and grief, but a thicket of slighter terrors, things to do with helplessness and whining.

Shortly, his father began hawking up sputum, and this became a kind of gagging. He was inclined to cough on his slobber—needed someone to lift his head and help him swallow his saliva. For a moment Ĉejo couldn't keep his hands from going on pushing down the beater of the loom, pressing the thread tight and even. Some neighbors' faces were registering alarm before he was able to make himself stand and go in. Bleakly, he helped his father's shoulders off the floor, waited for this spasm to be finished, wiped the spit with the edge of his hand, dried it on his trouser leg. His father's eye followed the movement, his right hand stirring vaguely. In a moment he murmured to Ĉejo, an unfathomable, insistent plea. Ĉejo looked away, sighing. He didn't know which eye he should be looking into, the fixed or the roving.

His father had to be helped to sit on the toilet—his body wouldn't support itself. He had to be propped against a repozo or turned from one side to the other every little while if he were lying on the floor; someone in his family had to spoon his food, sponge his sweating limbs, shave his cheeks, pull his shirt on over his head. And one or the other of their household had always to be showing in, overseeing, and turning out the stream of people who came to sit with him, bringing their extravagant reassurances and overly fervid prayers, their gossip and pointless jokes, believing this was help he needed as much as medicaments and therapy. Ĉejo thought bitterly that more of them could be helping to wipe his anus and his leaking mouth, to hold his head up when he choked.

"I'll get you up," he said in a bare whisper. "You need to pee. Here, sit, I'll get you up." Humberto helped him ineffectually, clubbing about with his left leg and arm. He could stiffen his left leg to hold his weight when he was upright, and he stood leaning into his son's body, breathing harshly. His penis had stiffened too—he was prone to useless erections since the stroke had brought him down in the corn field. Women had been teasing him for it. Even Ĉejo's grandmother was likely to laugh and say something lewd when she was helping him to urinate, or to bathe, but Ĉejo was ashamed of their shamelessness, and he pushed his father's thick penis down in the neck of the bottle silently. After a little pause Humberto got his stream of urine going and the two of them stood together thoughtfully watching the piss rising steaming in the glass. A little dribble spilled over the edge of the bottle onto Ĉejo's hand. "Paĉjo," he said on a long note, uselessly angry, and Humberto mimicked him, "Ahg," on a long note, guttural, meaningless.

"Do you want to come out to the loĝio?" he asked his father sorrowfully. "Watch people? I'm at the loom." Humberto made an inarticulate noise and twisted the left side of his face in a grimace—who knew what he understood? But he let Ĉejo bring him out of the apartment, clubbing along on one leg, and when he was seated, propped against a wicker repozo, his left eye watched people at their work, as they sorted seeds or straightened bits of old wiring, wrote notes for committee business, sharpened maĉetaj. People talked to him from time to time, but some of them spoke as they might have to a child or someone they barely knew.

An old woman, Pata Vilasenor, used his feet for winding her yarn while she told him a long, complicated story about an argument she had had with someone on the Metals Committee, a disagreement over the design of a thermocouple. Ĉejo sat at the loom and went on silently with his rug-making while Pata went on talking. Humberto's eye wandered away from the woman; he began to watch Ĉejo throwing the shuttle, bringing down the beater in a hypnotic rhythm.

Ĉejo's grandmother and his cousin Alfhilda came up onto the loĝio. Alfhilda squatted beside Humberto and studied her feet while Leona stood over her disabled son and her grandchildren and briefly unburdened herself to Pata Vilasenor. She had taken Alfhilda over to Kantado ŝiro because some people thought there was a boy living over there who might make a match for Alfhilda, but that boy would grow up stupid, Leona was saying. He had a mother who was loud and arrogant, bragging of things her son knew—what could be more stupid than that? Ĉejo looked at Alfhilda and she shrugged her thin shoulders, disinterested. They would be at this business for another ten or fifteen years; Ĉejo's own marriage hadn't yet been settled on, and he was years older than Alfhilda.

The old woman, Pata, at once began to tell tedious stories of marriages she had arranged in her own family, and Ĉejo's grandmother fell silent, nodding politely as she lifted her feet one after the other and fingered crumbs of dirt from her sandals.

Some people were in the kitchenhouse boiling tikisko, and maybe it was the smell of their cooking that began to make Humberto's mouth run with water; while Pata went on talking tiresomely to Leona, Alfhilda wiped his drool with the edge of her hand, wiped it again, and cleaned her hand on the hem of her shirt. Finally she stood and leaned into Leona, speaking to her in a whisper Cejo wasn't able to hear, then she squatted beside her uncle again, stroking his hand soothingly as Humberto began to shift his weight more and more restlessly and mutter secret words. When finally old Pata took her yarn from his feet, patted his ankle kindly and wandered away, Leona sighed. "That woman talks too much," she said quietly. "And her daughter is the same way. I wonder how they can keep from starving—they don't want to stop talking long enough to chew their food."

Alfhilda said, wiping Humberto's lip again, "Doesn't she know it's time for people to eat their supper?"

Cejo helped her to lift his father by the arms and bring him to sit inside the house. It was sweltry in the evenings at this season of the year, and other households ate their evening meal on the logio, or they slid open the pasado walls of their apartments to let the slight, cooling draft blow through, but the loose right corner of Humberto's mouth made his eating a strenuous, sloppy ordeal, and Cejo thought it was a humiliation for his father if they spooned his food into his open mouth while people who were not his family members watched them do it. He had pushed his family into a habit of shutting the walls of their apartment, eating in isolation, in the hot, dusky rooms. Now they fed Humberto slowly from their own plates, sweet mangoes and boiled cassava root, and wiped the dribble from his chin, while Cejo's grandmother and his cousin argued about Pata Vilasenor—whether it would have been rude to tell her she was talking too long, and that Humberto was needing to be fed.

Heza Barfor came into the house with cotton-silk seeds tied up in a manta, and she sat down without speaking and began methodically to pull the floss out of the seed pods. She seemed not to notice that the other members of her household were eating. It was Ĉejo's grandmother who had boiled the root of the cassava and beaten it to a pulp the day before, and she said in a hurt tone, "Don't you want to eat? Can't you wait to do that another time?" as if Heza's failure to eat the cassava were a personal affront to her.

Heza looked up in surprise. "There's that big old ceiba tree that stands over there between Alaŭdo and Esperplena. People have been gathering in the seeds as they fall." She had no eyebrows, only a few wiry sprigs of hair above the inside points of each eye to suggest where her brows should be, and she lifted these in a questioning way, as if she were asking something: *Is this a sufficient answer?* She never would answer a question herself in a straightforward way. Ĉejo's grandmother looked away plaintively. In a moment, though, she brought up with Heza this matter of Pata Vilasenor talking too much, and Heza took Leona's part in it, coming down on the side of politeness. After that, the two of them began to trade stories about Pata's family, old anecdotes and hearsay going back to women who had been old when Heza and Leona were children. Ĉejo stopped listening. He wandered off into a daydream about Katrin Amundsen, following her into the musky shadows of the corn field, lifting her shirt, putting his mouth upon one of her nipples.

"Did Olava Morgan come and show your grandson how to lay hands on your son?"

Ĉejo's penis was searching inside his trousers, and he looked between his grandmother and her friend in a flurry of self-conscious confusion, but it was his grandfather, standing there, who had asked this question of his wife. Old Petro had been sick with the plague and stalled in a long convalescence, imagining himself not yet well, but well enough to complain: This restless night-time thumping of his son's was keeping him from sleep. He'd been living in his brother's apartment to escape it, or to escape his wife's pitiless good health, but every little while he shuffled home to proclaim his lingering illness.

Ĉejo's grandmother was helping Heza with the cotton silk and both of them were fixed on this work, their hands stripping the floss from the seeds. She said, looking toward Ĉejo,

"I forgot to ask. Did she come? Did she say you've got the hands for it, Ĉejo? You know, mine are worthless, I told her that, I told her she'd have to give this work to my grandson, he always has had a thin skin, I told her, for letting invisible things come in."

Heza turned her head, peering at Humberto anxiously as if it might be possible to see Olava's work in his face. "Did she get this eye to close, yet?" she said. She put her work down and touched the tip of one finger to Humberto's eyelid. When she pushed it down gently, it rose open again slowly, and his crooked mouth released a clicking sort of sound—anger, or a sour laugh. He flopped his left arm vaguely. "Ga!" he said with bitterness. "Ga!" Maybe he was offended by Heza Barfor's finger pushing down his eyelid, or he might have been frustrated with Olava's rijki therapy. It was impossible to know. Maybe he just wanted to go on being fed. Heza murmured, "Oh, that's to be expected," as if the two of them were carrying on a lucid conversation.

It was Heza's belief that he understood all of them as well as he ever had, and she had half-persuaded Alfhilda of it: Sometimes Alfhilda tried to go on sharing with her uncle the parts of her life she had always shared with him. Now she leaned toward him, whispering beside his neck. "There is this pea sort-of vine we've found on the northern continent, it fixes nitrogen in the soil so this other plant, something like a draba mustard, will grow with it, and the draba gives off a smell and keeps this certain fungus away from the peas. Anejlisa said it was a perfect little arrangement. *Elegant,* she said." She bared her teeth for him in a shining grin.

The left side of Humberto's mouth shuddered with the effort to speak. His eye strained in its socket, demanding something of her. Alfhilda was always in fear of her uncle's angry eruptions, and she cast a quick pleading look toward Ĉejo. Why was she looking to him for a remedy? He felt overburdened, oppressed, and shrugged his shoulders impatiently.

His father's mouth went on working, while Alfhilda stroked his hand and whispered urgently about edible seaweeds, and bacteria that might protect plants from dying back in a mild frost. Ĉejo, against his will, began to feel Alfhilda's anxiety. Perhaps Heza felt it too. She suddenly quit her hand work, cleaning the cotton silk, and held out to Humberto a long sliver of mango pinched between her thumb and forefinger. "Here, it's sweet, a mango, do you want it?" Humberto's lips twisted, retreating from the offer, but the wildness abruptly went out of his face. He sighed and gazed off into the middle distance. Alfhilda, sighing too, lapsed into silence.

Ĉejo's grandmother opened the pasado walls of their apartment as soon as they were finished with eating, and then it was possible to hear families noisily washing their dishes, children getting into trouble, old people arguing with their older parents, chickens fighting and posturing. On the loĝio of the house there was to be a Weekly Meeting for Business, and some people began to go out there and sit down. Ĉejo fled quickly onto the loĝio himself, escaping his family, escaping care of his father, and distancing himself from his family's usual place at Meeting by sitting with Udo Blades and his family along the wall of the kitchen. Udo moved over to make room for him, but they were both silent. He and Udo had grown up together, yet the easy alliance of their childhood never had become friendship—Udo always had been inclined toward superstitious fears and aversions, and Vilef always had been at Ĉejo's right hand, a totem of horror.

As small children were sent off to play in neighbors' houses, gradually the quiet that people practice before a Meeting began to rise up and wash over other noise. The seventeen adults of the house were beginning to prepare themselves for thinking about business. They were studying the boards of the floor, or searching for peace behind their closed eyelids. Ĉejo mournfully watched his grandmother and his grandfather let their son's clumsy weight down to the floor at the family's usual place in front of the bathhouse wall.

"Any announcements?" Luizo Medina said, and people who had been meditating lifted their heads and looked around. Luizo was clerk of the Weekly Business Meeting, a short old man with a poorly repaired hare-lip and a lispy voice, proficient at keeping to an agenda and getting through a Meeting in a

timely fashion. There were a few things announced: a woman
giving a public reading of her poems; a change of venue for
Waters Committee Meeting; odd jobs needing doing; things
available for trade. Then Luizo opened the Meeting by formally
listing all the pending business matters, and he reminded people not to wander too far off from the agenda. No one had to
follow the order of his list; an agenda only defined limits. It was
common, in fact, for a single question to rise up, and speaking
begin to focus on it. Then other matters would go undecided,
held over for another Meeting or put in the hands of a small
committee. Not many things, after all, concerned everyone.

On Luizo's agenda was a long report to do with the New
World's zonal soils, and Celia Fuĝinaka read this aloud, not
every word of it but the gist. Some of it people already knew:
There were great tracts of lifeless sands and gravels, moraines
and glacial outwash and the abandoned diluvium of transient
lakes—a dead and stony lithosol—and vast ice-scoured and
stream-eroded slopes with immature soil profiles. There was
mature soil under the grasslands and in the shallow valleys, but
typically the A horizon was thin and gray, leached of iron and
aluminum, with the minerals deposited in a dense hardpan in
the illuviated B horizon. Short summers and low temperatures
and the soil's sharp acidity discouraged the biological process:
The layer of humus was a discrete and undecayed litter of stems
and twigs, leaves, petals of flowers, the mummified remains of
insects and small rodents. The Geological Arts and Sciences
Committee had been saying that if people tilled the grasslands
soil it would quickly lose its scant organic content and the loose
silt would blow off on the wind. It was this committee which
had been sending down to Farms Committees a steady procession of Queries to do with cultivation. The Alaŭdo Farms
Committee, Ĉejo knew, had been sending back a steady string
of Advices, ranging from digging-sticks and peat-drills to very
ancient, cautiously provident strategies of slash-and-burn.

But now the people studying soils had got through looking
at all the new information from the balloon surveys and they
wanted people to know: There were intrazonal soils in the de-
pressions of glaciated plains, in bogs and marshes underlain by

thermal basins. The heat and dampness in those places encour-
aged decay, and so the soil in the wetlands was enriched with
the remains of grasses, sedges, rotting marsh plants. Where the
C horizon was clay or loam, the soil scientists thought the valleys could be drained and made tillable. They had sent a Query
to both the Designs Committee and the Waters Committee,
asking those people to look at feasible plans for drainage fields.

A few times people interrupted Celia to ask questions or
make comments. Had the Ceramics Committee been brought
into this planning? someone wanted to know. After all, what
was a drain tile but a big piece of pottery? Someone else said,
well, there were other ways of draining a field, metal pipes and
tubes—wouldn't it make sense to just adapt and relocate the
systems that were already in place on the *Dusty Miller*? Had
the engineers thought of that? And inevitably, two or three
confused people wanted to talk about the difficulties of living
above a marshland—would houses be prone to sinking? would
people be able to walk across the ground without fear of falling
down a mud hole? But this was a report, not a Query, so Luizo
tried to keep everyone from too much turning aside.

When Ulfo Amsfred began his habitual stump speech—
"We'll have a much harder time down there, no matter if this
drainage works. There'll be more deaths, we'll have to work
harder, life will be more dangerous—" Luizo made use of it to
shift the talk away from soil, bringing up a question sent over
to them from Monthly Meeting, this matter of whether they
ought to give up trying to make the New World amenable—
whether they ought to build a biosphere flat on the ground
there.

"They want to know what we think, in general. And then the
questions that would have to be addressed if we began to plan
seriously to do this." He said *"theriouthly,"* pushing the tip of
his tongue against the cleft in his upper lip.

Knuto Mursawa's words—*We live in this world as in the
body of God*—had long since gone clear around the ŝiro—all
the ŝiroj. People were ready to speak to the question. If this had
been a Meeting for Worship they might have waited, might
have expected a reasonable silence to give weight to their words,

but old Karla Asida stood quickly and said with fierce heat, "This work we've already done, all this research and planning on how to live on the New World, I suppose that's all wasted, then, if we build a roof and live under it, eh?" She looked around at them resentfully, as if the research and the planning were all work she had personally accomplished, and the idea of a biosphere was a personal affront to her efforts.

Ĉejo didn't know what he felt about the biosphere plan, but he saw other people giving back Karla's look without speaking. No one thought she was raising an important issue. At the edge of his mind, Ĉejo began to repeat, *theriouthly addrethed theriouthly addrethed,* his tongue following his brain, pushing against the front of his teeth in a reflex of silence that mimicked Luizo's delicate lisp.

Hugo Lagrimas stood and said, "It's one thing to keep a closed system like the *Miller* running along without too much trouble, but building one is another thing, eh? We've got a smithy that makes steel for needles and knives, and they turn out a new light pole now and then, little machine parts, tools and whatnot. We haven't got the know-how, haven't got the raw goods or the machinery—have we?—to build a thing like this"—he gestured broadly with his two hands, a motion that took in the whole of the *Miller*'s metalline sky—"this big and difficult."

Ruben Bera, old Pata Vilasenor's son, had arthritis in his hips—people didn't expect him to trouble his body to stand up. From where he sat on the floor of the loĝio, he said, "They're thinking that we could dismantle the *Miller* and move it piecemeal down to the ground, that's what I heard."

Luizo said, "Is that right?" and looked at Laŭdia Ortega. Laŭdia's brother was a design scientist, an engineer. None of the people living in this domaro were scientists; for that kind of wisdom and apprising, they had to ask people in other houses, other family members and neighbors.

Laŭdia said, nodding, "Not a part-for-part rebuilding, but reusing the materials, anyway, the joists and sheathing, in a new architecture."

Someone murmured irritably, "Well, they ought to have said

so in the first place. What kind of a Query is it that doesn't lay out the circumstances of things?" Someone else answered this, but the only part of it that Ĉejo heard was the naming of Isaba Aguto, clerk of the Alaŭdo Monthly Meeting.

Their own experience was with small projects of farming and transport, small constructions of plumbing and electronics—they didn't have the knowledge for arguing—but they started blindly down the path, raising questions of engineering and technology, general difficulties they imagined might come from dismantling the *Miller* and reassembling it on the New World. Would people go on living inside the *Miller* in the early part of this project? What would be the living conditions for people working down there on the New World, building the new place? There would be excess heat, surely, from the taking apart of the toroid—how were the engineers thinking this heat would be discharged? Maybe a land-bound biosphere wouldn't need an absolutely closed system; maybe it would benefit from an exchange of air, of water, with the New World's own envelope? There must be particular tools and machinery needed for taking this big structure apart; would they first need to devise, build, test, perfect, the very means themselves?

Luizo spoke every little while, keeping people from too much arguing, keeping them from following a question too far. "All we're about, is to flag the stones in this field," he kept saying.

Eventually, Pata Vilasenor stood alongside her son and said, "What is the point of taking the *Miller* apart and rebuilding it down there? If we're going to go on living under a roof, shouldn't we just go on living right here? I think it's crazy, this scheme. And going down to live on the New World, that's crazy too. If the Maintenance Committee thinks this torus will last another fifty years or one hundred, then maybe we should let our grandchildren be the ones to worry about finding a new place to live. If we're going to go on living under a roof, we ought to just stay right where we are, is what I think, where old people with tired hearts can move up on the altejo, eh? and go on living easily. And people with arthritis can go on without the weight getting into their bones."

Maybe Ruben was sorry to have his mother bringing up his unlucky health in this sideways manner. His face became bright; he looked intently into the palms of his hands. His mother went on without seeing this, saying, "If we go down there—under a roof or not—many of us will die, it'll be a hard life, like Ulfo always is harping on. On that New World, I think Ulfo is not far off, I think we'll have a hard time of it." She looked around at her neighbors doggedly. "I don't see why we need to come out in the sunlight. We're doing pretty well, after all. It's like Knuto Mursawa said: This place is an Eden, it's the body of God. Only he didn't take it far enough. We ought to just stay right here, inside God's body, that's what I think."

Pata's leading turned them in a new direction. Instead of going on arguing about steel manufacture and know-how, Irma Lindberg slowly stood and gave them her own reasons for wanting to abide in the old *Dusty Miller,* a complicated argument to do with people on this world having to be mindful of every detail of their living environment, their souls and minds put to work always in keeping the whole world from collapsing, every act an act of conscious worship—for what else was it but worship, eh? loving and protecting this soil, these trees, these animals, against the void of space. Irma thought their ceaseless life-giving work made them completely and fruitfully human. On the *Miller,* she said, there were certain human potentialities that hadn't been in reach of people on the Earth.

This seemed both mad and rational to Ĉejo—irresistibly appealing. A quietness settled into all of them. Maybe other people, like Ĉejo, were waiting for sense or understanding to come out of the two women's speaking.

When Humberto made a small noise, a meaningless sound, Ĉejo's family ignored this distraction as if it had nothing to do with them. His grandmother's eyes were shut, her mouth in a pucker of concentration. She had a longstanding fear of leaving the *Miller,* and a longstanding resolve to live long enough to accomplish it. Ĉejo wondered: Did she think this planet-bound biosphere stood at the intersection? Ĉejo's grandfather, old Petro, sat beside his wife, his hands clasped behind his neck and his elbows pointing downward; he stared along them as if he sighted down an azimuth to the floor. A morbid torpor was in his face. Probably he wasn't thinking about people's leadings but yielding to his recent habit: sighting down the short end of his life. Alfhilda's face was creased and intent. When she saw Ĉejo looking toward her, she rolled her lower lip down thoughtfully, displaying a pink gum.

Sesilo Hurtado got slowly to his feet. Sesilo was married to Alfhilda's mother's sister. He was known for a certain stew he liked to make, of sweet potatoes and eggplant, tomatoes, summer squash, ground peanuts, and seasoned with ginger, garlic, coriander. In Ĉejo's family, this stew was moderately famous. "Where there's a hardship," he said, "generally there's a grace to be found in it," and people nodded, as if Sesilo had said something they all understood to be true. "On that world, eh? it's all hardship, and I wonder: What is the saving grace?" He looked around at his neighbors before offering them his own considered answer: Maybe that marginal landscape would force them all to economy, frugality, where a rich world might make them prodigal. There were old, historical understandings, available to anybody who would read the old books: Humans tended to be destructive exactly in proportion to their belief in abundance. It was people of meager lands who had gone on longest, on the Earth, holding to an economy of sharing and of thrift. "Maybe it's in a bare-bones existence that we'd be enriched," Sesilo said. "Maybe the hardships would be a good thing."

After Sesilo had spoken, Pia Putala stood and said that hardship was the sort of thing people liked to romanticize and think about endlessly, but there were plenty of hardships everywhere. "We don't need to go down to the New World to find hardship," she told them, indicating their own world with her hand.

Someone else said, Sesilo's argument about the destructiveness of humans might be a reason for them to keep to themselves, up here in the *Miller*. If people carried the possibility of apocalypse inside them, shouldn't they seclude themselves behind barriers?

People had finally come around to what the question was, and they went on speaking to it without the clerk needing to keep them to a center path. "The New World, it's forbidding of people—all that cold and the long days, the stony soil. This place, the *Miller,* at least it's made for people, eh? as the New World was not." "This world we've made in the *Miller,* it's simpler by orders of magnitude than any natural world—we can keep it going ourselves, it's not confusing to us." "We've got a life and death reliance on each other, right here, eh? It's our hardships binds us together."

Until recently, Ĉejo had had a habit of not listening to much that was discussed at a Meeting for Business—it was always tiresomely repetitious. People always were bringing up questions of sanitation and repair, arguing whether a diseased tree ought to be cut down, and what should be planted in the vacated space. He would often drowse dully, or wander in daydream. When there was a matter that concerned him, he fidgeted restlessly, waiting for it through tedious negligible discussions. But these days, everything circled endlessly around the New World. There were always Advices and Queries from Monthly Meeting, and matters people felt had been overlooked by Quarterly or Yearly Planning Committees. Lately, Ĉejo kept his attention scrupulously focused, and cast around in his mind for an opinion on every question. When the issues had to do with farming, sometimes his mouth opened and words came out—this, he had lately realized, was what people meant by The Inner Voice.

He didn't have an impulse to speak on this matter of how to live well and where to do it, but he wanted to hear every word spoken, and Humberto went on restless and noisy, shifting and banging his left leg, his left hand, and muttering meaningless phrases. Ĉejo became restless himself. He and Alfhilda exchanged glances. If he gave up sitting with Udo Blades and went over there where his father was, nothing would be accomplished by it—he didn't have a gift for quieting his father's noisy outbreaks—but he suffered from dim guilt, as if it was in his power to put an end to the distraction. He wanted someone who was already sitting over there, his grandmother or Heza or Alfhilda, even old Petro, to bring his father inside the house, so people could go on with the Meeting without this noisy commotion. In the same long braid with guilt was something like embarrassment, and aggravation.

For a while his family went on ignoring Humberto, but finally Heza began to whisper to him and then to Leona, and finally, when no one was speaking and Humberto's steady muttering was filling up everybody's silence, Ĉejo's grandmother stood up to pull at her son's arms. Heza helped her, and they got him standing. But then Leona looked out at people and said, pushing her lower teeth forward, "My son, Humberto, wants to speak to this Meeting."

People turned their heads in surprise. Ĉejo's father was braced on his left leg, his right leg trailing heavily useless, the fingers of his right hand curled like a flower against his thigh, and the two old women were standing there steadying him in their arms. His mouth was loose at the right corner, the shine of spit on his chin. His long eyes were unpaired, the one moving restlessly and the other staring, a vitreous bubble in a sagging fold of eyelid—maybe that eye was sightless. His mother kept his hair untangled and clean, but he never would sit quietly for it to be cut; it hung in a ragged curtain over his brows, caught in his eyelashes. His look was ferocious, pitiful.

His mouth shaped two words with agonizing care, two meaningless sounds, something like, *Forbar! Ardo!* Some people looked at him gravely and some other people looked away. Ĉejo studied his own hands, the line of black under a thumbnail—a horizon of soil. There was a long, following silence. Silence was a language people understood, and an expectancy and patience began to find its center in the stillness. Ĉejo went on looking at his hands, but then, irresistibly, he looked at his father. Humberto's working eye was moving among the faces of his neighbors, focused on someone, and then someone else, and someone else. When the eye came around finally to him, Ĉejo was surprised by it. His father's look behind the scrim of his uncut bangs was tender and reasonable, entering into the silence.

He felt suddenly at the edge of something—an abyss, or a continent.

Humberto grappled again with his tongue, and his urgent

whisper when it came out was meaningless and unknowable, but the feeling in it overleaped consciousness, passed into Cêjo's brain as a vivid, feverish intuition. He thought, *What is a human being for?* imagining this, or something equally solemn, something that reverberated through all the nights and days of their lives, must be what his father was asking them all. In the silence afterward, while people were considering Humberto's impenetrable question, Leona took a better hold of her son and closed her eyes. Heza, on his other side, fixed her look somewhere indefinite, somewhere in the center of the stillness.

Cêjo understood that something had come onto the logîo with Humberto's painfully achieved words, his unknown syllables, and that people were waiting to see what it was. And when his father began again, pressing on them his mysterious, necessary truths in hidden phrases, fluent silences, then the thing all of them were waiting for seemed to enter into his voice, where it became familiar, became allusive, and Cêjo wondered how he had ever thought there was but a single pronunciation in the sound of a word. He thought Humberto was speaking to them in his own language or theirs, in the bones of their ears or in their blood, his words a sigh.

Are we thinking we've created something? he was saying. *Are we thinking, because we've put ourselves and some other creatures inside a container, that this container we've made is Eden? There's only one Creation, eh? and we're among its members. What is this torus except a smaller circle within a larger one? Are we thinking we can go on living forever inside the little circle of each other's arms, without returning? without joining ourselves to the cosmos? without letting our arms open to touch the arms of the rest of Creation? What is this torus except a solitude? There isn't any meaning in anything except in its relations with other things—what is the anther of a flower except in its relations with the bee, eh? And what is the meaning of people who have uprooted themselves from ancient soil and are trying to go on living in a container of air and water, separate from the rest of the Creation? What is that meaning except a skeleton of bones from which the soul has escaped?*

There was a charged silence, a resonating peace, in which all of them were enclosed: the completeness and consciousness and life of the Meeting. At last someone murmured, or the air stirred in a coherent way, and Humberto's afflicted body moved slightly finding a new balance against his mother's breast. His tongue touched his lips silently as if it might be feeling around inside his mouth for more to say. Finally he sighed, and Heza and Leona stirred in the wake of that breath, letting his clumsy weight down on the floor and then sitting themselves, sighing too.

People waited in a long silence. Eventually, Udo Blades's mother stood. Her lips were moving in a whisper before she had quite got all the way to her feet, as if she spoke out from the middle of something: "... we're in the care of Wisdom beyond our knowing. Are we thinking we are God, then? What is God doing, freed of the obligation to order the waters and the skies?" She looked around at people thoughtfully. "I wonder, what is our ambition, in building this roof? Is this an issue of our trying to manage things? Do we think we've got control of everything here, because this place is small and simple and we're in charge of it? It's so obvious we're in control, I guess we may have forgotten we're not in control. And I wonder if those people on the Earth, because it was so clear they weren't in control, forgot that they were."

Cêjo had lost her leading, by the end, wasn't certain if she had finally argued for or against their going on living in the *Dusty Miller.* Was she saying the *Miller* was a living organism? or a dead mechanical object they were laboriously keeping alive themselves? When he looked out through the open logîo of his house, across the crowns of the breadfruit trees to the incongruously huge architecture of the Alaŭdo spoke holding up the roof of the sky, his confusion was charged with agitation, excitement: In the uncertainty itself, there seemed an indefinable meaning.

He was surprised when his own body stood up—surprised by the words coming out of his mouth: "If we make a container and put things inside it—what is left out? Are we thinking those things aren't valuable?" He quickly sat again, his shuddering knees unwilling to hold him.

Verner Bjornson, whose mother was a cousin of Ĉejo's mother, later stood and said, "People weren't built in God's image, eh?" He sat again and then looked around for agreement, but Luizo, also looking around, said that people didn't understand what Verner meant, and prompted him to get up a second time and explain himself. "Well, it's this business of the ŝimanas," Verner said, standing again. "We're living in a mechanical thing, eh? and we got to work hard to keep it from coming to ruin. People can't be expected to carry such a burden, can they?—knowing it's our human intervention prevents the whole world from collapsing. We weren't meant to be god-like in this particular sense, were we? I wonder if maybe that's the cause of so many people going insane—the ŝimanas, eh?" He filled his cheeks with air and rolled the little balloons around thoughtfully. He was small, with bulging eyes, and this grimace turned him to a toad. If he hadn't been saying something weighty, somebody would have teased him for making himself so ugly. When he let the air out of his face, Verner said, "People suffer from this knowledge," looking around as if this was intended to clear up any last little confusion about his meaning. Then he sat down beside his wife.

Immediately Sven Fuĵino stood and said, "It's true, there's no escaping the possibility of apocalypse—people just carry that possibility inside them. But nothing in life is certain, eh? Nothing but the circling round of things." And he brought up an old Quaker tenet, a belief in the progressive revelation of God's will through the ages. In order to discover new truths, they must look, each time around, for ways to widen the circle. "New paths around old habits," someone else said, and Sven nodded.

Between long silences, other people spoke: "This New World is how God created it. What are we thinking? that God's work needs remaking?" "We ought to be listening to this New World instead of asking it so many questions." "We ought to be asking whether there's a place for us there, and what it is." "If we want to live there, it ought to be on the old terms, eh? as the old Quakers lived, joining our hands to the world God made."

Gradually, people began to return to Sesilo Hurtado's lead-ing—that the marginality of the world might be a saving grace—and they followed that leading toward adaptive strate-gies, ways to live lightly on a fragile land. This time around, no one brought up drainage fields or tillage.

Cejo went on listening to people talk, but without looking at their faces. Once, he looked at his father. His eye was shut, his head bearing off loosely sideward as if he had been released, finally, from the burden of its weight. Cejo had a sudden, excruciatingly vivid recollection of his brother Vilef's heavy round skull balanced and swaying, a hibiscus blossom on a spindly stem.

It seemed to him that on the day of Vilef's birth his family had been set afloat above an abyss and had been straining ever since to make out what lay in the darkness below. Now in a flash of apprehension he realized he had never had Udo Blades's friendship and so never had lost it. And he understood, all at once, that his brother hadn't changed his life, only shaped it.

On this little eddy, drifting, he lost the stream of people's talk. Was it Heza's old voice that he heard finally? a few words, floating, transcendent in their meaning. *God's world,* she said. *Here we are, re-entering God's world.*

Ten

JUKO

Dazzling and tremendous how quick the sun-rise
     would kill me,
If I could not now and always send sun-rise
     out of me.
We also ascend dazzling and tremendous as the sun,
We found our own O my soul in the calm and cool
     of the daybreak.

Juko and her neighbor, Filisa Ilmen, helped Kristina from the tub when the old woman complained that the water was too hot, that her thin old skin was letting the heat through to her bones, but then both of the younger women got back in the water—Kristina hadn't yet become so old that she wasn't able to put on her own clothes, she told them.

While they went on talking about the man over in Mandala who was a hoarder, Juko watched her mother-in-law stooping over her pants, putting her clean knobby feet in the leg openings, shakily pulling up the trousers around her hips. Kristina's solidity, her sturdiness, was still in the bones of her broad face and hands, the wiry patch of her pubic hair, the splay of her feet, but she had seemed to shrink in the last years until now her skin was a loose fit, slumping in little shirrs at her breasts and elbows, buttocks and knees. And after the plague had finished with them all, the old woman never had recovered her whole strength. She had always been thin but after the plague her collarbones stood out from her neck in long delicate arches as if

they might be the scaffolding of wings, and there was fragility
in the sprung bones of her shoulders and hips, in the tender dark
cups of her inner thighs as she stood bowlegged getting her
pants on. Now her hands rattled the paper as she lofted lines
on a drafting board. Other people had to thread the needle
when she took up a piece of sewing. She was prone to fall asleep
at unexpected times—talking, sitting over a bowl of unshelled
beans or a lapful of reading—her chin dropping irresistibly
down to her breastbone and her eyes sliding in a secret search
behind the closed lids.

At such times, watching the spittle gathering at the edges of
the old woman's mouth and her uncombed hair trembling with
her breath, Juko would fall into an impatient, resentful melancholy. Her own mother had died at forty-seven, a bacterial in-
fection of her lungs; her father's mother had died in her sleep
at fifty-three; her mother's mother, bleeding out from a torn
uterus, hadn't survived her own youngest child's christening.
Humberto's mother, Leona, was as absolutely lost to her as if
she had died with her grandson, Vilef. Juko had thought, in
marrying Bjoro she had acquired a mother who was proof
against that lineage of early death. She had imagined Kristina
still standing flat-footed and erect at ninety, brandishing a cane,
going on stubbornly well. Her failing health was an unexpected
defeat, an offense, but who should be blamed for it?

"When she sweeps up the dust from the floor of her house,
her husband gathers it into bowls and keeps it," Filisa said in-
sultingly, and this made Kristina curl back her long upper lip.

"Maybe he thinks he'll get enough dirt to grow carrots in."

With little enough to share, it was their practice to share
everything, and this man Rajdaro Furbo was widely known,
defined by his selfishness. He stored corn in baskets in his
apartment. He was contemptuously tolerated, his family
pitied—gossip and scorn were the chief line of enforcement in
their lives.

"Does he think he's living alone?" Filisa gestured with her
thumb. "Does he think, if his children are fat, his family is living well?"

Kristina was sliding her feet shakily into her sandals, looking down to find the toe loop, frowning. "I don't blame him for it; he's crazy," she said. "Only I blame his wife, what's her name, you say? Helena?"

Juko let out a small scoffing breath through her lips, *Puh.* "For what? For sweeping her house?"

Kristina was shuffling off, sounding the tile floor with her sandals, and she waved a hand irritably without looking back.

Filisa knew this miser's wife, Helena, from having served with her on the Pacema Sewage Committee, but she seemed to take Kristina's point of view without a qualm. She said, nodding, casting her answer toward Kristina, "Maybe she ought to bring those hoarded things out and give them to other people, eh? And if that old shithole gets mad, she can divorce him."

In a flurry of dim exasperation and bewilderment, Juko thought of saying, *A wife can't be held accountable for her husband's corn, any more than his sins.* But she was following Kristina with her eyes, the old woman already through the doorway and her bent shadow moving across the openwork of the pasado wall, and in a moment she only said bleakly, "Maybe she doesn't want a divorce."

Filisa turned her head toward Juko, a canny look. "Well, maybe not," she siad, as if these were weighty words, a pronouncement. Juko's own marriage was the object of neighborhood gossip and speculation, she knew, and people doubtless were asking Filisa, who was an old neighbor, a friend, for news and judgment. Probably now Filisa would tell people, *Juko Ohaŝi doesn't want a divorce. Oh, she said it was to do with Rajdaro Furbo's wife, but I could see, it's her own marriage she was talking about.* Juko shifted her weight in the water, looking away from Filisa rudely, stung by the truth in this presumption. Her life had become melancholy and insupportable; her marriage felt broken, unfixable; but she didn't want to be divorced again.

"Who knows why Helena del Rio stays married?" she said unhappily. *It might be my mother-in-law and not my husband that I go on living with, will not separate myself from.*

"Well, some families think divorce is a scandal," Filisa murmured. "Or maybe she thinks, because he's crazy, it wouldn't be right to leave him." She gathered up her mouth. "Or maybe she likes the way he touches her in bed, eh? doesn't want to give that up?"

Juko had kept silent with her friends and her family about the thing that had happened between her and Bjoro—obscurely, she imagined that if she didn't speak of it, it might become far-away, equivocal—but she had become impatient in these last weeks, expecting illogically that people would stop making their jokes about sexual matters, out of kindness to her. Yet Filisa Ilmen, heedless, lifted her hands out of the water in order to make a lewd gesture in the steamy air: "Or maybe she likes to be let alone, and Rajdaro keeps her happy by sleeping with his corncobs." Filisa's face was round, her nose wide and flat; when she grinned, a crease folded across the bridge of her nose in a childish way. "Or maybe it's Helena who sleeps with the corn," she said, laughing, making that childish face, and then Juko was irresistibly drawn into it, delivering an insult common in women's bathhouses: "Any corncob will do—what's the use of men, eh?" In the gibe was a small, satisfying loosening, a release from inexpressible bitterness and anguish.

Filisa laughed again, rocking back in the tub so that her breasts broke the water. She floated, eyes closing sleepily, the cups of her ears flooding. Her breasts stood up like the soft brown crowns of earth in a field beset by gophers.

They got away from talking about Rajdaro Furbo, began to trade reports of their children, to gossip about other people's children, and complain about their parents. That got them started on other things, matters of aging. Women liked to say, when they were old enough to be done with the business of being women they could finally be persons. In their old age women were expected to make a lot of noise, be disapproved, be fearless. Filisa, grimacing, said she always had been loud and disagreeable, and who could stand her if she worsened? As if it were all part of the same thing, she said, "I'm getting to a rough place, myself—me and Leo—between the woods and the fields." She meant an old axiom, *The forest is always waiting at the edge of the fields.*

Juko was pierced by a sudden wish to confide in Filisa: to

say, *I'm at that place myself—in the rough weeds;* to say that she had not let Bjoro into her body since the night of the *Ruby's* homecoming. But Filisa went on with a flat reporting of the habits of Leo's that bored and offended her, and gradually Juko's urge to speak went out of her. Someone on the outside of the pasado wall was shaking a long mat, the person's shadow moving, bending, swinging arms, in the interstices between the upright bamboo. Juko watched this without seeing it, listening indifferently to Filisa Ilmen's complaints. Leo shirked small decisions, she said. He habitually asked for answers she had already given. And what was this proneness he had, for making himself scarce when there was argument between his mother and his wife?

They had been married a long time, she and Leo, their youngest child by now twelve or thirteen. Filisa was at an age celebrated for women's sexuality and men's erratic emotionalism. Couples who didn't divorce at the end of their child-rearing years often ceremonially reaffirmed their marriages then, when fidelity was a more difficult sacrament. It was a recognition of a hard truth: There could be no possibility of allegiance, of faith, without the possibility of choice. Juko understood what Filisa was asking. *Should I go on being married to my husband?* She understood that Filisa was listening for the answers inside her own mouth.

"Humberto Indergard—he's marrying, I heard," Filisa said suddenly. "Has he got so much better, then? I thought he was crippled, his mother had to wipe his mouth for him when he ate. Who's this woman? Someone his mother chose for him? A carctaker wife?"

"I don't know," Juko said in surprise. She had heard from her son that Olava Morgan, the kura, had begun to keep company with Humberto, and she had thought Olava was walking out with him to bear up his weak right side. If they were sleeping in the same bed, Ĉejo hadn't said. Were they marrying now? She didn't know. Olava Morgan was a big, beautiful woman, had gotten to be fifty-five or sixty without ever deciding to marry. Maybe Olava wasn't the woman people were talking about. Or maybe Humberto's coming marriage was a matter of gossip and rumor. People said it was Humberto's words that had cleared the way on this question of the New World, and now some religious people might be searching his life for signs and portents; maybe this was a guess that had jumped wide of the mark, something trailing illogically in the wake of wonder.

Filisa's thinking may have been going down this same way. She said to Juko, "It was God's voice coming out of his mouth, eh? How else to explain it?" Her body had settled in the tub so that the front of her face was the only part above the waterline, a small, crested island fine-grained as a dune. From between her damp lashes, she peered thoughtfully into the crosspoles of the bathhouse ceiling. "It's a mystery. The world's a strange place. We go along imagining it's ordinary, and then something happens and we're reminded: It's all inconceivable, every bit of it. Cockroaches. Bananas. People speaking in tongues. Why the hell ever did we get to thinking it was commonplace?"

Juko's own faith and practice always had been mundane. She valued the Quaker way of silence for leading people into scrupulous listening, slow judgment. A few times she had seen a certain power rise up out of the silence of a Meeting and bring speakers to places they never could reach alone, raise them to a kind of eloquence they never had shown before and perhaps never would reveal again, but if she didn't know what this power of the Meeting was, she always had accepted its presence in the world without presupposing some kind of junction with God. She and Kristina had spent years arguing such questions, all the proofs and rebuttals wrung out of both of them by now. When they had heard of Humberto's speaking, how all at once he had made himself understood, Kristina had pulled up her mouth, had nodded without surprise. "Music is in you; it awakes and comes out when you're reminded by the instruments," she had said firmly, as if this were part of their longstanding argument, a persuasive finding.

"I guess none of us can stand to know it every day," Filisa said, answering something else. "We'd be crazy, eh? if we always stood balanced at the edge of the mystery, looking out at the world with wide-open eyes. We got to take it in little glimpses through our fingers."

Juko said, murmuring, "Or send someone else out to look."

Filisa rocked her head, pushing a wake across the water. "Well, yes. We sent Humberto, eh?"

Juko had been keeping away from Humberto's sickbed, and telling people it was because of old Leona's rancor toward her. She didn't know if this was true. Humberto was someone who'd always been apt to complain about little maladies, her years with him a litany of queasiness, twinges, lesions and loose bowels, and for months after Vilef's death he had been chronically sick. Now he'd fallen down with a stroke. A few times she had sent along to him, by way of her son, some stupidly trite words of pity and support, but she had not gone to sit with him herself. There was a core in him, of helplessness and pathos, and she was impatient with it—or afraid of it, as a kind of proof of what might be at her own core: an unfeelingness, an indurate heart. But this gossip about his remarriage made her feel anxious and nostalgic. She yearned suddenly to say to Humberto every small thing that had not been said between them. She wanted to say: *I once loved you for your perfect acceptance of our imperfect child.*

She was fifty now, her menses had been erratic and skimpy for more than a year. Maybe she would be finished with that part of her life entirely, before long. How was it possible that she still remembered exactly the way her body felt, the hugeness, the intimacy, of harboring a child inside? And the absence afterward, the unexpected pang of becoming solitary again— she never had forgotten that. She was struck all at once by a flurry of precise physical remembrance, bare of nostalgia, the body's memory: the salt-burn of her milk letting down, the briny-sweet taste of her son Cejo's toes, the smell of his feces, Vilef's narrow, membranous breastbone—the palm of her hand cupped to the heated pulse there.

She stood up suddenly from the tub, sighing. In the close, humid heat of the bathhouse she combed her damp hair, smoothed her chapped hands, heels, knees with coconut oil, put on her shirt and sandals, tied up the strings of her trousers, while Filisa sat on in the water. "I think sometimes, when you set your mind to work at understanding your life, that's when you lose sight of it," Filisa said thoughtfully. She was looking into the ceiling, her tongue exploring her teeth. Maybe it wasn't meant to be advice for Juko.

Juko gathered up her towel and unclean clothes and went out, padding in flat bare feet along the narrow poles of the pasado to the door of her own apartment. People were waiting inside—Ĝan Sorensen, Svalo Smit, Dagmar Lopez, the three of them sitting with Kristina, talking quietly together while they waited. Bjoro was waiting with them, sitting in a half-lotus as if he might be meditating, his palms resting across his knees. When he saw her, he flushed slowly. She stood at the threshold, her bones taking on weight. "Oh hell," she said, from a kind of tired helplessness.

The three Clearness Committee people looked up at her, laughing, understanding. Dagmar said, teasing her, "Don't cry, Juko. Hey, we started without you, but it's a long work to find a clear way out of troubles. There's enough to do—you won't be left without." Ĝan, grinning, said, "She looks happy to see us, eh? She's got a good attitude. She wants to try to find a way through, doesn't want to do any dodging."

Juko didn't think any of this was funny. She gave Kristina a look. The old woman was sewing, her eyes fixed on her hands, but she knew Juko's eyes were on her. She made a small, flatulent sound with her lips and tongue. "Should I have let your marriage go on being sick to death, then?" she murmured.

The Clearness Committee people looked from one of them to the other. Dagmar said, not yet becoming entirely serious, "Are you blaming Kristina for bringing us into this? Did you think your troubles were a secret?" She gestured loosely, the swinging of her hand taking in Bjoro where he went on sitting as if none of this concerned him, his face turned from people, a mask of disinterest. "A husband and a wife can't stop sleeping in the same bed—hell, the same house!—without neighbors seeing it, you know. Anyway, people heard your shouting. Some people think they know what's the matter between you and Bjoro, and they asked us to help you find a clear way through. Maybe you should thank them, eh? for bearing witness. Maybe you shouldn't be looking around for someone to blame." Her voice was low, good-humored.

Juko always had liked Dagmar Lopez, a woman her own age whose sense of humor was on the sour side, whose laugh was a pleasure to listen to, low and chuckling. But now she said bitterly to Dagmar, the words spilling out from a jumble of shame and anger, "Maybe you should look around for someone else to counsel. I don't need help finding a place to put the blame in my marriage." From the edge of her eye she saw Bjoro drop his head and then lift it, seeming to search the ceiling. *Don't look up there for it,* she thought angrily, irrationally.

People on Clearness Committees were respected for their patience, and for a certain kind of graceful common sense, a considered or instinctive wisdom. All three of them looked at her quietly, Dagmar's face becoming serious but not taking on any offense. Svalo Smit said in a flat, reasonable way, "Where do you put it? This blame?"

She meant to look deliberately at Bjoro, to deliberately name him, but in a moment she let her armload of dirty laundry heavily down to the floor and sat down with it, her eyes fixed upon Kristina's hands, the bird-like clench, fingers stiff as pin feathers as they pulled a needle through the cloth, in and through, in and through relentlessly. Juko's mouth when she finally opened it said sorrowfully, "If there's a way not to blame my husband, you'll have to help me look for it."

Ĝan Sorensen nodded. He turned his head toward Bjoro before turning it toward Juko again. "I don't know if there's a way not to blame Bjoro. But there's always a way out of troubles, eh? and we'll all of us look for it." He didn't say, *Sometimes the way out of disease is death. Sometimes the way out of a troubled marriage is divorce.*

They let a fairly long silence clear the path a little. Then Dagmar said quietly that people had begun to know there was trouble in Bjoro and Juko's marriage on the night of the *Ruby*'s homecoming. She said that people knew there was trouble in their marriage when Bjoro butt-fucked his wife as if this were an entitlement rather than a matter for mutual consent. She said, looking from one of them to the other, this was something everybody knew, or supposed to be true, and if it wasn't, then Bjoro or Juko ought to say so now.

Juko's body filled with heat; there was a dim ringing in the bones of her skull. She had fixed her eyes on a point in the wall behind Svalo Smit's shoulder but was blind to it, her seeing turned inward following a shifting confusion of memory, the fine pale hairs along the curve of Bjoro's knee lifting to straddle her, the hollow below the hinge of his jaw clenching and then loosening, the involute plaiting of the rug pressed beneath her eye—an incomprehensible landscape, dim and vast.

"Some people think Bjoro is ashamed of his behavior and hates his wife for this shame," Dagmar said in a little while. "Some people think Juko hates her husband for his behavior and is ashamed of herself for this hatred. Anyway, everybody knows that Juko and Bjoro have given up having sexual relations with one another since the night of the *Ruby*'s homecoming. And that the person who came home inside Bjoro's body is not the same person who went away in it but somebody else, somebody who can't see a clear way through. And that the person inside Juko's body has lately become solitary—she thinks she's living alone, eh? anyone can see this." Dagmar looked at Juko and at Bjoro without seeming to expect either of them to reply. "So people have asked us to help Bjoro find a clear way, and take Juko by the hand so she can stand up with the rest of us and stop this crouching down."

There was a longer silence while people waited for an inner stillness. Juko's head kept up a clatter of noise, meaningless and distracting. She did not look at Bjoro but began to be conscious of the precise placement of his body in the close air of the room, the weight and balance of his head carried at the top of his spine. She didn't know what she was feeling except a buzzing, unfocused anxiety. The Clearness Committee allowed the silence to stand and stand until it began to seem solid, a support, and finally it became possible for her to bring a few words out: "I don't want to be known as the woman who was twice divorced."

She was surprised by the pitch of her voice, low, a murmur of piety and self-disgust.

"I wonder," Svalo Smit said, "who *would* you want to be known as?"

She went on being surprised, separate from her mouth, from the words that finally came out, dismally sentimental: "The woman who was married so long that she and her husband would finish each other's sentences." Fragments of dialogue, pointless and unidentifiable, unwound themselves in her brain, the voices of old people overlapping one another in an amiable, winding braid of storytelling.

Without seeing it, she felt Bjoro's head turning. The turning of her own head brought the frame of reference around, a disconcerting sideward slip, a coriolis effect, and then he said, looking at her, "Do you want me to be that husband? the one who finishes your sentences?" with something in it that was anguish, and something else, a wildness, a charge. He may not have been asking her anything. Maybe he was angry with her for disclosing a maudlin side; their history together had been agreeably bristly, unimpassioned.

"Yes! You!" She was angry too, and wild, and the surprising thing was that she began suddenly to cry, a choking cough of grief or denial. Maybe Bjoro cried too; he put his face down in his hands. She didn't know what she wanted from him, but not weeping, and she hated him for it suddenly, remembering that she had thought this was something left behind in her other marriage, with that other husband. Swiftly she was finished with tears herself. She stared bitterly across the casement of the pasado wall, up the narrow slope of the tube to the houses and fields of the Bonveno ŝiro.

Svalo Smit said mildly, "As far as that goes, I wonder if you want to be that husband—eh, Bjoro?"

Bjoro reared his head, exactly as opossum sometimes will do, a kind of blind searching, and when he found Juko he twisted the heels of his fists against his eyes harshly. "I want to go on being married," he said. His voice was rough, hopeless. In his long homely face there was something unfamiliar to her, a desperation that transcended loneliness. In that look, it was impossible to separate the gentle from the terrible, the suffering from the harm—what should Juko understand from that look?

She turned from it in a confusion of anguish, as if he had deliberately peeled back a bandage to show her an ugly wound.

"My wife never did finish my sentences, but she retold everything I said," Svalo said after a while, uncomplainingly. "She said I never could get it right, eh?" He was an old man eighty or more, and had been divorced from his wife after their children were grown.

The Clearness Committee might have gone on talking in this vein, a mild bantering—they may have thought this was a bridge to something—but Kristina said suddenly, bitterly, "I don't know what all this talking about unfinished sentences has to do with my son covering his wife's back." Then unexpectedly she gave Bjoro a furious look, her lips twisting, "What were you thinking? What were you thinking?" she said to him, and went on glaring at him a moment—his burning face. Then she pulled her head down again, going on with sewing. Her lips were drawn up in a tight gather as if she had just now sewn her own mouth shut. They all could hear the slight hush of thread drawing through the cloth, and the stick of the needle.

"What do you want me to say, panja?" Bjoro said to her, spreading his hands. "I was crazy. I told Juko that. I went crazy! I don't know what I was doing, why I was doing it. Shall I go on apologizing for that until you make up your mind how much penance is enough?" He looked around at all of them. "I don't know what I should do, after I apologize to my wife," he said angrily. "After I tell her I want to go on being married. What's the next thing I should do? I want to have sex with my wife again, but she never comes into my bed. What is the next thing I should do?"

Gan said, in the habitual way of Clearness Committees everywhere, "Oh, well, I don't think any of us know the answer to that; it's not our business to tell you what you should do, after all."

Bjoro made a sound, a low hissing of unhappiness, of frustration, and looked off from everyone.

"You say your wife never comes into your bed," Svalo told him after a while, "but as far as that goes, you never come into your wife's bed either."

Bjoro said fiercely, "My wife doesn't want me coming to bed with her." Juko believed this, herself. *I won't let him in my bed!* she was thinking, but in the silence, when those words didn't speak themselves out of her mouth, she knew that she had been lonely for his weight lying by her in the night, his back against her hips, his whispering in the darkness. The loss of her husband's company distilled itself into a pang of longing. It was her body, not her bed, that she didn't want Bjoro coming into.

When she spoke, finally, the words that came out were a bitter chiding. "I don't have any interest in having sex. You've made that a hateful thing. What do you think? That if we lie in the same bed, we must have sex?"

Then Dagmar said, nodding, "There's nothing wrong with Juko keeping celibate, eh?" She thought and then she said, "Everybody knows how it is with women who miscarry, how their bodies go on feeling the effects of grief and they have to wait for that to be finished before they get pregnant again, or they're liable to lose the new fetus, too. It seems to me, this is what Juko is doing, waiting a while, letting her body get over this grief, before she lets her husband into her again. There's a healing that has to take place."

"In Bjoro, too, as far as that goes," Svalo said, and Ĝan, nodding, told everyone that celibacy had a well-known value, especially in treating sexual matters.

The silence after that had a different quality, the vague weight of satisfaction; probably the members of the Clearness Committee were thinking a little progress had been made. Juko couldn't have said what the progress was. Something pent-up had been released; maybe that was all.

They went on talking a little while more but it was no longer a counseling. Dagmar asked Juko if it was true, this gossip about Humberto marrying. "I heard it was Olava Morgan he was walking out with," she told Juko. Kristina, without looking up from her sewing, said pointedly that Olava was a woman who had no interest in marrying. "People have too much empty space in their minds, that's where this kind of stupid gossip comes from," she said, mumbling in irritation.

They drifted off to discussing the New World, and Humberto's magical leading, and the *Dream,* gone out ahead of them to put a new landing party down in the southern archipelago. Bjoro listened to this talk dourly, not joining in. When Ĝan Sorensen asked him if it was true—from the face of the land there was no seeing the curve of it?—Bjoro gave back a harsh look. Juko thought he wouldn't answer. But then he said, staring away from them all, "I think of the sky." She saw that he was flushing slowly. He said bleakly, enigmatically, "It's the lack of incurvature on the sky."

After the Clearness Committee people had gone home, Juko and her husband and her mother-in-law went on sitting silently inside the apartment. Juko drew her unclean laundry into her lap and began searching along all the seams with her thumb and forefinger as if she believed she might find a place where some stitching had come apart. She didn't look at Bjoro, but felt him watching her hands.

"I miss the settledness of things, Juko."

What did this mean? She wasn't able to answer. Then he stood, grunting, and went down the ladder, out of the house. She began to fold the shirt and trousers, the towel and shorts, went on folding and refolding them in her lap while Kristina went on with her sewing.

"What is it, anyway, this business about Olava Morgan marrying Humberto Indergard?" Kristina asked her finally.

Juko looked at her. "I don't know. Do you want me to ask Ĉejo?"

"We ought to go over there and ask Humberto ourselves."

"That woman, his mother, doesn't want me in her house."

"Oh, she can go to hell. What does she think—that the mother of Humberto's sons shouldn't come and see Humberto when he's sick? She can go to hell. I always have liked Humberto Indergard but his mother must be a fool." She looked at Juko. Her eyes were rheumy, the lids trembling, but the look she gave was hard and intent. "Where is that house he lives in, over in Alaŭdo, eh? We ought to walk over there now. We ought to sit down with Humberto and talk with him."

There was something Juko had wanted to say to her once-husband: She remembered the impulse but not the substance.

What she felt now was her old determination to stay away. "I don't want to go into Leona's house, Kristina."

Her mother-in-law looked at her. Then she looked away. "Well, that's an old matter, eh? Settled."

A heat rose up the back of Juko's neck. "Yes. It's settled. That marriage, that child's life."

Kristina turned her head again, her mouth loosening sorrowfully. "Well, I don't know what that old woman is thinking—" she said after a while. "—what she's blaming you for."

Juko understood that this had nothing much to do with Leona Arntsen. After a long silence something yielded in her and she said without looking at Kristina, "Do you remember how a child will sleep tangled? How you want to straighten their bodies on the bed? My son Vilef slept so light—so light, Kristina. If I pulled his legs out straight, he always would wake and cry."

She didn't know why this memory had come up in her; or why, in a few moments, an ancient, latent culpability came out of her mouth: "Some people think sailmenders and other space-going people should keep themselves childless; the rads are higher for people outside. Maybe Leona thinks I'm to blame for making that fey baby." She grimaced—a concealing, joyless smile. "Or it may be she just blames me for not loving him more."

Kristina pulled her chin down. She said nothing, and then she said, "It's bad luck, is all it is. You know my son has gone out in the boats for twenty years, eh? and both his children were born whole. Who does that woman blame for her grandson Ĉejo, born whole?" After a long silence she sighed. "Ah, Juko," she said, as if this naming were a benediction.

They walked around to the Alaŭdo ŝiro, Kristina tired and slow, leaning into Juko. "Old age is not all it's cracked up to be," she muttered once, and flashed a sour grin.

One person, a woman they didn't know, was in Humberto's apartment, separating seeds from cottonsilk. This required them to sit down politely and help her get the work done, before it became possible to ask where Humberto was. "People are digging up the malanga taro, eh? this time of year," she said. She went on pulling out the seeds with her quick old fingers while she gave them an earnest look, drawing her skimpy brows forward. Juko didn't know if this was an answer.

They left the apartment and asked a man who was gathering eggs: Where was the field of taro planted? Looking for it, walking up the narrow beaten footway between the Ring River and the tiers of Alaŭdo fields, they saw a woman digging a test hole at the river's slack edge and when she stood up it was Leona— Humberto's mother—her trousers rolled at her thighs and her bare old legs glazed with mud. She made a sound when she saw Juko, a breathing out. In a moment, the old woman's chin convulsed and she deliberately stooped to her hole. Juko's impulse was to say something serene, something commonplace, as if there was no history between them, but her brain was suddenly filled up with too much that was consequential.

Kristina said, when they had walked past Leona, "Was that woman your mother-in-law?" and Juko said irritably, "You're my mother-in-law."

The big heart-shaped leaves of the malanga taro were brown and dead, and Juko's son was standing out in the spent field digging up the tubers with a wide-tined fork while Humberto sat at the edge of the field watching the work, his weight on one haunch with his other leg outstretched. Kristina put her hand on his scalp, petting. The shaky, weighted turning of his head was obscurely evocative: Juko's heart turned with it. Someone had cut his hair very short, baring around his ears a curving bow of skin that was pale and tender; his face had become bony, unfamiliar, asymmetrical. He looked at Kristina and then Juko one-eyed without surprise, or he had lost the knack for displaying it. "Ha," he said, twisting his mouth.

Ĉejo came out of the field and the four of them sat together and talked about the taro harvest, and a repair someone was making to the plumbing under a nearby domaro, and rumors and gossip to do with the people crewing the *Dream*. Humberto sat clasping one hand with the other, his outstretched leg trembling slightly, his bidden eye following people as they spoke. It was an effort for him to speak himself, the words thick and slow, but Ĉejo had developed an ear for making out his father's meanings, and sometimes Juko understood the gist of Humberto's words from Ĉejo's responses. It occurred to her, watching the two of them talking slowly back and forth, that if Humberto had once stood at the center of the Light, he was standing somewhere else now. But gradually she understood some of his words herself. When they were arguing about an opossum that had become a pet, Humberto said laboriously, "Gives up. Rightful. For safe," and his eye moved from one of them to the other. When he looked at Juko it was an old look, natural and dear, his brows rising in that self-effacing way, and she was pierced suddenly with a sad, indefinable longing. *None of us are standing in the old places,* she thought.

She and Kristina made a slow way home in the afternoon light. When they were stepping over the narrow channel of the mezlando aqueduct, she said, "Oh hell," and stopped suddenly, straddling the little ditch. "We forgot to ask about Humberto's marriage." Kristina shook her head, going on up the footway without slowing, beginning the easeful climb to the high houses of Pacema.

Their rooms were empty, mournful with the yellowing light of dusk. Juko and Kristina did not speak, sitting over separate handwork. When Kristina's chin fell to her breast, when she began to snore softly, Juko studied her sleeping. She thought of going out quietly, going onto the sail. After a while she did.

In these last weeks, the little orange sun had gradually become a source of light. Now in the blackness, objects were bright. Inside the exo, in sunlight, Juko's skin was warm, and on the shadow side of something, cold. The purity of the unreflected light was a comfort, clarifying. She went out to the field called the Wayward Gate and climbed to the head of the flymast. The sails were a vast wheel of light, luminous in the perfect blackness. From the head of the mast, it was possible to see the edge of light bound to the blackness in an intricate, inextricable coherence. Over the broad, bright field of the sheet she became exact, contained, a foot or an elbow like an oar dipped in still water moving her precisely. In the soundlessness, the depthlessness of space, there was the sense of a slight shudder, a susurrus on the black brightness. She floated on it, drawing her body through the light.

Vintro

(Of many debts incalculable,
Haply our New World's chiefest debt is to old poems.)

That time when the *Migremo* fell into the sea, I was standing
with my sister Kikuma in a small open boat in the Ŝiblingo
Fjord below the houses of Holds Loneliness, getting in the
kelp with rakes. Little squalls of rain came and went, but in the
still air between them the sea was green, the color people call
marblua, and the skin of the water was lacquered, glossy, beneath a colorless sky. A puso weather was moving in from the
northwest but we weren't worried yet, only watchful. We were
working between the beach and the stacks, a kilometer or a kilometer and a half from the shore, riding a heavy sea anchor, and
the boat had a high waist, tipped up horns, it was built for han-
dling a surf. Both of us had heavy-weather gear. And the puso
weather would be a while getting here: The cloud wrack was
faintly bluish white, lit by the Sea Is Groaning ice fields that
stand off the coast there. We wouldn't begin to worry much
about the weather until the belly of the clouds, moving toward
the coast over the open water, became the griseous color people call Water Sky.

There was another, bigger boat within shouting range, five people in it. One of the five, Adria Berelo, had a progressive disease of her muscles, a dystrophy. All of them kept this in their minds—it was a serious matter—but they were not governed by it, and no one in that boat was solemn: There was a good deal of talking going on and laughter, and Kikuma and I in our own boat sometimes yelled over there to ask what was making those people laugh; I guess we suffered a little from feeling excluded, deprived.

Kikuma and one of the men in that other boat, Davido Ĉekli, began to trade insults back and forth over the water. They were longtime kite fighting opponents, and you know how it is with kite people—when they aren't crossing their strings they're crossing words. They think when people are gathered in one place, digging roots or laying out kelp in wracks, and then stopping to eat their lunch, if you raise a kite it's an open challenge, and they want to be the last one to hold the sky—they coat their strings with ground glass. When the *Migremo* came apart, the two of them were shouting their gibes and I was laughing, and you know how it is when thunder is so far off you can only hear it in your bones? That was how I heard the breaking up of the *Migremo,* just in that way, its shudder going through the air as a dull booming, and when I lifted my head, looking, there was a daylight star scribing a long arc across the overclouded sky, trailing embers and ash, going down to the western sea. "Hey. What," Kikuma said, turning to look. "Hey, Ana, what did we see?" and I wasn't able to think of how to answer.

People say, all truths wait in all things. Here is something waiting inside something else: When I was a child we would go up, summers, to that place people call Embracing, and live in my great-aunt's latajo on the steep west side. You know how a latajo's walls are open? How they let in the air and the daylight and people's voices—the whole world? From the inside of that latajo you could look the long way out onto the maltejo, or up the long slope of land to where the mountains broke above the alta, and at night when Kikuma and I were lying in our bed we could see the old stars, and the little new star sliding like a bead

of ice over the roof, and it seemed as if you could look a great
long way up into the sky.

Once in the winter, after my family had moved back under
the berm at Having Wind, I went up on the alta looking for
some particular stones—some of us were laying out the pattern
of a vocero on the flat of the plain—and I came up to Embracing and looked into my aunt's latajo and the light that lay inside it was a certain color, had a certain quality. That was in the
years people call the malsataj. Do you remember those years?
The famine and the hard living? People were making their winter tea from pouring hot water over gravel, in those years.

Later in my life, when I flew in a balloon over Holds Loneliness and saw for the first time the color of the deep ice along
the edge of the glacier, I thought of that latajo, the light inside
it, lying empty in the winter. And later when I was standing in
that boat in the Ŝiblingo Fjord watching the long curve of fire,
the *Migremo* falling over the edge of the sky and into the sea,
I remembered the way the land looked when I was hanging
from that balloon above Holds Loneliness, everything seeming to move in sweeping arches, the stones off the shore standing in long curving palisades, and the breaking sea rolling slow
and broad, grayed with sand, and the long grasses streaming
under the wind, and the falls along the edge of the fjord flying
on the breath of air, upward like smoke, and the beads of rain
falling so fine that it was still possible to see the sun and the violet sky, but spreading the light in a great, brilliant, doubled
cielarko, its shining feet seeming to rest on the oxbows of the
mountains with the tongue of the glacier framed within it.
That's why the people of the coast have that certain look behind their eyes, I was thinking then. That's why they don't
want to live anywhere else.

So afterward, after I had moved into my sister's household
at Holds Loneliness and was standing in that boat on the Ŝiblingo Fjord getting in the kelp, and the *Migremo* fell out of the
sky in a flaming arch, I didn't think of people's deaths—that I
was standing watching people dying. I was thinking of the winter light inside an empty latajo, and the way the beads of ice in
a fine rain bend the light in a vivid rainbow.

Afterward, a little while afterward, there was a moment while I wondered if it was the old *Miller* giving up its orbit at last, but somebody in the other boat yelled, "Was that the *Migremo* falling?" and then I remembered the *Migremo* had been up there getting salvage from the empty houses, the feral woodlands, inside the torus, and coming down today onto the long landing field southeast of Divided. I wondered if the people over at Divided, listening on the uplink, had heard the dull clap, had felt it shuddering along their bones.

We watched the tendril of smoke thicken, become a brume of steam rising out of the sky line. Kikuma said quietly, "Are they lying in the Owl Strait, Ana? Off the Mizerido estuary?" and then someone in the other boat yelled out, "In the Owl Strait, looks like!" After a bit, those people in the other boat put their oars in the water and rowed over to us so they wouldn't have to keep on shouting. We looked at one another. Then people began saying how much sea they thought was between us and the wreckage of the *Migremo* and how quick they thought we could get across it, and whether our little boat, the *Pulls Together*, being quicker than their big boat, the *Keeps Steady*, ought to wait up or go on ahead without waiting, and whether it would be better to run on across the strait to the Goes To Grass Islands and lie snug, after we'd got the *Migremo* people aboard, or try to beat back along the lee of the cape, back here to Holds Loneliness.

We didn't want to get out in the Owl Strait and not be able to make land when the puso weather came in from the sea— we didn't want to go down into the water with the *Migremo*. But no one said this. No one said, The winds are northwesterly. No one said, Look, that puso weather is over there, over the ice. Only Magdalena Ulsen's young son, earnest and distracted, said, "There won't be anyone alive, do you think?" and Magdalena looked around sorrowfully and said "Oh, I suppose not," and began to coil up the lines in readiness for getting under way.

There were five of them to get their anchor up, their mast on the wind, and they were off ahead of us, beating west-northwest around the little skerries, the Fisted Rocks, but when we stepped our windpipe the *Pulls Together* made a little twitch, taking a breath, and skated off nimbly on the light air.

I had to look behind once, to the heavy white foot of the glacier and the berms of Holds Loneliness cockling the steep last downhill at the head of the fjord, and seaward from the berms the fretwork of low stone walls sheltering people from the sea winds, and below on the outwash plain that once was a glacier, the cobble of the beach, mossy bogs and hummocks of grass where terns hunted down the fingers of the streams, and people laid out kelp in long wracks, drying in the wind.

I don't know what I was looking for.

We passed the *Steady* in the open water west of the Fisted Rocks and when they fell behind us we dumped wind and kept them to our starboard side. Kikuma steered off the ragged brume, south-southwest into the Owl Strait. The Comes-Between Cape reared its head along the port beam, a great prow of basalt pocked with indentations and ledges, a summer nesting place for thousands of ribb'd gulls but now a many-roomed empty house. In this season of the year, the *vintro,* people like to visit those rooms—when we sailed into the Owl Strait looking for the *Migremo* there was a tiny figure, maybe it was a woman, standing high up on the whitened bluff of the cape, watching our boats, or looking out toward the smoke of the wreck, or offering something into the sky. I've climbed up there myself. On a clear day you can see the Goes To Grass Islands riding in the strait like boats, the tidal currents running so fast through the channels there, they drag long wakes astern. But there was no seeing the islands in that weather, the day the *Migremo* fell, and anyway people don't climb the Comes-Between Cape only for that view across the Owl Strait. When people are feeling the weight of their own lives, they want to see the life other animals are given, and there is something mysterious and revealing about the discarded machinery of birds' lives. In abandoned flakes of eggshell, emptied seed cases, the hollow stems of cottongrass, in the delicate attenuated backbones of fish and the teeth of desiccated crustaceans, you can sometimes glimpse the bare and intricate structures of God.

The mountains of Abides were shrouded in cloud, so when

we had come clear of the cape it was the long thin line of the escarpment that fixed the eastern edge of the sea. Westward, there was no line dividing the sky from the sea, and in the distant bourns of the strait we could not see the islands. Southward lay the long spine of Resting-Waiting; in other weather it might have defined the whole southern range of the horizon, the narrow peaks impounding the cirques of old glaciers, the steep headwalls streaked with snow and stone, but it was hunkered, like Abides, beneath a lowering sky. Sailing up the Owl Strait in this kind of weather, you're at the edge of the world, engirt by emptiness.

The little estuary of the Mizerido was bound in shorefast fog, so we kept an ear out for the voices of seeking-browns, those brief and reluctant flyers wintering over in the brushy aits of the Mizerido. We took our bearing from the faint ululations of their barks, and veered west by northwest, crossing and re-crossing the *Steady*'s tack, our two boats scribing a braid on the water. Gradually the column of smoke from the *Migremo*, blowing off eastward, became flat and gray, indistinguishable from the overcast, and then I went up on the bowstalk to look out for the wreckage. The wind was cold and dank. For a while I called down to Kikuma, stupid questions or remarks about the boat, and I kept looking over to the northwest where the puso weather was stalled above the ice fields. But after a while I got finished with that.

You know how it is when your mind enters into a silence with the land? when you give up speaking, and you give up listening for gulls or watching for a shift in the weather, and just begin to place yourself in the world? That was how it was when I was up on the bow stalk looking for the wreckage of the *Migremo*. Long patches of ruffled water, families of the great silver-backed balenoj going up to their wintering place in the By Far fjord; squalls of rain shadowing the sea; rafts of flag-dippers, gray-green against the gray-green water, the yellow bills of those seabirds seeming to slide like a scurf of petals on the water: I recognized and understood these patterns of light in a dreamy unvoiced way while I waited for my eye to take in what was not of the land—floating plastic, aluminum, the sufflated exo of a dead person—and say it to me on a breath, like a word spoken aloud—*There.*

We came off the wind, steering for a big piece of a shattered bulkhead, ribbed white, streaked with soot, and we grappled with the kelp rakes, getting it up into the boat. None of the people on the *Migremo* were known to me, not even their names, but in the illegible letters on the smooth facade of that bulkhead, beneath great flakes of sodden ash, broken blisters of paint, I could see their faces. That piece of wreckage was a ghostly thing. Kikuma and I passed a sorrowful look between us.

We beat a zigzag path over the water, going after a sudden swarm of flotsam—more plastic and forced aluminum, a spongy piece of batting, a tangle of flash tubing. We shouted our finds to the people in the *Steady,* and they called theirs back—*a ravel of wiring! here's some webbing! got a piece of a bolster, looks like, or a seat!* We went off to gather up a flotilla of broken crates, and when the *Steady* was a distant white figure on the water someone over there shouted, the voice feeble, indeterminate across the wind. We raised up from what we were doing and looked. A person gestured with upraised arms. I understood something all at once, with my body, with my blood; and I took hold of the tiller, brought the boat around wallowy on the waves. "They've found one of those people," I said to my sister.

There had been four, crewing the *Migremo;* one of them was tangled in nylon line in a wrack of bladderweed that Adria Berelo on the *Steady* had pulled up to the side of that boat with a rake. This was a small woman, young as my daughter, her white exo breached at the chest—pale rags of fat and muscle flapped from the hole. Her face was open and calm, her mouth slopping in the gray lees of water inside the exoskull. Her eyes examined the sky.

My daughter, when she married, might as well have stuck her finger up my nose. That man she married, Armando Fujino, had been married twice before—he had proven to everybody but my daughter that he couldn't be a decent husband—but he was shameless, and my daughter was stupid, and we hadn't spoken a word to one another since that day, though the Clearness Committee came around every little while and tried to counsel our quarrel. When I saw the face of that dead woman, the woman who died in the *Migremo,* her face broad and brown as my daughter's, I didn't think about our quarrel. I thought of how, in the afternoon when you sleep the dormeto, and wake before other people, you can try to be as still as everyone else, or if you haven't been married very long or are lying with a lover you can have quiet intercourse. Or if you're a child you can whisper until you wake someone up. I thought of how, in the weeks before my daughter was born, I slept restlessly, and took up a habit of going out of my own house and standing in cold bare feet at the narrow fenestroj of other houses, bending to peer through the wavery panes of glass at the shut eyes of sleepers. In the low winter daylight, people sleeping have a solemn expression, they breathe quietly, lying loose and still, children tangled on a mattress, married couples sleeping face to face with their knees pressed together, sisters lying down without touching, a grandfather wrapped up with his little grandchild.

A few times people woke up startled to find me peering through their windows while they slept—I may have had a brief, mild renown that winter, as a crazy person. But in those last weeks while you're waiting for a child to be born, you're expected to be restless, beside yourself. I wonder what I was looking for in the faces of those dreamers? The face of that dead woman made me think of an old poem, something about the newborn emerging from gates, and the dying emerging from gates; how, when the wildest and bloodiest is over, all is peace.

Three people on the *Steady* pulled this dead woman up into their boat and laid her body on the deck, and Adria Berelo sat with her under cover of the aft tarpaulin. The swells were slapping against the boats by this time—in the bottom of the *Pulls Together,* in a slurry of blackish water and kelp, our tangle of salvaged plastic and aluminum slid around and knocked against the ribs of the hull—but we went on hunting. We were a fit match for seas running a couple of meters, and then we'd begin to think about getting off the water, out of the weather. We gave up bringing in every little piece of wreckage, though—we remembered why we had come out into the strait. Finding that woman's body had rekindled in us a longing to find the bodies of the others.

For a while we veered here and there after indistinguishable shapes on the water, and when one became a company of wandering-tatters, or a cracked piece of plastic or metal, or a baleno breaking the surface to breathe, we veered away after the next. Hunting for a body on the sea was something some of us had done before—Kikuma had lived along that coast for thirty years, and once had gone out into the channels of the Goes To Grass Islands looking for the bodies of her brother-in-law and his daughter; I had been on the *Eye of the Moon,* when a murso breached under the stern of the boat and a woman, a cousin of my sister's friend Eŭnisa Pare, was swept over the side. There is a certain image you learn, the discrete shading, form, drift, that distinguishes a dead body from other things, and gradually we recollected it. Then we became more deliberate, more intent, carried along by the tide, peering for that particular shape lost on the water, and now and then steering around the edges of tangled alĝo, leaning out from the heaving boat to scratch through the jams with our long-handled kelp rakes.

A silence came into the hunt and inhabited it. The near water was blackish now, glossy, but my eye was drawn far out, to the edgeless gray billowing of the sky, the sea. On the smoky distance it was only the birds who measured the world, gave it dimension. Some plum gulls sprang suddenly up—a shifting figure of birds rising into the sky and vanishing on a soundless blackish flash of wings—and then Kikuma said to me, "Look." I saw a chip of white sliding down the pitch of a wave, and when it came up again and down the next slope, it became an exo spraddled on a broken piece of a hatch cover.

We quartered the waves, crying out strategy to one another for making intersection with the drift of the raft; we were signalling the *Steady,* too, with lifted arms, useless shouting, until they made us out and brought their windpipe around to follow us.

We were wary of having that heavy piece of steel pitching

alongside our little boat, our hull of paper and aluminum, reeds and string, so I made a line fast to the girdle of my overalls and waited, crouching along the gunnel, while Kikuma brought us near. When the raft slipped laterally, lifting gently up to meet us on the swell, I leaped out and scuttled onto it, clutching a bent end of rebar, scrabbling my boots in the hook of a steel step. I shouted, holding on in the cold wash of the sea, and paid out my line as the *Pulls Together* veered neatly off again without a bump.

My heart had come up into my throat—I had to wait to get a breath before I could make my hand let go its grip on the rebar and touch the gloved wrist of the exo. The body was lying front-down, the suit breached up the back. In the ragged purplish rift were the crenelations of vertebrae. The hands were outspread and clenched on the coaming of the hatch—a death clutch I thought, but when I touched the arm, the fingers of that hand opened and closed, taking a new hold. The faceplate was down in the spillover on the surface of the hatch—it was maybe with my mindseye that I caught sight of a man's mouth in a rigor of terror. I shouted to Kikuma. She made a glowering face and shouted back, a wordless gusting noise, and I knew she hadn't heard what I'd said. But she brought the tiller around and let the boat come into the wind, veering to close with us again.

I put my line through a D-ring at the man's hip, cinching him loosely to me, and then I peeled his fingers from the hatch and grappled his loose weight into my lap. His skin was pallid, translucent, and his eyes fixed on me with dreadful yearning. I put my head close to the faceplate but when he didn't speak, I wasn't able to think of anything to say myself.

Sometimes we are reminded. I suppose I had in my mind those few years while I was clerk of the Waters Committee, while I lived at Prolonged Singing with my in-laws. We never were done with repairing the fluejo, over there—those people at Prolonged Singing are still repairing them, aren't they? That domaro is situated along the edge of the fault scarp and the culverts and aqueducts are prone to break every time the earth shakes; in a hard quake walls slip, roofs let down their loads, people die. Do you know that little river over there? the Crouches by a Grave River? the one that long ago agreed to share itself with those people? the small water wheel that powers their machine shop and their mill? One time there was a strong seism and the housing for the pilot rod broke away from the tube in the wheel. Next day two of us were fitting a new draft tube below the little dam, and while we were doing that repair there was another harder tertremo. It sat me down in the tailwater. Birĝita Ŝiomi was crouching between the draft tube and the dam head, and in the moment before the struts broke and let down the dam on her, she looked over at me. Sometimes we are reminded: All of us live steadfastly in that moment, the one between hope and the exercise of God's will.

I pulled the man's loose weight up over my shoulders and when the *Pulls Together* came alongside, I let out my shout again. "This man is still living!" Kikuma's face opened in surprise. Coastal people say, piloting a boat is one of those things like playing the flute or writing poems—you are given it or not, and no amount of apprenticeship or striving will bring it to you. Kikuma never had been one of those people, but she delicately maneuvered, bringing the *Pulls Together* alongside and then pulling away again time after time without much banging against the hatch. And she went on being patient, not yelling much advice, while I crouched there with that man slung over my shoulders, getting up my nerve, imagining I was waiting for a perfect alignment.

The lacuna between the boat and the raft always was shifting, capricious, and I think it was finally on just an instinct of motion that I went plunging outward. His weight made me awkward, top-heavy, or I was clumsy; I struck the gunnel hard with my shins, there was a breathless pitching moment—I saw Kikuma lunging for me—and then the cold breaking of the sea. I lost hold of him or let go, stupid with surprise, grappling along the sliding hull in an urgent confusion. His breached exo must have taken on a quick weight of water, because when he sank to the end of my line he pulled me like a millstone and I lost hold of the boat and sank with him, straight down.

I had been afraid, waiting to jump, but now I wasn't afraid. How quickly our ties and ballasts are cast off! I was of the Owl Strait suddenly, my elbows resting in fjords, my palms outspread on the cobbled beaches. Inside my body there were forests of lichens, galaxies of starfishes and lamp jellies, and in my bones the shields of turtles, the teeth of balenoj. I felt in my blood the long slow tide, straining after the sun—I was water, and its unknowable alchemies, dreading nothing, simply streaming and alive. This was one of those times when your mind and body cohere and you understand suddenly what the poets say: To die is different from what you had supposed, and luckier.

Then inexplicably I began to rise up through the muffled darkness toward the dazzle of the daylight—Kikuma was hauling me up—I remembered I was tied fast to the *Pulls Together.* That was a curious moment: I had a sense that I must now make an accommodation to the world, as if I had lived a long time under the sea. Then my sister's hands took a grip in my hair. I reached up blindly and caught the rail and the boat heeled over steeply—she pulled me across the gunnel, washing in on the sea, and I knew as soon as I was in the boat that the knot binding me to the *Migremo* man had come undone. Kikuma pulled the end of the line into her lap and then she clambered back to the tiller to get the boat turned into the wind while I sat cold and shaky among the salvaged wreckage. The *Steady* had come up behind us on the starboard side, and people over there were shouting back and forth with Kikuma but I didn't try to hear what they were saying. I was too cold and wet through to take pleasure in my survival. I looked out over the water for birds.

The domaro where I lived after I married is the one people call Becoming Death, though its older, truer name is Prolonged Singing. At that domaro, before I was born, a man killed his young daughter by drowning her in the water where they were bathing. Or she died without his help, going down in the water silently while he was looking away. In the hot springs there, black-legged pipes raft on the water, and the little side-by-sides live in it, they don't seem to care, those birds, that the water is scalding hot. Their outcry, the slight splashing of the water, the rustle of their wings among the clouds of steam is unending, and after a while you just begin to not hear it.

One day some of us were bathing in that hot springs. You know how it is sometimes, when you see something? when there is a moment? when your eye is drawn to something vanishing? and in that moment something sacred is made known? While I was soaking with other people in the stone basin of the bath—I remember we were shouting harassment to Nona Asaki who was repairing the tiles of the conduit by the outtake of the spring; I remember there was a weather moving over the sky but it was a facila wind, a squall bound for somewhere else—I felt a sudden glimpse of those birds—pipes, side-by-sides— their voices like exclamations, and the fleeting dip and rise of their bodies in the steam. And in that moment I thought, They are calling the name of that man, the one who looked away, whose eye was caught by birds, just as his daughter sank. And that time when I was in the *Pulls Together* with Kikuma, after a man had come loose from my line and gone down into the sea, I looked out over the water to see if any birds were calling my name. But then Kikuma said to me, "Ana, here, get warm," and she peeled away my soaked clothes and put my arms in dry sleeves, my legs in dry trousers; she folded me under a tarpaulin.

I was grateful, exhausted. We were laboring through heavy seas with the edge of the puso weather whining in the windpipe, but I didn't try to hold this or anything in my mind. I lolled in the bottom of the boat, my skull rocking dumbly among the sliding scraps of salvage. While Kikuma was steering for a lee shore, I suppose I stood up from my life and let it stream around me in a clear cataract. I was freed from time, not lying inside a dream but standing in the compass of heaven where everything goes onward and outward, nothing collapses—and when I lay down in my life again we were beating northeast along the Comes-Between Cape. When I looked over the gunnel of the boat, across the strait toward the Fisted Rocks, there was a break in the sky and the sun broke fleetingly across the water in a long bright reef—the puso weather had gone over our heads toward Abides.

A bird's wing brushing your shoulder—or a fortunate weather while you're traveling—how can these small blessings of the land be set apart from God's will, any more than the bloody death that is inescapable, inherent in the world? When you open a hole in the earth by setting aside the turf with a spade, when you lay in the frame for a house and place the fenestroj to accept sunlight, and then mindfully replace the turf— when you do this work with skill and love and you stand at the edge of the field looking at it and see only the smooth grassy rise of the berm, isn't that a moment as vital and defining as a sudden death, bloodshed, cataclysm?

I think of the Woman's Frozen Toes, between Having Wind and Divided. In winter, the climb up from Having Wind is icy and relentless, people have died, even in good weather—it's a fine place to bring your body and soul together. But from the crack between the Woman's Toes, you can stand on your skis and slide down to Divided: It's all gradual downhill and wide turns, intermittent glimpses north and northwest across the shoulder of the mountain or south to the distant summits of Sisters Getting Homesick. A lot of people use that way over to Divided in the winter, and on particular days in a certain kind of weather, once you've got over the Woman's Frozen Toes you only need to set your skis in the tracks other people have laid in the snow and push downhill, a long lazy run.

For a while when I was still green, I was in love with someone who lived at Divided and one winter I made that climb over Woman's Frozen Toes three or four times—my brain was in my sexual organs that winter! Skiing down, it's most all in the cold shadow of the north side of the mountain until the last bend of the track where the ŝildo stones crouch in an open field close-shouldered under the snow, and on fair days the sunlight, crouching among the stones, leaps out brilliant, blinding. That time when I was in the *Pulls Together,* sitting up to look out toward the Fisted Rocks and the mouth of the Ŝiblingo Fjord, when the sunlight made a brief long glare on the water, I remembered suddenly the winter I had climbed over Woman's Frozen Toes—I remembered how it was, skiing out from the shadow of the mountain into the unbroken glare of the ŝildo field, how I was blinded by the light—how I flew down the red darkness by the brief fierce burning of my heart.

No one stood on the beach waiting for us. Daylight was seeping out of the sky by then, the overcast taking up blackness slowly; they thought we had long since gone to shelter among the Goes To Grass Islands, or been caught by the puso weather and overturned in the Owl Strait. So we were left alone to haul out the boats along the lee shore, and our tiredness came out in a muttering of complaint and disagreement. We argued over who would carry the dead woman's body, and which of us would keep her in their house until her family came after her. When that was settled, there was quarrelling over whether we ought to carry everything, all of the *Migremo* salvage, up the steep path to Holds Loneliness, or only drag it a little way and pile it up like a cairn of stones among the drift at the foot of the scarp, and let other people carry it up in the morning of the next day. Finally people just did as they liked, and it was the big, unwieldy pieces that were left behind on the beach, while glass and wire, small plastics and aluminum, damaged crates, the metal globes of xenon fixtures, those bits and pieces went up the path with us, shouldered or dragged or carried, behind the body of the unknown dead woman slung in a hammock of canvas between Kikuma and her friend Davido Ĉekli. What I carried up in a cracked plastic box were dozens of bound books, sodden and heavy, and masses of stained wet paper. Nothing is ever wasted, or can be; if the Library Committee gave up trying to salvage the books, people of the Paper and Ink Committee would slurry the wet pages, re-form and dry them.

That climb from the beach up to Holds Loneliness is long and steep. My shins ached from striking the gunnel of the boat, so I trudged painfully, scuffing my boots. I had to stop every little while and shift the big crate to the other shoulder, and then Adria Berelo, Paŭlo Medina, Magdalena Ulsen and her son, one after the other went by me, some of them not even excusing themselves for this rudeness, and leaving me finally to be the last.

The air was sharp, hoary; in the rucks of the fjord where the light was already gone, the cold fog people call *griza* was cleaving to the stones. I don't know why a fog, by diminishing the world, declares its vastness. But in a while I stopped climbing up through the narrow rift in the land's edge and stood there leaning into the uphill rock, holding the box of books. I think I may have cried a little. A person, ambiguous and small, came downhill out of the fog—became Kikuma. "What," she said in surprise, and she took the box out of my hands and peered at me across the edge of it.

You know how it is between sisters in their middle age? that old old friendship, how loose-fitting it is? the comfort and safety in it? how you can let silence lie between you without it taking on any weight? how you can let words out of your mouth without wariness or precision because you know your sister will listen to what's worthwhile and let the rest fall out of her ears into the air? how you can be surly, unreasonable, stupid, in the certainty of her grace? We had hardly spoken through this long day, but I said, gesturing impatiently as if this was something we had already argued about, "Oh, this leg hurting, and this damn crate too heavy, I was left behind with the ghosts, eh? Something. My stupid daughter. A dread. I don't know." I was by then crying bitterly.

Kikuma looked at me, shifting the weight of the box. Then she turned sidelong to me and rubbed her cheek along mine. I clung to her until I was finished. Then she said tenderly, "Let's go up, Ana," and I followed her along the narrow notch, the dark lead rising to Holds Loneliness.

When we came out at the head of the fjord it was not yet night—the sky was dark but holding the light beneath it as a hand cups a flame—and the wind had fallen utterly away. The other people had already gone to ground ahead of us, and from the edge of that fell there's no seeing the fenestroj of the houses, or the light cast out from those windows into the shadowed swales—it was a world without humankind in it, the land falling and rising and falling like swells of the sea. Across the shoulders of the berms the long wiry stems of the pinion poppies stood erect, holding their seedheads above the myriad shorter grasses, the brindled pelt of false skipper and flywing, hightail and boozy. Against the darkening sky, over the black water of the fjord a flock of bush owls hunted mites and moths, their dip and rise profoundly synchronous, silent. On the flanks of the glacier there were patches of shadow, thousands of pew larks with their twig-legs folded under, lying together in sleep. Out there were sand hares, flicker lemmings, hermit mice, in galleries and corridors under the ice. And in the waters of the Owl Strait, bowfish were choosing a home for eggs in the crevices of a man's relinquished vertebrae.

There is something about that particular time of day, the failing of the light; at twilight, when the air is cold and still and uncolored, when something moves in it the whole world sees it. As I was standing there at the top of the beach path—standing inside my memory of that day as if it were a stream of light— I came to a magic place in my life. I saw that man from the *Migremo,* the one who had fallen into the sea with me and drowned. Something moved apart from the birds, and I saw that man where he walked among the ŝildoj of Holds Loneliness, looking for a stone to give his name to.

Kikuma stopped with me, looking up the long slope. If she saw the man herself, she didn't say, but stood with me in silence while I watched him wade the swift white stripe of the Bears Grief River, and while I watched him walk across the hip of the hill, his shape gradually becoming indistinguishable, a part of the darkness. Then I said, "Well, he's gone now," and we trudged tiredly across the rocky mezlando, going home with that box of wet pages. People call this world *Reiradi,* an old word that has a tangled meaning, but something like circling back, or maybe returning. I wonder if those pioneer people, the ones who gave the world that name, I wonder if they were thinking of times like this one, coming home late and cold, carrying a weight.

This time I'm remembering, when the *Migremo* fell, we were living in a house with Kikuma's husband and my niece and our old parents, and a cousin who had quarreled with her husband. Our family's relief made itself known in a little stream of jokes at our expense, while they brought forward bowls and spoons and placed them in our hands and watched us eat our soup. My mother began to sort through the box we had brought up from the *Migremo,* and before long she was standing the wet books open, ruffling their pages with her thumb. When she had a field of books spread in front of her on the floor she stood up and turned around facing the other way and began again, setting out the rest. Then when she was done, she was in the center and couldn't step out and we had to help her move the books and make a path for herself.

My mother has an old, religious reverence for books. I value them myself, though my mother's experience of books is not mine. In her childhood people looked to books as a repository of wisdom about the land; in mine, people looked to the land itself. The child knows the world more sensuously than the adult, and I think my mother's understanding of this world, even after seventy years, is intimately linked to the fusty smell inside the covers of books, the thickened, buttery texture of the old paper, the sibilant sound of the pages slipping across one another. Mine is in waxy panes of riverine ice, in the smell of a mouse's old bones and the spiny rustle of a ring-eye's nest. The landscape we inhabit as children, inhabits us.

When I had eaten my soup, I had an odd compulsion to go out again in the darkness and look among the ŝildoj for the stone I had seen that ghost giving his name to. I said something else to my family—that I had a compulsion to go to Davido Ĉekli's house and sit with the dead woman. They sighed and reasoned briefly with me—this was something that they understood, but it could wait for the morning of the next day. Still, no one argued very strongly to keep me inside. I suppose they knew what I was doing, though I hardly knew it myself. I put my arms in my coat sleeves again and went out through the darkness between the houses.

The twilight calm had drifted off on the light, and the wind was cold again, a glaciejo wind, dry and lashing. I put my head down to climb the steep alta to the ŝildo field, walking among the stones in a misery of cold, hunching my shoulders, waiting for something to be revealed. If that man's ghost was there, he didn't speak. At the high edge of the field I stood looking seaward across the long black downsweep of the grass. There was a fine violet line marking the boundary of the sky—a vanish-ingly delicate memory of the sun. And then something was re-vealed after all. That dark filament of light illumined an early, childish memory:

Something more than a hundred years ago, people had buried an old woman in the ground east of my parents' domaro, and at Having Wind they were always telling this woman's story—why she wasn't burnt, how she had wanted to lie down in the earth after all those years apart from it. No one knew where this grave was—in my childhood, the people who used to know that were already corpses, their names given to sîldo stones, their souls living in the spaces that connect one blade of grass, one crumb of sand, to the next. What I remembered, standing at the edge of the sîldo field above the houses of Holds Loneliness, looking out at the violet line of the sky, was a time, as a child, when I stood on the berm of my parents' house watching the weather coming. It was angviso weather, that time, a weather without any experience of abruptness; it moved slowly at an angle toward me out of the east. Between me and the weather the brown grass was sunlit and I thought, When the shadow of the weather crosses the grass I'll see the sunken place where that pioneer woman's bones are buried.

When I first stood there on the roof of the house looking, there was nothing but the land itself, it seemed all one piece and unalterable. But then I became what I was seeing, and my eyes gave life to even the smallest things—blue stems of moss, the veiny ruts where meltwater sometimes ran, a turnstone, a dead-drop of shed feathers, the wind pushing the grass over in an image resembling a human head or a flight of birds. The weather rode very slowly across the grass, and in the shadow there was a deep old silence, and whispering into it was the land. I sup-pose that was the first time I heard the earth speaking, as in-explicably coherent as an old book in a forgotten language, transcendent in its meaning.

Now I walked across the sîldo field, across the crackling grass to the bank of the Bears Grief River and stood there a mo-ment, peering into the blackness, hoping I might yet see the ghost of that dead man, the one I had lost to the sea. But the urgency had gone out of the air, out of me, like a breath, and when I started down again toward the lighted fenestroj of the houses, I thought, That pioneer woman is still there under the grass, alive in the body of the world.

Glossary

altejo: highlands, nearest the ceiling; narrow terraces along the upper edges of the torus's inhabited interior

avino: grandmother

caparajo: loose, lightweight drawstring trousers

dankon: thanks; thank you

domaro: a large multifamily house containing several apartments

exo: pressure suit

kremaciejo: crematory

kura: doctor; nurse; healer

lavejo: lavatory

librajo: small laptop device for reading electronic books

loĝio: a covered, interior porch; the public space, the open middle, of a U-shaped domaro

maĉeta: farm implement for weeding and for cutting canes

maltejo: lowlands, in the trough of the torus's inhabited interior

mezlando: midlands; broad terraces along the middle reaches of the interior of the torus

mortafesto: funeral; wake; a celebration of a life that has ended

paĉjo: diminutive, affectionate name for a father

panja: diminutive, affectionate name for a mother

pasado: the exterior corridor of a domaro; a narrow porch that circles the house beneath its overhanging eave

plantodomo: greenhouse

repozo: wicker chair-back for floor use

sadaŭ: attic of a house, used for storage

sutaĝo: the open underneath of a domaro built on poles

ŝimanas: a spiritual malaise; exaggerated feeling of isolation and loneliness, leading toward depression, alienation, suicide

ŝiro: neighborhood; village; consisting usually of ten or twelve apartment houses. There are eight siroj: Esperplena [Hopeful], Senlima [Boundless], Pacema [Peaceable], Alaŭdo [Lark], Kantado [Prolonged Singing], Bonveno [Open Arms], Mandala [Circling], Revenana [Daydreaming]